A Sparrow Falls

Vicki Olsen

Magnolia Books, llc
Little Rock, Arkansas

Grateful acknowledgment is made to Don Congdon Associates, Inc. for permission to use excerpts:

FAHRENHEIT 451   Copyright 1953, 1981 by RAY BRADBURY
DANDELION WINE   Copyright 1946, 1975 by RAY BRADBURY

Scripture quotations from The Authorized (King James) Version. Rights in the Authorized Version in the United Kingdom are vested in the Crown. Reproduced by permission of the Crown's patentee, Cambridge University Press

All other quoted scripture is from works in the public domain.

DEDICATION

To my late parents, Louis I. Watts and Esther Hardcastle Watts, and my brothers Louis W. Watts and Michael R. Watts, who made up our happy, stable family and contributed to an ideal childhood free of the anguish suffered by Sarah Jones. Every child should have a family like ours.

ACKNOWLEDGMENTS

My thanks to friends and family who helped and encouraged me to complete this book.

Special thanks to my brother, Michael Watts and his wife, Lynnette. They spent hours poring over the manuscript and giving needed advice, suggestions and encouragement.

Of all those who helped me, no one took greater interest, nor followed the progress of this book more closely than Mary Schooley. When we met in the fall of 1964, she was Mary Henderson and we were entering our sophomore year of high school in Mountain Home, Idaho. Her input was invaluable when I needed to test my memory of what it was like to be a teenager in 1965. I love you, Mary. This one's for you!

Are not two sparrows sold for only a penny? And not even one of them shall fall to the ground without your Father knowing. (Matthew 10:29)

"Only God sees the sparrow fall, but even God doesn't do anything about it."
—**John Steinbeck, The Winter of Our Discontent**

A Sparrow Falls

Tolerance, Arkansas 1968

Until she was fifteen, Sarah Jane lived in a tumbled down farmhouse on a graveled county road on the outskirts of Tolerance, Arkansas. Her father gave her little attention and her mother, Dee feared raising her husband's ire. Theirs was a marriage of convenience where the love never grew.

Otis, Sarah's father had a habit of drink. But the drink never succeeded in silencing his demons and he seemed set on crushing the dreams of his family.

Now she is twenty and she is leaving this house again. Of all things in the world the one she most desired was to leave— leave the sagging porch, leave the peeling paint, and leave this town behind. Gone ... gone forever.

She reaches down and brings up a framed picture. The dark eyes of a chubby cheeked toddler look back at her. Her finger traces the bright ringlets of red hair. She kisses the rosy baby cheeks. Her hand trembles slightly as she bends to lay the photograph into the dented and scratched suitcase.

Packing the last few things carefully laid out on the bed she looks around her bedroom at what she is leaving behind. Pressed and dried yellow rose corsage pinned to her bulletin board, fifteen Nancy Drew books—she'd given up on collecting the entire set, Dolly, one eye closed, the Bible she got the day of her baptism, and the picture of Jesus hanging on the nail where she'd had hung it that same day. *I was mad at Him for so long.*

She picks up the suitcase, starts out the door and turns to take one last look. She goes back, takes the picture of Jesus off the wall and tucks it under her arm. Around her neck is a pale-yellow ribbon tied to a small gold cross and two wedding bands.

This is the story of Sarah Jane Jones--and of something more.

From the time we are born our story is molded by the books we read and the people who come into our lives and those who go out; good or bad, brief or lasting, living or dead. We are bent and broken, shaped and reshaped into who we were yesterday, who we are today and who we will become tomorrow. But is the person we become a reflection of the people we encounter or of the choices we make? Are we what we make of ourselves--or of what others make of us? Are we punished for our sins, or for the sins of others?

You tell me.

Vicki Olsen

ONE

Ecclesiastes 1:3
³What profit hath a man of all his labor which he taketh under the sun?

I n 1935, one week before her seventeenth birthday, Dee Ellen Finton's brother decided she should marry Otis Jones. Their widowed mother insisted that somewhere in all of Hallard County there must be a more fitting husband for her daughter. Dee was a beautiful girl. She wore her red hair swept back from her face in waves gathered into a loose knot against her neck setting off her blue eyes. The rich textured skin of her face remained unmarred by her harsh childhood. Only her slender hands bore the scars from tearing the soft white fluff from the sharp bolls of cotton plants.

"For goodness sakes, he's ten years older than she is. She's just a child."

"Not a child at all, Momma. She's older than you were when you had me."

"Otis already buried one wife. Now he's after another one. Poor Adah died bringing that little boy into this world."

"Dee could do worse. He owns his land, meager as it is…not a landless sharecropper like us. She could do a lot worse."

"Well I suppose, bless his heart, the man just needs someone to look after that baby of his'n and keep house. But I don't see why it should be my girl." She wiped her hands on her apron and brushed her eyes with the back of her wrist. She knew the choices. Her husband died of swamp fever, leaving their oldest son with the responsibility of five younger sisters and a brother; and the Great Depression continued to take an unrelenting toll throughout

Arkansas. She supposed Jesse needed to get all the girls married off sooner rather than later.

Early Saturday morning Otis pulled on his cleanest pair of overalls and tucked his late wife's gold wedding band into the bib pocket. He stopped by the Finton place on his way into Tolerance for his weekly errands.

Dee stood by the door and clutched a little bag of clothing. Otis grinned through his tobacco stained teeth. "We'll get on with the marrying soon as I finish up my business in town."

Timidly perched on the ragged seat of the Model B Ford Dee fondled a tiny gold cross on a chain around her neck. Despite Otis' stoic and unspeaking demeanor, she dared to throw an occasional glance his way. His calloused hands gripped the steering wheel in an effort to avoid the ruts in the sun-baked country road as he mouthed a pinch of snuff against his gums. Fate in the form of her brother had selected this man as her life partner.

She was reminded of her daddy when Otis brought an empty whiskey bottle to his lips and let the dissipated snuff juices slide down through the neck. This sight always repulsed her.

Dee followed Otis past the five and dime, Carson's Feed Store and the drug store operated by young Doc Murphy, finally stopping at Planter's Bank to make a payment on his crop loan. Not until Otis had crossed all the errands off his list, did they drop by the courthouse to say *I dos*.

Before he climbed back in his truck, Otis spat tobacco juice onto the sidewalk. "You gonna make me a fine wife, ain't you?"

By this time Dee wondered if she'd been dealt a very bad hand and could only manage a timid nod. Otis pressed his tobacco stained lips against hers. She held her breath to avoid the foul stench of his mouth. After he released her from his grasp, she was fearful of wiping her mouth, afraid she would offend him. "Yep, me and you, we're gonna get along just fine."

Her cheeks were suddenly warm. She stared straight through the broken windshield. Tires wobbled, and boxes bounced in the back of the truck as they made their way toward her new home where she would take on the duties of wife, and mother of Otis' eight-month-old son Floyd.

It didn't take long for her life of planting and picking alongside Otis to rob Dee of the beauty nature had provided. Her red hair became drab and lifeless and her creamy white skin, creased and weather-beaten. Even her eyes lost their luster.

Some men are blessed. Things come to them without thought or effort. Others are doomed to toil without return. Otis Jones was among the latter. Although he seemed resigned to his fate, he did not take it gracefully. He did all things with few words. Emotionally absent, he seemed to have an endless capacity for misfortune. A simple man, his reading was limited to the newspaper and his conversation limited to the weather.

Dee--after bearing three spirited sons, suffering a miscarriage and a stillbirth--gave birth to a baby girl with cherry pink cheeks, a curly mess of ginger red hair and bright blue eyes. Sarah Jane came along just after the youngest boy, Kenny Ray, turned five. Sarah's birth was like a tonic, bringing much-needed contentment and warmth to Dee's otherwise bleak life.

Scratched out of a marginal patch of what they call bottomland, the Jones farm lay between the Saline and Caddo Rivers near Tolerance, a community of about 1,000, in the eastern foothills of the Ouachita Mountains.

The sloping terrain of Hallard County had encouraged centuries of erosion to steal the nutrients from its shallow soils. Along the many streams that drained the upland watershed, the valleys were narrow and prone to flooding. Otis did what he could to bring his land to life but was always beaten by the weather or the price of cotton or the cost of seed. A crop lost to floods was a common occurrence.

From before the Civil War until early in the twentieth century Hallard County had been a major cotton producer. Otis planted cotton in 1939 but by 1945 most of the many cotton gins had closed due to lack of demand. Cotton fields were replaced by peach orchards until 1953 when late freezes followed by early springs destroyed the peach crops. Looking for a way to make ends meet, Otis signed a contract to haul pulpwood to the paper mill in Camden.

He swallowed his pride and borrowed money from his brother to buy a beat-up log truck. Before he carried his first load the paper mill announced a cut in production.

Dee accepted her position as keeper of the house, nurse, and conciliator. She derived a sense of security from her role and took refuge in knowing without her there would be no family. She loved her children, but she rarely hugged them or kissed them. She seldom laughed. She never cried.

Adah's child, Floyd grew to mimic his father's increasingly dour and brooding ways. A doltish, yet sturdy and stolid boy.

With each birth, the evidence of Otis' bloodline seemed to grow weaker. Dee's firstborn; Otis Junior exhibited limited imagination, however, possessed great energy and, if told what to do, would do what was expected of him but little more.

Jim Ed was tall and handsome, positive and shrewd, a hard and determined worker, always trudging onward in the hope of something better. "Well, that's all right," he'd say. "We'll make it next year." He inherited his father's almost black hair and his mother's deep blue eyes.

With Dee's red hair and a face full of freckles, Kenny's mild manner and even temper set him apart. What he lacked in size he made up for in eagerness. Of all her boys, Kenny least embodied his daddy, and for that reason, Dee was partial to him.

Sarah, a gentle and sweet child made everyone near her just a little bit more cheerful with her constant laughter and good humor.

Dee came to love the quiet of her Saturdays. With Junior, Jim Ed and Kenny loaded in the back of the faded red pickup truck, and Floyd next to him in the cab, Otis pulled onto County Road 5 and headed into Tolerance where they joined the other farmers who flocked to town for weekly errands. Without the men underfoot Dee could go about her washing, ironing and her gardening in peace.

The temptation to escape the solitude and mingle with other women on the town square provoked no allure for her. She held little interest in the prattle about misfortunes and the gossip about neighbors. She preferred the refuge of the farm. Only her dread of Saturday evenings stained the serenity of her solitary days.

With Hallard County being a dry county no store-bought whiskey could be found, still, it was a known fact you could always buy a drink in the kitchen of ol' man Scarborough's boarding house. There were a few bottles of cheap bootleg whiskey and jars of homemade 'shine tucked away in the pantry for his regulars whose wives' sense of sin put drinking whiskey at the top of a portentous list, followed by card playing, dancing, and gambling. Otis counted among those regulars. He never drank at home and he never came home on Saturday until he was drunk.

1949

Dee pulled the string attached to a solitary naked bulb hanging from the ceiling. The darkness of the room enveloped her.

Moments ago, she'd been standing in the next room, where she watched Sarah sleep. Letting the peace wash over her she'd taken in the sweet innocence of her baby. *There is nothing so beautiful as a sleeping child--free of care. If only you could have this peace forever; this wonderful sleep, so restful and quiet.*

Now alone in the room she shared with her husband, she stared into the darkness letting her eyes adjust to the dim moonlight. She plaited her hair into a single braid while straining to hear the popping cylinders of the old truck.

As headlights broke the darkness and gravel crunched under tires, she scrambled into bed and lay still. She waited. She didn't dare move. Hardly breathing, she pretended to be asleep and prayed that this time in his drunkenness he would fall to sleep at once and let her be.

From the kitchen came the familiar sounds of Otis and the boys as they returned home--stifled voices, the thud of the icebox door as it opened and slammed shut, the faint thump of cabinet doors and the muffled clatter of dishes in the sink and finally, the tap of the boys' bedroom door closing.

Pungent with whiskey and sweat, Otis appeared in the doorway of their bedroom. He faltered and momentarily leaned against the door-frame to steady himself. There he stood for a moment as he looked around the room. As if to offer a toast he raised his bottle and took the last swig. Whiskey spilled down the front of his overalls. He staggered across the room and placed the empty bottle on the nightstand.

Dee caught a glimpse of him as he stood for some time, unsteady on his feet, staring down at her before he clumsily stripped his stocky 6'2" frame to his patched boxer shorts and tumbled into bed next to her. Tensing as his sour breath assaulted her neck and his sweaty hands pulled at her cotton nightgown, she lay motionless as a rag doll while he climbed on top and invaded her. Grunting and groaning until he reached his satisfaction, he rolled off her and fell into a snoring slumber.

Lying alongside her husband there was no comfort. Tears burned in her eyes and hopelessness crawled through her belly. She had done her duty; fulfilled her marital responsibility, just as she did his laundry, washed his dishes, cooked his meals and reared his children.

Certain he had fallen asleep and with the rest of the house quiet, she left his bed, silently went into the kitchen, washed her thighs with a wet rag and retreated to the porch. Huddled in the wooden swing, she pulled her knees to her chest and tucked her nightgown around her legs. Sitting in the moonlight, motionless for hours, fearful of making the chain creak, she didn't feel sad or upset or remorseful. She simply did not feel.

The clear and cool night flaunted a sky full of stars. The budding trees stood still, no wind stirring their bony limbs, as the frogs and crickets provided a melancholy serenade.

Without an ounce of self-pity, she imagined life away from Tolerance and away from Otis and contemplated what adventures might be waiting in that vast world.

She watched the sky and wondered if some other woman might, at this moment be looking at the same stars, dreaming of a better life.

Only during these solitary vigils did she permit herself to dream. Dee knew leaving Tolerance would never be possible. There was no way to provide for her kids and she could never leave them behind. Despite their rough ways, her boys were a blessing to her. If she must put up with her hard life and her husband's demands, so be it. Her hope was for Sarah. Hope for a better life--one Dee could only dream of.

TWO

Proverbs 18:15

[15]A wise heart shall acquire knowledge: and the ear of the wise seeketh instruction.

1954

It was a hot day in September; ordinary in every way except it was the day after Labor Day and Sarah's first day of school. Plenty nervous about starting first grade she walked down the rutted dirt road towards Cold Fork with her ten-year-old brother Kenny.

His curly mop of copper red hair shone brightly in the morning sunlight and his long eyelashes were blond against his ruddy cheeks. "You're lucky. You get to go to the new school. We used to have another school until a big tornado knocked it down. I was in the first grade. It scared the daylights out of me. The teachers took us all down to the courthouse and we all hid in the basement. Practically the whole town was in there."

Sarah didn't find any comfort in his story about the whole school getting wrecked by a tornado. *What if a tornado comes and blows the new school away while I'm in it?"*

Kenny continued to talk. "Afterwards, Daddy took us into town to see the mess. It hit Tolerance real bad; flattened the sawmill too." His blue eyes sparkled against his freckled face. "I saw car parts hanging in a tree and Mr. Connor's Ford pickup turned upside down right in the middle of Main Street. It was pretty neat. And that old water tower, it was still sitting up there big as you please, just shining in the sunlight with everything around it flatter 'n a pancake."

She wasn't listening. *Who cares if the town got wrecked in the olden days when I was just a tiny baby?*

"Jimmy Frank's little brother, Darrell, he got kilt. A whole bunch of people got kilt. I didn't know any of them except Darrell."

Sarah looked up at Kenny and tugged at her rust-colored pigtails. Momma braided her hair way too tight and it pulled at her scalp. When she complained, Momma said they had to be tight, so they would stay in all day.

Her words whistled through the gap left by her missing front teeth. "Kenny, that stuff about dead people kinda makes me scared. Can you talk about something else?" She wrinkled her freckled nose and thought about being a first grader and wished she wasn't afraid to talk to other kids. First grade was scary enough without Kenny's dumb story. *If I make a friend, we could cut out Betsy McCall paper dolls. Playing paper dolls would be a lot more fun with a friend.*

Kenny picked up a rock and threw it at nothing in particular. "Anyway, the school we go to now is in the old Pentecostal church—the one they had before they got the new one."

Their cousin, Becky Sue, told Sarah all about first grade and how she shouldn't be scared because it would be fun. She said you had to learn to raise your hand, but the hardest part was not talking. Sarah wasn't surprised that Becky Sue found the not talking part troublesome. Becky Sue didn't go to school in Cold Fork; things might be different where she went to school. Becky Sue told her that she would learn to read *Dick and Jane.* Sarah already knew how to read; Kenny taught her this summer. *I'll be good at first grade. I can read, and I can draw really good and I always color inside the lines.*

Sarah wore one of Becky Sue's prettiest outgrown dresses. She liked it even though Momma had to let out the hem and sew a grosgrain ribbon along the hemline to hide the old stitching line. Momma sewed ribbons over a let-out hemline on most of Sarah's dresses.

By the time they reached the schoolyard Sarah had heard too much about the big tornado and Becky Sue's shoes hurt her feet.

Kenny waved to some friends and ran off to join them leaving Sarah on her own.

With a restrained hopefulness, she scanned the schoolyard for a familiar face. Children of all grades gathered in the dusty yard outside the small stone building. They milled around playing and talking about what they did over the summer, many seeing each other for the first time since school let out last May. Some had new lunch pails and stiff shoes, although most were like Sarah with brown paper lunch bags and scuffed shoes.

Deep in the crowd, Sarah spotted a girl from Sunday school. They weren't friends, but she knew her name... Mary Alice Johnson. She was a first grader too. Sarah stood on tip-toes hoping Mary Alice would see her. She did, and her face lit up right away. She moved through the crowd toward Sarah until another girl tapped Mary Alice on the shoulder and they ran off together.

Clutching her lunch bag, Sarah edged toward a cluster of girls gathered on the cracked pavement that had once been the church parking lot. Some jumped rope, some played jacks, and others talked and laughed in small groups. Standing back, she listened to a conversation and waited to be invited to join the group.

A short, fleshy girl with large green eyes peered from under uneven bangs and watched Sarah lurking like a glum shadow. Giving Sarah a hard look she stuck out her tongue and turned her attention back to her friends.

Sarah wanted to go home where nobody would stare at her or make fun of her. She sniffled and looking back to see if anyone noticed, walked away from the others to the edge of the pavement. Before she could turn and run for home, kids all around started to chant, "The bell, the bell. Get in line."

Mr. Miller, the Principal and 6th-grade teacher rang a bell mounted near the door. "Line up and enter the building in an orderly fashion," he barked. "Find your room and go directly to a desk."

Sarah was swept into the crowd of children who shoved into the building and pushed in every direction trying to get to class. She was overwhelmed and confused. *I wish I could find Mary Alice and follow her.*

All of a sudden Kenny grabbed her hand and led her to an open classroom door. She looked up at a printed card slipped into a metal frame attached to the wall; *Grades 1 & 2 Miss Green.*

She peeked through the door. A sweet-faced blonde woman stood at the front of the room writing on the blackboard. The teacher turned and smiled. No longer afraid, Sarah joined the children pressing into the classroom; Kenny dropped her hand and hurried down the hall.

The 1st and 2nd grade shared a classroom and a teacher because there were only eighteen students in both grades combined, counting the Adams twins, Debbie and Donna.

Sarah scooted into a desk in the back row. She sat up straight and attentively watched Miss Green. *She's pretty. I bet she's nice. Maybe it'll be okay.*

Miss Green pulled the door shut behind her and looked around the room. A wall of open windows allowed a stir of air and a swarm of flies into the classroom.

The teacher folded her arms, cleared her throat and waited for everyone to notice she was ready to start class. They gradually looked in her direction and quieted down.

"Thank you. Well done. Welcome first graders and welcome back second graders. My name is Miss Green and I will be your teacher this year." She pointed to the blackboard where she had written her name.

She writes so pretty.

"Call me Miss Green, not *teacher*. To help you remember, I wore a green dress today." She also wore a string of pearls and high heeled shoes.

I wish Momma would dress like that.

Sarah eyed the twenty-six cards fastened to the wall above the blackboard, each with two images of one of the letters of the alphabet lowercase and uppercase.

Becky Sue was right—she said we would to learn to write our letters. When Kenny tried to teach me to write my name, he said I can't make my S's worth anything. He kept saying they're mostly backward, but it's really hard to make them go the other way, and that's bad because my name starts with S.

"All right students," Miss Green said smiling. "Now, everyone stand next to his or her desk and look at me." She paused to give them time to stand. "Well done. Thank you. When I call your name, you will move to the desk I point to. The first grade will be on the right side of the room and the second grade on the left. I will be seating you alphabetically starting with Audrie Tillie Brown. Audrie take the first seat. Tell me what you prefer to be called."

"Yes, ma'am, I go by Tillie, ma'am."

When Miss Green had called every name, Mary Alice Johnson was sitting next to Sarah because they were both "J's."

Sarah noticed the hem of Mary's plaid dress didn't have a ribbon sewn to it. *Probably because she's not tall like me.*

Mary Alice Johnson told Miss Green she wanted to be called *Mary*. Sarah decided she would be just Sarah, instead of Sarah Jane.

Everyone looked up as a crackle and a squeal came from a speaker mounted above the chalkboard. When the squeal subsided, a man's voice said "Please stand. Ricky Stone from Mrs. Anderson's 6th-grade class will lead us in the Pledge of Allegiance and the Lord's Prayer."

Using her yardstick, Miss Green pointed to each word as the voice on the intercom recited the pledge. *I never heard of this before. Some of those are really big words.*

After Miss Green passed out the Dick and Jane books and gave the second grade a list of spelling words, she took a break from teaching for a while. She pulled a book from a shelf and settled into the chair behind her desk.

Sarah watched intently. *Wonder what she's going to do?*

Miss Green opened the book and read aloud. "Charlotte's Web. Chapter One, Before Breakfast. 'Where's Papa going with that ax?' said Fern to her mother as they were setting the table for breakfast."

Sarah sat mesmerized. Her chin rested in the palms of her hands. Miss Green made her voice go high and low, rough and smooth in a special way as she read.

Seconds before the start of recess, Miss Green closed the book. The class gave a collective moan. "We'll read more tomorrow," she promised.

The buzzer sounded signaling recess. As the children started toward the door, Sarah stood off to the side, but Mary grabbed her hand and led her to the playground. "Come on, we're going to jump rope with the twins."

"I've never jumped rope. I don't know how." Her blue eyes grew round.

"First you have to learn to turn. We'll turn and let Debbie and Donna jump first. They're second graders and they're really good jumpers."

"What do I do?" Before they even started to turn the rope, Sarah's palms were sweating.

Mary handed Sarah the end of a rope and showed her how to wrap it around her hands. Mary stood at the other end. "Everything will be okay," she assured Sarah. "They're the best at red hot peppers… when we say red hot peppers; we have to turn the rope as fast as we can. When someone misses, it'll be my turn to jump and then yours."

Sarah hoped the other girls wouldn't miss, so she wouldn't have to take a turn jumping. She imagined she would trip and fall, and everyone would point and laugh at her.

Mary turned the rope and Sarah followed her lead. Mary and the twins started to chant.

Mabel, Mabel, set the table.
Do it as fast as you are able.
Don't forget the Ketchup, Mustard, Salt and
RED HOT PEPPERS

By the time the rope caught Debbie's foot and she took the end of the rope from Mary, Sarah had learned the rhyme.

I'm playing jump rope with second graders. Becky's right. First grade is fun.

❧

At the end of the day, Kenny looked for Sarah outside the school. When she bounded out of the building he asked, "So, how was your first day?" …and the floodgates opened.

She started with, "I made a new friend! Her name is Mary," and hadn't stopped until they reached the drainage ditch running past the road. She stopped long enough to take off her shoes and socks.

"Wait up!" Sarah dug her bare toes into the velvety silt, stirring up fine dust as she scurried to keep up with her brother's long legs. She carried her school shoes, the socks carefully stuffed inside.

"…and we got divided into three reading groups and guess what? I got put in the highest group with some the second graders. I think they are the slow readers. What do you think about that?"

School opened a whole new world for Sarah; a world where she could jump rope, and where she felt validated by being in the highest reading group.

"We took turns reading Dick and Jane--Miss Green asked who would like to erase the board. Mary raised her hand and got picked. It looked like fun. There's a special blackboard eraser and she rubbed it across the chalk lines on the board and it rubbed the words away. I wish I wasn't afraid to raise my hand to erase the board in front of everyone--Do you know Joey Carter?"

Kenny rolled his eyes. "No. Why?"

"He can snap his fingers and whistle and break sticks with his hands."

"Is he your boyfriend?

Sarah blushed, tilted her head back and looked up at her brother, her dimples showing. "Don't be silly."

"Don't be thilly," he said mocking her gap-toothed lisp. He pulled the ribbon from her braids, hoping she would take a breath and stop talking.

She arched a brow. "Stop it. I'm telling Momma you're being mean to me!" She pulled the elastic bands from her thick braids and ran her fingers through her hair, careful not to tangle the strands, freeing her heavy hair.

Biting her lip, Sarah looked around and lowered her voice. "Leighton Shipps wet his pants right after lunch. I don't know what happened exactly, but everyone started to laugh, and he started to cry, so they started calling him a *pants wetter crybaby*. Miss Green got mad at everyone. I didn't laugh 'cause I felt sorry for him. I didn't say anything 'cause I didn't want anybody to think I'm friends with the pants wetter. Besides, he makes all kinds of weird mouth noises. Anyway, he had to go home."

Kenny snatched a mimeographed sheet from Sarah's clutched hand. "Whatcha got there?"

"Stop it, Kenny!" She grabbed it back. "I need that. It's my list of school supplies. I need a pencil and a box of crayons and a writing tablet. Mary said she wanted the big box with 16 crayons--Miss Green said we can only have eight. Mary said I could come over to her house and color and ride bikes after school."

She paused, "Kenny... I don't have a bike."

"Sarah Jane, Daddy won't let you go anywhere after school. You have to go right home and do your chores."

After a moment she grinned and said, "That's okay; I don't know how to ride a bike anyway."

THREE

Hebrews 5
⁴And no man taketh this honour unto himself, but he that is called of God, as was Aaron.

1957

The hillside in back of the house sprouted green with new leaves unfolding on bushes and trees. Barefoot and shirtless, Junior and Jim Ed ambled toward the pond with long cane poles balanced on their shoulders. Red and white bobbers dangled from the line. "Grab them worms," Jim Ed called to Kenny.

"Can't," Kenny hollered back. He considered fishing a waste of time.

The older brothers smirked and exchanged knowing glances. "Weird-o would rather do homework," Junior mumbled under his breath.

Kenny made his way to the kitchen, took off his outdoor things and hung them on a hook near the door. Sarah sat at the kitchen table, engrossed in her homework. As he came around the table Kenny reached out and gave a gentle tug on her pigtail and untied the ribbon.

"Ouch! Stop it!" She slapped at his hand. "I hate when you do that."

She finished her assignment, neatly creased the notebook paper lengthwise and carefully printed her name on the outside.

"I never knew third grade would be so hard," Sarah complained. "But I like Mrs. Johns, she's nice. I'm glad I'll have her for fourth grade too."

"Yep. Be glad ol' lady Turner left. She was my third-grade teacher. Talk about uggh-ly and mean. Looked like a witch; had a wart right here." He gently poked the middle of Sarah's forehead. She pushed Kenny's hand away but couldn't control a small giggle.

"Need help with your spelling words?" Kenny sat next to her and curled his legs under his chair.

Dee opened the icebox and selected two eggs for her cornbread batter. "I reckon you'd make a fine school teacher one day. You're so fond of helping your sister with her school work."

"Oh, no Momma, that's not what I'm gonna do. I'm aiming to be a preacher like Brother Leon," Kenny answered. "Brother Leon told me I got *The Call*. He said only a chosen few get *The Call* and I'm one of the lucky ones. He gave me this." Kenny beamed as he pulled a pocket-sized New Testament from his blue jeans.

"If it's God's will, so be it," said Dee. "Best not tell your Daddy about them plans, not just yet."

"Don't worry, Momma. I know how it is."

"I want to be a preacher too," echoed Sarah.

Kenny snorted. "Gee willikers, don't be silly, Sarah Jane, girls can't be preachers."

"Can too!" Sarah folded her arms across her chest and petulantly stuck out her lower lip.

Dee broke into a smile. "Sarah Jane's right, there have been some right fine lady preachers." A thoughtful expression formed on her brow. "Why, when I was just a girl, Aimee Semple McPherson came through town and held a tent meetin'. She looked might near an angel all dressed in white and preachin' the Word. It was truly a sight to see."

Despite the freedom to roam the square when she came to town with her family on Saturday, Sarah usually found herself at Hallard County Library, immersed in a book, escaping to an imaginary world.

The fly in the ointment of this experience was Miss Maynard, the pinched nosed librarian who viewed herself as queen, ruling proudly over her domain. She supervised *her* library according to a strict code of silence and decorum. Sarah's pride still stung from the humiliation inflicted on her the time she laughed out loud when she discovered the farmer in Animal Farm was named Mr. Jones—like Daddy.

Looking down from her imposing height, Miss Maynard issued a reprimand in her high–pitched whisper. "Sarah Jones, this library is not a fun-house. Children are not meant to be in the library unsupervised, reading books that are meant for grown-ups." She snatched the book from Sarah's hand. "It is my job to keep these books out of the hands of children, lest they be corrupted."

Today she would risk the wrath of the old biddy for a worthy mission. As she approached the library, she saw her accomplice. Mary waited on the library steps as planned.

The girls hurried through the glass and wooden doors determined not to ask the skinny, pinched nosed librarian for help. Sarah and Mary combed the shelves of the children's section of the library desperate to find a book about *"Amy Simple."*

They looked at every book in the children's biography section but the book still eluded them. With defeat quickly sinking in, Mary asked, "What next?"

"The adults' section is humungous, I'll bet it's there," Sarah whispered.

Mary looked shocked and shook her head. "Miss Maynard won't like that. You know kids aren't allowed in the grown-up books."

"I really, really want that book."

They moved away from the shelves, sat down at a nearby table, kept their voices low and made their plan.

"We'll get in trouble if old prune face catches us. She'll be lurking around."

"I don't care; I've got to find that book. You keep her busy and I'll sneak to the biographies and find it."

"Sarah, that won't work. She'll know we went to the grown-up section when you check it out. Besides, I need to hurry. I'm supposed to meet Patty at the Palace Theater at 3 o'clock. We're gonna see *Forbidden Planet*."

Sarah thought for a minute. Her eyes lit up. "I'll sneak it out of here under my coat."

Before Sarah could execute her plan the bony librarian, her heavy thick glasses perched on the tip of her nose, hovered over the girls.

Mary muttered, "Gotta go," and dashed out the door.

Sarah wiped her sweaty hands on her dress and told the woman what she wanted.

Looking over her glasses, her thin lips pursed, her eyes squinted. She poked her long skinny finger in Sarah's face. "Why in tarnation would you want that?" She motioned for Sarah to follow her into the grown-up section.

Sarah tip toed behind the librarian, fearing her steps would cause the floor to creak. Miss Maynard pulled the book from the shelf and returning to the front of the library stamped the book card. Looking down her nose she handed the book to Sarah and promptly resumed filing in her card catalog.

Avoiding eye contact with the woman, Sarah shot a wary darting look at the clock, tucked the book under her arm, pulled a dime from her pocket and headed to the theater to join Mary and her sister, Patty.

Sarah rushed through her evening chores. As soon as she'd done the supper dishes and taken the trash to the burn pile, she retreated to her room.

She snuggled under the covers and turned on her bedside lamp. The dim bulb cast a shadow over the black and white photos of *Sister Aimee* enveloped in flowing white robes and wearing a long white dress embellished with a cross that covered her chest. Sarah found herself immediately transported to a fantasy world where a farm girl from Canada grew up to hold revivals attended by standing-room-only crowds and preach the gospel on the radio and in movies.

She was on page 104 when Otis noticed the light coming from under her door and bellowed, "Turn off that dang light and quit wasting electricity, girl."

She lay in the dark and thought about the pictures of Sister Aimee, angelic in her beautiful white robes. Before drifting off to sleep Sarah vowed that someday, Kenny and everyone else would see--a girl can be a preacher. Her robes would be even more magnificent than Aimee's.

It became a Saturday morning ritual to gather a congregation of dolls and her stuffed bear Fluffy and deliver her sermon under a revival tent fashioned from bed sheets. Mimicking Brother Leon, she first condemned them all to hellfire and damnation before promising eternal salvation. Unfortunately, she discovered too late, that the baptismal waters of the bathroom sink would render the sleep-eyes of her favorite doll motionless. Undaunted, she declared it a miracle when the left eye worked its way partially open, permanently leaving Dolly winking with one eye opened and one eye closed.

FOUR

Psalms 100
[1] *Make a joyful noise unto the Lord, all ye lands.*
[2] *Serve the Lord with gladness: come before his presence with singing.*

On a hot Saturday morning in September, as summer continued its fight against giving way to fall, Sarah ran barefooted. Wearing Kenny's hand-me-down blue jeans, she dipped her hands in the rain barrel and splashed her face with water still cool from the night air.

While gathering eggs she discovered a cluster of little round holes peppered on the sandy ground under the eaves of the house. Retrieving the longest, most sturdy straw from the kitchen broom she squatted, ready to doodle for doodlebugs. She spat on the end of the broom straw, dipped it into the dirt to form a tiny ball of mud, like Floyd taught her, and carefully inserted it into a hole. Floyd was a good big brother. He taught her lots of things, like how to tie her shoes. And he never teased her the way her other brothers did.

Lowering her mouth as close as possible to the ground to make sure the doodlebug would hear her, she chanted *Doodlebug, doodlebug, come out of your hole. I'll give you a dollar, or a bag full of gold.* She sat back and waited for the broom straw to wiggle. She let loose a triumphant squeal and pulled the straw from the hole with the worm-like insect attached.

"Did you catch one?" asked Kenny on his way to the barn.

"Yep, sure did, and it's a good 'en too."

"You better stop your doodling for now. Momma wants a mess of blackberries."

"Hot diggety; blackberry cobbler," exclaimed Sarah.

Following Kenny into the barn, she grabbed a bucket, then, pigtails flying, set out toward the field.

24

"Put on your shoes and mind the poison ivy," Kenny called after her.

"You're not the boss of me! I can go barefoot if I want too."

Sarah whirled around remembering the time she'd stepped on a bee with her bare feet. She found her shoes in the middle of the yard where she'd kicked them off and without a word, sat in the grass and slipped them on. *Just in case.* She shrugged. *That bee left its stinger in my foot and it stung the bejeezus out of me.*

Sarah sighed. *Kenny thinks he knows everything! He's always right and he's mean to me. Sometimes he makes fun of me and calls me names. I hate him!*

Her resolve softened as she recalled how gently Kenny had scraped the stinger from her foot with his fingernail and smeared baking soda paste on the bump to soothe the sting.

He's not always mean to me. Sometimes he looks out for me, even takes the blame so I won't get in trouble. Once, he gathered the eggs and fed the chickens, when I forgot. Daddy caught him and blistered his butt.

She tried not to remember--she wanted to stay mad at Kenny--except it was hard.

After he finished whipping Kenny, Daddy had grabbed Sarah and lifted his belt, then said, "You ain't worth my trouble."

He swatted the back of her head. "Go on, girl. Git."

By the time she reached the trail that led along the fence line, she was still thinking about the times she'd done something wrong, but Kenny had been the one to get in trouble. *Seems I always get him in trouble, even if I don't mean to. It's not always that way. Sometimes he gets me in trouble. Like that time he called me names and made me cry and I threw my book at him. He didn't get in trouble for making me cry, but I got in trouble for throwing the book...it didn't even hit him.*

Sweet honeysuckle, blooming white and yellow covered the fence. Sarah pulled a blossom from the vine, inhaled the heady scent and pinched off the little green bud where the flower connected at the stem. She sucked sweet nectar from the tip.

As she worked her way down the row the honeysuckle gave way to wild blackberry vines. She filled her bucket with ripe berries, singing her favorite song from Bible School. *I got the joy, joy, joy, joy, down in my heart....* Her song trailed off.

From deep inside the thicket something moved. *Something's hidden in there!* She stood stark still and again listened for the thrashing sounds. It moved again. She turned to run but stopped in her tracks when a low whimper traveled from the undergrowth.

Moving closer, her pulse throbbed in her throat as she pushed back the prickly vine. Tangled in the dark shrubs, a small, black and white spaniel looked at her with fearful eyes.

"Oh, you poor thing." She knelt in front of the stray and slowly offered her hand for the mandatory sniffing ritual. The dog gratefully licked Sarah's hand as she untangled the furry prisoner from its thorny cage. "Oh, you're so sweet. You look just like Spot in the Dick and Jane books. I should call you Spot, but instead, I'm gonna' call you Joy. Is that okay?"

To show her approval, Joy jumped into Sarah's lap and cleared every spot of dirt and sweat from Sarah's face with her velvety tongue. Sarah fell over and giggled helplessly. Then, together they dashed back to the house as fast as their six legs could run.

"I'll swan, Sarah Jane, slow down, you're always on the run," chided Dee as Sarah slammed the bucket of berries onto the kitchen table.

"Momma I found a dog and I named her Joy--can I keep her? I'll take good care of her. I'll feed her, I promise. Please, Momma. Come see her, really, she is sooo cute."

Dee wiped her hands on a dishtowel and followed Sarah to the yard. Dee's heart softened watching the smile grow on her young daughter's face as she hugged the dog's neck.

"We'll see," promised Dee. "You know we gotta ask your daddy and she'd better not chase the chickens. And you better bathe her now; you and that dog are both full of ticks."

Sarah and Joy rushed to the barn.

By the time Sarah heard the voices of Otis and the older boys returning from the field for dinner, she had de-ticked and bathed Joy and was brushing her with an old hairbrush. Otis gave a stern glance toward the dog. "Where'd that fella come from?"

Floyd reached down and rubbed the dog's ears. "This here looks like a good dog," he said and gave Sarah an encouraging wink.

"Oh Daddy, I found her all caught up in the blackberries. Can I please keep her?"

Otis took a long look at the dog and then, to everyone's surprise, he said, "I'm guessing a dog might help keep rats out of the barn. It stays outside, and it better not chase the chickens."

When the house grew silent that night, Sarah slipped out of bed and quietly stole to the barn where she spread her pink quilt on the hay and snuggled next to the dog. "Joy, please don't chase the chickens."

FIVE

2 Samuel 11-12, 14

11-12Now when she had brought them to him to eat, he took hold of her and said to her, "Come, lie with me, my sister." But she answered him, "No, my brother, do not force me, for no such thing should be done in Israel."
14 However, he would not listen to her voice: but, being stronger than she, forced her, and lay with her.

Floyd sat on the back stoop of Scarborough's boarding house paring wooden curls from a twig with his pocket knife. Through the screen door, he listened as the two men discussed the weather, the dropping price of peaches and the rising price of cotton seed. Of all the men in Tolerance, Jefferson Davis Scarborough was the only one Otis spoke more than two words to. Likely Scarborough's whiskey, rather than his charm loosened Otis' tongue.

With each shot of whiskey their voices grew louder and the banter more lively. Floyd languidly waited for his daddy to get his snoot-full, so they could head home. It would have been more enjoyable to join his brothers with their Uncle Ed at the drive-in movie, but someone had to drive Otis home and that had become one of Floyd's regular chores—driving Otis home on Saturday nights.

By the time he was sixteen, Floyd was a big, stocky kid over 6 feet tall. He had a brutish look about him that matched his doltish languor. School had become very difficult for him and he couldn't learn to socialize. He carried a chip on his shoulder and expected to be treated with disdain. He was never disappointed in this expectation and became increasingly aloof and defiant. He was awkward and shied away from girls for fear of being hurt.

The third time he was sent home from school for starting a fight, he had no trouble persuading Otis to let him drop out and work full time on the farm.

27

As usual, Dee was not asked for her opinion, but since she knew that his abilities would forever limit him to the most menial kind of work, and that one more full-time hand on the farm might allow the other boys to stay in school, she was pleased with the decision.

Otis signed a new contract to haul pulpwood to the paper mill in Ashdown and taught Floyd how to drive the beat-up pulpwood truck. The extra money came in handy.

"Where you at Floyd?" Otis called. "Get in here and have a drink with me and Jeff."

Floyd cocked his head. Not sure he heard his daddy right he got to his feet and sauntered through the back door. The stench of cooked cabbage and boiled eggs hovered in the air.

"Pa, you really gonna let me drink with you?"

"Hell yes, ain't you almost seventeen?" A cigarette dangled from his lips. Squinting against the smoke, Otis signaled to Scarborough. "Pour my boy a drink. Reckon it's time he learnt to be a man."

Scarborough, a nearly blind, chain-smoking blowhard, grinned as he placed the shot of whiskey in front of Floyd who downed it in one flinching gulp. The second went down easier.

Floyd sat silent. His eyes watered his throat burned, his head grew a bit fuzzy and his lips a little numb. The men grew rowdy.

"I ain't seen that pretty li'l ole gal, May Nell around here lately," Otis said, his words slightly tangled. "Ain't she still a-workin' for ya?"

"She comes around now and again." From behind thick, wire-rimmed glasses, Scarborough narrowed his eyes. "Mostly she stays shacked up with that no-good Ellis boy." He grimaced and shook his head. "I don't know what that gal sees in him--boy ain't got the sense God gave a goose." Amused at his own observations, Scarborough grinned at Floyd and winked a milky, yellowed eye.

Slack-jawed, Floyd soaked up the drunken talk as it turned more graphic and the men leered and laughed. His head filled with boastful lies--fantasies conjured up by high school boys while jacking off to girlie magazines, they kept hidden under mattresses.

He had never caressed female flesh. Now he listened to the brazen descriptions of May Nell fondling Jackie Ellis and imagined her sweet smell and the pinkness of her young breasts. He began to picture himself with May Nell as her breasts filled his mouth and her hands tugged at his zipper. He struggled to control an uncomfortable throb between his legs. His eyes flickered from Scarborough to Otis. He desperately hoped they would not notice the swell of his crotch pushing against his jeans.

A trickle of relief ran through him when Otis pushed back his chair and said, "Gittin' dark out there, guess we better be headin' home, boy."

Staggering across the Johnson-grass and gravel yard, Floyd held onto his daddy for support.

"Better give me them keys." Otis held out his hand and Floyd dropped the keys between his fingers.

It was usually Floyd's duty to drive his drunken daddy home, but this time Otis dragged himself to the truck, slumped across the frayed upholstery and settled behind the wheel. He prodded the stick shift on the steering column, ground the gears into first and headed the truck in the direction of home.

As they made their way down the washed-out dirt road, Floyd considered the rite of passage he had just undergone. No longer relegated to the back stoop, he'd been welcomed into the world of adult men; invited to claim his masculinity. While in school, his natural hostility caused him to be a loner. He'd been an object of ridicule among his peers. Now with a new sense of belonging there came an implication of privilege.

These fuzzy thoughts were interrupted as the bump, bump, bumping of the truck finally got the best of his unsettled stomach. "Daddy, I think I'm gonna throw up," declared Floyd. His head hung out the window.

"You go right ahead, boy. Ain't nuthin' to be ashamed of. I've puked up my share of good whiskey and bad."
Floyd brushed the flecks of vomit from the side of his mouth and rested his spinning head against the seat-back. He recalled the images of May Nell he'd conjured up while he listened to the men talk. He'd become a man, entitled to the pleasures of manhood.

Floyd sat in the kitchen, elbows on the table, his head between his hands. Otis shoved a glass of cold buttermilk in front of Floyd. "Here, boy, drink this. If it don't settle your stomach, it'll make you earp up the rest of that whiskey. Either way, it'll give you some relief."

Floyd fixed his eyes on his old man as he staggered into the bedroom groping for the doorframe and closed the door.

He nursed the buttermilk. A reluctant eavesdropper, he listened to the familiar muffled sounds coming from just a few feet away; hearing the sneer of his father's voice as he hurled abuse at Dee. "You ain't asleep! You think you can pretend. I've' got my rights, give me what I want." Grunts and moans joined the murmurs and thumps. He closed his eyes wishing he could shut out the only sounds in the otherwise silent house.

With his eyes closed, the room began to spin and swirl as if he'd just gotten off the Tilt-o-Whirl at the county fair.

His eyes moved toward the door of Sarah's room. A tiny cubicle created by enclosing a portion of the porch two years earlier, when Sarah started school and Dee had deemed her too big to continue to share a room with her parents.

The groans continued from his parents' room. Images of May Nell came back into Floyd's aching head. He pictured her low-cut blouse and her white breasts exposed for him. They were his, there for his pleasure. The relentless urges returned with an unbearable urgency as the rhythmic sound of squeaking bedsprings filled his ears. When the noise finally stopped, Floyd knew Otis had fallen into a stuporous sleep.

Floyd moved quickly across the linoleum kitchen floor toward Sarah's room. Carefully avoiding the creaky board just outside Sarah's door, in an almost hypnotic state he reached for the knob and pushed the door open.

The moonlight filtered past the organdy curtains and highlighted Sarah's faded nightgown. A pink and white quilt had been kicked to the foot of the bed and her arm curled around Fluffy, her toy bear.

Floyd stumbled on a rug next to her bed. Kicking it aside he sat on the edge of the bed staring at the brown bear with the limp red ribbon around its neck. Fluffy had shared Sarah's pillow since the day he'd won the toy bear for her at the County Fair, the year she 'd turned four.

The throbbing in his groin grew more powerful and memories of Fluffy and the fair gave way to images of May Nell *shacked up with the Ellis boy*. May Nell *and her white breasts*, May Nell *and her rounded ass*, May Nell *and her succulent lips*, May Nell….

SIX

Luke 12:2

[2] But there is nothing covered up, that will not be revealed, nor hidden, that will not be known.

Floyd held the stuffed bear in his clumsy hands. The glass eyes shiny as black pinheads caught in a dim filament of moonlight and glared at him. His head throbbed with pain while he pondered that dark stare for a long time.

Eyes fixed on Sarah's pale skin as she slept; he ran his hand over her hair and brushed a few strands from her forehead.

Images of May Nell zipped through his head, crowding out reality. Confusion replaced clarity as a succession of emotions emerged from the blackest caverns of his mind. Clenching and flexing his fist, he opened his hand and let the limp stuffed toy fall to the floor.

He touched himself.

Groggy with sleep, Sarah stirred. "Floyd? Is it morning?"

"No, it's night. I just wanna show ya somethin'. A game."

"I don't wanna play. I'm sleepy. Go away."

"I have some things to teach you. Secret things. Dontcha wanna know a secret?"

Her eyes popped open. "I like secrets."

He put a finger to his lips and shushed her. "It's called *look and touch*; only big kids can play. If I let you play, you can't tell nobody. "

"I'm a big kid."

Unzipping his pants, he pressed her hand to his underpants. "Do you know what this is?"

She shook her head.

31

"I'm going to show you how this works. Now touch it. It's part of the game."

Something moved. Her fingers pulled away as if they'd been burned.

"Only special little girls get to play. Do you want in or not?"

"It's weird. I don't like it."

"Go ahead, touch it again."

Sarah hesitated, nervous, but feeling special. She'd been trusted with an important secret.

Reaching into his underwear he rubbed himself.

She didn't want to look at him or at what he was doing.

"Touch it," he said again and grabbed her hand.

Scared but curious, she knew it was wrong to look. Boys look different than girls…down there… once she'd seen her brothers skinny dipping in the pond, but she'd looked away after only a glimpse.

She shook her head again and pulled her hand away. "No, I'll look but I don't want to touch it."

Her bed rocked with the motion of his body.

Her eyes closed, but the scenes continued to play behind her eyelids. He moaned, and her bed stopped rocking.

"Never tell anyone. It's a special secret." He pushed himself to his feet. "It's going to be *our* secret. I'll buy you a present if you don't tell."

Frightened, she nodded and turned her back to him.

"Don't forget, if you tell anyone, Daddy will be mad at you for playing the game. You'll be in trouble."

Tears slid down his cheeks. *Floyd wouldn't make me do anything bad…but I don't like this game.*

⤴

In the quiet darkness of her room, she jerked awake, her pillow damp with perspiration. Confusion filled her when she first opened her eyes—had it been a bad dream?

She waited, anxious for the faint tinge of dawn to outline the edge of the curtains and send away the crowded maze of images in her mind. Her hand reached for Fluffy to comfort her, but he wasn't in his usual spot by her side. Instead, he stared at her from the floor, judging her with reproachful glass eyes. *He watched the bad thing happen.*

Curled into a fetal position Sarah pulled the sheet tight around her shoulders, a shield against the outside world.

Beyond her window, life went on as usual. The stillness of the night gradually gave way to a curious medley, the sounds of a new day on the farm; the bawling of Sweetie waiting to be milked and the crowing of a rooster in the distance. A blue jay squawked at the chirr-chit-chit as squirrels answered one another and birds chirped in the trees. But something had changed; something inside her.

The memories flooded in...*I did something wrong.* She wanted to erase the images from her mind... tried to wish them away. There was no place to hide from reminders of those terrible minutes with Floyd; they lurked everywhere. *This is our special secret.* They had done the bad thing here, in her bedroom.

Floyd's words pounded in her ears... *if you tell, Daddy will be mad at you for playing the game.*

He's my brother. I've been good. I did what he told me to do. The thought that he would do anything wrong, anything to hurt her was too complicated. *He's gonna buy me a present.*

The gray shadows vanished into morning light exposing the realities of the night, but the confusion of uncertainty remained. *Why can't everything be normal again?*

Floyd's right- I'll get in trouble. I'll get punished... and maybe Floyd too.

Her finger traced the letters on the cover of her book of Children's Bible Stories. Sometimes people did things they weren't supposed to. In the Bible, people did bad things all the time. Adam and Eve did a bad thing and got kicked out of the Garden of Eden. Cain killed his brother and got sent away. And Salome had someone chop off the head of John the Baptist after she'd done a special dance; Momma said that's why Baptists aren't allowed to dance.

Lost in these thoughts, the soft tap at the door went unnoticed.

"Sarah Jane, you awake?" Kenny peeked into her room. "Momma's got hotcakes and sausage ready."

"You're not dressed," he sounded surprised. Sarah always got up early on Sunday morning to get ready to walk the mile up the dirt road to the white clapboard church in Cold Fork.

"I know you're not asleep, you don't have to pretend."

"Go away, Kenny. Tell Momma I don't want to be at Sunday school today."

"You sick?"

There were no words for this feeling.

Today the thought of going to church made her ashamed. Brother Leon had been doing a lot of Hell-fire preaching lately. *What if I get burned up by hellfire in front of the whole congregation?*

Kenny picked Fluffy up and sat down on the side of Sarah's bed in the same spot Floyd had occupied the night before. He gently touched her shoulder. Her body stiffened under his touch. "What's wrong Sarah Jane?"

She remained silent, unable to answer his questions.

Kenny tried again to coax her, but she just shook her head and continued to avoid his eyes. *He won't like me anymore because I'm bad. It's wrong to lie, but crossed fingers cancel out a lie.* She crossed her fingers.

Suddenly, without the slightest transition, unable to stifle the burdensome guilt any longer she uncrossed her fingers and whispered, "I have a secret."

New emotions welled in her. Apprehensive about Kenny's reaction, her stomach tightened. She didn't want to tell but couldn't hold back the guilt any longer.

"It's about Floyd." Her voice faltered through clenched teeth. "You better not tell. Not even Momma... promise!"

Curious, he moved closer to Sarah. "I promise. Cross my heart and hope to die."

Little by little Sarah told the story.

"Floyd came in here last night. He smelled like... like Daddy when he's drunk. Kenny, it scared me. He made me do things I didn't want to do. And made me promise not to tell."

"What kind of things?" He listened in silence as the wretched secret ripped out of her.

Between sobs, Sarah described what happened.

It was a memory she tried immediately to close off. With the telling, Sarah felt lighter as if Kenny now held the burden for her.

Kenny's eyes turned dark. Tears of anger formed. She knew he didn't know how to comfort her.

Momma leaned over the bed and placed the back of her chapped hand against Sarah's cheek, then against her forehead. "No," she said, "you ain't got a fever." She cradled Sarah's face in her hands and kissed her cheek.

"Can I stay home with Daddy, please?"

"All right."

Dee tucked her hair under her favorite hat, grabbed her Bible and headed out the door with Kenny.

From the many years of being married to Otis, Dee had developed a great capacity for silence. She and Kenny walked down the sun-baked dirt road toward Cold Fork Missionary Baptist Church saying little.

Kenny watched the sunlight bounce off the chintz fabric of Dee's Sunday-best dress. His *cross my heart and hope to die* promise to Sarah weighed heavy on him. It would be comforting to hold Momma's hand, but twelve is too old for that.

A blue pick-up truck slowed as it approached and the dust it kicked up billowed around them. The driver waved. Kenny waved. Dee nodded.

Luther and Ruby Williams owned the farm a mile up the road from the Jones place. Once, years earlier, they'd stopped to offer Dee and the kids a ride into Tolerance to attend the First Methodist Church service. Dee thanked them kindly but said she would just as soon walk to Cold Fork to the Baptist church. As they drove off Dee grunted and allowed that the Jones family didn't need Methodist charity.

Later Sarah asked Kenny to explain Methodist charity. He told her Methodist are richer than Baptists and don't have to go to prayer meeting on Wednesday night. Episcopalians all live in town, are even richer than Methodists and don't have to go to church every Sunday and Catholics aren't Christians because they worship idols. Sarah decided Episcopalians had the best deal and wondered what one needed to do to be an Episcopalian.

When Kenny and Momma crossed the gravel parking lot of the church, it was almost full of old farm trucks covered in dust, and the music spilled from the building.

Kenny sat in his usual spot on the hard, wooden pew where they sat every Sunday morning and every Wednesday evening. His mother's wrist rotated back and forth as she worked a colorful cardboard fan. A print of the last supper covered the front side with *Keep Cool with Compliments of Stephens Funeral Home* printed on the back.

He struggled with his secret as the congregation sang *Blessed assurance, Jesus is mine!* As he studied Brother Leon's perfectly coiffed and stiffly sprayed hair, he struggled, and he prayed for deliverance from the dilemma. The secret created a burden too heavy to carry alone.

He received an answer to his prayer when Brother Leon grasped his hand and through perfectly straight white teeth affirmed "Jesus loves you," as Kenny left the church.

Dee had joined the women under the trees to exchange gossip and recipes. No one remained inside the church. Kenny worked to gather the courage to confide in Brother Leon. "Brother Leon, can I ask you a question?" He didn't wait for an okay, instead, just blurted out his question. "If you promised not to tell a secret, but it is about someone who did something bad, should you tell?"

"Well son," answered Brother Leon, "that can be a hard question to answer. A promise is your word and you should never go back on your word. But if someone tells you a secret and it puts them or someone else in danger then you are obliged to tell somebody."

Saying her farewells, Momma made her way in his direction.

Brother Leon continued. "Maybe I can help you through this…"

Kenny ducked his head and muttered, "Thanks anyway. I'll talk it over with the Lord." He slipped past the preacher and bounded down the church steps.

Kenny said nothing as he and his mother left the parking lot and started toward home. They were almost home before he had the courage to blurt out, "Momma, did you know Floyd got drunk last night?"

"No, Kenny I didn't rightly know that. But then, I suppose that's between Floyd and your daddy. I don't get into their business. Your daddy don't much like it when I do."

Momma's right. It wouldn't do no good to tell her. Telling it would cause trouble with Daddy. Always an obedient child, he avoided conflict whenever possible. *No, it's best not to tell Momma.*

When the farm came in to view, relief spread through him at the sight of the empty driveway. *The log truck's gone. That means Floyd's gone.*

Inside, Sarah sat at the table eating a bowl of cornflakes and reading the back of the box. She looked up when Kenny came through the back door. Dee's bread bowl rested next to her elbow overflowing with the entire contents of the cereal box.

"Hey, Kenny I found the diving frogman. This one's blue. It's mine…you got the last one." She held up the plastic toy in triumph.

"Look at this mess Sarah Jane, you know better." Dee tried to give her a stern look but hid a smile. "Help your sister get the cereal back in the box instead of all over my floor. I need to get started frying up the chicken."

"Floyd's gone to Texarkana," said Sarah.

Kenny looked confused. "What for?"

"Don't know. Daddy said he'll be back on Thursday."

SEVEN

Proverbs 14
[32]The wicked is banished in his wickedness, But the righteous has a refuge in his death

The family had gathered around the supper table when they heard the roar as the big truck pulled onto the gravel drive. Kenny held his breath and looked at Sarah.

He saw the concern on her face as they waited for the door to open.

Floyd stepped through the back door not stopping to wipe his muddy boots, a half-smoked Camel tucked behind his ear, his cheeks lightly peppered with a patchy growth of facial hair.

The first gusty hint of fall swept through the kitchen before he could get the door closed.

Without washing his hands or speaking he plopped down next to Jim Ed and stuck a fork into a slice of ham.

Jim Ed turned back to Junior and continued his conversation about their high school football team.

Kenny glared at Floyd. Should he tell his daddy what Floyd did to Sarah? It made him uneasy to feel such contempt toward his brother for putting him in this position. Searching his Bible for answers only caused more concern. Over and over he read *Matthew 5:22...but I say unto you, that everyone who is angry with his brother shall be in danger of the judgment.* There was no way to reconcile what he read in the Bible with what Floyd had done to Sarah. He wanted to talk to Brother Leon about his feelings, but that required him to talk about what Floyd did. The weight of the matter pressed heavily on him. He felt helpless to do anything about it.

He glanced across the table at Sarah who looked at her hands, down at her plate, into Kenny's eyes, anywhere but at Floyd. *If only he hadn't come home.* The knot in his throat made it hard for food to go down.

"Momma, may I please be excused? I have a belly ache." Sarah's voice was almost a whisper.

Otis grunted and gave Dee a dirty look.

"I'll be back to clear the table," Sarah mumbled looking toward Otis in conciliation.

"Don't worry, I'll help Momma," Kenny said, giving Sarah a nod.

Sarah closed the door to her room and took a shoebox from a shelf, found her small red spiral notebook and opened it.

At the back of the notebook, she listed vocabulary words to learn. In the front, she kept a detailed list of the books she'd read, complete with her reviews. Most books got five stars, and none got only one star. On a separate page, all thirty-three Nancy Drew books were listed in order, with a red asterisk next to the ones she owned. They'd been checked them off one by one as she read them.

She wished they all had a red asterisk. She hated to return the books she'd check out of the library to skinny old Miss Maynard.

Carefully straightening the books, she pulled number 10, *Password to Larkspur Lane* from the shelf.

She fluffed her pillow and shoved it against the headboard. *I wonder if I can put together all the pieces and solve the mystery before Nancy.* She settled back on her pillow, opened the book and escaped to a world where a girl had the freedom and intelligence to solve mysteries. She stopped once to add *Delphinium* to the list of words to look up in the dictionary at school.

The happiest part of her day was spent reading in bed; a time to explore other places and take refuge in the book in her hand.

Her greatest source of pride came from reading more books than any other girl in her third-grade class. Miss Maynard told her she should be a 5th grader to read Nancy Drew and handing her *Stuart Little* said, "This is what girls in the 3rd grade should read."

She read it, but found a story about a mouse with human parents to be quite stupid. She didn't care what Old Boney Face said. Nancy Drew's much better, it's about real people.

A knock on the door brought her back from River Heights and her friends Nancy, George, and Bess. Kenny poked his head in. "Everything's gonna be okay, I'm gonna look after you. No need to worry." Then he closed the door and left.

If she were as clever as Nancy, she would know what to do about Floyd.

The kitchen was hot, too hot to stay inside. Dee and Sarah retreated to the coolness of the porch. They sat on the swing; a mess of purple-hull peas filled an enamel bowl resting between them. Fresh from the garden the peas were plump and moist; they popped from the pods with ease.

Dee seemed lost in thought as she rocked the swing back and forth and softly sang, *Rock of ages, cleft for me. Let me hide myself in thee.* Momma sang this hymn often. Sarah wondered what cleft meant. She looked it up in the big dictionary at the library. The definition didn't help. No matter. Momma's singing always made her feel safe.

"Momma, do you think Floyd will get drunk like last Saturday?"

Dee stopped rocking. "Well, I don't rightly know," she answered. "But Floyd's might near a growed man and it would be between him and his daddy." After a long thoughtful pause, she asked, "Why are you and Kenny both troubled about Floyd's drinking?"

Sarah looked down at her purple stained fingers. "I didn't like the way he acted when he got drunk last time… that's all."

Sarah knew saying anything about Floyd would bring trouble, so without a further word, she dropped the subject. Besides, Kenny would take care of things. The past two nights since Floyd returned from Texarkana Kenny sneaked into Sarah's room and slept in a chair next to her bed, acting as protector through the night until just before dawn when he quietly left her room before the rest of the family got up.

This morning the old pickup left the farm with Daddy behind the wheel and the boys piled in the back. They headed to Tolerance for the Saturday routine. Fear of what might happen that evening weighed heavy on Sarah's mind.

Long after Dee had sent her to bed, Sarah lay awake listening for the sound of the truck pulling into the yard. Her stomach did a somersault whenever she heard the slightest noise.

A car door slamming jolted her awake. She heard the faint squeak of the screen door, the sound of work boots on the kitchen floor, the hushed voices of her brothers as they headed to bed. Sarah chewed her lip.

In the silence, the floorboard outside her door creaked. Fear grabbed at her stomach. The doorknob turned. The door slowly edged open.

Through the darkness, Kenny peered in at her with concern on his face. She knew Floyd must be drunk again.

Without a word, Kenny took his place in the chair.

With Kenny there, she'd dozed.

Her eyes snapped opened. Someone moved around in the kitchen. The icebox door opened and closed. A chair scooted across the floor. Sarah stared at the light seeping around the edges of the door. The glow blackened for a moment. She took a breath and held it as the door opened. A large dark figure appeared in the doorway, briefly illuminated by the dim light from the kitchen. The door closed again.

Floyd loomed over her; his eyes blank and stupid. She felt his hot, whiskey tainted breath on her face as he pulled at her blankets.

Before Floyd could make another move, Kenny, wild eyes flashing, pounced on his back and knocked him to the floor. His knuckles crashed into Floyd's jaw. The rage on Kenny's face frightened Sarah as he pummeled Floyd's face with both fists.

Sarah cried out.

Otis, wearing only his stained boxer shorts, crashed into the room with Dee tight on his heels. "What's all the commotion?" He pulled the boys apart and placing himself between them, grabbed the back of their undershirts and dragged them into the kitchen.

Jim Ed and Junior appeared.

Dee rushed to Sarah's side. With arms encircling her, she tried to calm her daughter's sobs. With labored gasps, Sarah told Dee the whole story.

In the kitchen, Jim Ed and Junior watched as Otis, Kenny, and Floyd shoved one another and shouted.

Otis hauled off and punched Floyd in the face. As blood gushed from his nostrils, Floyd dropped onto a chair and threw his body across the kitchen table. He buried his face in his curled arms and began to whimper. "I'm sorry. Daddy, I'm sorry."

"Daddy," Kenny said. "Floyd's got to leave. You can't let him hurt Sarah Jane anymore."

"You stay outta this, boy," yelled Otis. "Don't be telling me what to do. Now git, before I knock you into next Sunday!"

Dee came into the room. Maintaining a respectful distance, she declared in a quivering voice, "The boy's right Otis, Floyd needs to leave here right now."

Otis stopped mid-stride and returned Dee's sudden show of boldness with an incredulous dazed look.

"All y'all... 'cept Floyd, out!" He waved his arm toward the bedroom.

Dee and the three boys scrambled to Sarah's room. They heard only a muffled exchange before Otis finally declared "...and don't you ever darken the door of this house again. I'm ashamed to have my blood flowing through your veins."

"But, Daddy...," stuttered Floyd.

There was a scuffling sound and then the door slammed.

"Y'all git back to bed," Otis bellowed. He pounded his fist on the kitchen table with such force it rattled the teacups in the cabinets.

There was never any mention of that night again.

The reflection of the sun bounced off Fluffy's glass eyes for the last time, as Sarah buried him deep in the burn pile with the morning trash.

EIGHT

Ephesians 4:29
29Let no corrupt speech proceed out of your mouth, but only what is good for building others up as the need may be, that it may give grace to those who hear.

1958

Otis took the first portions and crammed a hot biscuit in his mouth. Only then did he allow the rest of the family to pass around the bowls filled with fried chicken, mashed potatoes and cream gravy. When Dee was growing up, saying grace had been a part of the supper ritual, but early in their marriage Dee learned Otis had no tolerance for what he deemed "such nonsense."

Carefully chewing with his few good teeth, Otis settled back in his chair, his shoulders slumped. "Was a time a fella could make a respectable living growing peaches around here, but that just ain't the case no more. There's folks cain't even eat these days, things being what they are."

"Ain't had a decent peach crop since them late freezes killed all the peach buds in '53. We didn't get half a crop this year, and there ain't no chance for a late hay crop neither.

"Them Mexican pickers has just about quit coming through here on their way back to Mexico. Ain't enough work to keep 'em here, so they been headin' straight for south Texas instead."

He buttered another biscuit, and holding his knife in his hand, watched the butter melt into the warm bread. "We gotta figure some way to make the land show us a profit. I about come to the conclusion we might be better off if we just pulled up them peach trees and used the land for something else."

Junior nodded in agreement. "The Allen's bulldozed their trees last year, and they're using the land to graze cattle. Carl Edward says things is a lot better now."

Sarah frowned. If only she could think of something to help the family. Maybe then they wouldn't be mad at her. It made Daddy mad that Floyd had to leave. Maybe if she tried a little harder, then Daddy would love her.

She remembered the 4-H Club members coming to her class to tell everyone how much fun they have in 4-H. They were having a contest to raise baby goats. She could win a blue ribbon for the best goat and even go to the County Fair. That would make Daddy proud. Then she'd be useful and worthy of his love, like the boys. She twirled her hair nervously. Her eyes darted from the fried okra on her chipped dinner plate to her daddy's worried face. Filled with pride and anticipation she paused, licked her dry lips and looked up. "I could raise a baby goat."

Otis ignored her.

She turned her eyes toward Kenny seeking comfort. He gave his head an almost undetectable shake.

Feeling a mixture of hurt and defeat she tried again. "At school, they told us you can make cheese out of goat's milk."

Otis grunted. His tone said *shut up*. "Hell's bells, are you crazy in the head, girl. A goat's 'bout as worthless as tits on a boar." Bits of food spewed from his mouth as he spoke. "We ain't goat farmers." He turned to Dee with a scowl. "This is your fault, the way you're raising her, encouraging her nonsense. Dang nanny goats!"

Sarah saw the loathing in his eyes. She bit back a sudden urge to cry.

Jim Ed put down his fork. "The Allens aren't the only ones to pull up their trees. Sonny Akins said his daddy's been talkin' to some guy from a chicken producer. He came from up around Springdale. The Akins' are about to add two more chicken coops to their place. The fella said he would give the farmers the chicks and the feed at a discount, then pay them to raise the chickens."

Otis leaned in conspiratorially. "You sure about that deal? We ain't got money to be a-wasting. That Akins boy ain't got the good sense of a turkey."

Jim Ed's voice became more confident. "Sonny's a smart guy. I don't know much about it myself, but I asked him a bunch of questions."

Visibly skeptical Otis said, "Guess it won't do no harm for you to go down yonder and talk to that chicken fella. Seems we ain't got much choice in the matter. Gotta make some kinda change 'round here."

Jim Ed's jaw clenched. He looked uneasily from Otis to Junior, and then back.

Sarah drew a deep breath and reached for her napkin. The tears she held back began to burn in her throat. She sniffed and blew her nose.

Otis snapped his fingers. "Girl, I'm gonna whup you good if you don't stop that sniveling. Now cut out the nonsense and get away from the table. Let the menfolk talk serious. Dee, it's time you stopped coddling this one."

Sarah shoved her chair away from the table and went to her room.

She wiped tears from her eyes as Dee entered her room. "Want me to brush your hair, baby?" asked Dee in her soothing voice.

"Yes ma'am," sniffed Sarah.

Dee sat beside her on the bed and hummed *Rock of Ages* while she brushed and plaited Sarah's hair.

NINE

1 Samuel 17

[34] And David said unto Saul, Thy servant kept his father's sheep, and there came a lion, and a bear, and took a lamb out of the flock: [35] And I went out after him, and smote him, and delivered it out of his mouth: and when he arose against me, I caught him by his beard, and smote him, and slew him.

Sarah's feet dangled from a tire swing that hung from the crotch of the big oak tree. Her tongue flicked at the Popsicle stick catching a sweet dribble of red liquid before it reached her fingers. Squinting against the sunlight she sang *"This little light of mine, I'm gonna let it shine, Let it shine, Let it shine, Let it shine."* Her long tan legs peeked from beneath the uneven hem of her simple red and white checked dress.

Joy rested at Sarah's bare feet, and together they watched the bulldozer circle around to make another assault on the row of peach trees. The dozer had worked all morning ripping the roots from the ground and shoveling them into large heaps.

Otis ordered the driver to leave a small stand of trees near the house; enough for the family and a few bushels to sell to the city folk at the roadside shed.

Sarah was happy to know they would still have the smell of the orchard. The sweet aroma of the trees loaded with ripe fruit had been a part of her life from her earliest memory. Changes always made her sad.

Sarah sucked the last icy chunk from the stick and hopped from the swing. She tossed the stick to the ground and picked a dandelion, caught her breath and blew. Hundreds of seed parachutes drifted apart and soared out into the grass.

"Come on Joy." Sarah bent to pick up her book where she had carefully left it against the tree. "Let's go to our special place."

Joy gave a few barks and quickly bounded off toward the fields. Sarah followed close behind hardly feeling the thorns and rocks beneath her calloused feet.

When the black and white dog reached the peak of a small ridge she stopped and waited for Sarah to catch up.

The pair nimbly maneuvered the path along a ravine high above a meandering stream.

Once they reached a clearing under a hickory tree, Sarah went about getting everything ready. She removed the lid from a weather-beaten wooden crate, pulled out a tattered quilt and spread it on the cool grass.

This had been her secret place since before finding Joy. No one knew about it—except Kenny, and he wouldn't tell.

At first, she'd bring Fluffy and Dolly and read to them. But now she was too big to read to a doll and… Fluffy—he'd been buried along with some bad memories.

Besides, now she had Joy.

The cozy spot in the dappled shade provided a place to let all her worries go and to let her imagination wander off and explore unbelievable places.

She pressed her back against the tree and opened the book.

"So Joy, today we get to start a new book. Old Prune Face let me have it with just one dirty look this time. I sure do wish we could buy the whole set and not have to worry with Pruny, don't you?"

The crash of the bulldozer against the trees resonated across the fields.

Sarah reached out and rubbed Joy's head. "Don't even worry about those ol' peach trees. Kenny says everything will be alright and we'll get to have a lot more chickens now. I like the chickens, don't you?" She took Joy's chin in her hand and looked into her brown eyes. "You won't chase the new chickens, will you?"

"All right, here we go. Let's see what mystery Nancy Drew will solve this time." She opened the book and began to read aloud. "The Whispering Statue. number fifteen. By Caroline Keene. Copyright 1937 by Grosset and Dunlap, Inc., chapter one. An Unpleasant Companion. page one. *'Oh, that was a beautiful drive, Nancy! Your ball must have gone at least two hundred and twenty-five yards!'*

Sarah stopped to explain to Joy. "Don't that beat all? They're playing golf at a fashionable summer resort. Nancy's father is a rich lawyer, so they can

46

afford to stay at a fashionable summer resort... I wish Daddy was a lawyer, and then he'd be nice like Carson Drew. Maybe I'll marry a lawyer when I grow up. We'll live in a white house with a picket fence and roses climbing on it and he'll buy me a convertible roadster like Nancy's." Joy tilted her head to the side, her long ears flopping.

"This is a roadster. Sarah held up the illustrated page to show Joy. Don't feel bad, girl, I didn't know what a roadster looked like either."

Crouched on the quilt beneath the tree, Sarah continued to read the story aloud. *The caddy gazed intently toward the ravine as he answered in a voice scarcely above a whisper: "The haunted bridge, that's what I'm afraid of, and so are the other boys."*

Joy rested her head on Sarah's thigh and settled in as if to find out more about the haunted bridge. "I'll bet Nancy's not afraid of a silly haunted bridge! We'll find out directly...just wait."

She continued to read, stopping from time to time to explain a passage. She didn't hear the birds singing in the trees and didn't notice the dragonfly hover over a leaf and flitter away, nor the green lizard that stopped by and listened for a while before going about his business.

"Nevertheless, it took courage,' replied her father. 'If you hadn't had it, you never would have been able to say farewell to that ole ghost."

The end

Sarah closed the book and looked toward the horizon. "Oh shoot! My stars and garters it's almost dusk. Joy, we're in trouble again. Mamma's gonna have a hissy fit."

They took off running trying to beat the dusky darkness.

Just after sun-up, Jim Ed and Junior moved from mound to mound and dropped blazing torches into the piles of uprooted trees. The green wood whistled and popped as it caught fire. While the fires burned, filling the fresh air with the sweet smell of smoke, the brothers began to nail smooth pine ship-lap boards over two-by-four rafters for the roof of the new chicken house.

"That green wood sure puts off the smoke, don't it? I'm afraid this laundry is gonna stink of smoke." Dee lugged her basket of wet clothes to the clothesline and set it down. She stayed for only a second to watch the fire lick at the broken trees. "It's done been washed, nothing to do but let it dry." She turned and disappeared into the house.

Sarah reached into the clothespin bag tied to the sagging clothesline and clipped the edges of a clean, damp towel to the line. She pinned row after row of freshly washed laundry to the line and watched the glowing ashes rise through the gray smoke and curl toward the morning sky to be extinguished by the warm breeze.

By day's end, the supplanted trees were reduced to smoldering cinders and were replaced by a row of new chicken coops, complete with nesting boxes ready for two hundred energetic chicks.

"Shoo! Git!" Sarah kicked at the brazen blackbirds that gathered to eat with the chickens. She reached into her pail of seed and table scraps and scattered a handful onto the ground.

"Heeerrreee chick, chick, chick! Here Blackie, here Chirpy, here Penny...come on girls, come and get it." The hens flocked around Sarah's feet, clucking and pecking at the ground. Another handful of feed started a frenzy of squawks. Heads jerked, and wings flapped as the chickens strutted stiffly around her.

Sarah looked after the family flock while the boys saw to the contractor's chickens. She'd given names to her favorites in hopes they would never be chosen for the frying pan.

The queen of the flock, Peaches, a fat brown and white hen pecked at Penny with an unrelenting viciousness. Sarah inserted her foot to separate the two hens and shooed the bully away. "Stop it, there is plenty for everyone."

She rounded the corner of the barn and stopped short at the gruesome sight. Her breath halted in her throat. Partial remains of at least four hens lay scattered about on blood splattered straw. Bits of raw flesh still stuck to the feathers littering the ground. She stood frozen, watching Joy forage through the bloody scene, feathers covered in chicken blood clinging to her fur. Carefully, she backed away, as one back away from a snake.

Otis' warning echoed through Sarah's head ... *she better not chase the chickens.*

For a brief moment, Sarah considered hiding the carnage. *No one would miss four chickens.* She pushed the temptation from her mind and took off in search of Kenny.

Finding Kenny with Junior and Jim Ed at the end of the chicken yard, she ducked around the corner hoping they hadn't seen here. *I need to talk to Kenny alone. Junior might tell Daddy what happened.*

Her stomach churned. She prayed. Leave!

Instead, immediately all three brothers stood over her. Her lips tingled and her hands were clammy. Hoping against hope nobody would say anything, she kept her eyes forward. *If Daddy finds out, I'll get a whipping I won't forget.*

"Something wrong?" Kenny asked.

She looked from Kenny to Jim Ed to Junior. Hesitantly; anxious for some guidance, she motioned for her brothers to follow.

"We got problems," Jim Ed said, as they approached the devastation.

Kenny pulled Joy from the carcasses and stomped his foot and swatted her bottom. "Beat it!" She growled and retreated, tail between her legs. Kenny surveyed the area with his eyes and shook his head. "Looks like a 'coon or maybe a 'possum got to the hens last night."

Junior and Jim Ed nodded in agreement.

The boys took a few steps away from their sister for a brief, whispered conversation. She strained to hear what they said but could make out only a few words... *Daddy...trap...dog.*

Kenny returned to her side. "Don't worry," he said. "Daddy'll believe me. He'll see your dog didn't do it."

Bit by bit, her breathing returned to normal, but her hands continued to tremble.

Then reality set in. Her chin trembled. "He won't believe you or he'll believe you. Either way, he'll be really mad. I'll get a whipping."

Kenny stayed by her side as Junior disappeared into the barn.

Minutes later he returned with Otis lumbering behind him, a pinched look around his eyes.

"What happened here?" Otis asked, his tone acid. He looked the situation over for a second, raised his eyebrows and gestured toward the dog. "Fetch me a chain!" he yelled. He walked away shaking his head in disapproval.

"Why did you tell him?" Sarah mumbled to no one in particular.

After the dishes were done Sarah and Dee joined the others in the living room. Dee took her normal spot in the overstuffed rocking chair and picked up her crochet basket.

Sarah sprawled on the floor next to her brothers listening to the latest episode of *Gunsmoke* on the radio. They waited for Marshall Dillon to either kill or lock up all the bad guys. Usually, he just killed them.

As the radio announcer listed the sponsors, Sarah managed to gather all her courage and with clenched teeth and shaking hands—openly defiant— she looked at her daddy and declared– "Joy didn't kill those chickens...it was a coon."

"We'll see what we catch in that trap," Otis growled. He looked her over for a second and turned back to his newspaper, making it clear the conversation was over.

With the question of what killed the chickens left in the air, Sarah slipped into the yard, past the water pump and the clothesline to the tool shed where Joy was chained to a fence post.

Joy pulled against the chain and whimpered. Sarah's heart clutched in her chest. Poor, Joy. She didn't understand. She'd never been tied up before. Instead, she'd been free to run in the fields. Free to chase squirrels and hunt for rabbits; but she'd never killed anything except a rat, never.

Sarah plopped onto the grass next to her dog. "Are you all right girl?"

Joy pushed her wet nose into Sarah's hand and stared up at her.

"I'm sorry Daddy chained you up...you didn't do anything wrong." She reached out and rubbed behind the dog's ears and up and down her back. The fur was soft and warm against her hand. Joy rested her paws on Sarah's lap and licked a spot on her arm.

"It'll be okay. I promise. I know you didn't do it." She rubbed Joy's head and sighed heavily.

Sarah dug into her pocket and pulled out a napkin stuffed with bits of meat and half-eaten biscuits. "I saved you some scraps when we did the dishes. It' alright, no one saw me."

Preoccupied with Joy's impending fate Sarah didn't hear Kenny approach. She sucked in her breath and jumped at his voice coming out of the darkness.

"Oh, it's you." The relief in her voice was undeniable.

He sat down next to her in the dirt. "Don't worry, Sarah Jane, we'll trap it."

"How long does it take to trap a coon?"

"Depends."

"What if we don't catch the coon? Please don't' let Daddy shoot Joy. If you don't catch the coon, he'll shoot her for sure,"

He looked troubled. "There's nothing I can do."

For the first time in her life, she knew Kenny couldn't fix everything.

The sound of furious barking roused Sarah from a troubled sleep. Barefooted, she raced toward the chicken house, the hem of her nightgown dragging in the dirt.

Joy pulled furiously at her chain, whining as Sarah rushed past her.

The trap was empty. But Kenny had cornered a nasty possum against the side of the barn. The possum let out a contemptuous hiss and flailed its arms with a clawing motion. Breathing hard Kenny stepped across the straw-littered ground gripping the .22 rifle they kept leaning near the back door. He paused, briefly scanning the situation, squinted through the sight and aimed the .22 between the eyes of the drooling predator.

He stopped, lowered the rifle and with a commanding gesture ordered Sarah, "Stay back."

A surge of adrenaline pumped through Kenny as the possum opened his mouth wide displaying a single row of razor-sharp teeth. It lunged forward and let out one final hiss. There was a loud timbre as Kenny pulled the trigger and the possum sprawled to the ground.

Sarah silently thanked Jesus. She gritted her teeth and affirmed under her breath, "I knew she didn't chase the chickens."

.

TEN

Psalms 55
⁵Fear and trembling come upon me, And horror has overwhelmed me.

Sarah liked Sunday school. Miss Dotty told Bible stories by putting cut out figures on the flannel covered board. The story of Jonah made Sarah think of Pinocchio when Geppetto got swallowed by a whale. She didn't believe anyone could really live inside a whale.

The story about Ruth was one of her favorites, especially the part where Naomi and Ruth get jobs in the fields. Boaz rides up on his horse and sees how pretty Ruth is and she sees how handsome he is, so they get married; just like Cinderella and Prince Charming.

She didn't like church as much as Sunday school. Mostly, she liked singing the songs. Mamma's face looked calm when they sang *Rock of Ages*. Sometimes Sarah would check the hymn board on the wall next to the pulpit. She liked to peek ahead in the Hymnal and mark the next song like she'd seen Momma do.

She never understood the preaching. When Brother Leon started the message, her crinoline petticoat scratched her legs and she got sleepy.

But today she didn't feel sleepy. Today Brother Leon had her full attention. Why she wondered, why would anyone want this? *How can this be a good thing?*

She studied the colorful picture on the church bulletin clenched in her hand. An airplane has crashed into the side of a flaming building. The streets are littered with mangled cars and trucks. And there, in the lower right-hand corner is a white church. It sure looks like Cold Fork Baptist Church. Tombstones are knocked over and white shrouded ghosts float from the graves and fly up into the sky. Above it all, in great beams of light, Jesus hovers above a city. His hand is raised in an inviting gesture, but below, the city is in chaos.

Along the bottom of the page, large-seriphed, jagged red letters spell out *The Rapture.* This sermon wasn't boring. She didn't want to lay her head in Momma's lap like when she was little, not today.

Brother Leon read from 1 Thessalonians.

> *For the Lord Himself will descend from heaven with a shout, with the voice of the archangel and with the trumpet of God, and the dead in Christ will rise first. Then we who are alive and remain will be caught up together with them in the clouds to meet the Lord in the air....*

"Oh, what a wondrous and glorious day it will be for those who are ready. Jesus will come. Believers will be caught up into the clouds, and Jesus will call them to come home to Heaven." Brother Leon closed his eyes, raised his arms, and turned his face to heaven. "And woe be to those sinners who have not received Him, for they will be left behind. Be ready. Be ready to meet Him when He comes."

Sarah's eyes widened. She moved closer to Kenny. This did not sound like a glorious day to her. Squirming in her seat, she looked around to count the people in the church. She wondered just how many would go to heaven in the rapture; would there be enough room for her?

She started ticking them off. Brother Leon and his family would go. Sister Dorothy Jo, who played the piano, the Adams twins, who always sat on the front pew wearing fancy store-bought dresses; they would all make it ahead of her. Momma and Kenny, they would go for sure. *That makes nine.*

Brother Leon continued, his voice reaching a roar. "As sure as we all sit here, He will return! The rapture will take place in the twinkling of an eye. You better be ready at that instant; we cannot count on there being another day in which to get ready. The Lord will not take out an ad on the radio. Yesterday is gone, tomorrow is not promised. Today is the only certainty you have."

She wasn't ready for Jesus to take her *with a trumpet blast* and *in the twinkling of an eye.* Being taken from earth and transported to be with Jesus in **Heaven sounded horrifying. Wasn't Jesus supposed to protect her, not snatch her out** of her bed like a monster from a movie? Weeks after her brothers took her to Texarkana to see *Creature from the Black Lagoon,* she still had nightmares. But *that* was just a monster movie, *not real like this.* Brother Leon would never make up such a dreadful thing.

"After the rapture, many will look for their missing loved ones, but they will never see them again. All those who do not know the Lord will be left behind! Mother's will be separated from their children, husbands from wives. Don't be left behind! Receive Jesus as your Savior now. Now is the time of preparation."

If Jesus loves all the little children, why would He take them from their mothers? Why would He leave them behind in the rapture?

This didn't sound like the friendly Jesus they learned about in Sunday school. Jesus is supposed to protect the little children from bad things. How do you pray for Jesus to protect you when He is the one you are afraid of?

"Now turn in your Hymnals to hymn number 527 and praise the Lord with your voices."

When the trumpet of the Lord shall sound
and time shall be no more
And the morning breaks eternal bright and fair
When the saved of earth shall gather over
on the other shore
And the roll is called up yonder I'll be there
When the roll is called up yonder
I'll be there

I'm not always good. What if I won't be there when the end of the world comes?
One person will be taken and another beside him will be left behind.
What if Kenny and Momma get "raptured" and I get left behind all by myself? What if the bad thing that happened with Floyd keeps me from going to Heaven with Momma and Kenny? What are the 'unpleasant consequences reserved for the unredeemed?'

Sarah had been awake listening to the sounds of the night for an agonizingly long time. Only the rhythm of tree frogs and crickets outside disrupted the quiet of the house. A dog barked in the distance.

Joy stirred, her ear twitched. Sarah had snuck Joy into the house once she was certain that Daddy was sound asleep. *I wonder if dogs get to go to the rapture. Maybe Joy will go without me.*

Humid air drifted through her opened window and saturated her cotton sheets. She craved sleep to relieve her from these frightful thoughts. Closing her eyes didn't bring sleep, instead came visions of skeletons soaring skyward from open graves.

On the clock at her bedside, a plastic ballerina poised on tiptoes and wearing a pink tulle tutu, stood still. The radium numbers glowed green. The hands pointed to 1:30.

Please, Jesus, help me...please don't let me be left all by myself. Please take me in the rapture. She wasn't sure she wanted the prayer to be answered.

The powers of her imagination exploded. Thoughts of Jesus became confused with thoughts of the Devil. Who would protect her from this scary new Jesus she had learned about? *I wish I wasn't afraid to go to heaven with Jesus.*

She turned the tiny knob on the clock and watched the ballerina spin round and round to the tinkling music. She loved the clock, a gift from Kenny on her 8th birthday. *I wish Kenny could stay with me until I fall asleep.*

Jesus is always watching. He knows everything you do. You can escape the darkness when the morning comes, but you can never escape Jesus.

She closed her eyes tight. An image appeared. It was her, with 666--the mark of the beast--carved into her bloody forehead. She opened her eyes; the image remained.

The ballerina stopped twirling. Sarah didn't dare put her hand out to wind up the music box again. Something in the darkness might grab her and drag her under of the bed. She pulled the covers tight over her shoulders. *Maybe I can put one finger out and see what happens.* Her finger crept from under the covers. Nothing happened. Her whole hand came out; still, nothing happened.

What's that in the corner? It's not moving... is it Jesus? Did he just turn his head to look at me? I can say 'be gone in Jesus' name' and it will have to leave unless it is Jesus. She closed her eyes. Opened them. The figure disappeared.

Is the bed moving? The rapture? 'Mother's will be separated from their children.' That was Jesus! Everyone has been raptured, except me. Joy's still here.

She wanted to leave her room but feared something hiding under her bed—the Devil—waiting to grab her foot the moment it comes within its reach. Finally, the fear of being left behind outweighed the fear of whatever was under her bed. Holding her breath, she stood on her bed and jumped far enough that the Devil couldn't grab her foot.

She shot across the cold floor to the bedroom where her brothers slept. Her feet hardly touched the ground. The door stood ajar. Barely breathing, she peeked into the room. A ribbon of moonlight ran across the room revealing a pile of clothing on the floor next to Kenny's bed. He *had* been raptured; only his clothes remained. Panic filled her.

Then the moon edged from behind a cloud casting a wide beam on the room, revealing three sleeping forms. The synchronized cadence of her brothers' breath assured her that she hadn't been abandoned. Not yet.

ELEVEN

Proverbs 12:10
*¹⁰ A righteous man respects the life of his animal,
but the tender mercies of the wicked are cruel.*

B rows knitted into a frown, Becky Sue asked, "What do you think it is?"
"Come on, girl. It's all right. We want to help you." Joy rolled over
obediently presenting her belly for inspection.
Sarah and her cousin stooped to get a closer look. Hovering over the dog,
they examined her swollen nipples.

I'm glad you came," Sarah said," You always know what to do. You're the
smartest girl I know-- almost as smart as Kenny.

She wished her cousin and aunt would visit more often...it seemed to
Sarah when Aunt Myra came to visit, Momma talked and talked and
sometimes she even laughed.

One time she overheard a little bit of conversation between Aunt Myra
and Momma. Aunt Myra told Momma she thought Daddy was rude and had
a quarrelsome nature. Sarah added "quarrelsome" to her list of words to look
up.

Sarah studded the nipples a little longer and finally concluded, "We better
get Momma."

The girls stormed toward the house with Joy at their heels. The screen
door slammed behind them as they ran, breathless, into the kitchen. Dee and
Myra sat at the kitchen table. They sorted piles of Becky's outgrown clothes
inspecting for lost buttons and loose hems.

Dee held up a homemade cotton dress for Sarah to admire. "I think this
one is just the right size." Becky's outgrown clothes were always *just the right
size* for Sarah.

"Yes ma'am, but...," Sarah clutched her side, struggling to catch her breath.

Dee put the dress in the mending pile and turned her attention to the girls. "What's got you two in such an all-fired hurry, anyway?"

Sarah inhaled deeply. "Momma, something is terribly wrong with Joy. Come see."

Dee looked confused, then worried. The women followed the girls into the yard where they found Joy. Her tail vigorously thumped the ground.

Sarah rolled the dog onto her back exposing her belly.

Dee took a quick look at the dog. "If that don't beat all."

"What's wrong with her, Momma? Is she gonna die?"

"Your dog will be just fine, but I can't say the same for them puppies she's carrying."

Sarah's eyes grew round and her mouth stood open. "Puppies!" the cousins squealed in unison. Jumping up and down, they threw their arms around each other. "We're gonna have puppies!"

"Your daddy is gonna have a conniption fit when he finds out," warned Dee. "You know we can't keep them. Your daddy won't stand for a passel of dogs around here."

"When do you think they will be born? Becky, you want a cute little puppy, don't you?"

The first light of dawn filtered through the window of the still dark room. Sarah slipped out of bed, brushed the tangled hair out of her eyes, and in a moment was dressed and rushing toward the barn without stopping for breakfast.

The sweet smell of fresh hay filled the dark, warm barn. Sarah squinted, trying to make out how many puppies Joy had piled in the nest of hay tucked into a shadowy corner of the barn. Five had been born last night before Dee made Sarah go to bed.

Her heart raced as she listened to the squeaky whimpers coming from the mound of black and white fur. There were six tiny balls, two solid black, and four black and white like their mother. Joy licked and nudged the puppies as they crawled over one another blindly searching for a nipple.

"Joy" she whispered, "I'm gonna call the black and white ones Spot, Buster, Fuzzy and Bo and the black one's Blackie and Shadow. Do you like those names?"

Dee had cautioned her not to touch the puppies for fear of upsetting Joy, but how could she resist? The unspoken message was for Sarah not to get attached.

She didn't hear Junior enter the barn as she cautiously inched her fingers toward the puppies. "Sarah Jane, Momma said, get in the house and leave them puppies alone. Breakfast's on the table." Startled at the sound of Junior's voice, she jumped and quickly pulled her hand away.

She stared at her empty plate, waiting for everyone to finish breakfast. *Hurry up, I need to check on the puppies. Jim Ed—stop talking about chicken feed.* For a brief moment she wondered if Daddy had poured another cup of coffee just to torture her, but at last, after what seemed like an eternity, Otis tilted his head back to drain the last swallow of coffee from his cup, wiped his hands on his jeans and stood up from the table. Breakfast was over.

Sarah hurried out the door, disappearing into the barn. She snuggled into the corner where the puppies were nestled against their mother. She put her hand out to Joy, allowing her to sniff. "This is just about the neatest thing that ever happened."

Carefully, she picked up Shadow, kissed him on his tiny wet nose, gently laid him next to an empty teat, and stroked Joy on her nose.

The rusty hinges creaked as the barn door opened and Kenny stepped in.

"You in here Sarah Jane?"

"Yes"

"Get to the garden and pick them butter beans before Momma tans your hide. She said them beans ain't gonna pick themselves. You best get your chores done before you play with them puppies."

She gave a shrug in Joy's direction, grabbed a bucket on her way out of the barn and shot across the yard to the garden.

It didn't take long for her bucket to fill up. She stopped picking just long enough to sit on the ground and watch a little green snake disappear into a row of pole beans. Her eyes shifted toward the house. Momma and Daddy stood on the back porch. She couldn't make out what they said, but Daddy seemed angry and her momma looked upset. It must be real important— Momma usually kept quiet and let Daddy have his way.

His stern voice got louder and shot through the air as he stormed from the porch. "I agreed to one dog, not a whole pack." He stomped past the rail fence that bordered the garden and went into the barn.

In a few minutes, Daddy emerged from the barn carrying a tow sack and headed toward the pond. Sarah's stomach churned; something was moving inside the sack. She dropped the bucket of butterbeans and ran to the barn.

Joy whimpered and frantically searched the barn. Sarah reached out and gently rubbed the dog's head. "I know girl, I'm sad too." Joy looked at her with large brown eyes glazed with distress. Sarah lay on the straw-covered ground next to her dog and stroked the soft fur.

At noon Dee came into the barn. She seemed angry. "I found them butterbeans all over the yard. You're Daddy weren't too happy."

"Yes ma'am, I'm sorry."

She looked into Sarah's eyes and her tone softened. "And have you forgot to feed the chickens?"

"Yes ma'am, I forgot." She sniffed and ran her palm under her nose.

"Well, after this don't forget your chores." Dee ran her fingers through Sarah's tangled hair and pulled it into a messy ponytail and taking a rubber band from her apron pocket, secured it.

Sarah sniffed again and paused for a moment to pick some straw from Joy's coat. "Mamma, Becky Sue wanted one of my puppies."

TWELVE

Mark 16
*¹⁶ He that believeth and is baptized shall be saved;
but he that believeth not shall be damned.*

All the windows were raised, but no breeze moved the heavy air. Dee's flowered dress, wet with perspiration, clung to her back. The singing and the praying were over, and the hard pew made it almost impossible for Sarah to *sit still and be quiet. Would the preaching ever end?*

Momma and Kenny seemed to be paying attention to what he was saying, but if Brother Leon would stop shouting Sarah could nod off.

Instead he waved his fist past his stiffly sprayed Elvis pompadour and shouted from the pulpit. He extolled the saving power of Jesus. Then, cupping his leather-bound King James Bible in his forearm like an NFL quarterback clutching a football, he shouted even louder. "Jesus said, *whoever acknowledges me before men, I will also acknowledge him before my Father in heaven...* Can I get an *Amen?*"

"Amen," the congregation repeated.

Dees' Bible rested in her lap as she waved a fan back and forth; the air carrying the fragrance of *Here's My Heart* cream sachet. The scent always reminded Sarah of the day Aunt Myra gave Momma a small gift-wrapped box on her birthday. Momma never got birthday presents or a cake or celebrated her birthday in any way. She seemed so surprised and thankful when she'd opened the box to find a pretty blue and white Avon jar. She'd patted a dab on her wrist and held it out for Sarah to inhale. *Mmmm—smells good.*

Sarah leaned in toward Dee and whispered. "Momma fan me. Please." Dee turned the funeral home fan in Sarah's direction and fanned her face, but her sweat dampened hair barely moved.

Brother Leon started listing sins; drinking, gambling, taking the Lord's name in vain, fornicating... *I need to add that to the list in my spiral and look it up in the big dictionary at the library.*

She wasn't sure if she was a sinner, but looking around, Sarah figured there were a whole lot of sinners in the room—especially the card playing kind. Her shoulders began to sag with the weight of all that sin. She crossed and uncrossed her legs.

"Now I am going to ask Sister Dorothy Jo to play as we sing hymn number 333."

One time, when they had sung four verses of the invitation hymn and no one went forward, Sarah overheard Mr. McCain tell his wife he wished someone would go up to the altar, so everyone could all go home. His wife whispered "Amen."

Just as I am, without one plea,
But that Thy blood was shed for me,
And that Thou bidd'st me come to Thee,
O Lamb of God, I come! I come!

Brother Leon's voice boomed above the voices of the congregation as they sang. "No one of us is saved by the faith of others. No one of us is forgiven by doing good deeds. No one of us is saved by attending church. The *only* way to be saved is to accept Jesus as your personal Savior, trusting in His death as the payment for your sins and in His resurrection as your guarantee of eternal life. Hallelujah! Praise Jesus."

With those words hanging heavy in the air, Brother Leon turned his piercing gaze toward the congregation. *Is he looking at me? He knows about Floyd!*

Suddenly overwhelmed with the terror of an uncertain eternal life, panic crammed her thoughts. *I don't want to go to Hell. I gotta get saved.*

Just as I am, though tossed about
With many a conflict, many a doubt,
Fightings and fears within, without,
O Lamb of God, I come, I come.

"If there is anyone among you who wants to dedicate his life to Jesus through the profession of faith and the act of baptism, please join me at the altar rail. Bow your heads and let Jesus into your hearts as we sing one more verse. If the Spirit of God speaks to you, please come. Is Jesus your personal Savior? Then come, come join me at the altar."

Just as I am, Thou wilt receive,
Wilt welcome, pardon, cleanse, relieve;
Because Thy promise I believe,
O Lamb of God, I come! I come!

Drawn by the Holy Spirit, fourteen-year-old Kenny leaped from his seat and started toward the altar. Before he had taken three steps, Sarah's small trembling hand slipped into his. He looked down into her glowing face and squeezed her fingers.

Opening her purse, Dee dug for her church hanky and wiped her eyes.

Skipping the handshakes and going straight for the hugs, Brother Leon greeted the children with "Praise Jesus. The Lamb of God who takes away the sins of the world welcomes you into His fold."

Sarah did not even notice that Sister Dorothy Jo switched from *Just As I Am* to *Amazing Grace*.

Sarah felt like Sister Aimee in the special white dress Dee had sewn for the occasion. *I wish Becky Sue could come to our church today and see me in my new dress.*

After brushing Sarah's ginger curls and tying them with a freshly ironed ribbon, Dee patted a spot beside her on the bed. Pulling a worn white box from her apron pocket, she slipped it into Sarah's hand. "Go on," she said, "Open it."

Sarah lifted the lid and her eyes widened. Nestled on a pad of once white cotton, a tiny gold cross hung from a delicate gold chain. "My Momma give this to me the day I was baptized," explained Dee. "It belonged to her once, and now, I guess it should rightly be yours."

"Oh, Momma put it on me; it's so pretty. I've never had nothin' this nice. Becky Sue is gonna be so jealous."

Dee's calloused fingers fumbled as she fastened the chain around Sarah's neck. She jumped, as the truck horn sounded, and Jim Ed hollered from the yard, "Let's go,"

"Good Lands o' Goshen! Hold your horses," Dee mumbled and gathered up her Bible.

Otis, sitting in his worn easy chair, wearing nothing but his patched boxer shorts, didn't look up from his Sunday paper as Dee and Sarah left the house.

Standing impatiently by the truck when Dee and Sarah came into the yard, Junior punched Jim Ed in the side. "Let's get this over with. I don't see why we gotta go sit in that hot church building, wasting the day, just because the little twerps found Jesus."

The two older boys had long ago grown tired of Brother Leon yelling at them from the pulpit every Sunday. As soon as they were old enough to overrule Dee's prodding, they'd decided to spend the day of rest fishing rather than going to church.

Despite ardent protest from Junior and Jim Ed, their momma had insisted they attend the baptism of their younger siblings. Both knew, on this occasion, she would win out over their objections. They'd gone about getting ready; grumbling while donning ill-fitting, seldom worn, but required, starched white shirts and tight shoes.

Kenny and Junior climbed into the bed of the pickup and Dee and Sarah rode up front with Jim Ed. Sarah liked riding to church instead of having to walk down the dusty road in her Sunday shoes. *If Jim Ed would go to church every Sunday, I wouldn't have to walk.*

Throughout the service Sarah fidgeted, nervously awaiting the moment she would have to stand in front of the entire congregation. Her anticipation made her oblivious to the scrape of the crinoline petticoat against her tender thighs. She stretched out her legs and studied her beautiful new patent leather Mary Jane's. Dee had pledged two weeks of her egg money before Otis would agree to such a "foolish" purchase.

From a framed picture on the wall, Jesus looked out over the congregation. Sarah thought he might be looking at her. Getting baptized would mean she would be able to take communion and eat the funny little wafers and drink grape juice from the tiny little glasses that looked like thimbles. She had always been envious and curious when the shiny trays were passed down each row, but she'd never been allowed to touch them. They were only for people who had been baptized because they were Baptist.

Now she would be a Baptist. Jesus would cleanse her of the bad thing Floyd did, so she could go to heaven in the rapture.

Brother Leon tried to explain what would happen, but Sarah didn't really understand. Kenny told her Leon would dunk her under the water to pretend she was buried in the water. Then, when he pulled her out of the water it would be pretending she was coming out of the grave, just like Jesus did on Easter, after he got killed on the cross. It sounded pretty scary. *What if Brother Leon doesn't yank me out of the water fast enough? What if he drops me and lets me drown? I don't know how to swim. If I drown before I get baptized, I might not get to go to Heaven…because of Floyd.*

Sister Dorothy Jo sat down at the piano and began to play the last hymn. As the final notes faded away Brother Leon stood in front of the congregation, but instead of the usual benediction, he raised both arms high and looked up in praise.

"This is a glorious day which the Lord has made. And to celebrate this glorious day, two of God's children have made the decision to become true Christians by entering a personal relationship with Jesus. Praise God!"

Voices from the congregation called out, "Praise Jesus. Thank you, Lord."

At the back of the altar, a heavy burgundy colored drapery slowly opened to reveal the baptismal pool; a large painting of a flowing river behind it.

Sarah was glad Kenny was with her as they made their way to the baptismal. Brother Leon's wife, Sister Laura Lee helped them into pure white robes just like the ones Aimee Semple McPherson wore.

The congregation began to sing.

> *Shall we gather at the river*
> *Where bright angel feet have trod*
> *With its crystal tide forever*
> *Flowing by the throne of God*
> *Yes we'll gather at the river*
> *The beautiful, beautiful river*
> *Gather with the saints at the river*
> *That flows by the Throne of God.*

Sarah's heart pounded as she stood on the top step of the baptismal tank and watched Kenny take off his Sunday shoes. A finger of sweat traced her spine and slid into the cleft of her underpants; the cotton dampened from summer heat and fear.

Kenny walked down the three steps into the water where Brother Leon waited.

Sarah's stomach clenched. She reminded herself to be brave, or she couldn't get baptized and go to Heaven.

Brother Leon laid his hands on Kenny. "As John the Baptist baptized Jesus, I baptize you in the name of the Father and of the Son and the Holy Ghost …" Placing a clean cloth over Kenny's nose and mouth, Brother Leon bent him backward. Kenny disappeared under the water and popped back up. "…. Buried in the likeness of Christ Jesus, and raised in the likeness of His resurrection, go now with the gift of eternal life. Amen."

I wish I hadn't walked to the front with Kenny… I'm gonna get drowned… if only I could swim…. I can't think of it now, or I'll run out of here in front of all these people. But what worried her most was…what if Brother Leon was wrong about not going to Hell and this was all wasted?

As Kenny exited the pool he looked into Sarah's eyes but said nothing. He put a hand on her arm and smiled. His eyes sparkled with ecstasy.

Her breath caught as she walked into the pool.

After it was over, Sarah and Kenny stood in front of the congregation and received new Bibles--not pocket-sized New Testaments like Kenny had, but full-sized Bibles with the Old Testament and everything. Brother Leon had written a personal message in cursive script in the front of each one. Sister Laura Lee gave them each a framed picture of Jesus like the one that hung in their Sunday school classroom.

After church everyone gathered in Fellowship Hall. That's where they usually went after funerals or weddings or for the potluck supper, but today they went there to celebrate Kenny and Sarah being baptized. They had oatmeal cookies and red punch. For once, Momma didn't say *only take one.*

On the way home, Sarah proudly sat in the *truck,* crowded between Jim Ed and Momma. Her new Bible and picture of Jesus rested in her lap. It had been a big day. She wished Mary Alice still went to Cold Fork Baptist Church so she could see how everyone had treated her special. She liked the feeling—being the center of attention.

She glanced down at the picture of Jesus. A handsome face, like a movie star, looked back at *her.*

By the time the truck reached the edge of the gravel drive at Jones Farm, Sarah had chosen the spot on her bedroom wall where she would hang her picture; a perfect spot where she would see Jesus from her bed and where He could watch over her while she slept.

Without stopping to take off her new dress, Sarah rushed to her bedroom and pounded a nail in the wall. She straightened the picture and sat on her bed to admire it.

She turned the Bible over and over in her hands and opened it. A bookplate was pasted inside the front cover. *This Book has been presented to Sarah Jane Jones by Cold Fork Baptist Church.* One more thing to make her feel special.

This is the biggest book I've ever had. I wonder if I can read the whole thing. If I'm gonna be a preacher, I got to know the whole Bible. I can't preach if I don't know the right stories to tell.

Being careful not to get the pages dirty, she turned to the last page-- page 194. That didn't seem like many pages for such a big book.

The mystery was solved when she discovered the page numbers started over with the New Testament. She opened her spiral to a blank page and added the numbers--819 pages! That's five Nancy Drew books. *I can do that.*

That evening, at bedtime, she opened her new book to Genesis, Chapter 1. Good news! It started on page five.

She read from the Bible every night before reading the next Chapter of Nancy Drew. Most of it was hard to understand, but the stories Miss Dotty told in Sunday school using the flannel-board helped a lot. Sarah read the story of Queen Esther four times. Esther got to be the Queen of Persia because she was so beautiful. She saved her people.

In Sunday school they got to color the flannel-board figures. Miss Dotty picked Sarah's picture of Esther when she told the story...because hers was colored the prettiest.

After starting with Genesis...*In the beginning* almost a year later, she finished the last verse of Revelations... *The grace of our Lord Jesus Christ be with you all. Amen.*

I did it! Read every word. It was the one big thing she'd done in her life.

But she still liked Nancy Drew the best...it was a lot easier to understand the words.

THIRTEEN

Genesis 3:19
19 In the sweat of your face you shall eat bread till you return to the ground,
For out of it you were taken; For dust you are, And to dust you shall return.

Stretched between two shade trees, a canvas banner snapped in the wind. Bold red letters promised "Revival Tonight." A few yards away, Cold Fork Baptist Church was clean and polished and coated with fresh white paint.

This was no ordinary revival. A famous evangelist from Oklahoma would bring his tent to Cold Fork for three days. As soon as Brother Leon made the announcement from the pulpit, stories of the sick being healed by laying on of hands spread fast; and accounts of people overcome by the Holy Spirit, speaking in tongues had worked up a powerful expectation.

On the night of the announcement, Kenny slipped into Sarah's room.

"What are you praying for tonight, Sarah Jane?"

"I'm praying so hard for Daddy to let us go to the revival."

Kenny squeezed her shoulders. "I know. Me too."

"Do you think strange things might happen before our very eyes?" She sparked with excitement.

"Maybe—you can never tell about these things. I want to go powerful bad—worse than I can tell you."

"We *have* to go. I can't bear not to. What if a real honest-to-goodness miracle ups and happens right here in Tolerance and we miss it 'cause Daddy won't let us go?"

"We won't miss it, I'll see to that… I'm still figuring on how to go about it."

Sarah nodded—Kenny would come up with a plan.

For days Kenny worked to gather the courage to approach Otis. As a rule, Kenny wasn't intimated by Daddy, but Otis' obstinance increased when it came to church activities.

"Daddy…" Kenny stared at the floor, unable to utter the next words.

Otis glared at his young son from behind the evening paper.

Gathering his mettle, Kenny looked directly into Otis' haggard face, "Daddy… you see…there's this revival at the church, and me and Sarah Jane, we'd like to go."

"What kinda nonsense has that preacher put in your head now?" Otis spit between his rotting teeth. "Dee, get in here and listen to what your idiot son is up to now. He wants to go to some magic freak show down at the church."

It didn't sit well with Otis that his two youngest children inherited more than his wife's red hair. He viewed Kenny's gentle nature and inherent goodness as signs of weakness. It was his duty to toughen the boy up for his own good. He'd allowed Dee to baby both of the young ones far too long.

Dee hurried into the room, wiping her hands on her apron.

Otis glared at her. "Ain't it bad enough these kids is wastin' all their free time at that church learnin' nonsense? Kenny spends too much time with that preacher fella--it ain't normal. When the boy ain't busy with his chores, he ought to be out fishin', not praying and listening to some crazy preacher tell fairy stories. You best stop encouraging this dang foolhardiness right now. It's time I made a man out of this one."

Dee rubbed her arm, her skin flushed, and her gaze darted toward Kenny. Her jaw set and she inhaled deeply through her nose and expelled the breath through her mouth. "It won't do no harm for them to go to that meetin'. They might never get another chance to see the likes of this." There was sharpness to her rarely contradictory tone.

Otis laughed at her as if she were the village idiot.

Crestfallen, Kenny turned toward Momma and shook his head. "It's okay, don't worry."

He dug in his heels and just looked directly at Otis with determination in his eyes like he'd not shown before.

After a minute, Otis took his paper from his lap. "You 'n your momma's like a couple of mules when you set your mind to something. It ain't worth my time to argue with you. But you ain't going nowhere until that last section of the backfield is plowed." His tone implied that failure to do so would be an offense that could not be overlooked.

❧

Instead of rushing to the kitchen for an after-school snack, Kenny headed straight for the barn. He tossed his school books onto a hay bale and climbed onto the seat of the beat-up tractor and started the engine. It shook a few times and then sputtered to a standstill. *Not today, please, don't act up today.* He hopped off and tinkering with the spark plugs, got the machine running. It spit, choked and shook its way to the field.

The crisp October air brushed against his sun-browned cheeks as Kenny drove through the pasture past the freshly tilled rows--the fruits of yesterday's labor. A hawk swooped down from the woods and flew over him. It flew away, its belly crimson in the waning light.

Otis always insisted on a fall plowing so the winter freeze could loosen up the soil. Kenny never objected to this task. These were his favorite days--the last days to enjoy the open air before the winter drove him indoors. The coolness of the air and the solitude allowed him to get lost in his own feelings —made him happy to be alive. *Could life be any better than this?*

As he reached the edge of the woods and the newly harvested back section, his mind was filled with thoughts about his future. Would he be a traveling evangelist or have a small congregation like Brother Leon? Whatever God's plan, he hoped he would always have a parcel of land to work. Somewhere he'd read a farm never really belongs to the farmer; he's just a junior partner in a relationship with God's earth. Nature is the one in charge; ruling her seasons and her elements. Thoughts of that partnership made his blood stir and rush through his veins. The country would always be a piece of him. *Yep, farming is a good life.*

From a black gum tree, a mockingbird broke into its evening song.

"Hey Mr. Mockingbird, are you here to give me your gift?" Kenny's eyes searched the braches for a telltale rustle of leaves. "Since you are singing me a song, I will tell you a secret. Tonight, I'm gonna stand up in front of my whole church and tell them how God has called me to a special purpose. No one knows except you, Mr. Bird. Daddy's not gonna be happy when he finds out, but it's something I just gotta do. It's a promise!"

The bird abruptly became silent and flew away disappearing into the woods.

Kenny laughed, kissed his thumb and blew a goodbye kiss.

Halfway down the second row the tractor jolted yanking Kenny from his daydreams. Annoyed, he jumped from the tractor. The right wheel had lodged in a furrow created by the first pass. *Why is everything going wrong today of all days?* He threw his weight against the machine and jockeyed it back and forth several times. The wheel rolled free from the rut.

On the next pass, the gears ground as Kenny popped it into fourth, and the tractor gathered speed. The revival would start at seven o'clock and Kenny wanted to get there early so he and Sarah could get a seat right up front. He planned to stay the longest and shout the loudest and maybe see a miracle happen. Imagine that?

～

At six o'clock, Sarah was ready for Momma to brush her hair. Smelling of soap and wearing her white Sunday dress, Sarah buckled the strap on her patent leather shoes.

"Kenny better hurry and get cleaned up," she fretted.

"Don't worry, honey, I just sent Jim Ed out to fetch him. I reckon he lost track of the time," Dee said. "You know how he gets out there on the tractor these days... he'd forget his head if it weren't screwed on."

The sound of running feet thumped across the wooden porch floor. The screen door slammed with a crack.

"You see, there he is now," Dee said, moving toward the kitchen.

Jim Ed burst into the house, his long legs taking huge strides.

"Daddy! Daddy! Daddy!"

"Son, slow down. What's the matter?"

"Oh, God, Oh God! find Daddy!" Gasping for air he waved a trembling hand knocking over a glass. Water spilled onto the table and trickled to the floor. "Find Daddy--now," his voice was shrill.

"What's the matter?" Her voice was more urgent now.

"Momma... The tractor...it's Kenny!"

"What?"

"Kenny. He's hurt bad. Find Junior. Help!"

Dee's face blanched. "No! No! No! My baby!" She grabbed the quilt from Sarah's bed.

The door slammed again and they were both gone, Momma and Jim Ed.

Sarah stood momentarily frozen to the spot. Her eyes wide, she took in the silence of the house and the sounds from the yard; gravel flying and the rumble of the pickup truck thundering away.

The sound of her heart pounding roared in her ears. "It's OK! It's OK! It's OK!"

Sarah broke into a dead run. The air caught her skirt held wide by her stiff crinoline petticoat and Joy nipped at her shiny shoes. She could run faster without them, but she couldn't stop.

Otis darted from the chicken coop with Junior on his heels.

Sarah ran even faster. Something fell behind her--her hair ribbon.

Wild with fear, they scrambled over the rutted furrows.

Coming to a rise, she caught sight of the pickup. Nearby, lying on its side, the tractor; pinned under it, Kenny, only his head and shoulders visible.

Using his bare hands to dig at the mud beneath Kenny, Jim Ed repeated again and again, "Hang on Kenny, hang on. I'm gonna get you out of here."

Sarah knelt beside Kenny. She looked into her brother's glazed, frightened eyes and rubbed the dirt from his smudged and bloody face. "We're here now, it's okay."

"I'm okay. Go away. Don't look. Go away, Sarah!"

He clutched her hand. "I'm sorry you didn't get to see a miracle," his weak voice barely audible, a stricken look on his ashen face.

With their bodies for leverage, Momma, Daddy, and the boys pushed. The tractor groaned and tilted freeing Kenny's mangled body. He let out a brittle moan and stared unfocused toward the sky.

Sarah's knees buckled, overcome with emotion at the sight of the torn jeans, soaked in blood and mud. "He's bleeding!

They swept past her and lifted the broken body into the bed of the truck onto the pink quilt.

Junior jumped behind the wheel and Otis ran to the passenger side shouting "Go, go, go!" as the rest of the family climbed into the back of the truck with Kenny.

The truck bolted across the field and turned onto the county road. Junior shifted gears; the engine changed pitch and they picked up speed.

Her face streaked with tears, Sarah watched Joy finally give up her race to catch the truck and turn to trot back home.

She looked down at her muddy shoes and stared at a smear of dirt and blood peeking from the folds in the skirt of her dress. "Kenny, don't die, don't die, Kenny. Don't leave me alone."

The truck recklessly bumped its way down the long gravel road toward Tolerance as Dee stoically stared into space through bloodshot eyes.

Kenny lay sprawled, unmoving, his head cradled in Dee's lap. She bent over him, holding her apron against a stream of blood running from his wounded brow into his eyes. "Don't give up, son." Kenny coughed; spit up blood and weakly clutched his momma's hand. She fisted her handkerchief into a ball and wiped the blood from his lips.

Embracing her son, she pillowed his head and mumbled over and over again "...the land has his blood. The land has his blood."

Sarah's fingers curled around the gold cross dangling from the chain around her neck.

The truck jolted as it bounced over a rut, snapping the fragile links of the tiny chain. She clutched the broken necklace in her small hand.

Sarah gasped through her panic and began to blather. "Momma, let's go to the church. The evangelist can heal Kenny. I know he can. Take Kenny to Brother Leon, he can help us. Brother Leon can help us, Momma."

Sarah lay on her bed clutching a fresh white carnation from the funeral spray. *When was the funeral? A month ago? Last week? Maybe today? Yes, it was today.* She still wore her new dress--Becky Sue's new dress.

It's a pretty dress, pale blue dotted swiss. Sarah liked dotted swiss. *Becky Sue didn't even get mad about giving up her new dress. I guess she's sad about Kenny too.*

Aunt Myra washed the old one. The blood and grass stains wouldn't come out.

The church had been filled to the rafters with tearful mourners who lauded the lovely service and tried to comfort Dee.

But all the beautiful words Brother Leon spoke and all the beautiful hymns, nothing could make Sarah understand why Jesus would let this happen to Kenny. Brother Leon said Kenny was is a better place. She didn't want him in a better place; she just wanted everything to be normal again. She wanted her heart to mend from the sight of life seeping from her brother's body.

Joy illicitly lay next to Sarah, the pink quilt bunched under her paws, her muzzle resting on Sarah's belly. "Are you glad I saved that quilt? Aunt Myra threw it away because she couldn't get the blood out of it. But I took it out of the trash. That's Kenny's blood, those dark stains; I want to keep it." Joy quietly whimpered and licked Sarah's hand. "Don't worry; nobody cares if you're in here. Nobody cares what I do anymore. Everyone's too sad. Are you sad? I'm sad. I think I'll be sad forever." The dog cocked her head to the side and looked at Sarah with sparkling plaintive brown eyes. "I know you want me to read to you, but I can't today. Maybe tomorrow."

"Brother Leon is a big fat liar; if that evangelist could heal people by laying his hands on them, why didn't he help Kenny—he didn't even come to the hospital with Brother Leon. Why not? It doesn't make sense. Nothing's ever gonna make sense again."

What if she pretended it never happened? Would it magically disappear? If she didn't believe it happened, then it didn't really happen. Maybe it was a mistake…a bad dream…a lie.

The picture of Jesus on her wall blurred through the tears in her eyes. She touched her neck. The gold cross had hung there since the day of her baptism, until now.

She had nestled the cross, with its broken chain, beneath layers of cotton in the white box and buried it in her dresser drawer.

The tears flowed down her cheeks. Kenny, her friend, her protector, her brother was gone. Her life would never be the same.

She took a deep breath. The tears didn't stop. When Kenny died, he took a piece of her with him to the grave--the carefree piece that laughed--the part that was a child.

Why did Jesus let Kenny die?

She was mad. She was mad at Brother Leon and mad at Kenny. She was mad at that phony evangelist. Most of all she was mad at Jesus.

FOURTEEN

Hebrews 10:26-27

[26] *For if we sin willfully after we have received the knowledge of the truth, there remaineth no more sacrifice that will take away sins,* [27] *but a certain dreadful expectation of judgment and a fury of fire, which shall consume those who live against God.*

1959

S arah yanked open the dresser drawer and began digging. Despite being the middle of October, it was the first day cool enough for a sweater. *Momma said the temperature must have dropped 20 degrees over the weekend.* Reaching for her favorite blue cardigan, she pushed her Bible aside. She stopped, curled her fingers around the edge of the book and looked up at the empty nail on the wall where the picture of Jesus used to hang...*should take that nail out of the wall...it just reminds me I'll probably go to Hell because I stopped loving Jesus.*

More than once she thought about tossing the Bible onto the burn pile along with the picture, but each time something stopped her. The picture and the Bible remained buried in her drawer along with a small yellowed box.

Sarah closed her eyes. A momentary sadness washed over her. Unable to shake the melancholy, she shoved the Bible to the bottom of the drawer and quickly covered it with a folded sweater.

The blast of a horn from outside caused her to jump. That would be seventeen-year-old Carl Edwards who drove the school bus his daddy owned. Carl seemed to take some bewildering delight in sounding the horn as he moved from farm to farm picking up the kids.

Last year, when the county decided to close the small schools and have all the kids go to a consolidated school in Tolerance, Sarah overheard Daddy say Mr. Edwards politicked for the consolidation so he could make money with that school bus. Daddy called it a *bunch of nonsense.* But Daddy called most changes *nonsense.*

Pulling on the sweater and grabbing her books and lunch, Sarah bounded out the back door into the crisp air before she even finished saying, "Bye, Momma."

The yellow bus rolled to a stop beside the mailbox kicking up dust from the narrow unpaved road. Carl pulled the handle to open the door, and Sarah climbed up the steps onto the bus. Carl's oily appearance caught Sarah's eye. Sometimes she expected the pimples across the wings of his nose to multiply before her eyes. It seemed to her that Carl never so much as frowned; he always just looked ahead with an aloof expression.

Finding a seat, she settled in. She liked to sit in the front to avoid walking past all the kids.

When Kenny died everyone seemed sad and treated her nice, but after a while, when it wasn't new anymore, they'd whisper and give one another knowing nudges as if to say--*that's the girl with the dead brother.* It was easier to avoid the whole thing by sitting alone, content in her self-enforced solitude.

Balancing a stack of books on her lap, Sarah pulled a *Classics Illustrated Comic* from beneath the pile and opened it. In that moment, the sounds of the rowdies at the back of the bus and the girls gossiping around her were drowned out by visions of Denmark and the handsome prince, Hamlet.

By the time the bus stopped in front of her school, the first bell was ringing and Hamlet lay dead. *Good night sweet prince: And flights of angle sing thee to thy rest!*

Sarah brushed away a tear and climbed down from the bus.

Mary had been Sarah's best friends since first grade. Now they were in different classes but had the same lunch period. *It's all about who you eat with.* Sarah could still sit at the same table with Mary every day and hang out after lunch; but lately, Sally Conroy had been sitting at their lunch table. Sally was in Mary's class.

Sarah neared the doorway of the cafeteria, joining the students pushing and shoving toward the aroma of yeast rolls and the pandemonium filling the hallway with the clatter of trays and clink of silverware.

At one of the long tables next to a group of sixth-grade girls, Mary and Sally were deep in conversation and laughing. *Where she sits in the cafeteria is very important- to some people anyway.*

There wasn't an empty chair next to Mary.

She could have saved me a seat.

Sarah dropped her crumpled lunch bag onto the table and slipped into a chair across from her friend. Mary looked up and smiled, but Sally kept talking as if Sarah's arrival had gone unnoticed. Her Annie Oakley lunch box lay opened on the table and her untouched sandwich rested on a sheet of waxed paper neatly spread in front of her.

I hate that lunch box.

Sally thought she was some kind of hot stuff because her mother's cousin from Little Rock played Annie Oakley on TV.

Sarah didn't believe her. *That's just bragging....*

Why can't we have lunch without her, just once!

One time Momma said. *Two's company, but three's a crowd.* She never understood what Momma meant--until now. It always felt like a crowd when Annie Oakley's cousin was around.

Sarah took her sandwich from the bag and tried to block out the sound of Sally's voice echoing against the hard tile walls. She fixed her eyes on cutouts of black cats and pumpkins with smiling faces taped to the walls around the room.

Sally continued to ignore Sarah and talked on and on, "...Judy is just completely boy crazy. It's a different boy every week--and because of why? ...Their looks. That's all she ever says. 'Oh, he's so cute.' As if any cute boy would ever like *her*."

Fluorescent light tubes flickering from the ceiling panels overhead seemed to echo the rhythm of Sally's voice.

"Don't you think Judy should start wearing a bra? You can see her boobies right through her shirt. Fat girls need to get a bra before skinny girls do. They need deodorant too--Judy needs it." Sally crunched a potato chip between her teeth and kept right on talking, spitting bits of chips with every word. "I'll bet she starts her period this year lots of fat girls start when they're eleven.

Mary looked at Sarah, her eyes wide with surprise. Sarah made her eyes wide in return as if to say, *Yeah, I know. I can't believe she's talking about that!*

They'd been friends with Judy in the fourth grade...until Sally decided she wasn't cool anymore.

Sarah thought it was mean to talk about Judy like that but was afraid to say anything. She wanted to be cool.

Sarah angled her head, narrowing her eyes and studied Sally's pert, little face with her honey dripped, perfectly cut bangs and thick, pencil-straight hair. Cropped at the jawline, it curved against her cheeks.

Instinctively Sarah put her hand up to the long single braid resting on her shoulder. Coarse, curly hairs sprouted from her head in every direction, escaping her thick braid. Momma taught her how to braid her own hair, but she couldn't do two pigtails. *I always make the part crooked.*

Mary took a deep breath. It looked like she might say something, but before she could speak, Sally's monologue continued. "Did you see what Betty Jo Shelby wore to church yesterday? I'll bet her momma went all the way to Dallas to get it. Guess you can do that when you're a doctor's wife. There's nothing like it in Texarkana, for sure. I wouldn't mind a dress from a store in Dallas. Betty Jo is always the prettiest girl in church."

Mary nodded and said, "I just love her new haircut, don't you?"

There they go, talking about First Methodist Church again. It made Sarah feel out of place and even guilty. *Maybe I should start going to church again. I'm big enough to walk there by myself. Momma wouldn't have to go.*

During the year that followed Kenny's death, Dee stopped going to church. Sarah figured Momma was mad at Jesus too. *She's been so sad since Kenny died. She doesn't care what any of us do.*

But the thought of going inside Cold Fork Baptist made Sarah sad. Just seeing the building made her want to cry. It held too many memories of Kenny.... *Maybe I could go to First Methodist with Mary and Sally. Mary's daddy got mad at Brother Leon about something and their family started going to First Methodist a long time ago. No... I don't have any fancy dresses from Dallas... Methodist people wouldn't like my clothes....*

Sarah tried to think of something to say to edge into the conversation. "I'd like to go to Dallas." *Good, Sarah that was brilliant.*

Sally looked at Sarah and said nothing.

Sarah looked back and said nothing.

She's stealing my best friend. I need to say something. What can I say?

She opened her mouth to speak...but, instead, her eyes followed a drop of mustard as it slipped from her ham sandwich and deposited itself as a bright yellow glob on her white blouse. She smiled weakly and dabbed at the spot with her napkin. *Great, just great!* She shrugged; certain everyone looked in her direction, thinking *what a klutz. And you think you can go to church with Betty Jo Shelby, the prettiest girl in the school, with the straightest blonde hair.*

Sally tossed a ball of waxed paper into her lunch box and nudged Mary. "I'm bored." Her gaze dropped down to Sarah's blouse. In her take-charge tone, she said, "Let's go see what's happening on the playground." Still staring, transfixed on the mustard, she said, "There's mustard on your shirt, Sarah."

The words pounded against Sarah's ears.

Mary made a sympathetic nod in Sarah's direction. "You coming?"

Sarah put down the smeared napkin but didn't look up. Her voice became slightly brittle. "No, I'm not finished with my milk." She tried not to cry. *No way, I'm going to the playground like this. Now I can be the girl with a dead brother and mustard on her shirt.*

Sally dragged Mary toward the doors to the playground and Sarah rushed to the girl's room to see how much mustard she could remove from her blouse before having to face her classmates.

Sarah shook her head, loosening the long braid, and ran a brush through her hair. Joy sat at her feet watching every movement. She cocked her head and her ears twitched.

Momma checked Sarah's reflection in the mirror. "Sarah Jane, are you sure? I still don't see no reason you should want to cut off your hair, it's pretty the way it is…so long and thick and it shines in the light. It's a sin to whack it off."

"Yes, ma'am. I'm too old for pigtails. I want my hair cut like Sally's." She motioned to her jawline with the back of her hand indicating how long she wanted her hair.

"Momma, *please* cut my hair."

Sarah took another peek at her reflection and went into the kitchen, set a chair in the middle of the floor, plopped down and waited.

Dee halfheartedly followed, wrapped an old towel around Sarah's neck and retrieved her scissors from the sewing box.

She pulled Sarah's hair into a low ponytail and fastened it with a rubber band, then taking a deep breath, tentatively reached out with the scissors.

Sarah held her breath and closed her eyes and pictured Sally as the scissors tugged at her hair. Clumps of red curls landed next to Joy's paw on the linoleum floor.

Dee pulled the towel from Sarah's shoulders, took in a deep breath and heaved a sigh.

"How does it look, Momma?" Sarah's eyebrows drew together, and she rubbed at the back of her neck.

Dee studied her for a long minute and didn't say anything.

Running her hand through the uneven tufts of hair sticking out from her head, Sarah hurried to her room. She stood in front of the mirror and examined the thatch of red straw frizzing and curling in all directions.

It doesn't look like Sally's hair. What a big mistake. I should never have asked Momma to do this!

Biting her lip, Sarah covered her face with her hands.

No wonder you don't have any friends, you're a freak!

She burst into tears and grabbed her hairbrush.

Joy laid her muzzle on her paws and whimpered.

"Stop looking at me," Sarah said almost angrily. "Momma did her best. ...Nothing in my life ever works out the way I picture it."

With no attempt to stop them, her tears flowed from the pit of her stomach and dripped down her cheeks.

She took another look at the lump of hair hanging over her eyebrows and the ragged rat's nest on top of her head. "This is all Sally's fault--Sally, and her perfect bangs, always lurking around Mary."

"Joy, I'm no good at trying to be like someone else— 'to thine own self be true'...that's from Hamlet."

She ran her fingers through her matted curls once more and reached for her book. *I have to go to school looking like a plucked chicken. Everyone will laugh at me.*

She took a deep breath "It's okay, Joy, I'll read a chapter of Nancy Drew to you. That'll make you feel better, won't it?"

By the time she finished reading, Aunt Myra and Becky Sue arrived with a bag of curlers and a can of hairspray.

"Your momma called. Said you could use a little help. We just need to show you how to put your hair up on curlers, honey. Your haircut will look just fine."

FIFTEEN

Leviticus 18:6
*⁶ None of you shall approach to any that is near of kin to him,
to uncover their nakedness: I am the LORD.*

The voice of Johnny Cash, warning his former lover she's gonna *Cry, Cry, Cry*, streamed from the box radio on the kitchen shelf. Jim Ed rested his elbows against the enamel table, poring over the numbers he'd penciled onto a lined tablet. Across from him, Otis stroked his stubbled cheek and fidgeted with his whiskey glass--his third--awaiting the verdict.

Jim Ed pushed the tablet aside. "Daddy, we got no choice, we gotta sell the log truck." He cleared his throat and tapped his pencil on the table. "I don't see how me and Junior can run the farm and still have time to haul enough wood to make ends meet."

Junior nodded and hunched his shoulders. "We can make more money if we stick to raising chickens and forget about hauling. We're just spread too thin as it is." He looked down. Stared at the table. "Besides, that old truck, it's about on its last legs." He hesitated. "With Kenny and Floyd both gone...."

Otis pounded his glass onto the table, splashing whiskey. "God took the wrong child. If He had to take one, why not take the girl, she ain't much use around here." He wiped his mouth with the back of his hand, waved his empty glass and spewed out a torrent of curses.

Jim Ed filled his cheeks with air and slowly blew it out. He signaled to Junior to refill the glass.

Junior turned the bottle end up, emptying it into the glass. He pushed the glass toward Otis and set the Wild Turkey bottle aside mumbling under his breath— "Time for a trip to Scarborough's"

There was a long, silent pause. The brothers exchanged knowing looks.

The drink calmed Otis. The drink always calmed him.

Jim Ed shifted in his chair and snapped a sidelong glance toward Junior.

Otis rubbed his swollen hands together, massaging the arthritis from the knobby knuckles. For years now, each night, they had watched their daddy soak his hands in Dee's strange concoction of stinging nettle, ginger root and what she called 'the magic'—smelling remarkably of onions. After soaking his hands he'd rub the stuff on his knees and legs. They both knew their daddy suffered a lot of pain, but his manly pride didn't allow him to admit it.

"Just 'cause I got the arthritis don't mean I can't do nothing—with a shot of whiskey and a beer--I can do damn near what I always done."

They all sat silent for a bit. There was nothing to say. The quiet seemed to bring Otis to his senses again.

"If you boys think its best, then sell the truck. But don't try to sell it 'round here. Ain't nobody got money enough to pay cash. Take it to that auction fella over in Texarkana.

"Sounds like a good plan, Daddy." Jim Ed patted Otis on the shoulder. "C'mon, let's get you to bed." He pulled at the old man's arm. Otis slowly rose to his feet and holding the table, straightened his body.

Jim Ed half-carried him into the bedroom, his large, lanky frame, a dead weight. He began to carefully help his father undress, fumbling with buttons. He had performed this ritual a lot in the year since Kenny died, and Dee had withdrawn into herself. If no one helped Otis to bed, as likely as not, he passed out sprawled across the covers fully dressed, leaving Dee to undress him and get into bed properly.

Otis sat on the edge of the bed, a blank expression on his face. He put his head in his hands and became tearful. "What's become of me?"

It's okay, Daddy. Let me rub your legs. It'll make you feel better. He knelt on the floor beside the bed and massaged the old man's legs while Otis constantly cursed him, "Dammit boy, be careful!"

Sarah daydreamed at the kitchen sink wiping the dinner dishes slowly with a tattered dishrag. A thud from Otis's bedroom pulled her from her thoughts.

"Junior, come 'ere." The slurred and muffled voice came from her parents' bedroom.

Great, Daddy's drunk and fell off the bed--again.

"He's gone to Texarkana, Daddy. With Jim Ed, to sell the truck." Sarah hollered, hoping he would fall asleep on the floor. But the call came again, louder and more emphatic this time.

She glanced out the window. A dim bulb created a shadow in the barn as Dee moved about gathering jars for tomorrow's canning. Two bushel baskets filled with peaches sat in the corner.

I wish Momma would hurry back to the house. I hate messing with him when he's drunk.

A third mumbled cry came, this time followed by the breaking of glass and a shout, "Goddammit."

Sarah could no longer ignore his pleas. *Now he's mad.*

For a moment she stood in the gray light of the doorway looking with disgust at the foul, snoring heap.

He stirred from his drunken stupor enough to mumble something incoherent.

She moved closer to hear what he said.

"...ain't dead."

"Who's not dead, Daddy?" *He's just jabbering nonsense.*

Avoiding the jagged shards of the shattered whiskey bottle Sarah reached for her daddy's arm, slung it over her shoulder and tried to lift him to his feet. Through clenched teeth, she begged, "Daddy, you gotta help me. I'm not strong enough-- C'mon wake up."

Too drunk to cooperate, he answered with a grunt.

Now partially awake, Otis managed to maneuver into a position leaning against the bed. His effort brought on a fit of coughing and choking. He wiped yellow phlegm from his mouth with his ragged sleeve.

For a flicker of a second, Sarah thought of leaving him like that. *Figure it out yourself, old man.* But deeper inside a sense of compassion moved her, making her ashamed. Her father needed her help; *I need to do what's right.* A small part of her knew this wasn't how things are supposed to be--it's supposed to be a father takes care of his children, not the other way. She couldn't look the old man in the face.

She struggled to lift and push until Otis collapsed face down across the bed, groaning and cursing. Rolling him over, she tugged his dirty work boots from his feet. The reek of dirty socks and body odor attacked the air. Without undressing him any further, she threw a quilt over him.

Grappling with the quilt he muttered as if riled. His knobby fingers grabbed her wrists with a sudden show of strength. He shoved at Sarah not seeming to understand her intent to help.

"Z'at you Dee?" He pulled her close, still mumbling. "Dee...you don't understand...."

"No Daddy, it's me, Sarah Jane. Let me get you to bed."

"Ya fool woman! Come 'ere an' hep me wid deesh overalls."

"Let me go, Daddy."

"Dee... din't *mean* to, Dee...." He lifted his bleary gaze toward Sarah.

"Why don't you let me go?" She struggled to get free.

His hot breath heavy with whiskey and cigarettes fell on her face.

Grimacing, she turned away.

He loosened his grip and clawed at the legs of his overalls.

"Ain't ya gonna rub my legs, Dee?"

The old man's bloodshot eyes glistened with wetness.

"Rub away the hurt."

He covered his face with his hands and began to cry wordless sobs dragged from far inside. Deep, gasping, painful sobs that shook his whole body.

Sarah stood helpless, watching him, her eyes filling with tears.

Unfastening the hooks from the shoulder straps she yanked at the legs of his overalls, not looking directly at him. She laid his legs across her lap and began rubbing them the way Jim Ed always did.

Taking hold of her wrist, he lifted her fingers off. "Quit tugging at me!" He grasped both of her hands and pulled her onto the bed alongside him.

"Daddy, no, stop!"

His touch horrified her as he groped her developing breasts.

"Shud-up Dee, I jush wad a li'l lovin'."

"Daddy, it's me... Sarah Jane, stop."

This is a mistake, some horrible mistake.

He held tight, fighting her attempt to escape his grasp.

"Be good, jus' lay still an I won' hurt you," he demanded, putting his hand over her mouth, pawing at her shorts.

In another moment, his hands started to roam under her clothes.

Her mouth went dry. Moving backward, she struggled to push him off, not knowing what to do. He wouldn't let her scoot away from him. It was useless.

He's too strong.

The stench of his body made her feel sick as he pressed against her.

What's he doing? I'm scared. Don't make him mad. Just do what he wants.

The sound of her heartbeat thrashed in her ears.

He crawled on top of her, his rough hands pulling at her cotton panties.

Her hands gripped the sheets, her knuckles going white, her eyes all the while trained on the door.

It was pointless to rebuff him. All her resistance went away with her surrender to the hopelessness of the situation.

...not really happening.

He groaned.

...can't breath

He was rough.

Lying flat on her back, her teeth clenched, she closed her eyes and separated herself from reality.

... A bad dream.... wanna die.

Feeling a scream gathering, powerful and fierce in the back of her throat, her body stiffened. With an abrupt snap, a switch in her brain tripped, and her scream was choked off. Her mind took control and a dazed lack of sensation carried her through the next long minutes.

She wasn't in her body anymore; from somewhere above, she watched the painful experience and waited for it to be over.

Please. God. Let it be over. Just let it be over.

...and then it ended.

The room filled with deep shadows of fading blue-gray twilight. Feeling the shudders subsiding, Sarah waited in silence. And when she heard the sound she waited for—the deep breath—the pause while the breath was held—the rasping release, she eased from the bed and crept to the small cluttered bathroom.

Looking away from the stranger in the smudged mirror, a scream gathered. Lifting her hand to her mouth and biting down hard on the back of it so hard she tasted blood. Filling the tub with blisteringly hot water she eased her body down into its painful heat.

Daddy didn't mean to do that to me. He thought I was Momma.

Nothing could take away the awful, dirty feeling that filled her.

She scrubbed at her skin until it bled, trying to rid herself of the filth clinging to her. But the feeling remained.

Straining her sore muscles, she grabbed the sides of the tub and slowly pulled her body up, her abdomen cramping painfully.

Sarah dried off with a rough towel and reached for the little green plastic container of April Showers Dusting Powder. Covering herself with the fragrant dust, the delicate scent reached her nose reminding her of the green and red wrapped package topped with a red bow; her first grown-up Christmas gift.

Daddy didn't mean it. He thought I was Momma. I didn't want to do it. It'll never happen again.

Tears accumulated, powerful and uncontrollable in her parched, aching throat and a horrible feeling, a sense of numbness filled her.

"No, it will never happen again," she said aloud.

SIXTEEN

Job 14:13

[13] "Oh that you would hide me in the land of the dead, and keep me secret, until your wrath is past, that you would appoint me a set time, and remember me!

A crazy topsy-turvy world whirled around her. Never catching more than a blurred glimpse flying past, she was blind to everything but a dizzy motion heaping color upon color.

It stopped.

The wave of dizziness passed. She twisted and twisted and twisted the rope on the old tire swing as tight as it would go and again let it unwind carrying her with it spinning in a circle. The wafting air, scented with a hint of freshly mown grass clotted with pungent smells, grabbed at her tight curls, tumbling them into her face.

Dizziness?--Confusion? What was it?

She was gone--had fallen into a deep dark hole to escape. It was the only way to survive the night. If she didn't believe *it* happened, then *it* didn't happen.

Horrific momentary flashes tried frantically to claw their way back inside her mind.

She longed for something--the smell of honeysuckle, the taste of wild blackberries, the feel of the breeze on her face as she ran--with Joy through the meadow. Anything. Anything, to simply make her feel different; to distance her from the feeling gnawing at her stomach.

With a new clarity she began to notice the sounds of the morning echoing through the fields; the rooster crowing and crowing again, Joy barking at the chickens and the chickens clucking their protest in return, and the cow in the barn begging to be milked, the pop and roar of the tractor in the distance. And the smells. The smells of the barnyard, hay, compost, chicken feed, manure.

The sun warmed her face, and she listened to a jay complaining in the trees. He never stopped his shrill rant. But his rants couldn't drown out the voice inside her head... *Daddy didn't mean it. He thought I was Momma. I didn't want to do it. It'll never happen again.*

The wash flapped in the wind, a pair of denim overalls swaying back and forth...his overalls. Dee came into the yard and started taking clothes off the line.

Momma hung that wash yesterday. She left it hanging out on the line all night. She's never done that.

Sarah watched for a second, then jumped from the swing as Dee batted at one of the sheets, struggling as it popped and waved on the line.

Dee began removing the clothespins and Sarah grabbed the bottom of the sheet. It had long since dried and stiffened. Each held one end of the sheet and together they folded it. Without a word and with Sarah avoiding Dee's eyes, they took in the wash.

Stretching her back Dee sighed deeply and bent to pick up the basket.

Trying to decide what to do, Sarah watched her mother walk toward the house. She followed as Dee disappeared into the house.

Sarah sat on the porch swing needing to think before going into the house. She didn't know what to say, how to start.

Momma'd be shocked and grieved to know what happened. Or maybe she'd be mad, think it was Sarah's fault.

Maybe it was my fault.

Dee moved about the kitchen. Sarah heard the low sound of a soap opera on the radio. *Momma's listening to one of her stories. Sounds like Young Doctor Malone.*

Sometimes Sarah would listen with Momma while she ironed or cooked, but usually, Momma sent her outside to play or do chores. *I guess Momma listens to those stories for the same reason I read my books.*

Dee came to the screen door and looked out; her hands and apron were white with flour. She watched Sarah for a minute or two and then wandered away.

Still wearing her apron, she came onto the porch, her hands wiped clean and sat down next to Sarah on the swing. The air around them was silent except for the buzzing of a mosquito and the sound of the tractor in the distance.

Dee cradled her hand in her lap

Sarah watched for a bit, waiting for Momma to find her words. The pain written over her face as she struggled with her thoughts filled Sarah with a momentary sadness for her mother.

Dee took hold of her daughter's hand gently but firmly and swallowed hard.

"Some folks drink to feel calm, some drink to feel joyfulness. Your daddy, he drinks to forget. But most times, it don't work. He's got a lot of demons to deal with."

Sarah nodded. A prickle of tears stung her eyes and she glanced away unable to meet those faded blue eyes. Momma was so clearly sad.

Dee leaned forward, her hand still holding Sarah's. "It's hard to understand why the world is the way it is or why folks do what they do. Sometimes they carry shameful secrets and they don't know what to do with it. Some folks do bad things, but that don't make them bad. You get scared, you don't like what they do, but you can still love them."

Momma knows! The guilt in her eyes said so. She saw that Momma didn't have the strength or understanding to face what happened. She placed no blame on her mother. *Momma doesn't know what to do either.*

"Your daddy worked hard for everything we got, every cent. Never got to finish school, but has his own land—ain't a sharecropper like some. He supplies us with a living and a roof. We ain't never been hungry the whole time we been married. He's a proud man—it's a hard kind of proud." Her eyes clouded with tears.

Sarah's mind returned to the hurt caused to the family when Floyd went away, the guilt she felt. Daddy, Jim Ed, and Junior, they all had to work harder because Kenny died, and Floyd got sent away. *It's my fault Daddy made Floyd leave.*

Somehow, she had to keep the house quiet—untroubled. She wouldn't cause more unhappiness. *For every one that curseth his father or his mother shall be surely put to death.*

The two sat for a moment letting silence sink in. Dripped in raw emotion, a shared sense of shame, each blamed herself. Both had been beaten in spirit and in body and in mind; each in her own way, so different, yet the same. There can be comfort in ignorance and lies, but once the truth is out there denial is no longer an option. Then there is no hiding from the truth. It is easier to keep the truth safely buried deep inside.

Sarah broke the silence. "Want me to help peel peaches?"

"Might ought to." Dee stood and looked at her daughter for a long minute, then went into the house.

After Dee left the porch, Sarah sat for a while. Sometimes she wished she wasn't still mad at Jesus. She missed sitting next to Momma in her Sunday dress, her Bible in her hand, Kenny standing beside her, singing *Rock of Ages*.

What if that evangelist hadn't come to town – Kenny wouldn't have been hurrying to finish the plowing- he wouldn't have died. What if Daddy hadn't started drinking so much after Kenny died- what if I hadn't gone to his room last night? What if, what if, what if…. These thoughts would lurk around and haunt her dreams forever.

Her eyes were red, but no tears fell. She went inside to help Dee put up preserves.

seventeen

Romans 7:18-20

[18] For I know that in me, that is, in my flesh, dwells no good thing. For desire is present with me, but I don't find it doing that which is good.[19] For the good which I desire, I don't do; but the evil which I don't desire, that I practice.

1961

From her desk in the back row of Mrs. Phillips' seventh grade American History class, Sarah scanned the blackboard and copied the first day's assignment onto a clean page of her spiral notebook.

There was a light tap on her shoulder and the faint scent of leather and oranges stirred around her. She looked up from her paper into the hazel eyes of Boyd Williams. He gave her a cocky wink and a quick twinge of excitement shot through her stomach as his hand brushed against hers. Pressing a folded note into her hand, he gestured toward Skeeter Akins in the desk next to hers.

She shuffled her feet beneath her desk and hesitated, trapped between her hunger to be accepted and her fear of getting caught.

She passed the tiny square of folded paper to her left.

Skeeter didn't reach for the note. He was looking at Mrs. Phillips.

Mrs. Phillips resettled her glasses on her nose, eyed Sarah sternly and rapped on her desk. "Sarah Jones, would you like to bring that note here so you can share it with everyone?"

The uneasiness in her stomach turned to fear and rose until it formed a lump in her throat. Sarah looked toward Boyd and shrugged.

She moved to the front of the classroom slowly walking to the gallows clutching the note in her hand. With the lies and excuses she could offer running through her mind, she felt the blood drain from her face.

"I would hate to have to send you to the Principal's office on the first day of school, Sarah. You will eat your lunch here instead of joining your friend Skeeter in the cafeteria."

Sarah looked up at her teacher with confused eyes. "Read it," demanded Mrs. Phillips. "Out loud for everyone to hear."

She wanted to blurt out *but it isn't my note*. Instead, she opened it and read aloud, "Meet me after school."

Titters floated around the classroom.

Great, now everyone thinks I like Skeeter. He's a creep!

"Get your books and move to this seat." The teacher motioned to an empty desk in the front row.

Sarah handed the note to her teacher, turned and looking down at her feet, began the long walk to her desk. With each step, her pulse pounded in her ears as eyes moved in her direction and the walls pressed in on her.

Sarah sat quietly at her newly-assigned desk, next to the busy pencil sharpener. Her eyes misted over as she imagined the students queued up waiting for their turn at the sharpener, while they whispered and looked at her.

With folded hands, she watched her classmates leave the room and dropped her head to avoid the smirks of the kids staring at her from the hallway as they shuffled past the classroom. She didn't need to raise her head to know glaring eyes bore into her.

She removed the waxed paper from her sandwich and took a tiny bite. Chewing it slowly, she wished she had some milk to help wash down the lump growing inside her throat.

Mrs. Phillips glanced at Sarah and then continued to grade a stack of papers.

The fluorescent lights hummed and sputtered overhead casting a flickering shadow onto Sarah's desk reminding her of a police interrogation in an old black and white detective movie at the Saturday matinee. *We'll beat the truth out of you if we have to.* She wanted to jump up and rat out Boyd like the *stool pigeon* in the movie.

❧

Outside after school, the kids gathered into tight clusters in a sea of clatter and banter, but the animated groups went silent the moment Sarah came near. Their silence and indifferent stares implicitly blocked her admission to the circle.

Feeling removed and out of place, she retreated to a secluded bench at the far end of the schoolyard. Her eyes fixed on her lap, she clung to the solitude.

Sarah's mind reeled; grappled to understand exactly what just happened. Playing back the scene and brooding over the past, her eyes moved to the small groups.

Everyone seems to already have friends--except me. Who wants to be friends with the weird girl? No one, that's who.

She hadn't had a best friend since Sally took Mary Alice away.

Pushing those thoughts aside, Sarah pulled a book from beneath her history book. She held *A Tree Grows in Brooklyn*, in her lap. Sometimes kids made fun of her—called her a bookworm. *Who cares?* She shrugged and opened the book, but before she started to read, Boyd came from inside the building and headed down the sidewalk.

Jerk! Your crummy note got me in trouble and you went scot-free.

Unexpectedly, he whirled around, retraced his steps and veered off in her direction. Before she could react, she looked straight into his confident smile.

"Hi," he said.

She glanced at him, then at the ground. A boy she scarcely knew, a cute boy, smiling at her. Her anger toward him faded. Keeping her head down, holding back gathering tears, she nodded and muttered, "Hi." She laid the book aside and clasped her hands on her lap.

He sat down with his back against the bench, his long legs stretched out in front of him, his feet crossed at the ankles and his arms over his chest. He was a town kid—didn't dress like the farm boys. His black boots were polished to a high shine and had steel taps on the heels that made an echoing sound with each footfall.

Something attracted her; not just the all black clothing he wore—a self-confidence he had in being different.

Not knowing what he was after, she felt confused. *That's the prettiest hair I've ever seen on a boy.*

He smiled as he watched her. "I think it's slicker 'en snot you didn't snitch. Most girls would've copped out."

Yeah, and most girls wouldn't have to eat lunch with zit-face Phillips.

Sarah turned her head slightly and twirled her hair around her finger. Her gaze returned to her lap. *He is sooo cute, I can't believe he's talking to me.* She chewed her bottom lip to hide the flicker of a smile that formed.

He pulled a guitar pick out of his pocket and held it up. "I play the guitar, sometimes. I can play *Ring of Fire*. Do you like Johnny Cash? He's from

Arkansas, you know."

She nodded. Hesitated, then said, "I like Elvis better. Can you play Elvis songs?"

"Sure." He leaned close, his breath fluttered against her cheek. "Want to come to my house and watch *Bandstand*?"

She agreed.

It never occurred to her, she could say *no*. She was blushing, flattered, confused. *Why'd he care about me?*

He wants to be my friend! The thought filled a hole inside her, the emptiness that comes with never feeling good enough to have friends.

They walked the first few blocks in self-conscious silence. Then, Sarah nervously said, "I can't stay long; I have to meet my brother at the Dixie Dairy. He drives me home."

"Yeah. I've seen you there."

"Really?" *I've seen you too…and you sure looked cool.*

"Yeah. I hang out there a lot. My sister works there. Sandy's there now. We can watch a little TV, then bug out; head down there if you want."

"So, is your mother at home?"

"Nah. Mom's working—at the dry cleaners."

For the first time it occurred to her, she would be in the house with him… alone.

"Here's my house," Boyd nodded towards a white house, with green trim, in need of paint. The roots of a large elm tree pushed up around its base and spread out in all directions, rising and falling through the rock-strewn ground. Sarah followed him across the grassless, gravel-covered yard to the back door without a word.

The hinges on the screen door gave a shrill cry as he drew it back. They stepped into an empty silence drenched in the smell of neglected damp mold mixed with the punch of half-smoked cigarettes and stale, overflowing ashtrays.

Sarah shifted from foot to foot, wanting to leave. Instead, she followed Boyd to the living room where he flipped on the television, tuned it to American Bandstand and adjusted the rabbit ears until the lines stopped jumping across the small screen.

"Want a Coke?"

Sarah nodded.

He pointed at the sagging couch and turned toward the kitchen. "Be right back."

After a second of hesitation, she sank down on the sectional sofa, snatching up the morning newspaper from the cushion and placing it next to her to create a boundary line.

The walls were filled with framed family photos—church directory photos from Olan Mills. Boyd, his mother and his sister—no father.

The curtains didn't hang right—as if they belonged on different windows in a different house.

His family was poor like hers, but unlike her, Boyd seemed to realize no shame in their poverty.

Dust mites floated in a shaft of sunlight filtering through the window shade and past the TV screen. Still just a bit uneasy, she watched the black and white image of Little Eva flicker across the screen, dancing to the *Locomotion*.

She was startled from her thoughts by the sound of taps on the wooden floor, as Boyd came into the room carrying two bottles of Coke and an aspirin tin.

"Got a headache?" Sarah asked.

"Nah, Sandy taught me this. If we drop a few of these into our cokes, we'll get high."

Lost in a combination of confusion and curiosity—she didn't want to seem square.

She was only slightly aware of Dick Clark's voice coming from the television.

Boyd tossed the newspaper onto the scuffed coffee table, tearing down her barrier, slouched next to her on the couch and propped his feet on the table. Dropping four tablets into a coke, he handed her the fizzing concoction and a straw.

She took a sip and pretended to like it. Tapping her fingers against the bottle, she brushed the hair from her eyes and waited to get high. Nothing happened.

What if he tries to kiss me?

Her stomach tensed and her eyes shot toward the unmistakable sound of someone turning the front door knob. She froze as she watched the knob turn. *Maybe his mother came home from work early…or his sister…They'll catch us here, alone together.* Her breathing grew unsteady.

The door opened. It was Skeeter with a ninth grader—Anna or Annie something-or-other. Without speaking or making eye contact, they headed straight to one of the bedrooms closing the door behind them.

Boyd nodded toward the closed door. His cheeks flushed, and his ears turned red. "He comes over here to make out whenever Mom's not here. That's what the note was about."

There was an uncomfortable silence. Boyd fidgeted. Sarah fidgeted.

"You wanna see my guitar?"

"Okay."

"Come on--it's in my room."

The words crashed against her ears.

He stood, took hold of her wrist and pulled gently at her arm.

Her shoulders tensed. She glanced around for a diversion. "Is that the bathroom?" she motioned toward the door that seemed the most likely candidate.

He nodded.

Pushing the door open she stepped inside the slightly shabby but clean room and flipped the light switch. A single bulb cast a dim glow onto the medicine cabinet mirror.

Why have I gotten myself into this? She came on her own, no one forced her.

She sat on the edge of the pink bathtub and eyed the pattern formed by the pink and mint colored floor tiles.

What next?

How much longer 'til I get high?

What's high feel like? How will I know when I'm high?

I don't feel anything different. That aspirin thing doesn't work on me.

Her eyes surveyed the room as if she were searching for an escape route. Her gaze stopped on a faded chenille housecoat hanging from a hook on the bathroom door. *Boyd's mothers. What if Boyd's mother comes home and catches me in his bedroom?*

Does he want to show me his guitar or does he want to make out, like Skeeter and Annie- Anna? Maybe he only wants to show me his guitar. I'd like to hear him play it.

I don't know how to make out...I never did it before. Maybe it would be okay if he just kisses me. I don't want him to think I'm not cool.

I'm pretty sure it's a sin to make-out. But he's really cute and I really like him.

Standing up, she looked at the frightened girl in the mirror, splashed cold water on her face, dried off with a towel, and put it back exactly as it had been.

She opened her purse and dug around to find her beige-pink lip gloss. An only slightly more confident girl looked back from the mirror as she ran the gloss across her lips. She reached into her bra, pulled the wadded Kleenex from the 32A cups and flushed it down the toilet, fluffed her hair and opened the door.

Boyd stood in the hallway.

She looked toward the closed door. *They're in there making out.* Her face grew hot and she didn't lift her eyes to his, avoiding even the briefest contact.

He took hold of her hand and led her down the hall to his bedroom.

The small room carried a distinctive boy smell—she recognized it from her brothers' room—a mixture of dirty socks and hair oil. Its plain walls were empty, save a bulletin board with pictures of cars cut from magazines pinned to it. The wood floors were bare, and the only furniture was a single bed and a compact dresser. His neatly made bed stood opposite the old dresser, painted green, with sags and brush marks. On top was a framed photo. A man in a WWII army uniform peered at Sarah from the faded sepia-toned photograph. In the corner near the dresser a very old, very sad, beat-up guitar leaned against the wall.

"This is her—my baby—she's a Gibson--belonged to my dad. I tell people my granddaddy gave it to him, but Mom told me Dad bought it in a pawn shop in Texas when he was in the army." He nodded at the photo on his dresser. "That's him. He got killed in a car wreck before I was born."

Sarah felt something familiar roll out from him; a wave of sadness that in an instant caught hold of her. She couldn't put her finger on it—but she knew that feeling of something inside; something that wouldn't seem to allow total happiness.

Boyd sat down on the bed and pulled his boots off. He slid his back against the headboard and put the guitar over his knee.

With no place to sit except the bed, she sat at the foot, keeping a distance between them and watched as he strummed a few chords, picked out notes and adjusted the tuning pegs.

He sat back for a moment as if trying to think of something to play, then smiled and slowly crinkling up his eyes, began to play the chords for Jailhouse Rock; his foot bounced to keep time.

She was taken by surprise at how good he sounded.

He finished the song; she clapped her hands together and smiled.

"I want to buy an electric-- I'm saving up for one I saw at a pawnshop in Texarkana." He adjusted the tuning pegs again. "I can play about 20 songs." He laughed; didn't look up and continued to turn the pegs. "Don't worry; I won't make you listen to all of them now."

He played a few more tunes—mostly Rockabilly then put the guitar down carefully.

The last one was a song Sarah had never heard before, but she loved it and clapped. He smiled.

"What's that song?"

"What? ...you never heard that before?"

He let his eyes meet hers and seemed to search her face.

She didn't understand; was embarrassed at how long he kept his eyes locked on hers. She felt her cheeks flush and dropped her eyes.

"I don't know the name of it," he said and wet his bottom lip with his tongue. "I wrote it, but I didn't give it a name."

Boyd moved closer, a light crisp whiff of his cologne drifted in the air around her making her weak and tingly.

"What do you think I should call it?" He touched her hair, moved his hand to her face and came toward her. Their lips brushed for an instant.

She swallowed hard, fighting the uneasiness in the pit of her stomach and moved to the edge of his bed.

"How do you learn to write songs?"

He didn't answer. Putting his arm around her he pulled her into his body.

She tried to keep her voice steady. "It must be really hard...to write a song, I mean."

His hand was at her back. He kissed her and eased her down against the pillows.

Her insides turned upside down.

He didn't seem nervous, seemed to know what to do. *I'm not the first girl he ever kissed.*

His hand was moving under her shirt--kept going a little farther with each kiss.

For several seconds, unsure of herself she didn't move. Looking anywhere except at him, she stared at a water stain on the ceiling.

He tried to slide a hand under her bra. Her hand pushed at his to stop him, but he continued his exploration, gently kneading her breast through the fabric, and kissed her again.

I like him, and he noticed me at the Dixie. Her heart beat faster as he pushed his hand under her bra again and this time she didn't stop him. *I want him to like me.*

A wave of regret swept over her, her body stiffened. "No! Don't!" She abruptly sat up. "I want to leave," she said. "Now."

Sarah hurriedly took her seat in Mrs. Phillips' homeroom. *Boyd's not here, good; I can't face him after yesterday.*

A few snickers from the back of the room were silenced by an icy stare from Mrs. Phillips.

The tardy bell rang. Boyd still wasn't in his seat. She relaxed—until Boyd strutted through the door, heels tapping, tardy slip in hand.

He took his seat without a glance in her direction.

Another ripple of snickers and a few whispers trickled through the room.

Straining to hear the whispers making their way down the aisle, Sarah shot a quick look over her shoulder.

All eyes in the room were turned to her, knowingly accusing.

Could she please disappear--like Alice--down a rabbit hole? Or better still-make them all vanish.

But, instead, there seemed to be an outbreak of dull pencils in urgent need of sharpening. A steady flow of kids wandered to and from the pencil sharpener. With the grinding of each pencil, curious eyes seemed to bore into her.

Not even pretending to pay attention to the announcements blasting from the intercom she spent the period crouched down, waiting for the bell signaling the end of homeroom.

The bell rang. She rose from her desk, smoothed her skirt and waited to regain her composure before moving toward the voices and confusion coming from the flood of bodies crowding the hallway.

Outside the classroom, Skeeter and Boyd exchanged angry whispers. Boyd's eyes met hers as she scurried past. Skeeter shook his head and Boyd lit into him again.

Arms full of books, she fought her way through swarms of kids bumping into each other as they streamed through the halls. Every face seemed to wear a smirk.

Rattled, she bumped against Mrs. Fisher, the hall monitor. Her books spilled onto the floor and laughter erupted around her. She grimaced and stooped to gather her books.

A girl bent to help, her pimply face dotted with Clearasil. She tucked her hair behind her ear and handing Sarah a book, shot her a look of commiseration. A short, pudgy girl yanked the arm of the Good Samaritan and pulled her away.

The muffled words Sarah overheard as the girls hurried off—*Boyd, all-the-way*—confirmed her fears.

Between each class, it was déjà vu as the hallway scene replayed; now aggravated by awareness of the lies being told about her.

By lunchtime, the morning had prepared her for the worst.... Rumors travel quickly around the school, but never more rampant than in the lunchroom—the gathering place of tacky, catty, snotty, girls with beautiful, perfect hair. But the worst came sooner than she'd imagined.

Making her way down the hall she saw out of the corner of her eye, two boys running up beside her. A hand reached out and slapped her on top of her head. They dashed ahead, turned around and began to taunt her.

Then out of nowhere, the sound of steel taps beating against the tile floor and a whiff of leather and oranges surrounded her.

"Leave her alone," Boyd warned. The two raced off laughing.

His brow rose above his large round eyes. "I'm sorry Sarah. It wasn't me. Skeeter's the one telling that lie. I promise it wasn't me. I told him to stop, but it's too late. I'm really sorry."

Sarah looked at him for a second without answering. They exchanged a momentary look of complete understanding. She looked away and then he was gone as quickly as he'd appeared.

A wave of noise and the smell of fish sticks primed her for entry into the lunchroom. Someone yelled, "I saved you a seat." Her spirits rose and then quickly fell as she realized the invitation wasn't meant for her.

She found an empty table, put down her brown bag and a spiral notebook and took her spot at the end of the milk line.

At last, making it through the slow-moving line, she sat down at the still empty table and took a bite of her sandwich. She stopped chewing as her eyes skipped to the notebook. Scrawled across the first page, in ornate script with a saucy little circle dotting the "i" were the words, "Boyd got cooties from Sarah the slut."

Why do they hate me? I never did anything to them.

Tearing the sheet from her notebook, she wadded it into a tiny ball and carried it, along with her uneaten lunch, to the trash can.

Why are kids so mean?

EIGHTEEN

Joel 2:24
24 The threshing floors will be filled with grain; the vats will overflow with new wine and oil.

Otis fixed his eyes on the recently oiled county road running past the farm. He clenched and unclenched his hands, inhaled a deep breath and blew it out as the shiny red and white Ford pickup approached.

Jim Ed carefully bumped the truck over the driveway dip, rolled to a stop near the house and got out. Stifling a grin, he approached his brother and father.

Raising his hand in greeting Junior smirked. "Bout time you got here. Daddy almost had apoplexy waiting for you to get back."

Jim Ed glanced at his daddy, then back at the truck. "Pretty, ain't it?"

He'd developed a quiet confidence over the past few years. Hard work, arthritis, and Wild Turkey took a heavy toll on Otis, shifting the full responsibility for the farm to the two young men. Jim Ed never seemed weighted down by the responsibility, but instead, embraced it. Junior was happy to defer to his brother.

While Otis had no fancy for business, Jim Ed developed a keen instinct, and no one in the family challenged his decisions.

Otis didn't like change. He regarded it with wariness and suspicion, but Jim Ed embraced new ideas and dreamed of growth. He never made excuses, never complained of too little sun or too much rain or the price of feed. To his way of thinking challenges were a fact of life.

As he took on more and more responsibility the farm saw more and more success. Had he been born into another family, one where his talents were nurtured, and education encouraged, Jim Ed might have gone far.

Otis studied the logo newly painted on the truck door...*Jones Family Chicken Farm- Tolerance, Arkansas* encircled an image of a white hen. For a split-second, a rare smile almost formed on his lips. He rubbed his hand across his gray stubble, lowered his head and shot a spurt of brown tobacco juice from between the gap in his rotting teeth. "Not bad."

Getting the nod of Daddy's approval, Jim Ed grinned again. It had been the right decision—a necessary one--to give up the orchard for chicken coops.

He said, as if to reassure himself, "Peach blossoms might smell sweet, but chicken shit smells like money."

Trying in vain to hide his pleasure Otis lowered his brow in a bogus frown, "I just hope you boys know what you're doing, putting all that money into this fancy get-up. Seems to me like a lot of dang foolishness—a sign on a farm truck."

Junior laughed. "All he's done for the last half hour is fret about how much you paid for that sign."

Dee's voice echoed through the open kitchen window, "Good lands 'o Goshen, what in tarnation is all the commotion about?"

Moments later, the old spring on the screen door screeched and the door creaked open and slammed shut.

Coming into the yard wiping her hands on a dish towel, with Sarah right behind her, Dee stopped short. "Well, I'll be."

"Look, Momma." Jim Ed held up a sign with the same logo as the one on the truck; *Jones Family Chicken Farm- Tolerance, Arkansas.* "It's for the fence by the road

"Oh, for land's sake, ain't we the fancy ones now?" There was a sparkle in her eyes that had been missing for years.

Sarah ran her finger along the satiny paint on the new truck. "Are we rich now or something?"

Jim Ed snorted. "I wouldn't exactly say rich. But we're rich enough to have a truck payment."

Dee didn't care much for money talk.

Satisfied that all the words on the sign were spelled right and the chicken looked like a chicken, she gave a brief smile toward her son and said, "Son, I'm a might proud," and headed back into the house.

❧

"Shoo!" Dee swatted at two flies circling freshly shucked ears of corn stacked in a dishpan. Sarah and Dee sat side by side on the porch swing and rocked back and forth with a bushel of corn at their feet and the dishpan resting between them. Sarah added another shucked ear to the mound and turned her eyes toward her mother. She studied the lines around her mouth, made deeper by years of smoking and the gaunt cheeks, weather-worn and dry.

Sarah tried to recall a time she'd heard her mother laugh. Maybe, before Kenny died. Surely she had.

Still searching her mother's face Sarah asked, "How old will you be on your birthday, Mamma?"

"I'll be forty."

Sarah wasn't sure if that was old. Aunt Myra was only two years younger than Momma but looked a lot younger.

Momma could be pretty if she would fix up a bit, wear a little makeup, care about how she looks. I hope I never get to where I don't care about my looks.

Some of the women in town cut their hair short to look like pictures of Jackie Kennedy on the cover of Life Magazine. Not Dee, she still twisted her long, graying hair into a tight bun pinned at the nape of her neck. *Momma's never worn her hair any other way.*

"Momma, when you were a little girl what did you want to be when you grew up?"

"Oh, we didn't much think about that when we was young. We just figured on getting married and raising a family." She stopped, looked off toward the horizon as if searching for someone. "I married too young and started having babies right away. I weren't but eighteen when I had Jim Ed." She sighed and picked up another ear of corn, but just sat looking at it. "Don't make the same mistake. There's a world of happiness out there; you just have to go find it." There were a few beats of silence. Seemed she wanted to say more but wouldn't or couldn't. With another sigh, she pulled at the husks.

When I grow up I'll get me a rich man to marry and Momma can come live with us so she won't have to work so hard. He'll be terribly handsome, too and I won't have to work. We'll live in a big white house with white pillars in front and roses in the yard. I'll have the latest fashions and …

"Howdy, Miss Dee, Miss Sarah Jane." Sarah jumped at the sound of the man's voice. She had not noticed him walking toward the house with a quick, forward-leaning gait. Now facing them on the porch he smiled almost apologetically.

His name was Linwood Croft, but he'd answered to "Cotton" since he was 'a tow-headed kid' growing up in the Ozarks of northwest Arkansas. Jim Ed hired Cotton as a full-time farm hand a year earlier when they finally showed enough profit to justify his wages.

"Whew." He pulled a faded bandana from the pocket of his strap overalls and wiped his brow. "Hotter'en a two-dollar pistol out here, ain't it? Heat's gitten' the best of me. I'm pure-D-tired." He stuffed the bandana back in his pocket. "Mighty sorry to bother you ladies. Reckon it'd be alright iffen I sit a spell?"

Dee nodded toward the steps, indicating permission. He took a seat, pulled off his old straw fedora and fanned himself with it. "This here hat belonged to my daddy," he said, studying a small hole in the brim. Then almost apologetically, continued. "I'm kindly partial to it."

Squinting up at the sun, he rubbed his hand over the rough stubble on his chin and thought for a moment.

"You know, my Granny worked every day, rain or shine—never a sick day. I always figured she feared if she ever stopped, she mightn't get started again. Shore-nuf, one day she sat down in her rocking chair, looked up to the sky and said, 'Jesus, Jesus, dear Jesus, I've lived eighty years and then some. Pardon my many, many sins, dear Jesus and take me to be with Thee forever.' Then if she didn't just close her eyes and that was that."

Cotton was the only person Sarah had ever known who hadn't been born and raised in Hallard County. He looked at life differently than other people. Momma said, 'he could sure spin a yarn.'

Middle-age had turned his once blond hair to snow white, and the childhood nickname still suited him. He still had a boyish look about him. Tall and lean but muscular, his face was darkened from the sun, his arms shiny with sweat.

A pleasant man, soft-spoken, he never said anything bad about anyone and from day one Sarah was at ease around him.

Her daddy called people from up around his parts *hill people*. He was always suspicious of *hill people* and he didn't make any exception for Cotton.

"I guess I'll help myself to a cool drink of water, iffen you don't mind." He walked to the pump and took the tin cup from a rusty hook and filled it to the brim. Three gulps emptied the cup. He wiped his mouth on his shirt sleeve and filled the cup a second time. He poured the water over his sun-reddened neck and then settled his hat on his head. Nodding a thank you in the general direction of the porch, he flashed a smile through his store-bought teeth. "Okie doke, best be getting on back to work now. I done sit long enough, ain't made it to eighty, not yet."

He placed the cup on the hook and looked up. His gaze lingered as if studying the white clouds in the sky. "Mighty fine day for feeling blessed, ain't it?" he said and walked away, without waiting for a response.

Dee's eyes followed him as he walked tall and erect toward the barn. "That man sure is a talker... talks a blue streak." She sighed. "Never knowed a man could talk so much."

As Cotton disappeared into the chicken coop, Sarah's attention went toward Otis. He shuffled through a jumble of old tires and rusty bed springs peeking from behind a patch of untamed Johnson grass threatening to overtake the barn. Taken aback by the conflicting demeanor of these two men she realized they were very likely contemporaries, but they seemed to come from different worlds.

NINETEEN

James 2:24
[24] Do you see that by works a man is justified; and not by faith only?

S arah woke before the first hint of sunrise with no smell of coffee coming from the kitchen. *Momma hasn't put the first pot on yet.* She dressed quickly and made her bed.

She measured coffee into the percolator and glanced past her own reflection in the window pane. In the semi-darkness of predawn, Cotton sat balanced on an old stump, his back to the barn. She put the pot on the gas burner and went outside to avoid waking the rest of the family. The aroma of coffee would soon enough have them milling about.

She walked across the grass toward the barn, the dew soaking her shoes.

Good-mornin' Miss Sarah Jane," Cotton said, never looking up from the peach he sliced with his pocket knife. Joy studied him with doggie eyes. He raised a peach wedge to his mouth then pointed to Joy with the tip of his knife. "Me and the pup here, we're having some breakfast. She said she don't much care for peaches, but she took right kindly to that slab of ham I brung from the boardin' house."

"Didn't mean to interrupt," Sarah said.

"Not interrupting a thing. Sit a spell. I got til sunup afore I get to workin'."

Sarah eased down onto the damp grass next to Joy, crossing her legs in front of her.

She had a special fondness for Cotton--liked to listen to him talk.

He'd worked for her family for some time, but he was still a mystery to her. Apart from knowing he lived alone in a room at Scarborough's Boarding House, she knew little else. She wondered if he'd ever been married if he had any kids. She figured if she waited long enough, he'd get around to telling her.

He'd said he didn't like to put down roots, didn't like to stay anywhere for too long, but he'd been working at the Jones farm for over a year. Once he told her that he was always thinking about leaving, but just never got around to doing it. *I guess as long as I know I can leave, I don't need to go nowhere.*

Taking a last bite of the peach, he tossed the pit into the grass and wiped his knife, then his hands on his overalls. Reaching into his pocket he fished out a book of matches and a pack of Camels. Tapping the pack against his hand he opened it, slowly winding the little red ribbon around the cellophane and tearing off a corner of the top. He placed an unfiltered cigarette between his lips and glanced toward the sky. "Bit airish this morning, ain't it?"

Sarah nodded and watched the ruby tip of the cigarette, glowing in the morning light. "Mamma said we didn't have much of a winter this year."

Cotton ran a hand through his thick hair. "I ever tell you 'bout the widder woman back home? She could prognosticate on the weather--had a whole heap of ways to know what was gonna happen."

Sarah liked to hear his stories about mountain folk in the hills that straddle the Missouri-Arkansas border but wasn't sure she should believe most of them. His sly, self-deprecating manner made the telling entertaining, even if not true.

"Did you know if a rooster crows at bedtime its gonna rain afore sunup? Well, it's the gospel truth." He pointed toward the chicken coop. "If you don't believe me, you just start minding 'ol Rudy there - you'll see."

Cotton flicked the ash from his cigarette and took another long drag squinting against the smoke. "Anyway, the widder--Miz Selmer--that was her name--she was mostly good at prognosticating 'bout the winter. She'd allus roast a fresh killed goose for Thanksgiving dinner. She'd carve it real careful-like, to make sure she didn't cut through that wishbone." He paused, held up his index finger. "That part is real important." He took a draw on his cigarette. "After dinner, she'd take that bone and clean it up real nice and put it on a shelf to dry out. In a few days, after it was good 'n dry, she'd take a fair long look at it. She could tell just by looking at the color iffen we could figger on a cold winter or a mild 'en. She'd hardly ever get it wrong."

As dawn broke the sound of a mourning dove filled the air. After a short pause, a chorus of chirping birds added a counterpoint to the dove's melancholy song. Cotton leaned forward and pointed his cigarette toward the sound of the birds. "Even when a body tries to deny God, he's still surrounded by His works."

He pulled a tattered paperback from his pocket. "I do some readin'," he said tapping the book on his knee. "Take this here book. It was writ by this little ol' Georgia gal--Listen to this... 'I preach there are all kinds of truth, your truth and somebody else's, but behind all of them, there's only one truth and that is that there's no truth.' I liked what it said, so I memorized it."

Sarah looked confused. "I'm not sure I understand what that means, Mr. Cotton."

He laughed. "Me neither but I like the words anyhow. Maybe if I think on them long enough, I'll figure it out. I just know some religions believe there's one truth and some believes there's a different truth and both think they got the only truth. Me, I think all of 'em has some truth, but none of 'em knows the whole truth. Only the universe knows the whole truth. I can't hold much store in any church that says they know the truth and the only truth. Now, if I was to say that around some folks, I'd be in a whole heap of trouble. But that's how I see it."

Sarah took the book from his hand and studied the cover. It looked like the cover of one of the dirty books Momma found hidden under Junior's mattress. A man sprawled under a tree and a girl sat next to him lifting his hat and peeking into his face. Red letters spelled out *Wise Blood*. Above the title were the words *A Searching Novel of Sin and Redemption*. Sarah was surprised a woman would write such a book. *Flannery* didn't seem much like a girl's name either. But sure enough, the picture on the back of the book was of a woman.

"What's it about?"

"It's about this here fella..." Cotton tapped the cover, "...he starts a new church. Calls it the Church Without Christ and he goes to preachin' on the street telling folks Jesus is only a trick and they shouldn't believe him."

"I might like to read that book. I've read a lot of Nancy Drew books and *The Red Pony* and *Of Mice and Men* and a whole bunch more.

"If it's alright with your momma, I reckon you can have it when I'm done with it."

Joy lay at Cotton's feet waiting for him to drop a bite of ham. She got up and whined. He put his hand out for the dog to sniff. Her wet snout covered every inch of Cotton's hand and when she was finished, she licked the salt from his fingers. Satisfied there was no more ham, she wandered off to lap from a bowl of water by the barn door.

"Well, I'll tell you something, Miss Sarah Jane, if I'd been a rich man I'd have me a room full of books. I'm just an ignorant man but I was introduced to books when I was a young'en and that made a mark on me. My momma, she loved to read. She'd read to us from the Bible every day, but she had some other books too, mostly ol' Mark Twain. He was from Missouri--like my granny. When Momma finished the Bible reading, she'd take down one of them other books and read to us some more." He held the butt of the cigarette between his lips; smoke hovered over his head as he took the book from Sarah and thumbed through until he found the dog-eared page he was looking for. "Here it is…" He began to read out loud. "'I believe that what's right today is wrong tomorrow and that the time to enjoy yourself is now so long as you let others do the same. I'm as good, Mr. Motes,' she said, 'not believing in Jesus as a many a one that does.'"

Cotton closed the book, his thumb holding his place. "I think there's a lot of truth in them words. It's what my momma taught me. She always said to speak the truth and do your best. Just know what's right and what's not right. That's my religion; to know we should be good to each other…just because it's the right thing to do…not because we're afraid of God or the Devil or because we want some reward for being good. Some folks got it all wrong. They do good things because they think it'll get 'em into heaven. That's not gonna do it. You do good things 'cause it's the right thing to do."

Red sparks flew in the air as he took a long final draw off the cigarette and flipped the butt into the air.

Sarah felt less lonely around Cotton. He talked to her like she was a grown-up and listened when she talked. It made her want to tell him things-- things she'd never shared with anyone.

"I used to go to church and I got baptized with my brother, Kenny. Did I ever tell you Kenny studied on being a preacher?" She paused; looked down at her hands folded in her lap. "I thought about being a preacher too. But after Kenny died, well, I kinda fell out with Jesus."

Joy trotted back and curled up on the grass thumping the ground with her tail. Sarah reached out and rubbed the back of the dog's neck. "Mr. Cotton, are you a Christian?"

Fishing another cigarette out of his shirt pocket he lit it and studied the glowing tip for a minute. "That kinda depends on what you mean by a Christian—if you mean do I believe in the things Jesus said—I do. Do I try to live the way Jesus said we should? I do."

Rudy crowed. Waited. Then answered himself.

Cotton continued. "I read the Bible 'cause there's a lot of good lessons in there, but I ain't much for going to church and such. I believe in all the important parts--forgiveness, kindness, caring about people, and the like. But I don't cotton too much to some of the other stuff that goes on with church folks.

"Am I a Christian? I don't rightly know. Puttin' names on things never mattered too much to me. Sometimes folks start to believe the names they put on themselves, but just because a fella calls himself something, don't make it so…."

Surprise flickered over Sarah's face, then quickly disappeared. "I get it. Just 'cause you name a town Tolerance doesn't mean the folks that live there are forgiving."

"You're a smart girl."

"You think so?" Sarah grinned.

"I know so. You may not understand what I'm tellin' you right now, but after you think on it a while, it might start to make some sense." He flicked away the half-smoked cigarette smoldering between his fingers. "Some folks that calls themselves Christians seem to think there ain't much wrong with them. They figure if they just say they's Christians then they's all of a sudden good people. Bet you know a lot of Christians who ain't so good."

He stopped talking and looked into the distance. After a moment he sighed. "Now my granny, she was half Choctaw Indian. Indians don't think of it so much as religion; it's more like just their belief that they are connected to nature. That's the way I look at it too, live in peace with nature, not by a bunch of rules made up by folks."

Looking up at the sky he said, "Gonna be a nice 'en. I best get on over and check out them feed sacks. I saw an ol' rat snake around here yesterday. Snake'll break up a henhouse quicker 'en anything."

He walked away, stopped at the chicken coop where he bent and slipped inside. He came back out with a dozen eggs in a bowl and handed it to Sarah. "Breakfast," he said and gave her a wink.

Sarah took the bowl into the house. Dee stood at the stove lifting slices of ham from the skillet. The air was thick with the rich fragrance of coffee.

Leaving the bowl on the counter, Sarah said, "I better go milk Sweetie," and scooted out the door.

TWENTY

Leviticus 15:19
*¹⁹ The woman, who at the return of the month, hath her issue of
blood, shall be separated seven days.*

S arah is alone in the sanctuary of Cold Fork Baptist Church. "Why am I here? I
don't remember how I got here." The smell of burning candles saturats the air. The
sound of hurried footsteps frightens her. She realizes they are her own.

*A stripe of sunlight falls upon a large crucifix fastened to the wall. Christ's dead body
hangs from the cross, his head limp, his eyes shut. "That's not right...not in a Baptist
church...the cross should be empty.*

Where is everyone? Momma... Brother Leon?"

*At the altar an old priest, all in white—wrinkled flabby face—tiny eyes lost beneath
drooping lids, beckons to her, directing her attention to a simple pine box nearby. The lid
stands open. Approaching, she places her hand on the side of the coffin. The room is now
flooded with moonlight – not sunlight– the moon silent at the window. In the shafts of
light, she studies the blue-white pastiness of the corpse; his hands folded across his chest, the
nails perfectly manicured. A rustic wooden cross, red smears crusted across it, lies on the
body. Who is he? Who is that man? Where did he come from? He wasn't here a moment
ago?*

*Sarah looks up at the priest. He shakes his head sternly... as though blaming her for
something... and he is no longer a priest but instead, Brother Leon in his powder blue
polyester suit.*

*An old woman lays her gaunt hand on Sarah's shoulder and a hushed voice echoes in
her ear. "Never saw your daddy look so good. Doesn't he look wonderful? Looks like he's
asleep."*

*"It is Daddy." Until the woman said it, Sarah didn't recognize him. How could she
not recognize him? Now, she sees him and sees him and sees him. She will not--can not cry.*

"He's not sleeping, he's dead."

A smile forms on his lips and cloudy gray eyes shoot open.

Sarah slams her eyes shut, but still, she can see his mocking face.

A closet door opens a bit. The sounds of laughs and whispers come from within. A fly comes buzzing from the closet and circles the coffin which is now just a dusty cardboard box. With a snapping crack, the fly hits the window leaving a slimy stain.

The face of the corpse morphs. It's Kenny, not Daddy. She cannot see the face but knows it is him. She tries to see him but the head turns away.

All of a sudden, she is surrounded by laughter and curiously quiet voices. Rows of people sit in the pews, their faces turned toward her. Faces of kids she knows from school. The old woman glowers from the front row, peeling peaches into an enamel dishpan.

The old priest makes his way through the crowd, seizes Sarah by the hand and snatches her from the cluster shaking his head and crying, "Come away, don't look."

"You should look, he's only sleeping," shouts the old woman breaking into riotous laughter.

"Yes, you should look," shouts another.

Again, the priest turns and summons Sarah. She rushes to him and tries to clutch at his hand, but it fades and the old man is gone.

She awoke with a start, perspiring and anxious, sheets tangled around her legs.

Alert now, the anxious feeling that came with the nightmare lingers.

Memories of Kenny's funeral flooded her thoughts; people praying over him, saying he looked like he was sleeping. *How would they know — they'd never seen him sleeping? He looked dead with all the color drained from the flesh and painted with the garish colors of a doll's frozen face.* And when all the people who did not love him were through praying and commenting and mourning and watching his coffin disappear into the ground--when they'd all gone home, Kenny was not sleeping. He was in a dark hole forever, and Sarah would never see him or touch him or hold his hand again.

She adjusted her pillow and fought the tears. *Saturday, no need to get up yet.* It was tempting to draw up the blanket, close her eyes and sink into a nest of quilts. *Can't sleep… I can lay here feeling sad…or get up, go outside, read, listen to the birds, feel the sun…it must be nice out, the sun is peeking around the edges of the curtains.* She glanced at the clock ticking loudly on the nightstand. *Almost nine! I can't believe Momma let me sleep so late…guess everyone is finished in the bathroom by now.* Turning the covers back, she rested her bare feet on a small scatter rug beside the bed. An unfamiliar ache gripped her belly, and from that pain and heaviness, a sick feeling spread through her stomach.

Crossing the threshold of the bathroom, she glimpsed her image in the mirror. There were recent changes in her thirteen-year-old body. She no longer needed to stuff her bra with Kleenex to fill the A cups. She stared for a while at her reflection. The pretty girl looking back at her had grown tall for her age unleashing a desire to hunch over, trying to make herself small so she didn't tower over everyone.

She turned the faucet on and the tub began to fill with warm water. She pulled her nightgown over her head, dropped it to the floor, and slipped off her panties. About to climb into the tub, she noticed a pink stain on the crotch of her white cotton panties.

So this is it? This is what that movie at school was all about.

Momma had to sign a permission slip before she could see the cartoon about becoming a woman. Watching the girl who looked like Cinderella with flowers floating around her, Sarah wondered what the big deal was all about.

There had been a great deal of suspense as the sixth-grade boys were herded into the cafeteria and the girls gathered in the music room to watch the movie. That film and what she overheard listening to other girls provided all she knew about this normal event signaling impending womanhood.

Sarah had watched intently as the narrator explained what would soon be happening to her body. After the lights came back on, Nancy MacDougal boasted, "Heck, I didn't need to see that," shaking her head in disgust, small gold studs shining from her pierced ears. "I've done started my periods already."

It was while the girls filed back into the classroom, the boys watching them with knowing smirks, that Sarah heard Nancy, the newly self-appointed sixth-grade authority on menstruation, whisper to Sandra Webber, "Some guys say they can tell when a girl is having her period."

"Oh no, I hope not," Sandra whispered.

This information that boys might have some magical power of detection devastated Sarah. Excitement and pride over the prospect of having her first period commingled with anxiety...fear that others would know when she wore a bulky pad between her legs to catch the bloody discharge filled her with self-conscious dread. *What if I stand up and there's a bloody spot on my skirt.... It happened to that nasty Sally and I was glad everyone whispered behind her back.*

Sarah examined the spot on her panties once again. She puzzled over it. *Maybe I shouldn't take a bath. I'm not sure.*

113

She heard Momma in the kitchen and remembered. *Momma will know what to do. She has what I need.*

One afternoon, about a year ago, she and Becky Sue were watching the Cisco Kid and his sidekick, Pancho bring justice to some bad guys. As Cisco and Pancho rode off laughing in a cloud of dust, the girls overheard their mothers as they chatted away in the kitchen.

Aunt Myra talked in a loud whisper like she always did when she had good gossip to share. "Well, Becky Sue got her first period last Sunday. Won't be long before Sarah Jane has hers. I noticed she's starting to grow some little bubbies."

The girls exchanged embarrassed glances.

Momma lowered her voice, "I plum forgot about such; with the others all being boys and such."

"Sis, you better get yourself ready. It's-a-coming sooner than you think."

In the top drawer of Sarah's dresser was a booklet *Very Personally Yours.* It had been there ever since the postman delivered a large envelope addressed to Sarah. She'd torn a coupon from a Kotex ad in *Seventeen* and sent off for the free booklet and a personal calendar to mark off the days of her period, so she would know when to expect it each month.

When the package arrived, Sarah hurried to her room to rip it open. She had since spent a number of hours concentrating on the illustrations. Then she put the book away and waited for the special day to arrive.

Now, with the time finally here, Sarah didn't know what to do. She shoved a tissue in her clean panties and pulled on her clothes. Stuffing the soiled panties in her pocket, she went to the kitchen.

"There you are," Mamma said, folding her arms over her bony chest. "Everyone else done had their breakfast. I saved you a biscuit and a sausage patty."

Even while the cramping in the pit of her belly grew stronger, Sarah agonized over how to tell Momma. *This is so embarrassing.* By the time she gathered the courage to approach her mother, her mouth was dry. She didn't want anyone to know about her period; especially not Otis or her brothers. Her cheeks burned at the thought of them knowing. She wanted it to remain a secret between mother and daughter.

Unable to find the words, she pulled the panties from her pocket, bit her lip and held them out. "Momma," was all she could get out; her eyes said the rest.

Dee stood still for a moment, letting it sink in. She touched her daughter's cheek sweetly and brushed the hair from her eyes. "Don't be scared, Sarah Jane. It's just a normal, natural thing."

Momma dosed her with a tablespoonful of Otis's awful tasting whiskey, then tucked her in bed with a heating pad on her tummy.

Dee gently kissed her forehead. "Sarah Jane, you rest today, but this is gonna happen once a month for the next forty or so years. You can't go to bed each time it happens. You just learn to cope with life's troubles." Her eyes looked sad.

Lying in bed snuggled against her pillow she thought back to the day she got her first bra. She'd been excited but embarrassed. Before long, there was a new, constant worry when Junior made a habit of snapping the back of her bra through her blouse and asking, "What happened to your undershirt?"

He thought it was funny; was only teasing--it wasn't funny to me.

At least the boys at school didn't bother her with the teasing, they saved that for the girls they liked. *Maybe the boys would like me if I was prettier, or shorter, or had blonde hair...or maybe ...if Skeeter hadn't lied.*

Boyd...Floyd...Daddy, her mind would constantly return to those memories, all somehow mixed together, a muddled mess of pain, sorrow, and denial haunting her. She hated how it made her feel inside...dirty, ugly, confused.

TWENTY-ONE

Deuteronomy 31:6

⁶ Be strong and of good courage, fear not, nor be afraid of those people: for the LORD thy God, is who goes with you; he will not leave thee, nor forsake thee.

Carefully placing the last of the freshly pressed and starched shirts on a wire hanger, Sarah carried them to her brothers' room and hung them in the closet alongside two pairs of iron-creased khaki's folded neatly over hangers. She glanced at the neckties draped over a nail, remembering how Junior groused when Jim Ed shook his head and complained, "they're not in style anymore, gotta get some new ones."

How could those two be brothers? They were so different from one another. Junior complained every time he was forced to put on a tie. "It serves no useful function and it chokes my neck. And why should I shine my shoes to talk about chicken feed with some hillbilly from Springdale? Don't make no sense to me." But in the end, he always did what Jim Ed wanted.

Returning to the kitchen, she eyed a neatly folded stack of shirts ready to be put away—Otis' things. *I'll do it later. He's in there now—probably sneaking an after-lunch-drink. Pathetic. I hate him. Wish I wasn't here alone with him.*

It was rare for Dee to leave them alone in the house together.

She tried to block out the hate and the horror of the dreadful, familiar ritual… the sound of Otis on the front porch—not even trying to hide the whiskey bottle, the bang of the screen door, lights going out and heavy footsteps; then, the dread— waiting to see. On a good night, he would go to his room. On a bad night, she would feel her blanket pulled back and rough hands would fondle her. She learned to go away in her head until it was over, but each time it happened she lost a little more of herself and felt a little more alone.

That first-time …that's when she lost control of her life. Not a day passed without the memories piercing her thoughts; sometimes consciously thinking of what he'd done, other times, a dull ache in her mind, taking from her all simplicity and innocence of childhood.

Unplugging the iron and folding the ironing board, she headed for the pantry to store them away. *I hope he'll leave me alone this time.*

When she turned Daddy stood in the doorway. "Where's your momma at?" his voice hoarse and full of whiskey. His stubbled jowl had two days growth and seemed he hadn't bathed or changed his clothes. He raked a hand through his greasy hair.

"Aunt Willie May's sick," Sarah answered in a voice, deceptively calm. "Momma took her some soup. She'll be back directly." Her jaw tightened at the sight of him…the smell…*I wish he'd die.*

"Find me that bottle. I know your momma hid it." He teetered with his legs wide apart for balance. His voice got louder, his words slurred. "She hid it. It's here, I know it is."

If I give him the bottle maybe he'll get drunk enough to pass out and I won't have to mess with him today.

"She didn't hide it, Daddy. It's right here in the cabinet." Her voice was firm and pitiless. Sarah opened the cupboard and held out the bottle at arm's length.

Snatching it from her hand, he lifted the bottle and peered at the level of whiskey, then stared at her warily through rheumy eyes. His face dark and desperate, his eyes glared. He poured whiskey into a glass and waved it in the air, liquid spilled down the sides. Mumbling under his breath "Thinks she's smarter 'en me, puttin' it up there…." He raised his arm to gesture with his glass, lost his balance and fell against the table and toppled into a chair.

He took a swig, coughed and wiped his mouth with the back of his hand. Fishing around in his pocket, he pulled out a crumpled pack of cigarettes and a box of matches. He tapped the pack against the side of his hand and cigarettes spilled onto the table. Infuriated, he grabbed at them and fumbled them back into the pack. With a shaking hand, he got one into his mouth. He flicked the match head against the striker. The flame sparked and went out. Again, he tried. It didn't light and again smacking at the matchbox with an intensifying fury until he slammed the matches to the table and bellowed, "GODDAMNIT!"

Hoping to placate him, Sarah struck a match and held it to the cigarette clenched between his teeth. He pulled in the smoke.

The stench of alcohol mixed with tobacco, sweat, and urine assailed her.

He grabbed at her, his watery eyes fierce. Twisting her wrist, he growled and sprayed her with spittle, "Where you think you're going? Trying to get away from me?"

"C'mon over here...." He tried to hug her; his body nudging against hers, pushing toward the bedroom.

Her mouth quivered, fear and anger mounting. He'd never been this aggressive before.

She knew what he expected of her; to be passive, meek, submissive. Because of the fear ingrained into her, she had always done everything he said.

As his fingernails sunk into her arm, fear turned to rage.

No longer fearful, the realization that he couldn't hurt her more than he already had emboldened her. Maybe it was the light of day—maybe it was her newly formed womanhood—wherever the strength came from, she was somehow going to take control of the situation. She would never let him touch her again. *I can't do this. I can't be touched by him one more time.*

A kick of adrenaline shot through her filling her whole body with an unfamiliar power.

Resolute, she took a step back, shook her head saying *no* for the first time since the abuse started.

"I don't want to," she said. Her voice shook, but there was confidence in her posture—erect, head held high and eyes unflinching.

Unable to keep pent-up anger in any longer, words cascaded out in a stream of honesty. "I don't want you to touch me anymore and I don't want to touch you. I hate you."

He stopped at the door, his eyes blinked against the smoke of the cigarette between his lips. He took a drag, smirked and threw the smoldering butt at Sarah.

Wincing against the burn, she looked at him without expression, feeling nothing now but the hard stone in the pit of her stomach.

Pushing at her, he pinned her arms to her sides.

"Let me go!" She kicked at him, no longer able to bear the humiliation. Every breath she took in this house made her sicker.

He shoved her against the wall trapping her there, his arm against her throat, wheezing into her face with sour breath.

"Let me go." She tried to push him away.

"Let me go… I'll tell Jim Ed. I'll tell him what you been doing to me."

He loosened the hold on her neck and grabbed her hair.

A panicked strength ran through her. Terrified, she pulled away from him and ran on trembling legs, ran outside stumbling and nearly falling. The door slammed behind her.

Leaning against the wall for support, she felt her heart speeding. Shaking, she sat on the ground before her knees buckled under her. Through the screen door, she could see him sitting at the kitchen table, the empty whiskey bottle in front of him and a look of fear on his face.

What have I done? I still have to live in this house. She rested her head on her arms and sat, feeling astonished, numb and much older than her 13 years.

TWENTY-TWO

Psalm 56
² My adversaries pursue me all day long; in their pride many are attacking me.

1963

S arah stepped out of the pickup and onto the sidewalk into the vibrant glare of a cool, March, Arkansas sun. She abandoned her sweater on the truck seat, wanting to show off the pink shift dress she'd bought at a rummage sale in the basement of First Methodist Church. The label inside was from a nice department store. In especially good spirits, she entered Piggly-Wiggly. The dress gave her newfound confidence.

She moved quickly through the store checking off Momma's list and loaded the groceries and household supplies next to the sacks of feed in the bed of the pickup.

Hurrying across the street to the Rexall Drugstore she made her way to the cosmetic section to inspect the rows of pink and peach Cutex nail polish and tubes of matching lipstick lined up, side by side.

Wanting to confirm the colors in an ad, she headed to the magazine rack and began thumbing through the current issue of *Seventeen*. Lost in the pages, she jumped as a gruff, cigarette choked voice echoed from the back of the store. "This ain't no library. You wanna read it? Buy it."

Doc Murphy kept an eagle eye on teenagers who came into his store.

Derisive giggling erupted from behind a large photo of Bobby Vinton. The words "New Hit Single, Blue Velvet" were printed below his face. Not glancing left or right, Sarah returned the magazine to its proper place.

Brenda Sue Wilson and Betty Jo Shelby shuffled through a stack of 45 r.p.m. records displayed next to the Bobby Vinton poster. They didn't acknowledge Sarah but continued to shoot glances in her direction and giggled and whispered.

Brenda Sue nodded in Sarah's direction looking as if she swallowed something sour. Then, in a voice deliberately loud enough for Sarah to overhear, she asked, "My goodness isn't that your sister's old dress Sarah Jane Jones is wearing?"

"It sure enough is. Aunt Dotty gave it to Carol Ann for her birthday. She wanted to throw out the tacky thing, but Momma made her wear it when Aunt Dotty came to supper. After that, Momma let her give it to the charity sale at the church."

"Don't you think it's kinda bright?" Brenda Sue snickered. "And maybe a little too short?"

"She's so grody. I guess no one ever told her redheads shouldn't wear pink,"

Brenda Sue added, raising her voice. "I bet she's got cooties in that frizzy hair."

Sarah straightened up and fixed her eyes on them until they stopped talking. Her cheeks flushed pink.

Loud-mouthed gossipy pigs, rooting around in the dirt. I'll show you who's grody.

Sarah pondered the best way to escape and turned to leave, hoping they couldn't see the tears of anger forming in her eyes.

On her way out the door, she caught a glimpse of herself in the mirror mounted on the wall above the soda fountain. What she saw in the mirror wasn't what she'd seen in her mind's eye. She'd spent hours tugging at the tight curls trying to pull her hair into a trendy smooth style just to have the Arkansas humidity work against her, denying the desired result. Overcome by a stroke of rebellion, Sarah scanned the room for Doc Murphy's white coat, defiantly grabbed the *Seventeen* from the rack and hurried out the door.

She raced out the door onto the sidewalk, smack into Jim Ed.

"Hey there, what's the hurry?"

"Nothing, I just want to get away from those stuck up, town girls," Sarah answered, blinking through her tears.

"Hang loose. Come on, I'll buy you a frozen custard,"

They walked into the cigarette smoke-filled air of the Dixie Dairy and were greeted by the voice of Elvis coming from the jukebox and the smell of stale grease coming from the grill.

A group of older boys occupied two of the four booths and flipped through the song selection on the tabletop jukebox, arguing over what to play. Jim Ed dropped into a seat next to his friend, Frankie.

"Hey, little sister, come sit with me." Frankie's younger brother, Roy patted the red vinyl bench and pulled a comb through his dark, oiled hair.

Sarah didn't like it when her brothers' friends called her *little sister*.

She slid in alongside Roy, thinking he'd be cuter with a Beatles haircut, but, like most of the boys in Tolerance, he still wore long sideburns, like Elvis.

Tall and good-looking—the rugged type, his bicep flexed beneath the pack of Lucky's rolled into the sleeve of his white tee shirt. *He's the kind of guy a girl could go for.*

Digging into the pocket of his tight blue jeans, he pulled out a quarter. "Pick some sounds." He winked and pulled her closer.

Her hand hesitated over the buttons as she scanned the titles. *I need to pick the right song, so he won't think I'm square.*

"How about, *Only the Lonely*, Roy Orbison." Then, hoping to sound clever, added, "boss name, doncha think?"

He reached across her and dropped the quarter into the slot. She tried to stay calm as his hand skimmed hers.

Peering through the large plate-glass window into the parking lot, Sarah eyed a red Chevy Super Sport. *He has a great car...what if Brenda Sue and Betty Jo saw me riding in Roy's car, or maybe even driving it...They'd be so jealous. Me and Roy... a senior...I could learn some neat stuff from him. Then I'd be really cool.*

"You see that Super Sport? That's a bitchen car." Sarah said, pretending she didn't know it belonged to his brother.

"Yeah, it's Frankie's, but we share it."

"Neat. Do you think you could take me for a ride in it sometime?"

"Hey man, toss me your keys. I'm gonna take little sister for a ride."

Frankie pulled the keys from his pocket and slid them across the table. He gave his brother a hard look. "No racing!"

Roy took Sarah's hand to coax her from the booth and motioned her toward the parking lot.

Jim Ed delivered a glare toward the couple and shrugged as they walked away, Sarah's hand in Roy's.

With his elbow out the window, Roy backed up the growling Chevy, shifted gears, and revved the engine. The car peeled out of the parking lot, kicking up gravel and turned in the direction of the old ice house.

Sarah pressed close beside him and his hand purposely grazed her thigh when he shifted gears. As they rumbled past the Rexall, Sarah searched the sidewalk for a glimpse of the mean girls. *I wish they could see me!*

Roy looked over at Sarah and gave her a playful grin, showing one little dimple.

He is so, so, cute. I'm so lucky to be with him.

"I knew you and me would get along," he said in a low sexy voice. "Sometimes things just happen."

He pulled into a secluded spot behind the ice plant, a huge concrete structure built for making tons of ice to refrigerate boxcars. It'd been closed for years— ever since the peach orchards shut down. Now it was the favorite spot for teenagers to make out or knock back a six-pack.

"Nice girls aren't supposed to come here."

"Maybe I don't... y'know, like nice girls." He gave her that dimpled smile again.

Maybe I can be his girlfriend. That would show those girls. He wouldn't call me little sister anymore.

"You're not like...y'know...not like other girls...y'know you seem older...."

"Really?"

One minute he was talking and the next, his lips were on hers, his tongue probing, his hand creeping dangerously close to her breast, and then his thumb circled her nipple, through her dress.

She let his fingers wander under her dress and didn't protest at the sound of his zipper going down.

"I like a girl who knows what she's doing. Some girls play games, y'know... not you. You're not a tease."

Her desire to win his approval, to please him, blunted her sense of right and wrong and she made no attempt to stop him.

Afterward, she was still scrambling around for her clothes when he started the engine and turned onto the highway heading back to the Dixie Dairy. At once, feeling tainted and degraded, she regretted her decision. By the time they pulled into the parking lot, Sarah knew she would not be slow dancing with Roy at Gary's Sugar Shack on Saturday night. Whatever feelings she thought they could have for each other had only been in her imagination.

I'm the town slut. My name is probably on the men's room walls at the Dixie Dairy... probably at the Sugar Shack too.

She straightened her hair and vaulted out of the car.

Jim Ed stood by the door, his keys hanging from his fingers. "Ready to go?"

"Sure," she said trying to act like it was no big deal.

"Where did he take you?"

"Nowhere. We just drove around."

"He didn't try anything with you, did he?"

"Nothing happened." Sarah lied easily.

"Momma, Sarah needs you." Jim Ed lifted Dee's chin and looked into her eyes. "I don't mean to hurt you. Honest. But, Momma, you walk around here like a dead woman. That's not okay. You're not dead- Kenny is. Crawl out of his grave and take care of your daughter."

He drew up a chair and guided her into it, his face slightly averted. She held a stack of plates, remnants of dark syrup sticking to them. Hotcakes; her last remaining Sunday ritual.

He took the dishes from her hand, carried them to the sink, poured two cups of coffee and dropped into a chair beside her. He hesitated, carefully choosing his words, not wanting to stray a hairs-breadth farther than necessary to get his point across.

He lowered his head and hid his face in his hands as he had as a boy when he'd done something wrong. Reaching out her hand moved in gentle strokes through his hair.

It was hard to tell what went on in that mind or hers, all locked up tight. She seemed unable to feel anything but pain.

He didn't speak for a while, taking in the comfort of his mother's caress; then he raised his head and met her eyes.

She noticed a change in his face, a resolve in his eyes. She'd seen the growing strength in him, had seen how more than once, he used his charm, his loose easy smile, to calm Otis' anger, but this was the first time she'd been the object of his purpose.

"You're not the only one who lost something when Kenny died. We all did. But we never grieved for him as a family; we each took our grief alone." His voice quavered slightly. "He was a sweet kid and he should have grown up into a good man. But you've been putting a dead child ahead of your living child long enough."

"I really don't want to think about him." Her face was pale and blank; she couldn't even speak his name.

"Momma, Sarah lost the most. She didn't get to be a little girl. She wasn't but eight years old; didn't know how to grieve for a brother she adored. But she lost her momma at the same time. She was scared. She's still scared."

Her eyes turned from him and strayed to the cluttered table.

"You been neglecting her all these years. It's not just you, it's Daddy too; she's grown up without any parents… no one to teach her what right and wrong look like."

He rubbed his hand across his mouth, got up, poured a glass of iced tea and found some lemon in the refrigerator. Setting the glass in front of his momma, he sat back down.

"Momma, she's one of those kids—she worries about the wrong things. She cares too much what people think. She drifts along waiting for someone to come along and tell her what to do, where to go. She's whoever she needs to be, does whatever she thinks the group wants. She's turned into a pretty girl, the kind that attracts boys the kind that ends up with a bad reputation or a broken heart…or both."

Dee stared at him for a moment. Her eyes glistened as if he'd slapped her… a stinging slap across her face. She wanted to get away from the sound of his voice, from what he said; willing him not to say another word. Get away and not have to think about it. Silent and wounded, she wished that what she knew as the truth was somehow a lie.

Glancing over her shoulder to make sure no one was near, he lowered his voice. "We all know Daddy's nothing but a drunk…not much of a father…but he's who we got…sometimes you get a bad deal."

Staring down at his hands, he linked and unlinked them. "I know you've been dumped in a circle of hurts and disappointments; a lifetime of misery caused by another person. Don't let Sarah get stuck in the same prison of pain you locked yourself into."

He stood up, the outburst of emotion faded. He looked at his momma with a smile, took her hand and kissed the top of her head.

"I want you to know I understand."

TWENTY-THREE

Jeremiah 29:11-13
¹¹ For I know the plans I have for you, saith the Lord, plans of peace, and not of evil, to give you hope and a future. ¹² Then you shall call on me, and you shall go and pray to me, and I will listen to you. ¹³ You shall seek me, and shall find me, when you search for me with all your heart.

It was still early, not yet time to get up, but going back to sleep was out of the question. No matter how hard she tried to shake the dream, the images of the nightmare twisted together—kept forming in her mind. She's driving down Main Street in a pink convertible, *Seventeen* cover model Colleen Corby is in the passenger seat. The model tells Sarah how good she looks in the pink car. Sarah's hair is thick and straight and dark brown, cut into a perfect bob. The model has a mass of frizzy red hair and bright pink lipstick—the color of the car.

They drive past the school where girls stand side by side shaking the chain link fence that lines the playground. The model is no longer in the seat next to her. Now Doc Murphy in his white lab coat occupies that spot. His mouth moves but no sound comes from it. Yet, a raspy voice pounds in her head, repeating over and over again, *Exodus 20:15 Thou shalt not steal…Thou shalt not steal.*

She kicked the twisted sheet from her feet and sat there for a moment staring at the floor, before standing up. Pulling on a pair of hip-hugger bell bottoms and a fitted sweater, she yanked the *Seventeen* from under her pillow and found the pink dress wadded-up on the floor.

In the kitchen, she dug through the pantry, found a brown paper grocery bag and stuffed the magazine and the dress inside. She grabbed her copy of *Dracula* and an apple from a bowl and went outside to watch the sunrise. No need for garlic or wooden stakes. At the exact moment of sunrise, an

126

emotional catharsis would purge her of simple fears.

The birds were already singing a promise of a spectacular sunrise on this spring morning. She looked toward the east barely able to make out the opaque outline of Cotton's pickup already parked in its usual place by the barn. Her toes sank into the soft grass, cool and moist with dew under her bare feet. She didn't go back inside for shoes, instead, she found herself drawn towards the shadowy figure.

She had learned from him the transcendent peacefulness of a sunrise.

Sitting on the tailgate of his pickup, drinking coffee from a plaid thermos, Cotton looked toward the eastern horizon. She sat down beside him. He simply continued to stare in the direction of the horizon until the first glimmer of the sun peeked above the horizon.

After a few moments, he broke his silence. "God's peace and solitude; purty close to paradise, ain't it?"

He refilled his cup from the thermos. "Growing up in the mountains I spent a lot of time in nature leaving me free to think my thoughts. Sometimes out there all alone and at peace, I'd hear God's voice tell me he'd put all of this here for me. That can make a fella feel a might bit special. One thing I know for sure, rich folks don't get no better sunrise than us poor folks."

A tiny smile formed on her lips. "I guess I never thought of it that way. It must be a good feeling…to feel special, I mean."

Cotton dropped a comforting arm over her shoulder. She stiffened just for a second and then relaxed. He removed his arm.

He continued, "The way I figure it, we're all special, just some of us ain't figured it out yet. We don't always see ourself the way other folks see us." He looked at her with eyes full of wisdom. "Now what's got you up so early this morning? Certainly not a hankering to watch the sunrise with an old man," he laughed, tossing out the last bit of coffee from his cup.

Sarah unfolded her arms, her slender hands peeking out from the sleeves of her gray sweater. She looked down and shook her head. "Nothing. Just a bad dream about some girls picking on me."

"Sometimes hard to shake the feeling of a bad dream, ain't it?" He tapped a cigarette from a pack and struck a wooden match against his thumbnail. The cigarette glowed against the dawn as he sucked in the first long puff.

Sarah nodded. "It's not always just a dream. Sometimes the kids say awful things about me and some of them are not the least bit true." She lowered her head to hide her shame, knowing there was truth to a lot of what they said.

"You can't let silly little gossipy girls get you down in the dumps. You got to put it in its proper place. They's just trying to fool with your head so don't let 'em, then they lose. But if you let 'em, they'll tear you to pieces."

Sarah leaned her back against the bed of the truck and studied Cotton's face. The early morning light masked the insults of time, and she saw that he must have once been a very handsome man…still was handsome. Despite his apparent lack of education, there was a confidence about him. Something about him, she wasn't sure what, set him apart; made her feel he was a safe repository.

"Miss Sarah, you need to realize just because you look different from those other girls, don't mean you're not beautiful. The Bible tells us the sun has one kind of finery, the moon's got another and even the stars has each got a light different from all the other stars. Paul wrote them words in a letter to the Corinthians just about 50 years after they crucified Jesus."

He picked up a long stick and started to absent-mindedly draw lines in the dirt. I done a lot of thinkin' about God when I was a young'un. There's lots of time to think when you're out wandering alone in them hills. I don't think anyone can rightly understand what God is. Being alone in nature, that's about as close as a fella can get to understanding; better 'n being in a church house. It's hard to sit with nature all around you and not believe that there ain't something out there bigger than your own self. Sometimes you just have to listen to the silence to understand what it is."

Sarah thought for a second. "What made you ever leave the mountains?"

"Oh, just tired a' being poor, I guess." He scratched the whiskers on his cheek. "My papa was a good man, an honest man. But we never had much. He taught me to hunt and farm, to use tools and fix things. And once in a while, he give me a good whuppin with a switch; but only when I'd earned it."

His eyes again turned toward the horizon where the sun had fully broken through.

He flicked away the cigarette and sat silent for a moment. "Now, I guess I've just about talked your ear off and I'd better get to work before your brother gets a stick after me." He picked up his hat, straightened the brim, then putting it on his head, he went into the barn, climbed a few steps up the ladder to the hayloft and was gone.

Sarah picked up her paper bag and headed for the burn pile.

TWENTY-FOUR

Colossians 3:5
⁵ So put all the earthly desires out of your life: sexual immorality, uncleanness, lust, evil desire, and greed, which is idolatry.

The black and white image of Dr. Ben Casey flicked across the television screen as Sarah thumbed through a tattered copy of *Teen Magazine*. No point getting engrossed in the re-run; any minute Otis would come in, change the channel and chase her out of the stained Lazy Boy where she sat curled up. Her eyes occasionally strayed from the photos of back-to-school hairstyles to focus on a close-up of the dreamy Dr. Casey.

Junior paused in the doorway. He lifted his shirt tail and wiped a spot of grease from his cheek. "Did Dub Winslow call looking for me?"

"Nope."

"He's gonna buy my baby moons. Tell me if he calls."

Sarah pulled her legs up to her chest and rested her chin on her knees. "Yeah, Dub Winslow? White T-Bird convertible?"

"Don't play dumb. You know who he is. Everybody in Tolerance has seen him big-shottin' around town in that car. Those moons'll look sweet on it."

He turned to leave but stopped. "Suppose you...I thought if you'd come outside...I figure, you know, just say *hi*."

She stared back at him, frowned and shook her head. *Fat chance. Dub's a dweeb.*

Junior shrugged. "Just thought you might like a ride in his car and...you know...butter him up for me."

"Well, maybe I'm just not in the mood to cheer up your buddy. I have better things to do."

"Yeah? Like read a magazine for the third time and watch a re-run? Come on. Help me out here."

Sarah tossed it around in her head for a moment and then smiled, not really a smile, just a tiny uptick in the corner of her mouth. *Wonder what Betty Jo Shelby would think if I started dating Dub? He may be a dweeb, but his daddy owns the bank. I might be invited to the Winslow's big, fancy white house in town; the one surrounded by a picket fence covered with pink rose bushes.*

Dub wasn't handsome. He wasn't athletic, and he wasn't popular. She might have a chance with him.

She feigned disinterest. "Maybe. I'll think about it. What's in it for me?"

Junior turned away and headed toward the door. He called over his shoulder, "A buck."

Flipping off the TV, Sarah headed for her bedroom. *That's a new lipstick and matching nail polish and maybe a ride in a convertible.*

Tilting her head at different angles, she studied her face in the cracked mirror over her roughly painted dressing table. *I am pretty. I don't know why other people can't see that.* She opened the top drawer and rifled through it. Finding her prized tube of Cola Kiss lipstick, she leaned into the mirror, dabbed on a layer of beige lipstick, rubbed her lips together a few times, and blackened her lashes with mascara. She sat back to admire the result. *I can hardly wait to see the look on his face.*

By the time she buttoned the last button on her blouse, Junior called from the living room. "You comin? 'Dub's in a hurry."

"Hold your horses; I'll be there in a minute."

No time to tease her hair into a perfect smooth flip she pulled it into a ponytail, high on the back of her head. *Yep, I'm ready, but let him wait.* She put the lipstick away and smoothed her hair. *It's going to be different this time. I'm not putting out so easy. I'm looking to get me a real boyfriend.*

She paused on the back step to rub Joy's ears. Shielding her eyes from shafts of sunlight gleaming off the chrome hubcaps spread across an oily tarp on the ground, she watched Junior and Dub. Standing outside the barn, they seemed to be arguing over something. *Probably haggling over the price.*

They looked up when she approached. Dub nodded to Junior and handed him a wad of cash which Junior stuffed into his pocket.

"Hi," Sarah said as Junior walked away. She smiled just a little, keeping her head down and peeking at him from behind her lashes.

"Well. Hi, yourself." Dub grinned and let out a soft whistle. He was quite small, shorter than she realized--about an inch shorter than Sarah. Traces of acne nibbled away at his smug pasty face.

"What took you so long?"

"I wanted to make myself pretty." She tucked an errant hair behind her ear.

"Well, I'd say mission accomplished." His eyes flicked over her.

He thinks I'm pretty!

Dub grabbed her hand pulling her toward the barn. "Let's get out of the sun."

"I thought maybe we could go for a ride in your car—maybe with the top down."

A subtle change took place around the edges of his mouth, a hardening of his smile. He nodded toward a ladder propped against the hayloft. "Let's talk about it--up there."

This wasn't turning out the way she'd imagined, and she didn't know what to say…didn't know how to refuse. *I want him to like me.*

Sarah climbed the ladder ahead of Dub and dropped down on a hay bale, keeping her arms folded across her small breasts.

Dub threw himself onto the soft hay and gave it a pat, testing for comfort. Grinning, he again patted the hay. "Come over here, let's make friends," he said tugging at her hand, pulling her down alongside him. "I only let my friends ride in my car." He rested his hand on her thigh.

She tried to relax, act normal. It wasn't going well—her attempt at asserting her own wishes.

He moved closer, his hand crept a bit higher, moving toward her crotch.

It would be easy to give in the way she'd done in the past...the familiar reaction to her need to feel important, the longing to feel loved, to feel close to someone…no matter how fleeting. But a tiny voice inside her head kept saying *it's not too late to change.*

The breeze blew a strand of hair down over her forehead. She brushed it back into place and stood up, her back straight. "Maybe you've heard things about me. Some of the stuff you've heard isn't true," she said, rubbing her forearm. "I'm not like that." Smoothing the folds of her skirt, she looked away. "I'm a nice girl."

"Sister, I don't give a rat's ass what people say about you."

Biting her lower lip, she narrowed her eyes. "Maybe today we could get acquainted," she said feeling weak and exposed. What little confidence she'd gathered while dressing evaporated. *—this is my fault. I shouldn't have come up here with him.*

"You've gotta be shittin' me." He laughed a short derisive snort. "We'll get acquainted all right." He stood and grabbed hold of her arm. "I got such a hard-on I could barely make it up that ladder." A dew of sweat formed on his upper lip. "Now get over here before I waste it."

Her eyes flashed.

He tightened his grip on her arm, then released it. "Chill out. Jeez, what's your problem? I'm getting a little streamed here." His mouth twisted into a sneer. "I paid your brother top dollar. He told me you were interested in getting to know me, might show me a good time, if you get my drift."

Her cheeks flushed red. "If you want a good time, let Junior show you a good time!"

She twisted her body a half turn and tried to push past him, but he stepped in front of her and grabbed the front of her blouse, gathering a handful of soft fabric in his fist.

"You little tease, you climbed up that ladder ahead of me, so I could see up your dress. You know what I came up here for."

Newly tapped anger rose inside her. She shoved back, unlocking his grip. Dub stumbled backward and fell over a bale of hay.

By the time he recovered, Sarah had reached the ladder. Before she could make her escape his reddened face loomed over her, spewing curses. He reached down to pull her back into the loft and hooked his hand around her ponytail. She instinctively gave him one quick tug that caused him to release her hair and cost him his balance.

From the ladder, she watched in horror as he tumbled past her and fell to the ground.

"You little bitch! You've broken my arm."

Joy nipped wildly at his legs as he struggled to stand.

Sarah scurried down the ladder and ran toward the house.

From her room she heard raised voices, a car door slam, a motor grind over, the rev of an engine and the sound of spraying gravel as the car squealed onto the pavement. *I wonder if his arm is really broken...? I don't care...wish he'd broken his neck.*

Her blouse was damp with panic, but she had a sense of victory. She'd said *no*—stood up for herself. She'd fought that weakness with something inside that had taken root so gradually she'd hardly noticed.

❧

"That banker feller, Winslow, called up here. Said his boy got his arm broke when he come out here to our place." Otis glared at Junior. "Said you two got in a fight over some nonsense 'bout hubcaps. Hubcaps! Dammit boy, his bank owns the mortgage on this farm."

Junior threw a cold look at Sarah.

"You boys is driving all over town in that fancy- painted pickup with our name scrawled all over it. I guess he allows we somehow got rich. Wants me to pay some doctor bills."

There was a heavy silence, then Sarah spoke boldly and with strength she never knew she had.

"It wasn't Junior, it was me. I pushed him out of the hayloft."

Otis' gnarled fingers pulled at the straps of his overall. "What was you doing up in the hayloft with that boy?"

She stopped, frightened at the reaction her confession would let loose. Then quietly said, "Just talking."

"Just talking? You climbed up there to *just talk*? You take me for a fool?" He scowled.

She looked at him without expression, feeling nothing now but the hard stone in the pit of her stomach. "Yeah, you're right. I'm a tramp and why do you think that is?"

As soon as Sarah spoke the words a creeping fear squirmed through her.

"Don't you sass me, girl."

Otis raised his hand slightly as if he might strike her. She cowered. The fearful look of an animal that has been beaten and kicked by its owner too many times crossed her face. She just wanted a place to hide.

Jim Ed grabbed Otis' wrist and stopped his hand in mid-air. "Let her be. I've watched this long enough, the way you beat down Momma and Sarah Jane, it's wrong and it's gonna stop. I can't keep quiet about it anymore. And don't worry about the Winslow's. I'll take care of Dub…doubt he wants it spread around town that he got his arm broke by a hundred-pound girl."

TWENTY-FIVE

Psalms 35:15
¹⁵But in my adversity, they rejoiced, and gathered themselves together. The attackers gathered themselves together against me, and I didn't know it. They tore at me, and didn't cease.

1964

Sarah pushed open the door, rubbing it against the worn linoleum floor. The jingle of the shop keeper's bell mounted on the wooden door announced her arrival at *Hazel's Hand-Me-Down Shop*.

She'd been here before, looking for a copy of *The Catcher in the Rye*. Ever since hearing that the book was banned from the library, she'd been on a quest. *What could be so bad that a book would be banned?* She wanted to see what all the fuss was about for herself.

Scrunching her nose against the taste of dust floating in the air and the reek of not quite identifiable odors, she rushed past a khaki-trousered fat man who watched, unsmiling and silent from a wooden chair propped precariously against the wall. *Hazel's husband? Maybe Hazel? He's always here—gives me the creeps.* It was more than the jagged scar that disfigured the side of his mouth; something about the man wasn't right... the way his eyes followed her around the room...and he never spoke. She fantasized he'd returned home from war—like Paul Bäumer in *All Quiet on the Western Front*-- to find he didn't belong anymore...and he never spoke because he could only speak German.

Just find the book and get out of here fast.

She hunched her shoulders and moved in the direction of a table with a hand-lettered sign...*Books 10⍰ or 3 for 25⍰ and* piled high with musty paperbacks. The floor squeaked and bounced as she continued toward the rickety table.

Seconds into her search she spotted it…half hidden, tattered and dog-eared in an uneven stack of cast-offs. Sarah's eyes darted around the room to ensure no one saw her reach for the book. Her mouth dry and her throat tight, she grabbed two more books and slid the contraband between the more innocuous volumes.

Flashing the books at the still seated, still unsmiling Herr Bäumer, she placed a quarter on the counter and shoved the books into her purse.

He nodded and gave an almost inaudible murmur before she skirted out of the store into the sunlight.

She aimed for the sidewalk and hurried around the corner to the Dixie Dairy to find Jim Ed for a ride home.

The lunch crowd had thinned, and the place now took on the late-afternoon pack of teenagers drinking soft drinks, eating fries, and playing the jukebox. Sarah ordered a vanilla Coke at the counter and dropped onto the patched Naugahyde bench in the only empty booth.

She sipped the Coke and leaving the banned book in her purse, pulled out the other two. She laid aside *The Picture of Dorian Gray*, and picked up the small book *Anthem* and fanned the yellowed pages of the book, before flipping to the back cover. The photo of the author caught her attention—a woman sitting in a big leather chair, held a cigarette. Curious, Sarah read the bio...*Born and educated in St Petersburg, Russia, Rand moved to the United States in 1926…*.

The sound of snickers from the next table drew her attention away from the book. Two girls made a mock attempt to smother their erupting laughter as their male companion stared at Sarah and made a nasty face. Certain they were sharing a foul joke at her expense; she tried to ignore their loud whispers.

One of the girls, small, slightly plump, her hair brushed into a perfect blond flip, nudged the other girl, whispered something and sniggered. She stood and directing her question to no one in particular, asked, "Would you mind trading places with me? I can't enjoy my milkshake with Little Orphan Annie looking at me."

Amused by the reference to Sarah's frizzy red hair, they again erupted into giggles.

Sarah reached up and smoothed her hair. The laughter, shrill and burning, tumbled against her ears, stirring her insides. She closed her eyes and tried not to listen, wishing the earth would open up and swallow her.

Skilled at faking indifference, Sarah resolutely went through the motions-- pretending she didn't hear the painful words, clinging to the hope that someday she would be liked and accepted for being herself. She fumbled through her purse, found a dime and hurriedly inserted it into the jukebox, quickly punched B-8 without bothering to check the song title, and picked up her book again.

As *Town Without Pity* poured through the speakers. Sarah slumped lower into her seat, dismally regretting her selection. She put the song out of her mind; tried to at least.

The uneasy feeling of being watched came over her. She looked up to meet the girl's unflinching gaze. The girl kept her eyes on Sarah and mouthed the word "slut."

In the past, she would have run from the situation, but, a wild flash of anger came over her. Something in her came awake…a feeling of power where she once felt powerless. It had slept all these years while she'd tried to make herself small, trying not to attract notice or give offense, but she'd no longer shrink from conflict.

Turning contemptuously to face her adversary, she stared at the girl. Stared and stared until the girl looked away. *I win.*

Through the plate glass window, she caught sight of the Jones Farm pickup pulling into the parking lot. She jumped to her feet and shouldered her way to the door while the words blasted in her ears. *"it isn't very pretty what a town without pity can do."*

TWENTY-SIX

Matthew 6:34

34 Therefore don't be anxious about tomorrow, for tomorrow will be anxious about itself. Each day has enough trouble of its own.

*E*very day the newspapers and television were filled with news—good and bad— mostly bad. President Johnson's Great Society waged a War on Poverty and the Federal Trade Commission waged a war on cigarette manufacturers' advertising. The US began bombing North Vietnam in response to an attack on a US destroyer in the Gulf of Tonkin and Cassius Clay joined the Black Muslim movement and changed his name to Muhammad Ali.

On November 22, 1963, America saw the first televised assassination of a US president and two days later, a Dallas nightclub owner killed Lee Harvey Oswald—the accused assassin of President John F. Kennedy—live on the evening news. Then on March 14, 1964, in the first courtroom verdict to be televised in U.S. history, a Dallas jury sentenced Jack Ruby to die in the electric chair for the murder of Lee Harvey Oswald.

But these were not the things foremost in Sarah's mind on the first Sunday evening in September. Hair still damp from washing, hanging limp over her shoulders, she mused over the contents of the grocery bags nestled in the corner next to the TV. What could be done to Becky's annual offerings to make them more like styles from the pages of the *Seventeen* back-to-school issue opened on her lap?

Back-to-school, a freshman—the thought tied her stomach in knots. *What a nightmare! I will be miserable and embarrassed and probably humiliated before the first day is over. I don't know how to act in high school.*

Letting out a breath in a long-tortured sigh, she tossed the magazine aside. She shrugged. No sense putting it off any longer. Lying on the couch reading or watching TV wasn't going to turn anything in those sacks into a Mary Quant mini-skirt or a ribbed-knit sweater. *Aunt Myra still orders Becky's dresses from the Sears catalog. They're tacky, but at least they're not home-made.*

Becky outweighed Sarah by ten pounds but at five feet nine Sarah had grown six inches taller than her cousin. The sacks were no longer filled with outgrown hand-me-downs; but instead, last year's styles discarded to make room in Becky's closet for her new clothes.

Glad Becky doesn't go to Tolerance High-- no one will know I'm wearing someone's old toss-offs—like that pink dress I burned.

She looked at the clock on the wall above the television. *Almost time for Bonanza.* She adjusted the rabbit ears to get a better picture on the TV. *Wonder if Jim Ed's ever gonna buy that color television he keeps talking about. I'd like to see what Michael Landon looks like on a color TV.*

I should at least take a look at the dress I'll wear tomorrow.

She pulled the bags from the corner, dumping the contents onto the couch and began to sort skirts and dresses into three piles—those she could wear as is, those that could be altered to give them a new look and those she wished had been given to someone else.

Holding a wrinkled, flowered eyesore under her chin, she tried to imagine blending into the crowd wearing it. *Yeah-like that's gonna happen. Looks like a pillowcase!* She tossed it aside.

She pulled a plaid pleated skirt from the pile, cut the threads from the hem and pulled the ironing board and a can of Niagara Spray Starch from the closet.

As the iron passed along the fabric smoothing away wrinkles, Sarah fought back tears, uncertain if she cried out of fear of the first day of school or because her life had never been what she wanted.

She reached up and twisted a thick strand of hair around her finger. In a few minutes it would be dry enough to put on the giant rollers—rollers so big she couldn't sleep on them—and Dippity Do— so much Dippity Do, to get the ends to flip up.

She had almost learned to manage the stubborn curls with the help of Curl Free. But sometimes, when her hair refused to surrender the curl, Sarah would sit with her head on the ironing board while momma passed the iron back and forth to straighten her hair. *All the popular girls have shiny straight hair that holds a perfect flip...you can't be popular if you don't have nice hair.*

What had Cotton said about there being different kinds of beauty? She thought that was baloney. But the part about not letting the mean girls win; that part was true.

She wiped at her eyes and took a deep breath. One simple rule applied here--if she wanted things to change, she'd have to change. That was another true thing Cotton said.

About half of the one hundred or so freshmen at Tolerance High School would be kids she'd known from elementary school and junior high. She decided to pretend she didn't know them. The rest, the other half would be new kids--kids who didn't know her. This was her chance to erase the last two years--years she'd spent trapped inside herself, trying to win acceptance and soothe her ego by riding in cars with boys and agreeing to go with them to some secluded place.

She frowned. She could put those days behind her and never return to being the "easy girl." Over the summer she'd gained new confidence. Now believing she could escape her private hell and build a new reputation—to break away from the past that drove her into her shell of quiet anger and guarded disconnection. That thing that made her cower at the back of the classroom and avoid other girls. She would reclaim a piece of herself she'd lost along the way.

Her mind began to wander toward the future. In her daydream a guy was getting her number and making plans to see her again—take her to a party and to the Saturday night dance at the Sugar Shack. And there were girlfriends; friends who would care about her opinions on lipstick colors and hairstyles and the Beatles.

Sarah stared at her locker and tried the combination once more, this time stopping at 38 after 16; she listened for a click. No luck. She stomped her foot in frustration.

"Having trouble there, Sunshine?"

She turned at the sound of his voice; cocked her head to get a better look.

He leaned casually against the locker next to hers. He pushed back a mop of blond surfer's hair that had drooped adorably into his gray-blue eyes and flashed a toothy grin giving off an air of comfortable confidence.

She rubbed her sweaty palms on her skirt and twirled the dial on the lock for the third time. *I wish he wouldn't stand so close. Bet he can hear my heart pounding. How can I concentrate on the numbers...does he smell like ginger cookies? I think he's the cute guy I saw on the black motorcycle this morning. He's even taller than me.*

The lock clicked open. "Oh, thank goodness, I thought lunch would be over before I could get this dadgum thing opened." She spoke mainly to herself.

He reached around Sarah and grabbed the brown paper bag holding her peanut butter sandwich and tossed it into the air. Her heart stopped. *Not again. Please don't let the teasing start again.*

But as he caught the bag, he turned to her, made a deep bow and returned her lunch. He smiled and stuck out his hand. "Charlie Weeks at your service."

That smile of his, why did it have to be so entirely charming…almost infectious? *I think I could learn to like Charlie Weeks.*

"And you are…?"

Her cheeks flushed. She blinked at him and in a small, thin voice replied, "Sarah Jones."

"Well, Sarah Jones, you must be a freshman. I'm sure I would have noticed you if you'd been roaming these halls. Let me welcome you to THS, home of the mighty Tolerance Tigers." He took her by the elbow and escorted her down the hall to the lunchroom.

He led her around the long lunch line and past a table filled with girls. They had popular girl hair and popular girl clothes. To cinch her assessment—Brenda Sue Wilson and Betty Jo Shelby laughed and talked with two girls in cheerleader uniforms. She turned her head trying not to make eye contact. The laughter stopped. From the corner of her eye, she watched their reaction …shocked expressions and gaping mouths. A self-satisfied grin flickered into place on Sarah's lips.

Charlie Weeks seemed to like her. She wanted to keep it that way.

TWENTY-SEVEN

Job 6:8

*⁸ Oh, that I might have my request; and that
God would grant me the thing that I long for!*

Sarah closed her locker. Glancing down the noisy hallway she opened it again, pretending she'd forgotten something. *Wonder where his locker is. How long before first bell?* She pictured his grin, his hopeless hair falling into his eyes. *How long can I stand here before it starts to seem weird?*

Since lunch yesterday, a good portion of her time had been spent thinking about him; reliving, savoring every moment she'd spent with him, hearing, over and over again, every glorious word he'd uttered. A conversation with him looped through her head—one that always ended with him asking her out.

Now the negatives were creeping in-- the maybes... *maybe it's a mean joke...maybe he's just teasing me...maybe someone put him up to it...maybe he has a girlfriend....*

The maybes stopped ticking off when she spotted the top of his blond head bobbing above the crowd. She smiled to herself, almost shuddered with anticipation. He stopped. *Oh no! He's talking to Skeeter. Great, he knows Skeeter. Wonder what Skeeter is saying about me?* She squatted down on her knees pretending to look for something in the bottom of her locker. *Maybe he won't see me.*

She peeked over her shoulder. Charlie moved toward her. *I wonder if I can fit inside this locker.*

"Well, if it isn't Sunshine. I see you learned how to open your locker and here it is only the second day of school." He winked and smiled down at her.

A knot twisted in the pit of her stomach, excitement welled in her. She smiled back and hurriedly got to her feet, smoothing her skirt.

He glanced away and fidgeted with his watch, looked around as if checking to see if there was anyone within hearing distance. He lowered his voice, "Uh, wanna hang out?"

"What?"

"Wanna hang out with me this weekend? You know, come out to our farm and go horseback riding or something?"

He's asking me out! What do I say? "I've never ridden a horse." *No! No not that. I shouldn't have said that--he'll think I don't want to go.*

"You're kidding. I thought you were a farm girl."

"I am." She laughed. "A chicken farm. My legs are too long to ride a chicken." *How dumb- I can't believe I just said that.* "We do have a cow, but I've never ridden her either." *That didn't make it any better. Come on Sarah, get a grip. Now he thinks you're an idiot.*

He ignored her attempt at humor. "Riding's easy. I'll teach you right now. Sit up straight in the saddle, keep your heels down, toes in the stirrups, and most importantly, don't fall off. The horse has to do the hard part." Offering his arm, he said, "Now that you know how to ride, may I escort you to your class?"

After only a moment's hesitation, she laced her arm through his, blushing slightly, trying not to let it show how much his touch affected her. *I hope he can't hear my heart pounding.*

As they walked down the hall she could feel eyes on her and Charlie and hear the whispers as a group of girls passed by. Betty Jo shot her a nasty look.

ॐ

She stood on the porch dressed in jeans and a cotton shirt, her hair pulled into a ponytail. *Am I someone's "girl?" Not just any someone but Charlie—a wonderful someone. I could literally die from happiness.*

Without warning her life had changed in a very short time. Her narrow little world expanded beyond the place she'd inhabited only in her mind; that happy place she always believed to be merely around the corner. Fear of her past no longer held her back. For the first time since Kenny's death, Sarah felt normal. She had a new identity. No longer just the girl whose brother died…she was now *Sarah,* half of a team, *Sarah and Charlie.*

She looked at her watch—*Not yet nine*—then glanced down the narrow road, back to her watch and then, at the road again. *A watched pot…Momma says that all the time.* She dared not go back inside…*he might get here any minute.*

Ashamed of the untidy and run down house, she preferred that he not see inside, not yet anyway. *Better wait here.*

When Charlie first mentioned horseback riding, it seemed exciting and romantic; something out of one of her books, but now the reality was sinking in. Second thoughts tied her stomach in knots.

This morning, when her alarm went off, a tingle of excitement ran through her—*Charlie—our first date—today.* The sun peeked through her open window and the cool, crisp air bathed her room...*a perfect day for riding.*

She looked toward the road again; her feelings were mixed, caught between her desire to ride and her fear of falling off the horse—or just embarrassing herself somehow.

She looked up half hoping for rain—then they could go to the movies in Texarkana, or just hang out at his house and listen to records. *Such a beautiful blue-skied day, not a cloud in sight. Yeah, that's pretty much it...I'm gonna have to get on a horse.... Like it or lump it.*

Catching sight of Joy a few feet from the house, she sat down on the steps. The dog came to her wagging her tail and sat at her feet. Sarah reached over to rub Joy's grey muzzle. Joy licked the salt from Sarah's hand. "Yeah old, girl I know, and I love you too."

Above them, through breaks left by the thinning leaves of the pin oak that shaded the house, a squirrel rattled a branch.

In a light voice, Sarah said, "you know what I thought about the other day?" With an odd happiness and a stirring of sorrow, she recalled the day she found Joy. After seven years, she still remembered the feel of the dog's soft tongue against her dirty face. She gave her a good scratch down her back. "Remember the day Kenny shot that possum?" She choked on the words. "I don't think I would have made it without you. Kenny saved you, so you could save me." Her eyes grew moist.

Her breath caught and she stood as she heard the roar of a pickup heading toward the farm. Charlie downshifted and pulled his daddy's truck into the driveway, ripe acorns crunching beneath the tires. He wheeled around in a semi-circle and rolled to a stop, bringing the nose of the truck around to face the road.

Sarah stretched out her leg to give Joy another little rub with her foot. "Don't worry; you're the best friend I've ever had. That won't change just because I have a boyfriend."

Pulling off his sunglasses Charlie hopped out of the cab, but before he could come around to open her door, she had already made a dash toward the truck and jumped in. He closed the door and grinned at her.

Heat rising in her cheeks, her heart skipped a beat. *I like him, I just do. Something funny about liking someone, you don't know why…you can't help it, you just like them.*

He hit the gas and pulled onto the blacktop. "Feeling nervous?"

Sarah lied. "Hmm, not too bad," *Of course I'm nervous, I'm meeting your parents and I have to ride a stupid bucking bronco just to impress you.*

An uncomfortable silence filling the car, he turned the radio up loud. *Guess he doesn't know what to say either.*

She yelled above the music. "I like this song too."

He nodded and sang along. *My mother was a tailor; she sewed my new blue jeans. My father was a gamblin' man down in New Orleans.*

Windows down, they drove, music spilling from the radio, sneaking glances at one another until he pulled the truck off the paved narrow road into a driveway of crushed white rock alongside a pleasant country house.

Before Charlie could turn off the engine, a tall man with a lanky build that deceptively hid a work-hardened muscular body strode toward them across a small, dense lawn dotted with flower beds. The grin across his face was Charlie's goofy grin.

"That's my dad. Mom's in the house and my sister Mary Ann is away at college.

When Charlie's dad tipped his hat in greeting, a thatch of thick rust-colored hair escaped. "Where'd you find this pretty redhead?" he teased, gripping her hand with a firm but gentle squeeze. "Rusty Weeks."

Unaccustomed to compliments, Sarah lowered her eyes. An involuntary smile briefly forming on her lips; she felt the blood rise to her cheeks again.

"Call him Rusty…if you call him *Mr. Weeks,* he'll start to think he's important." Charlie laughed.

"That's right, you can call me *Rusty* and the boy can call me *Sir*." He winked at her. "We saddled Belle for you. Come meet her."

As they approached the barn she grew breathless, her nerves prickled and a trail of sweat dribbled down her spine, pooling at her tailbone. Meeting Belle made her even more nervous than meeting Charlie's parents.

Charlie took her hand. "Belle's a little strawberry roan saddle horse, real gentle. Nothing to worry about, we let kids ride her. Nice little horse." He seemed to sense her apprehension and did all he could to help her through it.

Hearing, but not processing his reassuring patter, Sarah steeled her nerves as they approached the barn and the sweet smell of hay and leather hit her nostrils. The enormous size of the animal intimidated her; the stirrup was higher than she thought it would be. Nothing about her said, *little* or *nice* to Sarah. She studied the situation for a minute, but finally, her sense of adventure and her desire to please Charlie surpassed her fear.

"Her mane is the color of my hair. Okay girl, we redheads must stick together."

Charlie looked at Rusty and shrugged. "Seems I'm out-numbered by redheads at the moment."

Still reluctant, Sarah took hold of the saddle horn and raised her leg toward the stirrup. Charlie helped her place her foot in the stirrup and the leather creaked as he lifted her into the saddle.

I did it – I'm on the horse and still in the saddle.

Belle grumbled softly and pawed at the ground telling Sarah she was tired of standing around and ready to go.

"What now?" Sarah asked.

"Try not to be nervous- she'll sense it."

Yeah, right.

Charlie pressed the reins into her hand, took hold of the bit strap, and walked the horse around showing Sarah how to use the reins. Then he stroked Belle's nose, talked to her in a low voice, and let go. The horse just walked without Sarah doing anything and slowly trotted away.

The bone-jarring bounce rattled Sarah a little. Afraid to turn in the saddle, she wondered where Charlie might be.

She took a deep breath when he rode up next to her.

"See, I told you, it's easy," declared Charlie. "There's a creek about a mile down the hollow--we'll ride down there for starters." He pulled his horse's head around, clicked his tongue and they took off down the trail.

Ears up and alert, Belle shifted to follow at a gentle gallop.

Sarah looked around from her perch astride Belle. The air never smelled sweeter and the sky had never been bluer. *I would have missed all this if I'd given in to my fears.*

When they got to the meadow, Charlie climbed off his horse. He helped her dismount, lifting her to the ground, but didn't release her immediately. He looked in her face for a long time, and then he put out his hand and pushed a wayward strand of hair from her eyes.

The afternoon sun sliced through the trees and lay in bright lines on the ground where the horses rested. Stamping their feet, they flicked their ears at the buzz of flies humming in the air and chomped at the metal bits in their mouths while they nibbled at wisps of grass.

"I wish you could see your red hair against that blue sky." With no pretense, he kissed her. Then he just stared at her with a big goofy grin. It was the first time she had delighted in a kiss.

TWENTY-EIGHT

Proverbs 27:9
*⁹ Perfume and incense bring joy to the heart; and the good counsels of
a sweet friendship refreshes the soul.*

S arah stood in Momma's kitchen wistfully looking about.
*New curtains and fresh paint! Yep, that's all it needs. After all, it's the first room
we see when we come in; no one ever uses the front door. I'm not even sure it opens.*

She bit her lip as her eyes fell on the peeling linoleum covering the uneven kitchen floor.

*Or better yet, a box of matches. That's it —fresh paint, new curtains, and a
bonfire.... That's the only way to improve this place.*

She wistfully recalled her second visit to the Weeks' farm. There'd been rain. She climbed from the truck, lowered her head and ran along the puddled driveway toward the porch, squealing and giggling as the water splashed up onto her legs.

Charlie pushed open the door and she walked into his mother's kitchen for the first time. The fluorescent light bounced off pale yellow walls warming the room like sunshine and swallowing the powerful gloom that lurked outside the windows.

She took another look around her momma's kitchen with its painted ship-lap walls, discolored porcelain sink, and worn floor. It was always scrubbed, smelling of Lysol, and yet it never looked clean.

Pulling her hair off her neck into a ponytail, she tightened the elastic, shrugged and went to the porch.

She found her mother gliding in the creaky porch swing, hunched over a dishpan heaped with freshly-picked pole beans.

"Whew. Goodness me, what in the world!" Momma cleared the sweat from her eyes with the edge of her apron and fanned her face. "A body'd think it was August instead of the middle of September."

Flopping down next to her on the swing Sarah grabbed a handful of beans and started snapping off the ends.

Dee nodded toward the dishpan. "This here's 'bout all that's filled out... found a few new potatoes, and some okra... not enough to put up."

Pushing against the floor with her bare feet, Dee moved the swing forward and back.

"Waitin' on Charlie?"

Sarah's cheeks flushed, she nodded and dropped the snapped beans into a bowl at Dee's feet.

They fell silent. The swing rocked gently under them, the rhythm relaxed and soothing, they snapped the ends and pulled strings from the beans.

"I've been thinking," Sarah said at last.

"What about, Sarah Jane?"

"I was wondering...would it be ok if I painted our kitchen? Maybe made some new curtains for the windows?"

Dee paused holding a handful of beans. "You don't want your fella to see our house, not the way it is."

Sarah wiggled in her seat and shook her head. "No, Momma, it's not that," she lied.

"Honey, I know how other people see us; you're afraid to let him meet us aren't you?" Her voice came out shaking and thin. "I don't mean to cause you shame."

The pain she saw in her mother's eyes made Sarah ashamed. She turned quiet as she realized how lonely her mother must be and how she accepted the way things were as the only way they could be. Sarah wondered what went on behind those sorrow-filled eyes.

"You know what I was thinking about the other day?" Sarah asked, trying to change the subject. "I was looking at a picture of you and Junior when he was a baby. When you got married you weren't much older than I am."

Dee stared into space twisting her wedding ring on her finger before she answered in a brittle voice, "Barely seventeen."

"How old was Floyd when y'all got married?" This was the first time that name had passed her lips since the night Floyd left. He was never mentioned by anyone...as if he'd never existed.

Dee pushed a stray tendril of hair behind her ear. "He weren't yet a year. I was the only momma he ever knew."

Sarah shook her head. "I can't imagine being married and having a baby at my age."

"It wasn't easy, and Junior come along that first year. But that's just what we did back then. My normal was different from yours and yours will be different from mine." She tried to smile. "Maybe when you're forty, you'll know what I'm talking about."

Would she ever understand? There was so much Sarah didn't know—had begun to wonder about. Sometimes things Cotton said or books she read caused her to think about things—deep in her mind things she couldn't quite sort out. Would she ever know who she really was or what she was looking for or why things happen?

She wanted to tell her momma of the secrets that held such power over her... the hurt she had gone through because of Floyd and because of her daddy. But she wasn't ready, still too ashamed to talk about it and some part of her understood there was no point.

They were interrupted by the crunch of gravel on the drive. Sarah bounced off the porch in one leap.

"Bye, Momma."

Charlie rested his arm on the window frame, the sleeves of his checkered shirt rolled up to his elbows, The Beach Boys vibrated through the open window. He raised his hand and nodded a greeting toward Dee. She nodded in return.

Sarah hopped into the truck and they drove off down the narrow road, dust billowing around the fall-blooming goldenrod and wild asters clinging to the sides of the ditches.

The road leading to the paved highway ran straight as a plumb-line. They passed an occasional farmhouse flanked by rows of chicken coops and separated from neighbors by nothing more than tilled fields.

Charlie sang along with the radio—*You'll Never Get To Heaven If You Break My Heart* ....

The warm air rushed through the cab blowing Charlie's hair. Little lines fanned at the corners of his eyes squinting against the sun. Being with him still caused her heart to flip.

I've been hearin' rumors about how you play around. Though I don't believe what I hear, still it gets me down... an uncomfortable pause connected their eyes.

Sometimes she caught him watching her as if he was trying to see inside her heart and soul. *Is this what love feels like?* No one ever made her feel the way he did.

Rays of sun faintly reflected off the dust-covered bumper of an oncoming rusted pickup. The driver tapped his horn and slowed as he neared. Face weathered and wrinkled he gave a slight nod, a tuft of gray hair snaking out around the edges of a John Deere cap pulled down over his forehead.

He raised an index finger slightly above the casually held steering wheel as he passed. Charlie lifted a single finger in response.

They had almost reached the Weeks farm when Charlie said, "Hey, do you know my cousin EmmaLee?" He shot a wary look at Sarah. "I forgot to tell you…she's at the house this morning."

Sarah groaned and looked down, at her faded jeans and madras shirt. "Great," she said. "She'll think your dad hired a new farm hand."

"Come on, Sunshine. She's just my cousin, not the queen of England."

"Good, because I left my diamond tiara in the barn."

"Darn it, Sarah, you're too grand for me."

"Shut up, Charlie."

"You could have let me know before you picked me up…you know…" she held her thumb to her ear and pinkie to her mouth, "Hello, this is Charlie. My cousin will be at the house today. Be sure to dress like a hobo so you can make a really great first impression."

When they pulled into the yard, Rusty was in the flower bed tying up a rosebush. Charlie revved the engine to annoy his dad. Rusty jumped aside just enough to let them pass.

Sarah hopped out of the truck and made a beeline for Rusty. He gave her a hug and a sheepish grin.

He punched Charlie playfully on his jaw. "I need to borrow the boy for a few minutes; I got a chore for him. Why don't you go on in the house and say *howdy* to the girls? I'll have him back before you have time to miss him—I promise."

Self-conscious of her hand-me-down shirt, Sarah approached the door with as much dignity as she could muster. As she reached for the knob the door opened. A petite dishwater blonde with a bright smile, hair teased and sprayed into a perfect flip stood in front of her.

"Hey, you must be Sarah, Charlie's 'oh-my-goodness-she's-so-pretty' girlfriend. I'm Charlie's cousin, you know, EmmaLee… Isn't that something? Such a voyage-to-dumb-city kinda name. My mother thought she was frown-flipping clever coming up with that one," she said shooting another sunny grin in Sarah's direction. "My brother's name is Robert…not RobBert, just plain Robert. But I get EmmaLee. Can you beat that?"

Sarah shrugged and flashed her awkward smile. *Say something clever. Don't just stand there staring at her.*

EmmaLee kept on talking while she led Sarah into the living room. She sprawled in front of a stack of Beatles bubblegum cards spread on the floor and continued to talk.

"You go to Tolerance High, don't you? I've seen you in the hall. I wonder why we don't have any classes together. I'm a happy-town freshman too. Do you know Stevie Burke? He's my hot-puppy boyfriend." EmmaLee pushed her hair behind her ear and let out a breath. "You're very tall, aren't you?"

"I...I suppose so, yes," Sarah answered hesitantly.

"I wish I was taller."

"Sometimes it sucks...I don't like being taller than the boys."

EmmaLee smiled at her as if they were already friends. "Lucky for you Charlie's tall. He gets that from Uncle Rusty, not Aunt Rachel."

She stopped talking and thought for a moment, appearing to ponder her next words. "Do you like the Beatles? Who's your favorite? Mine is Paul. He is fab-gear cute, don't you think?" She picked up *A Hard Days Night* album and put it on the hi-fi.

EmmaLee seemed to be exactly what Sarah had imagined she wanted in a friend. Someone who would not judge her by what others deemed appropriate. Someone who seemed to accept her just the way she was. She had the same natural charm and agreeableness as Charlie but with twice the animation.

Sarah stretched out on the floor surrounded by Beatles cards. "When I was thirteen, I was deeply and hopelessly in love with George. He's still my favorite." Sarah started to add that he seemed quiet and shy and stays in the background, but before she could take a breath EmmaLee barged ahead.

"Cool." She sat up and drained the last swallow from a bottle of Coke. She ripped open a pack of Beatles bubble-gum cards and began to search through them. She handed Sarah a card with a picture of George Harrison and gave a grin that showed a hint of dimples. "You can keep it. I already have that one."

"Want a milkshake? I can fix us one. Aunt Rachel has a blender. We don't have one. Do you?" Not waiting for an answer, she got up and started toward the kitchen.

It made Sarah dizzy, the way EmmaLee filled the room with energy; it was like being swept away in the surge of a hurricane.

TWENTY-NINE

Deuteronomy 32:2
*² Let my teaching drop as the rain, let my speech condense as the dew,
like gentle showers upon the tender herb, and as rain upon the grass.*

1965

Stretching her neck outward, Belle rubbed her forelock against Sarah's shoulder. Sarah reached out to stroke the horse's velvety nose. "Yes, Belle, I love you too…."

Belle's brown eyes blinked, and her ears pricked forward as she let out a soft nicker. She stamped a hoof and let out another nicker signaling she wanted to go.

Charlie held the mare's bridal while Sarah steadied herself in the saddle.

He finished cinching his saddle, tossed a rope across the saddle horn and was mounting his horse when Rusty rode up.

"We got a heifer out there, been in labor since early morning, but no sign of a calf. I'm fixing to go back out there and check on her. I'm afraid we might lose 'em both. Y'all tag along. I might need a hand."

Making his way to the pasture, Rusty shifted in his saddle and whistled for his mongrel collie, Lucky. Sarah and Charlie circled the corral and fell into step beside him, the dog trotting behind. With clear skies and a breeze from the south, it was headed toward becoming an uncommonly warm March day.

As they approached the first gate, Charlie swiveled in this saddle ready to dismount but stopped short as Sarah jump from her horse and dragged the gate open, its rusted hinges moaning. Letting the horses pass through, she swung it shut and double checked the latch.

Rusty gave Charlie a sly wink, his eyes glinting with amusement.

Lucky barked a noncommittal warning at a few grazing cows. Unfazed they ignored the intruders to their pasture, but nearby, birds flitted from bush to tree twittering in unison. Their sharp alarm calls spread across the meadow.

As Rusty feared, they found the heifer lying on her side, heaving in pain, with two little black hooves protruding from her body.

Taking a handkerchief from his hip pocket, Rusty pushed back his hat and wiped his forehead. "I'm thinking that calf's all cattywampus and we're gonna have to pull it."

"Pull it?" Sarah looked puzzled.

Charlie nodded. "Yeah, usually there's no problem, we just find a new calf running around one day. But sometimes with the first one, a heifer has trouble and we have to give her a nudge."

Sarah's brow wrinkled. "Chicken farmers don't have that problem; never had to help any of our chickens lay an egg."

Rusty knelt beside the heifer and laid his hand on her swollen belly. "Yep, sure as a cat's got climbing gear, she's in trouble." His voice was calm and soothing as he rolled up his sleeve. "We'll do what we can, girl, but I'd rather you'd done this on your own." The heifer seemed too weak to put up much of a fight as he slipped his hand inside. When it emerged, he had hold of the front legs of a calf. Charlie untied a coil of rope and dismounted.

Rusty wrapped a slipknot around the feet of the calf. He started pulling and the heifer bellowed loudly, trying to get up. A booted foot on the shoulder held her steady.

Sarah looked away. "Poor thing."

Still keeping one eye on the cow, Rusty tossed the end of the rope to Sarah. "Wrap the end around your saddle horn two or three times," he told her.

Sarah studied the heifer as she looped the rope. "What next?"

"Make sure that rope stays stretched tight."

There was no time to question before he slapped the rear of her horse and commanded, "Back, Belle. Back."

Belle inched back, and the cow bawled louder. Rusty strained to guide the wet calf as it slipped from its mother onto the grass.

Charlie released the heifer and stepped back. Rising to her feet the cow immediately turned her attention to the calf, licking it clean and dry. Rusty loosened the rope and the new calf bawled, got up on his legs and wobbled off behind its mother.

When Sarah dismounted, Charlie grabbed her, spun her around and kissed her full on the lips, "Good job, Sunshine." Her red hair pulled back into a tight ponytail glistened in the sunlight.

"By golly, you're handier than a pocket on a shirt, girl," Rusty yanked her ponytail. "You did that like you been doing it all your life."

While they made their way back to the house in the late morning sunlight, Sarah tucked away this cherished praise with a special sense of belonging.

Rachel kneeled in her garden, her face shaded beneath the broad brim of a straw hat. She looked up, her eyes bright, a smile on her mouth as the trio rode toward the house.

Rusty jumped from his horse and gave her a playful kiss. "Mother, you got yourself a new calf, but we had to give him a little bitty shove."

He winked at Sarah. "You should've seen this gal in action. I am tickled to death to see how she handles Belle, and she's a might bit prettier than Charlie." His forehead creased as he grinned. "I might have to trade him in for her."

She blushed easily, and Rusty knew it.

Rachel poked him in the side, "Oh hush, with your foolishness. You're embarrassing her."

"Charlie and I have more work to do." Rusty sighed and looked at Sarah. "You've done enough cattle wrangling for one day. Why don't you stay here with Mother and give her a hand with her garden? I'll bring the boy back directly."

"It would be mighty nice to have some company." Rachel handed Sarah a garden trowel and a pair of gloves. "Let's tackle some weeds." She pointed in the direction of a bed of daffodils in full bloom.

Sarah stopped to admire a patch of graceful ruffled blossoms and sucked in their seductive perfume.

Rachel picked one, smelled it and handed it to Sarah. "Don't they smell lovely, like orange blossoms and honey? I love sweet peas; they look like tiny butterflies and start blooming about the time the daffodils give up. When they're in flower, my house is full of bouquets."

Sarah nodded, biting her lower lip. "We've never had flowers in our house."

"I always say bringing flowers into the house is like bringing God's gift inside." She stopped for a moment, then continued, *and when the sun shines brightly, tend flowers that God has given.*

"That's beautiful. Did you make it up?"

She smiled. "No, honey, Robert Frost made that one up. But I do write a little poetry from time to time. It's not much to speak of, but it helps me relax and meditate." Her hazel eyes seemed to shift from amber to green when she smiled. "I tried to pass on my love of Robert Frost to the kids; didn't have much luck though. They'd rather hear their daddy's favorite poems more often than mine."

Rachel chuckled and shook her head. "Charlie's favorite is *The Cremation of Sam McGee* by Robert Service. Do you know it?"

"No ma'am, I don't think I do."

"Now Sam McGee was from Tennessee, where the cotton blooms and blows.
Why he left his home in the South to roam 'round the Pole, God only knows.
He was always cold, but the land of gold seemed to hold him like a spell; Though he'd
often say in his homely way that he'd 'sooner live in hell'."

"Silly isn't it? But it rhymes." She pulled on her gloves. "There are a lot of ways to nourish the soul and laughter is surely one of them; just as important as beauty... maybe more important."

Sarah liked that about Rachel, the way she talked, easy going, rambling; always seeing the positive.

Rachel pulled an intruding tuft of grass from the flowerbed and tossed it aside. "I think it was Rusty's sense of humor that made me fall for him. We were high school sweethearts." She looked off into the distance for a brief moment. "Charlie reminds me so much of his daddy at that age. He's every bit as charming and tends to get his way. Rusty always got his way too. No sense fighting it." She shook her head. "No sense at all."

"Yes, I know. I figured that out pretty fast."

"Once a Weeks boy sets his cap for you, you might as well surrender 'cause he'll win you over in the end." She touched Sarah's cheek.

It seemed so easy, so natural to be a part of this family--the way they lived, this house, this yard, Rachel's flowers. It was the life she'd always yearned for, but never knew existed outside of her books. How could she have possibly known this was normal for some people--for many people?

Seek the darkest corner of the room and try to make yourself as small as possible. Those were the lessons learned from her family. In her world, a family didn't laugh and talk and find joy in one another. In her world practicality always trumped beauty.

Rachel cut a yellow bud from the rosebush and held it between her fingers. "The yellow rose is the symbol of joy and friendship. Did you know during the Victorian times there was a secret language using flowers? Lovers would send messages through nosegays. But I think of flowers as God's promise that life goes on. The dead blossoms give us seeds to create new life."

At the mention of death, Sarah stared at the ground.

"My brother died." Tears rimmed her eyes. "I still miss him something fierce." She didn't look up and almost in a whisper she said, "it just about killed my momma."

"Yes, I remember when it happened… such a tragedy. No mother should have to bury her child."

"Kenny was good; he didn't deserve to die. He wanted to be a preacher you know." She blotted a tear from the corner of her eye with her finger. "I got mad at Jesus when Kenny died. Momma stopped going to church."

"You were so young then, how could you possibly understand? It's hard for anyone to understand the death of a child. It is for me. We have all kinds of questions about why and how, and we want the answers right away. But don't let your heart shrink and become hard."

She stared down at the rose for a moment before handing it to Sarah. "Faith isn't a one-time decision; it's a decision we have to renew every day. The Bible tells us, *Trust in the Lord with all your heart, and do not lean on your own understanding.* Sarah, don't be angry with God, trust Him. He knows what's best for you."

She nodded. "Miss Rachel, I guess you might be the smartest person I've ever known. You know something about everything, don't you?"

Rachel laughed and gave Sarah a hug. "No, honey, I am afraid that's not the case. But thank you for the compliment. I know a bit about books. I taught English before Charlie and Mary Ann were born, but there is a whole lot I don't know."

"I have a lot of books at home. Sometimes I borrow books from the library, but if I really like a book, I want to keep it. It makes me sad to have to return it. Sometimes, after I have returned a library book, I'll try to find a copy at Hazel's, so I can keep it."

"I know how you feel, honey. Books make fine companions and re-reading a favorite book is like renewing an old friendship." Rachel smiled. *"I ate them like salad, books were my sandwich for lunch, my tiffin and dinner and midnight munch. I tore out the pages, ate them with salt, doused them with relish, gnawed on the bindings, turned the chapters with my tongue!"*

Sarah's eyes brightened. "I know that one! That's *Fahrenheit 451.* I did a book report on it last year."

"That's right." Rachel's eyes sparkled. "What kind of books do you read?"

"I read Nancy Drew books. When I outgrew them, Agatha Christie took their place."

"There's nothing wrong with Nancy Drew. I read them too when I was a girl. Nancy often offers a direct path to Agatha Christie and it is a short journey to Sherlock Holmes and, suddenly you are at the door of Edgar Allen Poe, and that's when you're in English teacher territory."

Sarah laughed. "Yes, I took that trip. I also took a trip from Anthem to Fahrenheit 451 to Brave New World and 1984. I never thought of it as a trip, but I guess it really is like a journey...step by step."

Rachel stood, stretched her back and said, "Wait here, I have something I want to give you."

She disappeared into the house and returned with a thin volume darkened by time and worn by use. Her hand stroked the blemished leather cover. "My mother gave this to me when I was in school." She held it out to Sarah as if it were a treasure. "Here, honey, it is a gift for you. I hope you enjoy some wonderful journeys."

"For me? For no reason at all? Thank you, Miss Rachel, thank you so much."

Sarah looked down at the cherished book *Best Loved Poems*. The leather back was beginning to fray and the corners were rounded and slick. It fell open on its own accord to a well-thumbed page; *The Road Not Taken* by Robert Frost.

THIRTY

Ecclesiastes 11:9
*⁹ You who are young, be happy while you are young, and let your heart
give you joy in the days of your youth. Follow the ways of your heart
and whatever your eyes see, but know that for all these things God will
bring you into judgment.*

S arah sat at her desk watching the movement of the classroom clock, bit
by bit. The thin red hand did not move until the full second passed,
then it jerked forward, stopped on the bold number and waited for
another second to pass.

Her eyes moved to her notebook with the initials *CTW* scrawled here and
there. Using her finger, she traced over the initials. It seemed her life had
opened into a new world in the months since she met Charlie and EmmaLee.

On Sunday, she wasted no time calling EmmaLee to give her the news
about Saturday night. She tried not to sound too thrilled but failed miserably.
Sarah couldn't talk freely in the kitchen with everyone listening. Now, she
could hardly wait to tell EmmaLee every detail of how Charlie had given her
his class ring.

The bell sounded; its harsh tones resonating through the air signaled the
end of third period Algebra. Sarah tucked her pen into her purse, grabbed
her books and rushed into the hallway, echoes of the bell still hanging in the
air. Her pace quickened when she caught sight of EmmaLee's wispy ponytail
bobbing toward her.

"Let me see it. Let me see it," EmmaLee begged, bouncing on tiptoes.
One dimple formed among the faded freckles painting her cheeks.

Sarah extended her hand and presented an opened palm to EmmaLee,
holding Charlie's senior class ring--an undeniable symbol that she, Sarah Jane
Jones was going steady with a senior, a member of the football team. Dating
a popular kid made her a popular kid. But it meant more than that. She liked
being part of his family. She liked the way his confidence fed her own.

"How did he ask you? Were you in blissville?" Without missing a beat, she persisted. "Isn't it just paradise here and now? When did he ask? What did he say? Come on, let's ditch lunch and walk down to the dime store. You can give me all the details on the way."

Even with the coming of spring, it was a dreary morning, but the dank and chilly air could not dampen the girls' enthusiasm. As the girls walked toward the town square, Sarah took the ring from her pocket and slid it onto her finger, stretching out her arm to admire it again. "Of course, it's too big. I need to buy some ribbons, so I can tie it around my neck... like the other girls who're going steady."

"I guess me and Stevie are going steady, but he never really asked me...I'm sure when he gets a senior ring he'll let me wear it! Do you think Charlie knew he was going to ask ... or was it just a sudden notion?"

"Yeah, he acted all weird and stuff and I couldn't figure out what was going on. It really bummed me out. I swear I was afraid he was trying to get up the nerve to break up."

EmmaLee smiled. "That's crazy. How could you think that? Trust me, Charlie's nuts about you. I've never seen him so happy—he doesn't even pick on me anymore." She gave Sarah a light punch on the arm.

"You know me, I mean, you know I always see the bad side of things...I know...I can't help it.... So anyway, he had this quart of beer and he just kept sipping it, and offering me a taste, but not saying anything. I thought he'd never say a word."

"Were you about to die?"

"Gospel truth, it seemed like an hour--he just sat there, drinking and staring straight ahead."

Their gait quickened as they neared the five and dime. They entered the store and passed the clerk and a customer huddled together talking. The clerk's eyes followed the girls for a moment before she glanced over her shoulder at the clock.

"Ignore her. She thinks we're ditching school. Finish the story." EmmaLee whispered.

Sarah instinctively leaned in closer and lowered her voice.

"Well, then he finally finished the beer and took his ring off of his finger and put it on mine." Her cheeks flushed. "I thought I was gonna die." She grinned. "I think he had to drink all that beer to get up the courage to ask me. He didn't say anything, he just kept grinning at me with that silly grin of his. He was so sweet, I almost cried."

THIRTY-ONE

Psalm 30

[11] Thou hast turned for me my mourning into joyful dancing: thou hast taken away my sorrow and surrounded me with gladness.

Rebecca Evans shot forward into the parking spot in front of Dillard's department store and bumped the front tires of her station wagon against the curb. EmmaLee looked at Sarah and rolled her eyes. Shutting off the ignition, Mrs. Evans glanced into the rearview mirror. Her eyes unreadable behind sunglasses, she grinned. "I saw that, missy."

Sarah reached into her purse one more time and opened her billfold to make sure her money was still there. Thumbing through the bills, she counted again: *twenty-six dollars and some change.* Momma had no idea how much a prom dress would cost when she took her secret money jar from the pantry this morning and gave Sarah every penny.

Rebecca pumped an hour's worth of nickels and dimes into the parking meter while the girls lingered long enough to survey the window display of taffeta and lace dresses. It had not been difficult for the girls to convince Mrs. Evans the trip to Texarkana was necessary to find the perfect prom dress. A dress from the Sears catalog would never do for such an important occasion.

"Sarah, look at that blue one. It's like the one we saw in Vogue." EmmaLee bounced on her toes. "Mom, do you think they'll let us try it on?"

The girls exchanged excited glances as they pushed open the glass doors into the air-conditioned space with its high ceilings. In every direction, displays beckoned shoppers to take a peek at their scarves, their purses, their jewelry.

Not noticing they'd left Mrs. Evans behind, they quickened their pace and headed for the escalator. Riding up, Sarah peered over the rail at crowds chattering and shuffling across the highly polished marble floor below.

Stepping off the escalator onto the second-floor, the girls bolted toward the formal dress department. A middle-aged saleswoman, her dyed hair done up into a Beehive and sprayed rigid with Aqua Net, looked up from a rack outside the fitting room where she lined up yellow, blue, green and pink satin dresses.

She peered at them through cat-eye glasses and gave a fake smile. Her face wore a mask of layered makeup, colored an unflattering tint of orange, a shade darker than her skin She sniffed and returned to rattling hangers and pinning price tags to dresses.

By the time Mrs. Evans joined them, EmmaLee was rifling through the racks, ignoring price tags and pulling out dress after dress, holding each up for Sarah's approval.

The saleswoman lifted an eyebrow. She whirled around sending the overpowering scent of spicy rich perfume into the air. Her lips parting in a genuine smile this time she squinted as if sighting Mrs. Evans in the crosshairs of a rifle scope. "Let me know if you need anything." Her bracelets clattered as she rested a hand on her hip.

EmmaLee handed the clerk an armful of dresses. "You can put these in a fitting room, please." The woman hopped to her bidding.

Sarah drew in a long breath, lifted her shoulders in a shrug and continued to sort through the selection. She paused to pull a dress from the rack. Careful not to leave a smudge on the delicate fabric, she held it at arm's length, studied it, peeked secretly at the price tag. She placed it back on the rack. Squaring her shoulders, she ended her search and gathering a few dresses--none of them less than thirty dollars--draped them over her arm.

The saleswoman hustled toward the fitting room with another armload of dresses EmmaLee had chosen, followed by Mrs. Evans and the giggling girls. Mrs. Evans parked herself on an overstuffed chair outside the door. "I'll wait here for the fashion show," she laughed. "I want to see all of them, even if you think I'll hate them."

A few minutes later, the clerk pushed open the curtains of the dressing room, a blue dress...the blue dress from the window lying across her outstretched arms. Red glass stones set into her huge gold ring flashed under the lights.

EmmaLee tossed aside the dress she held and stepped into the one retrieved from the window. Sarah pulled the zipper through the satin and chiffon dress. The ruffles along the hem flowed around EmmaLee's ankles as she twirled around. She wrapped her arms around herself. "Isn't it just a piece of perfection?"

"It is amazing. You should get it for sure," Sarah agreed.

EmmaLee paraded from the fitting room to show her mother and admire herself in the 3-way mirror.

She caught Sarah's eye. "But what about you? Don't you want to try it on?"

"No, it was made for you,"

"At least try it on."

Having already examined the price tag, Sarah replied, "I'm too tall for that style. It looks better on you."

"Perhaps something with an Empire waistline," suggested the saleswoman who still hovered nearby.

Sarah bit her lip and fiddled with Charlie's ring hanging from her neck.

EmmaLee's eyes surveyed the accumulation of dresses "I think you should get the green one. You looked *shockingly gorgeous* in it!"

Sarah shook her head and picked at her nails. A quick smile crossed her lips. EmmaLee found many things to be *shockingly gorgeous* these days.

"I don't see exactly what I want here." She toyed with a lock of hair. "I think I would rather make my dress. That way I'll know no one else will be wearing the same thing,"

EmmaLee gave Sarah a knowing glance. "Then you should do that. You shouldn't get anything you don't want. If I could sew like you, I'd make my dress too. I don't have the patience you have."

A flush crept up Sarah's face as she met her friend's eyes, grateful for the tenderness she saw there.

Mrs. Evans motioned to the saleswoman and murmured, "We'll take the blue one."

EmmaLee hugged her mother, and the girls hurried to the fitting room where they wiggled out of the dresses and put on their street clothes.

Sarah headed for the sewing department while EmmaLee and her mother paid for the blue dress.

EmmaLee found Sarah crouched over the pattern books, flicking the pages back and forth. Looking up from the book she blew out a breath. "I have narrowed it down to two. I kinda like the Vogue pattern, but it costs $1.50 and McCall is cheaper."

EmmaLee placed a hand on Sarah's shoulder. "They are both beautiful, but I really think this is a perfect dress for you," she said, pointing a finger at the McCall pattern. "It will be *shockingly gorgeous* with a satin sash around the waist. Don't you think so?"

162

"Yep." Sarah agreed. She snapped the book shut and giving the pattern number to the clerk, began to scrutinize row after row of shimmering fabric. Spotting a bolt of gleaming yellow chiffon, light to the touch, Sarah knew this was the only choice for Charlie's *Sunshine*.

THIRTY-TWO

Proverbs 27
[17] As Iron is sharpened by iron; so one friend sharpens another

S arah rocked back and forth on the porch swing; her eyes repeatedly darted toward the road searching for a glimpse of Mrs. Evans' station wagon. She glanced at the picture she'd carefully torn from the pages of *Hairdo* magazine. Reassuring herself the hairdresser could make her hair look like the picture, she folded the page and stuffed it into her purse. EmmaLee had declared it *shamefully wonderful*, or was it *amen amazing*? Either way, Sarah would get her hair piled high and stiffly sprayed into place at Cindy Lou's Beauty Shop in Tolerance. She was excited and nervous. It was her first trip to a beauty parlor. EmmaLee made appointments for them both.

Her eyes held for a moment on a delicate yellow dress hanging from a hook on the porch. It billowed in the soft breeze.

EmmaLee was right; she would be *shockingly gorgeous* in that dress. Sarah recalled the rush of excitement as bits of organza, cut in the shape of pattern pieces, were gradually pinned and stitched into place. After hours of patient stitching, she'd stood on a footstool looking down at Momma's head, as she kneeled, folding the hem and talking around the pins in her mouth.

She was sad Momma wouldn't see her wearing the dress, all dolled up with her fancy hair-do. But the disappointment was tempered by the excitement of spending the night at EmmaLee's house for the first time. Most of all, she was happy that this special occasion would not be ruined by a drunken scene from her daddy.

❧

All giggles and smiles, the girls came through the door of the Evans house clutching square white boxes with *Flora's Fancy Flowers* scrolled in green script across the lids. Each box contained a carnation boutonniere, one dyed yellow, and one blue. The excitement swelled as Sarah glimpsed her bouffant hairstyle in the long mirror just inside the entry hall. Hurrying into the scrubbed and polished kitchen, the girls stashed the boutonnieres in the icebox, grabbed two Cokes and hurried up the stairs to EmmaLee's bedroom.

EmmaLee's room had always been a source of envy for Sarah. After she'd seen the lavender painted walls and white French Provencal canopy bed, she had gone home, looked around her room—tried to picture it with shelves crammed with Madame Alexander dolls and framed family photos. In the end, she shrugged, grabbed a book from the shelf and found a spot to read under a peach tree. There were no framed family photos in the Jones house, and Sarah never heard of Madam Alexander dolls until her eyes lit up at EmmaLee's collection.

Today she felt no envy.

Once again, she checked to make sure her shoes had been dyed to exactly match her dress, carefully hung the dress on the back of the door and placed the shoes on the floor beneath it.

She threw herself across the bed, sinking into the soft mattress and let her eyes drift from a giant poster of the Beatles to the shelf of dolls and mementos. Mindlessly running her hand across the frilly pink bedspread, she stared out the window. She could feel herself, her nose pressed against the window looking in; yearning to come inside, all the while knowing some things stay as they've always been.

EmmaLee propped up near the headboard; feet tucked beneath her, as Sarah's eyes explored the room. She'd been in Sarah's modest room only once. Now watching Sarah, she saw things for the first time and understood the disparity. Feeling a twinge of guilt and hoping to break the mood, she hugged a pillow to her chest and with a sigh, said "Can you believe that it's almost the end of our first year of high school? And even better, can you believe that we're both going to prom! It will be *funbelievable!*"

She nudged Sarah with her bare foot. "I'm so glad you're Charlie's girlfriend and we can be friends. Oh, and of course, I'm glad the sweet and lovely Stevie is my boyfriend!" She flipped on the radio. The girls sat stock-still and silent for a moment listening to Peter and Gordon sing *A World Without Love.*

"I used to feel like that-- before I met Charlie."

"But now you have Charlie…you won't have to be *locked away*," she laughed.

Sarah nodded. Her gaze returned to the magnolia tree outside the window. The lemony scent of its white blossoms drifted through the open window. She'd looked at magnolia trees all her life…strange how she had associated them with class and position.

"What do you think it's like to live on Old Orchard Road?" She continued to look at the tree.

"Like anywhere else, I guess," EmmaLee said.

Something shook loose in Sarah and touched a cosseted place. "Sometimes I think about what it would be like to be somebody and get somewhere in life. Seems like in this town all you have to do to be somebody is to live on Old Orchard Road. Betty Jo lives there. You just wait—someday I'll live there too."

EmmaLee listened in wide-eyed silence

"I'll live there with my fearfully rich husband in one of those elegantly grand houses and will have nothing to do all day but drink lemonade with my rich friends on my big porch and count the number of dresses I have in my closet; not a single one of them will be homemade."

"But, Sarah…" EmmaLee started to protest.

"Of course, you will come to drink lemonade on my porch. I will buy tons of beautiful things with my husband's money," she said. Her tone turned whimsical. "And the house will have a library with beautiful wood paneling. It'll be filled with books, all of them with leather covers. Then I'll leave Tolerance someday and see the whole world. I'll go to Dallas and St Louis, and even Paris. I'll see for myself what the rest of the world is like. I'm gonna be somebody important. You just wait and see."

EmmaLee looked sad and serious. "What about Charlie? You can't just forget about him."

Sarah's heart beat a little faster as the thought sunk in. Being with Charlie had given her an exciting new life—a happy life, and she adored him. But did she love him enough to give up her life's dream?

She recovered her cheerfulness. "You'll see. I am lucky to be pretty and I know how to use it," her eyes twinkled with devilish amusement.

Laughing, EmmaLee picked up her pillow and tossed it at Sarah. "Oh hush." The pillow sailed past her ear and landed on the floor. "Not me. I'm gonna have my own money; not rely on a husband to support me. Mother and Aunt Rachel were both Chi Omegas at Ole Miss and I'm going to Ole Miss too. I'll be a Chi Omega. I'm a shoo-in because I'm a double legacy."

Sarah wasn't interested in finding out what that meant—Chi Omega--legacy—but she liked the idea of earning her own money. At that moment, for the first time, she realized college was an option for her.

Her thoughts alternated between living on Old Orchard Road and going to College.

No one in her family had ever done either—lived on Old Orchard Road or attended college. It never occurred to her that a girl could go to college. She'd always been made to feel a woman is not complete without a man; that girls were a burden to their families and needed to marry well to be of value. New resolve began to bubble inside her. Perhaps a man is only half a thing without a woman. She could make it on her own if she went to college—yes, she would go to college.

Her thoughts were broken by the ring of the princess phone on the nightstand. "I bet it's Stevie!" EmmaLee jumped to reach for the phone halfway through the first ring. She smiled and purred into the phone. "Yes, Stevie. Well you know, we were just fixing to." Her lashes flicked up and her eyes sparkled. "Nope. Yes. Okay." She hung up the phone, lifted her hand to her forehead and pretended to swoon, falling onto the bed.

"They'll pick us up at seven," she said. "Guess we should start getting ready. You use my bathroom; I'll use the one in the hall." EmmaLee grabbed her robe and disappearing into the hallway hollered over her shoulder, "Use the Gardenia bubble bath."

Exploring the selection of bubble bath, Sarah found the Gardenia and poured it into the filling tub. The deep sweet scent hung in the air. She stepped into the warm fragrant water. A sigh of pleasure escaped her lips and her eyes closed. Taking special care not to get her hair wet as she slid down beneath the scented foam. She soaked and contemplated the evening ahead.

Before she met Charlie, all she wanted was to be accepted by others. Things like going to the prom had only been daydreams, and her daydreams always ended in disappointment and hurt.

Her attempts to escape—as misguided as they were--only opened the wounds further, left her hating herself for hoping. Stupid girl, stupid, stupid girl. And then, just as she had come to accept her life as it was—knowing her dreams were impossible—there was Charlie—giving her hope. Had this one thing changed everything?

Static on the radio, the sound of it being tuned from the other room, cut through Sarah's thoughts, and with a reluctant sigh, she forced herself to leave the luxury of the tub. Stepping onto the thick bathmat she patted herself dry. Wrapping herself in a towel, she padded into the bedroom.

EmmaLee sat on the edge of her vanity chair, smelling of bath powder and soap. She studied her image in the mirror. Sarah watched as she fussed with her make-up.

Turning to Sarah, she begged, "Do my eyes. Do them like Cher's. I bought some drool-worthy black liquid eyeliner. Check it out!" She pulled a small bottle from the mound of makeup piled on the dressing table.

A flutter of excitement tickled Sarah as she surveyed the brushes and pencils and powders and bottles of perfume spread across the table.

Sarah went to work with the eyeliner, carefully drawing a wide sweeping line along EmmaLee's lashes ending with an upward tail. She glanced at it and frowned. Something was missing. She pulled a photo of Cher from the bulletin board, studied it a moment and then added a dark line to the lower lashes. "Perfect!"

EmmaLee's eyes popped open. "Really? You think?"

"No peeking until I'm done." Sarah shuffled through the makeup to find the palest of pale pink, almost white, lipstick. She applied the lipstick before letting EmmaLee look. "Don't rub your eyes until the mascara is dry."

By the time the doorbell rang the girls had finished their makeup, slipped into their gowns and were admiring their reflections from every angle.

At the sound of the bell, Sarah started toward the stairs, but EmmaLee took hold of her elbow. "Let Mother answer it. Wait until they are inside. We can make a grand entrance down the stairs, so everyone can see how enchanting we look."

Charlie and Stevie, clad in white dinner jackets and holding florist boxes looked up at the girls moving one step at a time down the stairs, taking care not to stumble in their high heels.

"You look beautiful, Sunshine." Charlie beamed at Sarah, his thick fingers fumbling to remove a corsage from its box.

"You look beautiful too, Charlie Weeks."

Handling the corsage as carefully as a piece of broken glass, he gave it to Sarah and wiped his palm on his black slacks. She lifted the yellow rosebuds tied with organdy ribbons to her nose and drew in a deep breath. It smelled sweet and fragrant, like the flowers from Rachel's rosebush. Her eyes sparkled as she handed it back to Charlie. "Pin it on," she said with a tiny rush of excitement.

The color rose in Charlie's face as he stood close to her studying the filmy bodice of the dress. He took a deep breath, bent his head forward and with a trembling hand tried to pin the flowers to her dress. "Oh, man," he muttered as the pearl-topped pin pricked her warm skin. "Dumb klutz moment." He finally pinned the corsage to her dress and stepped back. It drooped at a questionable angle.

He shot a helpless look at his aunt. She smiled and winked at Sarah and re-pinned the corsage with ease.

"Wait! Let me get pictures." Rebecca insisted, grabbing her camera.

They all smiled while she struggled to pop a flash cube on to her camera. "Say cheese!" They blinked as the flash went off and then quickly escaped out the front door.

Cinderella on her way to the ball could not have been more eager than the foursome in Miss Rachel's new Pontiac Bonneville.

Magically transformed into a wondrous Paris street crafted of silver and blue crepe paper, the gym bustled with excitement. Cardboard stars covered in tinfoil hung from the ceiling and an Eiffel tower fashioned from chicken wire and cardboard completed the fantasyland. EmmaLee declared it to be *très extravagant*.

They scanned a sea of round tables with silver confetti sprinkled on pressed white tablecloths. "There, next to the column," Stevie said, pointing toward the back of the room.

For once in her life, it didn't bother Sarah to parade past everyone. They breezed past the table reserved for the prom queen and her court. Brenda Sue's head turned, her eyes coolly looking Sarah up and down as she passed. Betty Jo made eye contact, then pointedly looked away and whispering in Brenda Sue's ear, began to giggle. Sarah held her head high and kept walking, holding tight to Charlie's arm.

They danced in a crowded sea of satin and taffeta, and posed in front of the Eiffel Tower for the classic prom photo; Sarah's gloved hand held at her waist, resting in Charlie's hand. The evening passed quickly, swept up in a blur—and now, the band played the opening chords of the final song, signaling the end of a perfect evening.

"Gosh, I love this song." Sarah draped her arms around Charlie's neck, closed her eyes and swayed to the music. Charlie smiled down at her and pressed his cheek against hers; his lips against her ear, he sang along as they danced to The Dave Clark Five song, *Because.* She felt protected and safe in Charlie's arms; feeling him against her as their bodies connected. She wondered if Charlie meant the words-- or was he just singing along?

He pulled her even closer. Everyone in the room seemed to disappear, until it was just the two of them, barely moving. When the music stopped and they pulled apart, she was dizzy and flushed. *Maybe this is what love feels like.*

Sinking into a deep, soft chair, Sarah dug her bare toes into the plush carpet covering EmmaLee's bedroom floor. Wiping cold cream from her face with a tissue, she rested her head against the back of the chair and caught a glimpse of her prom dress, once again hanging on the door. *Shockingly gorgeous.* She smiled at the thought.

She whirled around and flopped down on the bed. "EmmaLee, have you ever been in love?" Sarah pensively stared upward at the lavender canopy and fingered the yellow ribbon holding Charlie's class ring. "I think I may be in love with Charlie."

"I suppose I love Stevie. We've been together since we were fourteen. He's the only guy I ever kissed." EmmaLee pulled a record from its sleeve and placed it on the turntable…The Kinks. While Ray Davies bemoaned the fact that he was *so tired, tired of waiting*, Sarah thought about Charlie. Surely, he'd heard the whispers about her. Did it bother him that she had *been around*, but they never had sex? The ugly reality was that the gossip was true. She had used her looks and sex appeal as a tool and it had gotten her nowhere. She got some attention, but those encounters didn't replace the acceptance she desperately sought. That need formed a vital part of who she was, had led her to a pattern -- to let someone else make decisions and take power over her sexuality. It was easier that way.

In the months since she and Charlie started dating, there had been times she had wanted to go all the way, but each time something had stopped them. Was Charlie *tired of waiting?*

Sarah's eyes narrowed. "Do you think the boys were disappointed that we didn't go parking behind the ice house and make out after the dance?"

EmmaLee winkled her nose, "Girls shouldn't make out unless they know a guy is heart-jittering serious about them."

"Have you ever gone all the way?"

"No! Of course not! That would be inconceivably sinful." EmmaLee looked stunned.

"Do you really think that it's okay to tell him *no* after dating for so long? Don't you feel guilty... aren't you afraid of being called a tease?" She had never been so frank with EmmaLee, with anyone, not even Charlie.

EmmaLee sighed and sat down on the bed watching Sarah. "Guys don't want to date a tramp, but they don't want a prude either." She propped herself up on her elbow. "You have to know where to draw the line. You have to tell them when to stop, 'cause otherwise, boys are just *divinely clueless*."

Sarah rolled onto her side and hugged her pillow to her chest; she could not rectify what she was hearing with her own experience.

"First date I had with Stevie, I told him no hanky panky for me until I get married. He said, 'okay.'" She lowered her voice to almost a whisper. "That doesn't stop him from trying every once in a while- but the answer is always the same. He knows I'm saving myself for my wedding night. I want it to be special."

Slipping Charlie's ring on her finger, Sarah held her hand out to let the red stone catch the light. Maybe he would exchange it for an engagement ring one day. But her wedding night wouldn't be special—not like EmmaLee's— it was too late for that. She accepted that she didn't deserve anything better. She put the ring back on the ribbon and toyed with the edge of her pillowcase. Her gaze was intense and serious. "You don't expect your husband to be a virgin when you get married, so how is it fair that he would expect you to be?"

"Sarah, you shouldn't talk like that. Guys don't want a girl who's been around." Sarah could see in EmmaLee's expression she was not judging her. "Nice girls don't put out. You have to be careful when you fool around; it is an amazingly short trip from nice girl to tramp."

All of a sudden Sarah felt like a bad person. She'd already taken that short trip and there was no returning to the nice girl side of town. Instantly, two images each seen through the scrim of time, flashed through her mind—her daddy pawing at her, and Dub's jeering face as he fell from the hayloft ladder. *Not now. Don't think about that now.* The images stuck in her mind.

"Sarah... Don't look like that!"

"Like what?"

"I don't know," EmmaLee muttered. "You...sometimes you look as though...as though you are heartbreakingly sad." Her gaze didn't leave Sarah's eyes.

Sarah looked away, stared up at the ceiling. "Life has not always been exactly what I wished for." Unexpectedly, a strong impulse to tell EmmaLee everything about the invasion into her childhood stirred her. For a long time, she had wanted to tell someone, someone she could trust, someone who wouldn't judge her. Needing to rid herself of the demons her family had cast on her she wanted to confide this dark thing. She wanted EmmaLee to accept her even when she knew the truth.

Sarah moistened her dry lips and bit by bit began to recount the things she'd gone through. At first, the sickening words only trickled, but then they came pouring out as she went on telling the whole dreadful story about Floyd.

Trembling, she recalled being subjected to her father's verbal cruelty; his constant criticism and hurtful sarcasm. She was sobbing by the time she finished with the telling, including how she had slept around in search of someone to make her feel loved. But in the end, she did not reveal everything about her father. How could she share that kind of shame with anyone? It was too painful, too filthy, too horrible. Her voice trailed off in a mix of relief and regret, and her disgrace and guilt did not diminish.

Two large, bright tears ran down EmmaLee's cheeks. Her eyes never lingered long on Sarah's face, but, she didn't wipe the tears away and Sarah didn't try to hide that she saw them. They sat together on the bed without speaking.

"Sarah, I'm glad you told me." She took her hand and pressed gently.

EmmaLee opened the window. The air wafting through the screen was warm and perfumed with honeysuckle.

Exhausted, the girls snuggled into the sheets, positioning themselves to catch the perfect breeze through the screens of the open windows, and fell asleep to the roar of the attic fan drowning out the hum of insects.

THIRTY-THREE

Song of Solomon 3
⁵ I warn you, O daughters of Jerusalem, by the deer, and by the gazelles of the field, that you not awaken love, until its proper time.

Peter, Paul and Mary, Blowing in the Wind, blasted from the transistor radio resting on the top of the dresser. Sarah turned down the volume and adjusted the antenna. She buttoned her blouse, looked in the mirror, and unfastened the top two buttons. Pulling a blue ribbon from her cache, she held it against her blouse and studied her image in the mirror. Nodding to herself, she threaded the ribbon through Charlie's ring and tied it around her neck.

She sat in front of her mirror pulling her hair free from fat rollers. As each long curl bounced out and recoiled, not sparing the hairspray, she teased it until it stood high on her head, then smoothed it into a perfect flip.

Leaning over the dressing table, she studied her face in the mirror. Her freckles had faded and her skin was honeyed and clear. *Like a china doll,* Momma always said.

I wonder what Charlie sees when he looks at me.

When they were not together she thought of him—thinking about when they would be together again. When she was with him—that's when she was happy. *I've stopped feeling lonely and I don't want to ever go back to it again.*

Her instinct said *trust Charlie.* He wouldn't dump her like others, in the past. He always treated her with respect, never made her feel cheap. She wanted to be deserving of the respect he'd shown. She had a say in the matter but wasn't sure how to separate her wishes from her fears. Scared of losing him if they had sex, she was afraid he'd move on if they didn't.

We may not be able to resist much longer. I'm glad Jackie Parker scared the pee out of us last weekend. Their passion quickly cooled when Jackie pulled his Ford

Galaxy patrol car behind Charlie's truck and shined his flashlight into the cab. All he said was "Move on." And they did.

It wasn't like Charlie was pressuring her or anything. She tossed her hair over her shoulder and reached for a small emerald colored bottle on her dressing table. Dabbing on a bit of fragrance, she lifted her wrist to her nose and took in a deep breath of the creamy amber and vanilla scent.

Perfect. Closing her eyes, she sniffed the sweet smell again.

For a few precious moments, she shut out the world and its problems and recalled her birthday.

"I bet you thought I'd forgotten," Charlie teased, handing her a small gift with a gold bow. "I wasn't sure what you wanted ...."

From the way he grinned, she could tell he felt rather pleased with himself. "Mom helped me wrap it," he admitted, then motioned to the gift. "Go ahead--open it?"

She didn't want to; wanting instead, to cherish the moment, prolong the surprise...the first time she'd received a gift from someone who wasn't family.

"Go on!" Charlie was growing impatient.

Sarah tore off the paper and opened the bottle of cologne.

"Try it. Do you like it?"

Gingerly dabbing out a drop on her wrist she offered it to him to smell. He sniffed her skin, nodded and continued to hold her hand against his cheek.

Her quiet thoughts of that day faded with the sound of Otis' voice sputtering from the living room. "Hey, Miss Highfalutin'. Turn down that gawd-awful noise. I can't hear my television show," His voice sounded more querulous than usual. "Get me another beer before you go running off with your fancy boy... and tell your momma I'm waiting on my supper."

A flash of animosity prickling through her, its intensity stunned her. *Pretty soon I'm going to be old enough to leave here.* She took a deep breath, steadied her shaking hands, and turned to snap off the radio. She glanced at the clock...ten past seven. If she didn't get a move on, Charlie would be here before she could get her daddy settled.

She turned back to the mirror to give herself a final viewing, checking her dark-rimmed eyes and rolling her lips together to make sure her pale, strawberry flavored lipstick was applied evenly. Confident she looked good, she went to the kitchen.

Momma looked up from the stove. She opened her mouth as if to say something but stopped. They exchanged a shrug and Momma dropped her eyes back down to the skillet and continued stirring the gravy. Sarah grabbed a beer from the icebox and then foraged around in the drawer for the opener. She punched two triangular holes in the top of the can and headed back to the living room.

A swell of stale beer and soured body odor remained in the air as Otis snatched the can from her hand. "Now get out of my sight!"

That's right, have another beer old man--stay drunk and watch your TV. Don't worry about what I'm up to or what time I get home--stay out of my business.

The crackle of tires on gravel sent her heart racing. She hurried to the door to make sure Charlie wouldn't come in.

Sarah hopped into the truck beside Charlie and slammed the door. She eyed the collection of old tires and rusting farm equipment piled next to the barn. It made her want to apologize for who she was. Why would Charlie want to be out with her when he could be out with a cheerleader who lived in a nice house, came from a good family?

Charlie punched the truck into reverse, whirring backward onto the pavement and images of her neglected surroundings faded.

They headed for town with the radio blasting the Beach Boys. Before reaching the underpass, they drove past the drive-in to see what was playing. Not that it mattered. Sarah was more concerned about who might be there. She wanted to go out in public, where everyone could see her wearing Charlie's class ring. She knew that once inside the drive-in, they'd just pile into the back seat of someone's car and make out.

"Everyone will be at The Sugar Shack tonight. That band from Texarkana is playing," hinted Sarah. "But if you want to go to the movie, that's okay."

"Your wish is my command, Sunshine." She liked the way he always called her *Sunshine.*

For the last dance, the music changed to a haunting, slow-moving melody that sent people into each other's arms. Charlie reached for Sarah and putting his arms around her waist pulled her close. She leaned into him; resting her head on his shoulder, closing her eyes and letting her body drift to the music.

He nestled into her hair and his lips grazed her ear as he sang softly. His hips pressed into her. She was reminded of another night-another dance when he sang to her. Feeling the heat of him, she let her body move of its own volition allowing the music to fill her senses and stir through her, taking her into her own private little world.

The song ended, but the music still echoing through their bodies, they remained locked together a couple of beats, wanting to hold on to the feeling, make it last forever. As they parted, their eyes held for a long moment.

Putting his arm around her shoulder, Charlie quickly led her through the crowd into the parking lot. It was almost midnight. The streets were quiet and the cool night air sweet and fresh.

He drove down a dirt road to a secluded spot in a small grove of trees and stopped the truck close to an old abandoned shack. He rolled down the window and sat for a moment before shutting off the ignition, leaving the radio on. For a long time, he stared thoughtfully out the windshield, the songs on the radio filling the silence.

"I loved this place." He nodded toward the decaying building. "That's the original farmhouse. My grandparents built it when they got married in 1915. After a few years, Daddy and Aunt Katie were born and the farm was doing ok, so they bought a little more acreage and built the house where we live now. We moved to the farm when Grandpa and Mamie moved into town. I was just a little kid then."

He filled a paper cup with coke spiked with rum pilfered from the bottle Rusty kept to one side in the kitchen cabinet--*for company*. Charlie put his arm around Sarah and they took turns sipping from the cup.

"Sometimes I come out here to watch the sunset. It's nice and peaceful." They kissed and held each other for a while. "I'd like to bring you out here to watch the sunset," he said and kissed her again. Then taking her hand he helped her out of the truck and tossed a tattered quilt into the truck bed. He let down the tailgate and grasping her around the waist lifted her up onto the edge. He leaned against the fender.

"Someday I'm gonna build my house here—under that elm tree. A brick house with a big front porch."

"One that wraps around the side?"

"One that wraps around the side."

"And a white picket fence?"

"Yeah, a white picket fence if that's what you want." He lowered his head, kissed her lightly, then drew back and studied her face in the soft light.

"Sarah, do you like being with me?"

"Yes."

"Do you like me?"

She took a firm hold of his hand, kissed it and rested her cheek against

176

it. "Yes, very much."

She smiled but he wasn't smiling back. He blinked back a tear. "Sarah, I would never want to do anything to hurt you."

The flood of emotion all but drowned her. How could she tell him she didn't want to get hurt again without admitting to her past hurts? She never wanted to be that girl again, always accepting her fate; the girl who was afraid of herself. She'd let go of the part of her that feared trusting him—the part of her that had been hurt and disappointed too often. It felt right relinquishing that trust to him. He was decent; she could see it in his eyes. There had not been much in her life that was decent.

He climbed onto the tailgate and settled next to her. With his arms wrapped around her, he eased her down to the quilt and laying his head in her lap, closed his eyes. She stroked her fingers through his hair and watched the stars flicker through the clouds. "I wish we could stay like this forever."

There were still shadows inside her. Shadows she didn't fully understand, but she understood her feelings for Charlie. She'd given herself willingly to others, others she didn't care about. Why not to him?

She had no answers. But when he wrapped himself more tightly around her and pushed his hips against hers, when he lifted the hem of her skirt, she didn't resist. It seemed right she should give herself to him.

THIRTY-FOUR

Ecclesiastes 11

*[10] Remove sorrow from your heart, and put away pain from your flesh,
because youth and the prime of life are fleeting.*

Seeing that Otis was not in his usual spot in front of the TV, Sarah grabbed the evening newspaper tossed to the floor next to his chair. Shuffling through the pages she found *Dear Abby* and dropped the remaining pages to the floor. The headlines about thousands of college students gathering in Washington to protest U.S. bombing in a far away country held no particular interest for her. Dimly aware of stories on the 6 o'clock news about a war in Vietnam, she sometimes listened with half an ear when President Johnson, looking tired and worried came on television to talk. Charlie's graduation held more interest for her than any of those things that didn't affect her.

She skimmed the advice column—nothing juicy today— just a husband complaining about his wife wearing rollers to bed. Once, years ago, with no one to confide in, she'd written a letter to *Dear Abby* asking Abby why Daddy hated her so much. Of course, she never mailed it. What if Abby printed it in the paper and Daddy figured out she wrote it? She took it directly to the burn pile and buried it in the ashes. EmmaLee was better than Dear Abby—she could trust EmmaLee with her secrets.

With a quick look at the living room clock, she let out a little sigh. Graduation starts at 7 p.m. and there was still much to do before then. Making her way to the bedroom, determined to think only pleasant thoughts, she shoved old troubles to a corner of her mind.

I'm not going to let you spoil this evening, you warped, hateful old man.

The last stitch sewn in the hem of her new dress, she glanced up. Her eyes lingered on the cork board and the dried yellow rose corsage pinned next to a photo of her and Charlie at the prom. Imagining his touch, she briefly skimmed her fingertips along her cheek.

Raising the threaded needle to her lips, she bit through the bright green thread and stepped into the dress.

A fragrant mist of hairspray hovered in the air as she turned her head from side to side, assessing her reflection in the mirror. With the scissors from her sewing basket, she trimmed her straight bangs just below her eyebrows and caught another quick look in the mirror, taking no notice of the cracked glass or her shabby surroundings, and gave herself an approving nod. Convinced there was not a strand out of place she picked up the can of extra hold hairspray and gave her hair another shot. *Just for good measure.*

Sarah admitted to herself she looked *fab* tonight.

Jim Ed pulled up in front of the high school stopping just long enough for Sarah to hop out. She scoured the swarm of graduates in identical caps and gowns assembling outside the building but didn't see Charlie's head towering above the others.

Inside the gym, the high school band tuned their instruments, the sound mixing with a muffled blend of voices traveling through the air. The labyrinth of folding chairs lined up on the floor rapidly filled with families dressed in their Sunday best.

EmmaLee bounced up from a seat near the front, her hand waving about to get Sarah's attention and pointing to a vacant seat beside her. By the time Sarah settled in a seat on the row with the Weeks family, the graduating seniors were moving around at the back of the gym lining up for the processional.

The first notes of Pomp and Circumstance hushed the crowd. As voices trailed off, the senior class filed in looking somewhat grown-up and dignified. Flashbulbs went off to the right and to the left as the graduates took their places in the cordoned off front rows.

Sarah swiveled in her seat to get a better view of Charlie as he marched by. He gave her a quick wink as her eyes met his. Feeling a rush of warmth to her face, she wanted to reach out and touch him, take his hand. Instead, she caressed the ring hanging around her neck.

Faculty, friends and proud families listened politely while the speakers droned through announcements and introductions and speeches with fancy words about going out and changing the world.

She kept her eyes on the back of Charlie's head, her mind wandering to her own dreams. It made her worry, how much she needed him…how much her feeling of self-worth depended on him, how much her plans for her future were wrapped around him.

Eager to have the ceremony finished so she and Charlie could celebrate with their friends, Sarah curled her fingers around the small box in her lap. Delight bubbled inside as she anticipated the look on Charlie's face when he would tug the ribbon free and open the box to find the chrome Zippo lighter engraved with C.T.W. in block letters. She'd lost count of the number of times she'd fondled the lighter, checking to make sure the jeweler had engraved the correct initials before she carefully wrapped the box in blue paper and tied it with a white ribbon.

She shifted in her seat and let out a deep breath when the valedictorian finally said "...in conclusion...," and took her seat.

But it seemed to take forever to get to the end of the alphabetical list of a hundred graduates. Her heart raced when they finally reached "W" and the announcer called Charlie's name. He walked across the stage, covering the distance in giant strides, to shake hands with the principal and receive his diploma.

Watching Rachel wipe her eyes, Sarah realized how fortunate she'd been to inherit this family. Keeping her gaze on Rachel's happy expression, she thought of the day Jim Ed walked across the same stage a few years back. Momma had been filled with emotion, every bit the proud mama. Jim Ed was the only one of Dee's children to stay in school long enough to graduate. Despite a great deal of grumbling, even Otis attended the ceremony. Sarah intended to make Momma proud to see another of her children finish high school...and she'd show Daddy-- she'd show him what a girl could do...a girl can go to college.

She had plans—and Charlie was a part of those plans. She would walk down the aisle to get her diploma and then walk down the aisle on her wedding day. Charlie would build a house under the big elm tree next to his grandparents tumbled down shack, and they'd live happily ever after. She'd go to college and be a teacher like Rachel.

Sarah cuddled next to Charlie as he dragged Main a few times searching for the other kids. A strange, worried look clouded his eyes; he scarcely said anything... and he didn't sing along with Herman's Hermits...he always sang along with that song.

The last few bars of *Mrs. Brown You've Got a Lovely Daughter* faded away behind the announcer's voice. "...and here is this week's number one tune…The Beach Boys with *Help Me, Rhonda."* The unopened blue box rested on the seat next to Sarah when Charlie parked behind the old ice plant. For Sarah, this place held bad memories, memories she chose to leave behind.

Reaching under his seat, Charlie slid a flat bottle of cheap white rum and a Coke from a paper bag and opening both bottles filled a cup. He gulped eagerly, then offered it to Sarah. They silently passed the small cup back and forth in the dark, his hand brushing against hers sending a tingle through her. She watched him, letting the rum work its magic, waiting for him to tell her what was troubling him. Charlie drained the last sip and tossed the empty cup out the window.

For a long time, he just stared at his hands still gripping the steering wheel. Finally, he blurted, "I joined the Marines."

Sarah fought to regain her composure. "Are you crazy? Do you think you're John Wayne or something?" she snapped. "This isn't a movie, there's a real war going on."

"Jeez, you don't have to sound so hateful. I've already been through this with my folks. They're plenty pissed off." He slumped as if the life had gone out of him. "They had plans for me to go to college and study agriculture and then come back here and run the farm. I knew they'd be mad but was hoping to get a little support from you."

She stared at him as if he'd stabbed her. How could he do this and not tell her? "Maybe if…." She bit her tongue. *Not tonight--don't fight with him, not tonight.* She wanted to understand, but her mind was a blur of half-formed thoughts and worries.

"I went down to the recruiting office in Texarkana with Mark Hopkins. They offered us a two-year hitch instead of the usual four-year enlistment. We signed up to leave in September. …the recruiter…."

"Charlie, how could you? Don't I mean anything to you?" Her fingernails dug into her palms. "How can you leave me all alone in this town?" She looked away.

"I can't answer those hard questions."

He paused as if searching for an answer "Look, it's join now or get drafted later. This way I do it on my own terms and use the G.I. Bill to pay for school. Sarah, this is my chance to get out of Arkansas and see what life's all about. If you're smart, your plans will include getting out of this place, too."

She choked back tears. "I thought…why can't we…we could leave

181

together."

Powerless to conceal her hurt and confusion, she reached past the gear shift and turned up the volume on the radio. Mick Jagger mournfully lamented his inability to get satisfaction.

She didn't want Charlie to know how much he'd hurt her. He seemed glad she'd momentarily dropped the subject.

She sought out his eyes in the darkness and fidgeted with the ring hanging from her neck. "But we're still going steady— right?"

"Sunshine, you can keep my ring, but at the end of the summer I'm leaving here, and who knows what will happen after that. We have the summer--beyond that, I can't make any promises." His face remained impassive. "I'll be gone for two years and I don't want you waiting around for me. Who knows, I might not even come back to Tolerance. I want you to go on with your life, without me in your plans."

The words made her stomach clench.

He touched her hair. "You look real nice."

All her pent-up confusion poured out. "Don't you love me?" She took his rough hand and kissed it. "I still love you."

"Don't. Don't love me now. Things are so mixed up. I can't deal with it right now."

"I'm sorry, Charlie, I was being unreasonable."

He paused. "I don't have the right to love anyone right now."

She looked up at him. Her stomach in knots and her eyes filled with tears. She snuggled against his shoulder. "I'm giving you the right. I want to be your girl. I want to wait for you. Lots of soldiers have girls back home. When two people care about each other...well, when two people really care...they make things work... even when it's hard. Don't you think so?"

He gently pushed her away and lit a cigarette. "That kind of talk makes me uneasy."

She tried to think of something to say but exhausted from the conflicting emotions running through her, the words had dried up.

He sucked the smoke deep into his lungs, held the smoke there and tilting his head back, expelled a cloud of tension, then lifting the cigarette back to his mouth, took another drag. Sarah watched silently as the orange glow lit his face casting harsh shadows for a few seconds. She studied the features of the stranger sitting next to her as the fire burned further down towards his fingers. Finally, as the last few embers dangled from the end of the cigarette, he stubbed it out in the ashtray piled high with discarded butts.

Charlie rested his forehead against the steering wheel and muttered, "I need to get home."

"You jerk!" Sarah lashed out at him, pounding his shoulder with the white-ribboned box. "Drop me at the Dixie Dairy." Her words were sharp with bitterness. "I'll catch a ride with Jim Ed." Unable to say more she just shut down, her hand trembling in her lap.

He started the engine and paused. She thought he might say something more, but he didn't. Instead, he drove toward the diner, pretending to concentrate on driving so he didn't have to look at her.

It hurt to see him avoiding her. All she could think of was the look on his face, that awful disappointment when he realized that she could not support his decision and instead had lashed out at him.

He pulled into the parking lot and didn't kill the engine. They stared at one another for a long time. She ignored the squeeze he gave her hand as she reached to open the door and jumped out of the truck. She didn't glance over her shoulder at him.

As he watched Sarah disappear into the diner, Charlie fingered the dented box she'd discarded next to him. He held it for a long moment before ripping off the paper. His eyes clouded as he examined the shiny lighter. His fingers traced the initials carved on the front. He turned it over in his hand blinked through his tears to read the tiny script on the back…the date, and *love, Sarah*. His impulse was to run into the diner and tell her he loved her too. Instead, he slammed the truck into reverse and set out in search of another bottle of rum.

⚬

Bo Hayward fiddled with his keys and studied his shoes, waiting for an answer from Sarah.

She bit her lower lip as her eyes surveyed the meager crowd at the Dixie Dairy. Jim Ed had already headed home before Sarah arrived. She pushed a strand of hair off her forehead and sighed. She had nothing against Bo. She'd known him most of her life; she just wasn't comfortable asking for a favor. Weighing her options, she reluctantly accepted his offer to drive her home.

As she slid into the passenger seat, her foot bumped against a bottle of Ripple wine on the floorboard. Closing the car door, she inhaled the familiar, almost comforting, odor of cigarettes and alcohol. *The smell of home.*

Pulling his car onto the street, Bo headed for the outskirts of town. He fussed with a cigarette and kept checking his rearview mirror, muttering under his breath. "Looks like Billy Ward's truck…been behind us for a few blocks. Someone with him…probably Dub. Those two…up to no good."

Sarah paid no attention to his incoherent rambling. Exhausted from fighting with Charlie she wanted to forget all about it, but she needed to think—try to sort out the many questions trapped inside her head.

Leaving the city limits Bo eased up on the accelerator and cracked the window. The car veered toward the shoulder, the tires hugging the furthest inches of the narrow blacktop as he groped the floorboard retrieving the bottle.

He chugged from it, then wiped the neck on his shirt sleeve and offered it to Sarah. Reluctant, at first she shook her head, but then reached for the bottle. The buzz from the rum she'd shared with Charlie had worn off and feeling numb again held its appeal. She tipped the bottle back and took a sip. It was sweet and bubbly as it went down like cherry cola. She took another mouthful and handed the bottle back, paying little notice of a faint light, barely visible in the passenger's side mirror. It glowed as it slowly encroached on the darkness.

By the time the bottle was near empty; Bo moved his car to the center of the road and pressed hard on the gas pedal.

Sarah now noticed the lights drawing closer. Bo must have seen the headlights in the distance, reflecting in his rearview mirror.

Dust-covered headlights loomed out of the darkness and traveling recklessly close to Bo's car, Billy's truck roared up beside them. Dub rolled down the passenger window and leaning out yelled something Sarah couldn't understand and raised his balled fist into the air. Interior lights were on and she could see the pair inside hollering and laughing. They seemed well on their way to being drunk.

Billy mashed on the gas and pulled directly in front of Bo, forcing him to hit the brake pedal. Bo punched too hard. The rear tires locked and the car fishtailed. He jerked the wheel the wrong way; the car hit the gravel shoulder and went into a spin. He braked to a stop on the road.

"Damn you!" His face flushed with a deep furious fire, Bo thrust his arm out the window and flipped the bird.

Billy pulled off the road into a clearing and Bo, half-drunk, followed despite Sarah's protest. He seemed scared but unwilling to admit it.

Intently staring at the truck, Bo gritted his teeth. "That dick. Dub thinks he can push me around, just because I work for his daddy."

Dub got out of the truck and in three long strides covered the distance from Billy's truck to Bo's door. The corners of his mouth quirked upward into a smirk.

"Hey Bo-Diddley, you got a church key we can use? Me and Billy, we're having a celebration and seems we've misplaced ours."

Sarah's eyes were on Dub now. His cocky strut reminded her of a banty rooster Momma used to have. She remembered how much she hated that rooster and the good dumplings Momma made after wringing his neck.

Dub poked his head through the driver's side window. Looking past Bo, he shot a smug wink toward Sarah. "You look mighty fine tonight, Sarah Jane. Where's Charlie-boy? He's gonna be bummed he's missing this nifty party."

Laughing, Billy moved toward the passenger door. "Hey, Bo you gonna take Sarah Jane over to the passion pit and kipe a feel? Ole Charlie will be madder 'n a wet hen if he finds out. He might just kick your ass for messing with his lady."

"Hell, she's no lady," challenged Dub. "Shit. She's put out for every dick in Hallard County. I did her when she was thirteen."

Watching Dub's face, Sarah tightened with uneasiness.

"Come on; y'all leave her alone," Bo pleaded, glancing at Sarah with a failed reassuring smile.

At that moment, the door behind Sarah opened and someone tugged her arm. Dub's leering face appeared beside her as he crawled into the back seat.

"I'm gonna get what I was promised way back when, bitch, and a little payback for breaking my arm. Do you and your little friend laugh about that when you're sitting on the porch?

She slammed her eyes shut and tried to block his words with the muffled chatter of *Sam the Sham and the Pharaohs* resonating from the truck radio. The wine Sarah had downed so readily, in an eager attempt to take the edge off her nerves tore at her stomach. Gagging, she opened the car door and got out.

"Come on, princess, let's rock and roll." Dub clamped his fingers into the tender flesh of her arm and yanked at her spinning her around, and grabbed her small breasts. She passively did not resist.

Billy sang along with the radio while Dub continued to dance and grope at Sarah. Her knees near buckled and the music from the radio sounded muffled and very far away.

Gagging again, she vomited. Clumps of puke dribbled down the front of her green dress and splattered on Dub's shoes. Dub looked down at his feet, indignant. A sinister look formed in his eyes. In a mad flurry, he rushed at her pawing at the front of her dress. A button flew off.

She squirmed away, trying to get some distance between them.

Bo shoved forward in an attempt to push Dub away, "Let's quit this now. Just get on away from her."

Scarcely registering what she was seeing, Sarah watched Billy take out his hunting knife and hold Bo back.

Dub grabbed a handful of her dress again. It tore as she reeled backward, her foot coming out of one shoe. She went down, buttons popping off.

"Billy, make him let her go," Bo begged.

Billy playfully poked his knife at Bo. "Easy," he warned.

Sarah recovered enough to push herself from the ground, her dress hanging from her shoulders.

Dub dragged her to the back of the pickup, put his knee between her legs and forced her down on to a dirty camouflage tarp. Sarah had the whole picture straight and clear; she was being put to the test to see what she'd do. She tried to pry his fingers off her but didn't dare to claw at him for fear of provoking him to greater anger. *You think you can hurt me? Go ahead and try-I can't be hurt anymore.*

He shoved his hand up her skirt and rubbed hard against her. Climbing on top of her, he breathed whiskey and tobacco into her face, as his fingers fumbled to unzip his jeans. She lacked the strength to shove him off. Gasping for breath, she whimpered for him to stop.

Billy moved toward the back of the truck to get a better view. Bo dropped to his knees and began to heave. He rose to run, but his feet stayed planted in place and his eyes reddened.

Her safe place emerged. Numb and silent, without protest, Sarah mentally retreated to her submissive cocoon. She seemed to look through him as though he were simply not present at all, her eyes fixed on the stars in the clear night sky and waited for it to be over as he rammed against her, forcing himself into her. For a moment it hurt so much she couldn't breathe.

He lasted only several swift seconds and abruptly it was over. He lifted his weight from her and looked at her scornfully. "Nobody hurt you—it's nothing you haven't done before."

As Dub climbed off, Billy hovered waiting for his turn. But before anyone could move, or speak Bo picked up a big stick and lunged toward Billy. He pulled him off of her and slugged him, sending blood pouring from his nose.

As if suddenly startled into reality, a solemn pall came over the group. A surreal quietness settled over them leaving a sense of abject revulsion.

His shirt covered in blood, Billy bounded into the driver's seat and started the truck. Dub clambered into the seat next to him, slamming the door. The truck lurched forward into the darkness.

Sarah watched the taillights fade in the distance and told herself nothing happened.

What took place that night was the kind of thing everyone in a small town knew about but only discussed in whispers.

THIRTY-FIVE

Luke 12

² For there is nothing covered up which shall not be revealed, nor secret that shall not be known.

The only words Bo spoke after they were left alone in the emptiness of the night were "I'm sorry, I'm so sorry." That's all he seemed to be able to say.

After Bo sat on the ground beside Sarah and cradled her in his arms, and after he helped her to his car and cleaned her up and left her at the door of the dark farmhouse, she had tucked the torn green dress into a grocery sack and hidden it at the bottom of the burn pile.

How many secrets had she buried in that funeral pyre over the years?

She knew the secrets of that night were safe with Bo. He would never lie about it; he would just never speak of it. There would be ugly consequences if he were to accuse Mr. Winslow's son of being a rapist. He didn't want to lose his job—custodian at the bank was a good job.

The rich smells of bacon and coffee roused Sarah from her fretful sleep. Freeing herself from the tangled sheets, for a brief moment, she tried to tell herself the hazy memories flooding her mind had all been a surreal dream. But as the fog cleared from her head, it took only a few seconds to sink in. The dull aching hangover and parched raw throat confirmed the certainty. Her last clear recollection was the sweet taste of Ripple. The soreness of her thighs confirmed there had been more. Unable to get her mind wrapped around it all, she laid her throbbing head back on the pillow and tried to remember, not really wanting to expose it to the light of day.

Rolling over, she tugged the quilt up to her chin. Charlie's ring resting on her copy of *Dandelion Wine* glittered in the sunlight. That's when it all came back to her in a flutter of panic. All the losses slowly caught up to her...her plans for a future with Charlie, her newfound confidence, all the things that mattered were no more. All gone! Gingerly she took the ring from the nightstand and held it, watching it sparkle through her teary gaze. *"And the sea moved her back down the shore."* She closed her eyes tightly and remembered a passage she had marked in the book… *"Some people turn sad awfully young. No special reason, it seems, but they seem almost to be born that way. They bruise easier, tire faster, cry quicker, remember longer."*

Before falling into bed last night, she had eased herself into a hot bath trying to soak away the pain and the dirty feeling. She wasn't sure how long she'd lain awake after climbing beneath the rough sheets--the last time she'd looked at the clock on her bedside table it had been past 3 am. Each time she closed her eyes, a memory flickered through a small slit at the edge of her consciousness; the angry look in *his* eyes and the words, *nobody hurt you. It's not anything you haven't done before* seared into her brain. The red marks left by the grasp of his fingers on her arms had now turned to purple bruises forcing her to accept the reality.

She sat up, threw back the covers and dragged herself out of bed. Wincing, she pulled her jeans passed her scabby knee and over her tender thighs. Staring straight into the mirror while twisting her hair into a ponytail, she studied her face. *Good, no visible marks to explain. Of course not, he's too smart for that.*

Unable to unlatch the reality that none of this was her fault, she wondered if she could have done more, should have done more to prevent it. She tried to hang on to the thought *nobody will blame you*--but she knew that wasn't true--they would blame the easy girl.

Whatever happened, whatever caused it--it's over with. *Don't think about it--just don't think about it.*

She finished dressing and went into the kitchen.

Busy at the stove, Momma didn't look up as she came in. "What happened to you this morning? It's late."

"I'm sorry Momma, I overslept."

"Guess you and Charlie must've had a big night of it, with him graduating and all. Heard you come in kinda late." She wiped her hands on her apron. "I'm running behind this morning, too. I forgot the biscuits." She waved her spatula toward a bowl of biscuit dough with a long wooden spoon sticking from it. "Finish those up and crack me some eggs into a bowl."

Robotically scattering flour on the countertop Sarah scraped the biscuit dough into the mound of flour and tried to shake off the flashbacks. Having no luck, she found herself frozen in the midst of reaching for the biscuit cutter, tears welling in her eyes, wondering where it all started to go wrong. No matter how hard she fought it, her brain worked against her. Her mind would not stop going around and around, asking *why?*

What should she do? She needed to talk to someone, but who? Charlie? He would want to hurt Dub and that would cause problems for everyone, especially Charlie. Besides, he'd be gone in a few weeks.

EmmaLee? No, she might tell Charlie—probably would tell Charlie. EmmaLee had a strong sense of right and wrong, but she saw everything in black and white, nothing in shades of gray. *She might blame me for getting myself into the situation and not want to be my friend anymore because I'm shameful and disgusting.*

And then the bare reality of her circumstances cut clean through her again. She couldn't tell anyone about what happened. Who would believe *Sarah the Slut?* Who could blame them if they didn't?

To face the worst parts, would mean she'd have to deal with it. It was easier to fall into her old patterns of denial and hold her shame close.

THIRTY-SIX

Genesis 38

*[24] And it came to pass about three months after, that it was told
Judah, saying, Tamar thy daughter in law hath played the
harlot; and also, behold, she is with child by whoredom. And
Judah said, Bring her forth, and let her be burnt.*

As July threatened to turn to August, the newspaper accounts of the war
were becoming more frequent. Sarah now had reason to take notice.
She sighed, folded the newspaper and placed it on the table.

Glancing out the window she saw Dee hard at work in her vegetable
garden. *Momma always looks happy in that garden.* For a few moments, Sarah
watched Dee gather seed from spent poppies and larkspurs to sow next
spring. She thought back to the day she'd brought home a small container of
seeds from Rachel's flowers and suggested Momma plant them along the
edges of her vegetable patch. *To brighten up the yard.* Momma shook her head
and said, "Flowers belong in flower gardens and vegetables belong in
vegetable gardens. This is a vegetable garden." Only after much urging from
Sarah, did Dee finally threw up her hands and give her reluctant consent—
but watched with silent disapproval as Sarah scattered the seeds. Though Dee
would never admit it, Sarah saw Dee's delight when the red poppies began to
bloom.

Sarah pulled a roll of sprinkled laundry from the icebox. Tuesday was
ironing day. Monday—washing day— everything got sprinkled and rolled up
like a cabbage and left in the icebox overnight. Momma insisted on
everything being ironed— every pair of pants, every shirt, napkin, and
apron—even the flour sack dish towels had to be smoothed under the hot
iron.

Returning to the ironing board in the living room, Sarah eyed the electric fan oscillating on the floor. Anticipating the moment when the gentle back and forth breeze would again swirl around her, she passed the iron back and forth across a starched cotton shirt. The warm air offered insignificant relief as a strand of auburn hair blew against her face.

The grey images of *Guiding Light* flickered across the television screen as she grappled with tangled thoughts about Charlie and about life; thoughts about who she was and who she wanted to be.

Since graduation night, things had been strained with Charlie. Even knowing their time together would be short they had wasted precious minutes. When they were together Charlie seemed moody and distant. Did the bitterness of her obstinate words still linger, or maybe he'd heard rumors? He'd changed; no longer the boy who teased her at her locker and kissed her in the field.

Or was she the one who'd changed— the one creating distance with her hurt feelings and resentment? She'd tried to convince herself what happened after they parted on graduation night had been his fault. His choices— choices made without asking how she felt, had changed both their lives.

Scrolling lines across the television screen drew her attention to the sober voice of a news commentator, "We interrupt this broadcast...." The picture flashed to a live feed of President Johnson in the press room of the White House. Looking gravely into the camera, the President started his speech as he always did...*My fellow Americans.*

...*Cutting into my story for a boring news conference.* She started for the kitchen to get a Coke when the president's words sent a shiver down her spine.

He would be increasing the U.S. military presence in Vietnam and doubling the draft calls to 35,000 a month. She adjusted the volume, fighting the strong desire to rip the knob off the TV. She sat stunned as he continued "...*I do not find it easy to send the flower of our youth, our finest young men, into battle. I have spoken to you today of the divisions and the forces and the battalions and the units, but I know them all, every one. I have seen them in a thousand streets, of a hundred towns, in every state in this union working and laughing and building, and filled with hope and life. I think I know, too, how their mothers weep and how their families sorrow.*"

Sarah clicked off the television and slumped onto the couch. Sitting for a few seconds trying to figure out what she just heard, trying to make sense of it. She burst into tears. *Charlie will be sent to Vietnam.*

Once more her world collapsed. That tiny bit of hope she clung to kept slipping out of her grasp. Worn down, tired and confused, she didn't want to make any decisions, but suddenly there were a lot of important decisions. She was scared. *Charlie will leave for basic training in just a few weeks.*

Something had to be done soon.

Last night, she'd been forced to face the truth—something she hadn't wanted to admit to herself. She'd tried for several weeks to push it to the back of her mind, even looked at herself naked in the mirror to confirm she'd not gained weight. But deep down, reality crept in. And then, just before supper, the smell of food sent her running to the bathroom.

When she returned to the table, Momma examined her with questioning eyes.

After supper, they'd cleared the table in an awkward silence. Placing a stack of dishes on the counter near the sink, Sarah started washing the dishes. Only once, as Sarah handed Momma a plate to dry, their eyes met. Again, Sarah saw the unasked question on her mother's face as she rubbed the plate dry with more force than seemed necessary before putting it in the cupboard.

Later as Sarah pulled her nightgown over her head, Momma tapped on her door, pushed it open and stood in the doorway waiting, watching for a short moment. She came in and sat down on the bed, motioning for Sarah to sit next to her.

Momma closed her eyes and sighed. Sarah turned away. If Momma looked deep enough into her eyes, she would see something troubling her, and she wasn't ready to tell her…not yet. Almost against her will, it seemed her gaze was drawn back to her mother's.

Taking Sarah's hand Dee sighed again and calmly said, "I wish we didn't have to talk about this, but we do. After four babies, I just might recognize the signs."

Sarah didn't want to voice it. Didn't want to admit it even to herself; but not wanting to admit it, didn't change the facts. Momma did it for her. Now that the words were in the air, she was forced to accept the truth.

Drawing strength from the concern in Momma's face and the warmth of the hand holding hers, Sarah admitted the reality to herself and to her mother.

Swallowing back the rest—knowing the whole truth wasn't needed now, she did not let go of the secret she'd held in so tightly.

Only one solution existed in Dee's world. "You have to tell Charlie the truth. He has to marry you."

Sarah wondered which truth she should tell him. What if the baby wasn't his? She pushed the thought out of her mind. Of course, it was his. He would do the right thing and marry her.

He wouldn't go off to the Marines and leave her here to face the scornful glares of the people of Tolerance secretly laughing at her behind fake smiles.

Pebbles beat against the mud flaps as Charlie turned the truck down the road that led to his grandparents abandoned homestead. Sarah had no idea why he showed up at her house after supper and casually suggested they go for a ride. She grew more curious.

When he came to the door, he seemed somehow different, more comfortable, more relaxed than he'd been in weeks. More like Charlie.

As they drove he hadn't said much, but it wasn't an uncomfortable silence. It felt good to be sitting next to him, like old times. She slid a peek his way, wondering what was on his mind.

He pulled around and coasted to a stop near the tumbled down shack, with the rear of the truck facing west.

Looking out over the sun-patched grass, his hands still on the steering wheel, he said, "I want to watch the sunset with you. I promised you a sunset, and I never gave it to you."

"And you never break promises." Her unblinking gaze never left the trees glittering with the light of sunset. She wished a hint of sarcasm hadn't been in her tone.

Charlie wrapped his calloused hand around hers and moved to the truck bed where they sat cross-legged on the tailgate waiting for the sun to disappear below the horizon. They sat surveying each other without exchanging a word.

The trees were unshaken by the breeze. Nearby, inspired by the sunset a bird began to whistle its night song. Amber rays bristled through translucent clouds making them glow sky-blue pink in the opaque sky. They watched for a long time without a word, till the ball of orange light touched the horizon and slowly slipping down, vanished. Sarah heaved a regretful sigh.

Charlie climbed into the bed of the pickup and leaned his back against the cab. "Come here; come sit with me," he said.

She scooted next to him. He wiped his palms on his jeans and rested one arm on her shoulder. They watched lightning bugs gathering just past the trees. The flying yellow lights multiplied, the swarm growing thicker before dispersing.

Charlie broke the silence. "I'm sorry, Sarah. So sorry."

She picked at her fingernails. "What do you mean?"

"I have been such a jerk." He ran his fingers through his hair. "It scared

194

me how much I care about you. I didn't want to rush things. I'm still trying to figure out who I am. That's why I joined the Marines; I needed to get my bearings." He took her hand. "I just thought we could both use a little time apart—a little space. I'm sorry for not understanding how you'd feel."

Sarah pressed her lips together trying not to cry.

As the tears were building in her eyes he shut his own. "Don't turn the tap on- you know I can't take that, not now."

Her voice, almost a whisper, "I thought you didn't care about me anymore."

He was quiet for a minute then looked at her. "I figured I could break it off with you—go our separate ways. I was wrong to think I could just cut you out of my life; I'm too dependent on you. You're a part of me. It took almost losing you for me to understand. I'd be stupid to risk that again."

At that moment she realized he needed her as much as she needed him. *He still wants me.*

Charlie kept his hand on hers. His voice shook. "I'm a bit scared and I've never been more pissed at myself.... we only have a few weeks before I go."

She sat for a time gathering her thoughts, figuring out how what he said changed things. Tears blurred her vision; she couldn't hold them back any longer.

"Come here now." Charlie drew her close, nuzzled her cheek to his chest and held her. With her face buried against his chest, she sobbed. His shoulders lurched. She froze with a surge of anger. She could tell by the way his shoulders moved he was laughing. *He's laughing at me. I'm crying and he's laughing.*

She looked up about to throw an angry question at him. Before she could lash out, she saw his eyes were filled with tears. He had broken out into uncontrolled weeping.

They held on to one another for a long time before they stopped crying.

Sarah sniffed, drew in a shaky breath and swiping her cheeks with her palm, wiped away her tears.

Charlie pulled back and gave her a serious look. "We'll take it one day at a time and see what happens. Then, when I get back, if we still feel the same way, we can maybe build that house right here. We'll sort it out. There's no rush."

"No rush," Sarah repeated, her voice almost inaudible. She quivered and eased his hand off her shoulder, turned to face him, but couldn't meet his eyes. She took a deep breath, closed her eyes and tried to imagine how he would react. Her hand cradled her abdomen. Quickly, before there was time to lose her courage, she blurted, "There's something I need to tell you."

She could feel the silence that followed as Charlie looked at her, waiting for her to finish.

"There's going to be a baby."

He sat looking down at his hands. In the blue darkness of dusk, she struggled to read the web of emotions playing across his face.

Trying to swallow her fears, she fought to gather the courage to tell the whole story; the baby was probably his, but she couldn't ignore another possibility….

He looked up; staring at her, his face like a frightened child, but his voice was decisive. "All right, then—it's going to be okay, we're in this together. You'll see. Don't be afraid. We'll just get married."

"There's something I haven't told you…- it's about graduation night… after the fight we…."

"Sarah, I told you I was wrong—it's my fault, not yours. I didn't mean anything I said that night. I was trying to cover my own feelings of guilt about making that decision without considering you. The thing is, I care about you- I love you." He took her hand, linking their fingers. "I'm serious about this. Whatever happens from now on, we stay together, and we get through this together."

She wanted to marry him, but not like this. He assumed he'd fathered the baby, never questioned her. Of course—that's who he is. *How can I take advantage of his trust? I can't. It's wrong.* "If you'd listen to me instead of telling me what we're going to do or not going to do, you'd understand…."

He didn't let her finish. "It's not just your baby, it's my baby too," he whispered. "It's about life going on; a reason to come home. It's something to hang on to—to be a part of something—something that's a part of me. I want my baby and I want to do right by you. Don't take that from me. Besides, you think Mom and Dad wouldn't be disappointed to think I didn't do the right thing?"

Lifting her chin slightly, she said, "I don't want you to marry me because it is the right thing."

"That's not what I meant— I'm having trouble getting my head wrapped around this—finding the right words."

She closed her eyes and held them shut. When she reopened them minutes had passed, but nothing had changed. She hated herself for not having the courage to be alone, to be confronted by accusing stares and whispers. She hated herself for taking the easy way out, knowing she should tell him everything. She hated herself for refusing to deal with her life and escaping into his.

She looked him in the eye. "You might start to resent me, think I screwed up your life, and I might start to question your feelings. I know you, you'd stick around."

"Sarah, can't you see how much I need this, do this for me. Don't you love me? Don't you want to marry me?"

How can I take that from him? It means so much to him to be the father. It's too hard.
"Yes, I want to marry you."

Pressing a kiss to her hair, his arms tightened around her and he laid his cheek against the top of her head. She rested her cheek against his chest. In the circle of his arms, she felt warm, cherished, and safe as they watched the stars gradually press holes in the gathering darkness above. Propping his head against a folded blanket, Charlie continued to hold her as they lay for hours watching the sky shift and change and listened to a coyote's howl.

Feeling the sun on her closed eyelids she woke at sunrise. Charlie was asleep, his arm still around her shoulders, his uncombed blond curls sticking up, making him look like a little boy. She smiled and smoothed his hair, running her fingers through it.

Well, Charlie Weeks, we slept together. You're my first. So this is what it's like to sleep alongside someone you love; to let down your guard, and wholly trust someone. Touching his cheek she rubbed her thumb across the light sprinkling of soft golden stubble on his chin and the wispy mustache of a teenager on his upper lip. *What are we doing? We're just kids.* She realized his face still belonged to a teenager, but things had change-*we've changed overnight.*

She pressed her temple against his cheek. He opened one eye lazily; lay on his back gazing at the morning sky.

"You could at least say something- anything, Charlie. Do it and get it over with I can take it. I can take almost anything now."

"Okay. Do you know what we're going to do today? We're going to get married. We'll go down to City Hall and get the license this morning, and then we'll get married. But first, we'll have to tell our folks. Are you ready for that?"

Sarah nodded.

"Good," he said, giving her a teasing kiss on the forehead. "You can tell Rusty."

"Oh yeah, right. I'm not an idiot."

"I'm not kidding. Please."

"I'm not telling him, you tell him."

"Tell him why we're getting married? Are you insane? He'll kick my ass into Sunday." Charlie smiled. "Maybe you could tell him after I leave for boot camp."

THIRTY-SEVEN

Genesis 2:24
24 Therefore a man shall leave his father and his mother and hold fast to his wife, and they shall become one flesh.

ou're the only girl I know who would be so excited about this old heap."Rusty winked at Sarah. "I'm glad it makes you happy. We got it for a good price."

"It's perfect." Sarah grabbed Rusty and kissed his cheek. "Thank you!"

The trailer had belonged to a deacon of First Methodist Church, who bought it for his recently deceased mother-in-law. Now, it sat shining in the sun filtering through the leaves of an elm tree in a corner of the yard behind the Weeks' house. A little rundown, a fresh coat of glossy white paint covered the beaten-up exterior.

A wary smile formed on Rachel's lips as her gaze moved from Charlie to Sarah. "I know, you had your heart set on having it at the old homestead, but there's no electricity or water out there."

Rusty grinned. "Mother didn't sleep a wink, worried you'd be disappointed." Sarah could see love flow through his eyes as he looked at Rachel. "I'm surprised at you—thought you'd be out there last night stringing wire so they'd have what they wanted."

Rachel reached out to pop him on the top of his head. He tried to duck, but her palm landed on its target. "Hush. You go on now. If you're finished with your silliness maybe, we can go inside and see what needs to be done."

Glancing toward Rusty for reassurance, with a squeak of the door, she moved aside to let Sarah and Charlie pass.

Stooping, Rusty squeezed through the narrow doorway. "They threw in some of the furniture- I think you can make it presentable. Might take both of you to get things the way you like 'em."

The refrain of Donovan's "Catch the Wind" rose from the stereo. Sarah sat alone staring at the freshly painted walls. *This song is so utterly sad. Why do I listen to it? Somehow it makes me blissful and miserable at the same time.* Running her hands over her stomach, she wondered if anyone noticed her expanding waistline.

With appreciation, Sarah looked around the sparse newly scrubbed-clean room. This would be their home until Charlie graduated boot camp, and perhaps beyond, depending on where the Marines decided to send him.

The buckled linoleum floor had been mopped and every surface from floor to ceiling had been dusted and wiped down before she collapsed onto the newly slip-covered couch and looked around the room. The project for sprucing up the worn kitchen cabinets didn't turn out as she imagined. It bore little resemblance to the photo in the House Beautiful photo that served as the inspiration.

So what? Their life wasn't a magazine picture. The place remained scuffed and worn, yet it served as a source of contentment, they'd created together.

Charlie teased her mercilessly when she suggested they hang wallpaper but finally gave in.

"Okay, Sunshine—you paste, and I'll hang."

She busied herself cutting strips of wallpaper and slapping on the paste.

"Don't use too much water," he cautioned looking over his shoulder as he climbed the stepladder.

Balancing on her tiptoes, she reached up to hand him a sheet of pasted wallpaper.

He pressed it to the wall. "Does that look about right?"

"Down a bit… now up. There. I think that's it."

Smoothing a bubble, he wiped his hands on a rag and stepped down from the ladder to admire his work. He watched the section of paper slowly peel away from the wall and drape itself over his head.

I don't think that works," he said, pulling at the paper. Frowning, he turned to look at her.

Blushing and looking down, a sheepish smile formed on her face. "So, what do you think?" she asked. "…too much water?"

Glue oozed down his face. Unable to resist the temptation, she pasted a scrap of wallpaper to the tip of his nose. "Is this too much?"

Shrieks of laughter erupted from both of them as he caught hold of her and lifted a bucket of water over her head, threatening to soak her.

"Uncle, uncle, I give," she cried, bracing herself for retaliation.

Taking a washcloth, she carefully dabbed the paste from his face.

"Too late." He tickled her until she giggled like a child…then touching her swelling belly he pulled her into his arms and looked deep into her eyes, gently touching her face. His grin made her heart pound faster.

"Don't worry, Sunshine, one day we're going to have the most beautiful house you can imagine."

He always knows how to make me smile. Sarah pensively twisted the tiny gold band on her finger. The images faded from her mind as she realized every passing day made it a little harder to smile. They'd barely had time to start their life together, to get to know one another and soon he would be gone. It was important to ensure the few memories he would take with him would be of the pleasant moments they shared. Despite the circumstances, these few weeks being Charlie's wife had been filled with happiness and the eagerness of youth.

Hers would never be the storybook life she'd imagined, but that didn't mean it couldn't be a good life. That had been driven home on the day she and Charlie went to City Hall to be married. Like any girl, she'd dreamed of her own wedding many times--a white dress, a fancy cake with a tiny bride and groom on top; family and friends.

Momma and Rachel had tried to make it as nice as possible. Momma made a pretty little coconut cake and Rachel decorated it with real flowers to match Sarah's bouquet of white and yellow roses from Rachel's garden. Rachel added a single red rose to the bouquet…to represent love.

Of course, Daddy didn't come--but her brothers came and Momma and Rusty and Rachel. EmmaLee insisted on being the bridesmaid and signing the license as a witness. It had been a wedding maybe not fancy; but a wedding. Charlie loved her, and she loved him.

Realization that it was almost dusk interrupted her reflection. *How did it get to be so late?* Time to get the cornbread and turnip greens fixed before Charlie quit the field and came in.

Supper with him continued to be her favorite part of the day. It was nice…felt natural. The two of them sharing a peaceful meal together. Chatting together. Laughing together. Being together. Other than this, they hardly had any alone time together.

Each morning, Charlie sneaked out of the trailer, trying not to disturb her, before sun-up to have biscuits and gravy or some other heavy meal with his folks before he and Rusty headed for the field.

Just before the sun was straight up in the sky and the two men came in to sit down at the kitchen table for dinner and a little rest, Sarah would join Rachel in her kitchen to get dinner on the table. When Sarah walked through the back door, Rachel would always say, "Our boys will be coming in soon, and they'll be hungry." It seemed as if the sanctity of carrying out the ritual served as a comfortable distraction; would be enough to prevent the eventuality of Charlie's departure.

Sarah would set the table, pour milk and dish up hot food. Everything would be ready and waiting when the men came in smelling of fresh sweat, engine oil, and newly turned earth. They'd go straight to the sink, grab the Lava soap and then plop into their chairs at the kitchen table.

Every day, after they were seated, Rusty would say the same blessing, "Thank you, Jesus, for everything that you have blessed us with. Thank you for this food to nourish our bodies. And thank you for making Sarah a part of our family and most of all thank you for our grandbaby. Amen."

As soon as the men left for the fields again, ready to stay until little daylight remained. Rachel would fill containers with fried chicken, potatoes, and green beans. She'd always cook enough at the noon meal to have plenty of leftovers for supper. *"No need to heat up the stove again and make the house unbearably hot."*

Sarah would carry the dishes to the sink and begin running a pan of dishwater. Rachel would make shooing motions with her hands. "Skedaddle."

Ignoring her, Sarah would finish washing the china.

After Rachel dried the last plate and put it in the cabinet, she would hand Sarah containers holding half of the left-overs and ask, "Now, do you have everything for supper?"

It all seemed natural.

The sound of work boots stomping on the front steps interrupted her recollections. She smoothed her hair and sprang to the door to meet Charlie.

He greeted her with a sweaty embrace and a peck on the lips. "And how was your day Sunshine? Something smells good in here. I hope that's my supper."

"It's ready. Go wash up. I'll put on some music." She turned up the volume on the radio. The lyrics to *Eve of Destruction* spilled from the radio and she quickly clicked it off, putting on an album instead.

Charlie slipped into the seat across from her and turned his attention to buttering a slab of cornbread. Not releasing the fork until his plate was empty; he polished off his supper in record time. Then, nervously, he pushed his fork at a single green pea rolling around on his empty dinner plate.

For the longest time Sarah didn't say anything, simply watched his face and tried to calm the butterflies crowding her stomach.

Eventually looking up, he squared his shoulders, but still didn't speak. Running his fingers through his hair he broke the silence.

"I talked to the Marine recruiter about a deferment, like you asked me to." He ran his fingers through his hair again. "He said there's not much chance because of some new law Johnson just made about being able to draft married men. Since I volunteered instead of being drafted, well, there's not much chance, not even with the baby coming. I'm really sorry Sunshine." His voice trailed off.

"Then, that's that," she said unblinkingly. Defeated, she scraped her chair back from the table and began to clear away the dinner plates.

On September 26, 1965, Charlie kissed Sarah goodbye and got on a bus to Dallas, where the Marine Corps put him and his fellow recruits in an old flea-bag hotel. The next morning, they were bused to the airport, boarded a plane, and sometime after dark arrived at the U.S. Marine Corps Recruit Depot, San Diego, California to join other boys being sucked into the thresher to be beat-up and spit-out as fresh young killing machines.

Vicki Olsen

THIRTY-EIGHT

1 Samuel 17
[33] Saul replied, "You are not able to go out against this Philistine and fight him; you are only a young man, and he has been a warrior from his youth."

Sarah dropped her schoolbooks onto the kitchen table next to a stack of paperbacks and poured a glass of milk. Charlie had insisted Sarah return to school for her junior year. Now that he'd gone, it was good to have something to keep her busy. Between school work and her cache of paperbacks from Hazel's, her mind stayed occupied.

Her waistline had started to disappear. Soon, there would be rumors and whispers and people counting on their fingers to determine how many months had passed since her wedding day. Being the subject of gossip was nothing new to her and at least Charlie could avoid the scorn brought on by marriage to the town tramp.

Rachel had talked with the high school principal and made arrangements to tutor Sarah once her little belly became so large as to shame herself and horrify the chaste. She would return to school after the baby was born in February.

A light tap sounded on the trailer door. Rachel opened the door a crack and came in.

"Sarah, honey, I have something that might cheer you." Reaching into her pocket she pulled out a small white envelope edged in pale blue. "It's from our boy— it's to both of us. I thought we could open it together." There was a sadness Sarah had never seen in Rachel.

As Rachel unfolded the paper, Sarah recognized the gold Marine emblem. The same pale blue as the envelope edged the paper. At the bottom of the page a drawing of two Marines, wearing backpacks and helmets, holding weapons in firing position left no room for doubt about the mission of the Corps.

Sun. Oct. 2, 1965

Dear Sarah and Mom,- oh, and you too, Rusty-

I'm here. The only thing I saw of San Diego was the pimples on the neck of the guy sitting in front of me on the bus. We got in at 9:00 Monday night and they kept us up until 2 A.M. issuing toilet kits and uniforms and basically jacking us around.

My toilet kit had everything, but a comb. No comb, because at the first stop, a barbershop, it took a barber about five seconds to shave me bald as a boiled egg and send me off to the next building of horrors.

We were run into a room with a bunch of tables with boxes and rolls of tape. We had to mail home all of our personal items. All I got to keep was my cigarette lighter and my Bible. If you received my box, hope you weren't too disappointed to get a box of dirty clothes instead of a gift for you.

The drill instructors screamed at us for about a minute telling us we had thirty seconds to take off all our clothes, put them in the box and seal it up. "Thirty seconds! Go!" You probably noticed the shirt I sent back had half the buttons missing and the shoes got yanked off without untying laces. Most of us made it in the time, but a few didn't. They got dragged into the hall and we could hear the DI's hollering and calling them names.

In the hassle, I misplaced some of my addresses, so if you will send me Stevie's address at college, I will be very thankful. Oh, and I was really glad they let us keep our lighters. Sarah, I think of you every time I use it.

The Marine Corps wastes no time letting you know who's running things. You have to start and end every sentence with "Sir". Like "Sir, yes, sir." To tell the truth, much of that first night is a blur. Everything happened so fast, drill instructors yelling at us and herding us from place to place like a bunch of sheep.

I would like to turn my head and just look around, but it is impossible. They want you to be robots with your eyes fixed to the front at all times. The DI's are really fascinating monsters. They each have their own individual act they put on for us. They even have a different voice for yelling at us than their normal voice. Kinda like the preaching voice, the Baptist preacher uses back home. It is going to be a long haul for the next 13 weeks.

After we finish here, we go to 4 weeks ITR. I suppose I will be home around the middle of January before going to my next training.

When you write please include any items on world affairs you think might be of interest to me. We have not been allowed to buy a paper yet and I have no idea what's going on. Tell me what's going on back home. But don't send any packages or anything but letters. If a private gets a box of cookies, he has to sit down and eat everything, including the postage stamps.

Say "hello" to everyone for me. I live only for bedtime and mail call. Please write often. Give the old man a hug for me.

Love,
Charlie

Sun. Feb. 6, 1966

Dearest Sunshine,

As you can see, I made it safely back to Camp LeJeune. It sure was good to be home with you and the folks and to see the gang again. You looked so good to me and I can hardly wait to meet that baby growing inside you. I sure hate it, I can't be there with you when it is born. I think it is weird, they will let you come home for a death in the family, but not to be there for your own baby being born. There is something wrong with the whole damned system.

I like the names you picked for the baby. I think it is good you want to honor your brother. I know how much you loved him and how much you miss him. So, I agree, Kenny if it's a boy and Keni if it's a girl.

I feel like we got some good honest talking done during our last few days together and I want you to know, I have faith providence has guided us to our proper place together. So I want you to approach the future with peace of mind. No way do I feel trapped into our marriage.

Monday, on the bus ride to Little Rock to catch my plane back here to North Carolina, all I could do was think about you and all the things we have done together and all the things you mean to me and how I have hurt you and all of a sudden (around Arkadelphia) I realized something very astounding- I love you. I mean, really love you. The old empty feeling down in the stomach hit me, that feeling something is wrong. I realized it's because I'm not with you. You have become simply a part of me and I feel un-whole when you're not here.

What do you think about this shit? It's got me turned around and I am really feeling depressed. I can't tell you how hard this leave has been on me. When I was with you everything was right, sort of mellow in a way. Now I feel lost and losing ground every day.

Sarah, I love you. I <u>really</u> love you. What else is there to say?

Charlie

Wed. April 13, 1966

Good Day Sunshine,

I received your letter and it is too much. That card you sent really put a warm feeling in me I haven't had for a while. The pictures of the baby are really great. They did wonders for my morale and made me very melancholy at the same time. I miss you both so much. I cannot believe she will be 2 months old tomorrow. Sorry, I could not be there when she was born, but what a wonderful Valentine she turned out to be. I sure am glad she has your red hair.

Tell her to stop growing so fast. I can't believe how quickly my time at home passed. I don't think I will be home again until just before I ship out for Vietnam. Then we'll get 3 weeks leave.

Our platoon commander told us today that we could receive packages from home. If you and Mom would send me some homemade cookies, I really wouldn't mind a bit. Don't if it is too much trouble (chocolate chip).

I've got to go. My rifle, (I hate that thing with a passion. I don't think most of these privates fully realize what its sole purpose is. To kill a man.) needs cleaning.

Write soon and send more pictures. I'm thinking about you at day and dreaming about you at night, and that's no lie.

> *I Love You,*
> *Charlie*

Sun. May 29, 1966

Sunshine,

Well, I've been in the Nam for over 24 hours, and it's been raining the whole time. I'm at a place called Chu Lai Airfield. Check the map we bought when I was at home and look for a giant mud puddle. Right in the middle of it you should find Chu Lai. What a dirty, stinking place this is, the whole country smells like piss.

I've been assigned to the 5th Marines, 1st Bn. They call it the 1/5. I don't have an address yet but I hope you will write every day and send me a bunch of letters when I finally give you a place to send them.

Guess what? I've been to Hawaii. Don't be too jealous. We were there for a whole 45 minutes. But at least I can say I've been there.

Tomorrow, I start orientation and then in 4 days, I'm just like the rest of them. There is no need to worry as I'm in the rear and because of the rain the helicopters can't get us into the area where my unit is. It could be one day or one week before I get to my unit. I'm in no hurry 'cause the NVA is hitting them pretty hard right now. This a.m. a chopper came in with medivacs and I keep hearing about 7 Marines being killed by a bomb the Cong hid in a drinking hole. Don't worry; I'll be careful where I drink.

I'm sharing a hooch with 6 other Marines. It's fixed up nice. Right now I'm sleeping on a cot with a roof over my head and a wooden floor, so I'm doing all right. I even have a light by my rack, so I can write and read in bed...

The airfield is right beside my hut and those Phantoms and Skyhawks fly out of here 24 hours a day one every minute or so.

Please write. Thoughts of you and the folks back home keep me going. You are my only Sunshine in this shithole. You and Keni. I look at the picture of the 3 of us constantly.

Love,

C.

PS. tell Mom and Dad I'm okay. I don't have time to write them today.

Thurs. June 2, 1966

Dear Sunshine,

Well, it's another rainy day in Vietnam. When they say it's been known to rain 40 days and nights you can believe it. As you can see from the envelope, I now have an address.

Do you think you could send me a CARE package? I sure miss Mom's chocolate chip cookies, (hint) and any other snacks you can fit in a small box. Some paperback books would be great too- you know what kind I like. Don't laugh but I would really like to have some Incredible Hulk funny books. I'm serious. OK?

Are you and EmmaLee glad school will be out soon? Hope your grades are good. Make honor roll or I'll make you suffer when I get back. I

Love You,

Charlie

P.S. I just don't want you getting too worried. Actually, I am pretty safe here.

Wed. June 29, 1966

My Only Sunshine in this God-forsaken-place.

Well, how's everything been back in the home front? Everything is really going good with me and I hope it's likewise for you. This letter is gonna be short because the light is getting dim fast.

Thanks for the new pictures of the baby- she looks more like you every day- lucky girl. She is beautiful. Can't believe how much hair she has.

I'm finally getting settled in with my unit. We're, pretty close to the DMZ but behind the lines and out of range.

It's pretty safe here so don't worry about me. The only danger I have here is incoming artillery every now and then, and we have pretty good trenches for that. I live in a tent with six other guys; they have bunkers dug to sleep in, so we don't have to worry about incoming at night.

I received the package you sent me. It was great. The food is all gone, but I'm still reading the books. Tell Mom the cookies weren't too smashed up and I will write her tomorrow.

No mail has come in since the 26th, but I'm hoping there will be some today. You don't know how much it means to me that you write every day.

Today, me and my buddy "Trigger" (he's the guy from Pittsburgh I told you about) had to fill sandbags and build a bunker where a mortar round came in last night. No big worry. It was at least 300 yards away.

He calls me "Johnny"— as in Reb, on account of we call the VC "Charlie." No lie. It's short for Victor Charlie (VC). We played cards last night, and I won $20 off him.

I wish you could see me because ever since I left stateside I've been growing a mustache. You might like it, and Mom would hate it. It's kinda reddish and the guys make fun of it. I would shave, but don't want to give them the satisfaction.

We put up mosquito nets over our cots today - one day too late. We had an invasion of bugs last night. I saw the biggest bug I've ever seen crawling up the side of the tent, the bugs are big over here - you wouldn't like that too much...

Well, can't think of much more to say except take care and don't worry.

Love,
C.

P.S. I have been reading the Bible a lot lately and there are some words to live by in that Book, no matter what your religion.

Sat. July 30, 1966

Dear Sunshine,

Well... No mail came at all today - the second day in a row without any mail. I sure hope the mail comes tomorrow - I need to hear from you to perk me up. Knowing you write every day helps-but just makes it more frustrating when I'm not getting those letters. Send more pictures.

Right now, we are restricted to the tents because we are supposed to go out on an operation. I don't know how often you get to write on an operation, but I'll write as much as possible.

Sun.

Got interrupted last night. There really is a war going on over here. We had an attack on another part of the base. You know how they say war is not like the movies show it. Well, they're wrong. This was exactly like the movies. A Huey was landing and bounced then flipped upside down right behind our tent. One of the guys was thrown out of the helicopter. It was so dark outside it took us a while to find him. He wasn't breathing, but Doc did mouth-to-mouth and got him breathing again. They took him to the field hospital, but we haven't heard a report on him. Needless to say, we were all a little shook up.

I've enclosed a picture my squad leader took for me so you could see my mustache. He said you should tell me to shave it off. In the background is the bunker me and Trigger built. (Oh, to answer your question—we don't call him "Trigger" because he looks like Roy Rogers horse—it's because he likes to keep his finger on the trigger.)

By the time you receive this letter, we will probably be in the bush. Remember, I can't always write when I'm out there. So, don't worry if you don't hear from me for a couple of days.

Have you been receiving the allotments? I hope so.

Well, got to go. Can't think of much more to say for now. Take care, and please send a package. OK?

Love,

C.

Sun. Aug 21, 1966

Dear Sarah,

My company just came back from a 21-day operation and we got hit pretty bad.

For the last 9 days, we've been sitting on the top of a hill. We hadn't been in any combat at all. This morning we moved in on a village looking for Viet Cong. I think we found maybe one.

Then at 0900, all of a sudden, we realized we were targets. The NVA mortared holy hell out of us. Actually, I wasn't scared; but it kind of gets on your nerves when you don't know where the next round will hit.

After it was all over, we headed into base camp for our three-day stand down. I got some clean utilities and I finally got to take a good hot shower. I just got back and feel a little better. Boy, did I stink. I must have washed a half inch of mud off of me. The monsoons are coming in and we are living in mud as usual. The shower is about a mile away, and we all go down in a group on a little vehicle called a mule... when I get back home, I want to get one of those mules for the farm.

Going to the bathroom is still a major undertaking - especially at night - because we only have one now, and it's about 100 yards away.

There's not a mess hall so we've been eating C's for a while. Please don't worry too much about me, as if you won't. I *promise to take care of myself. I am counting the days (274) to when I will be with you and that beautiful baby girl again. What a beauty she is- just like her momma. Send more pictures. I carry that last picture you sent- the one of you and Keni with me. Thoughts of home keep me going.*

Thurs. Sept 29, 1966

Dear Sarah,

We got mail three times last week, and I got a whole mess of letters from you. I got a letter from EmmaLee and one from Aunt Rebecca. It's a real boost.

Guess what? I got promoted again...or at least they say the warrant is in for Corporal. If it's the truth, it means your allotment should go up soon. It is a meritorious promotion. I was a Lance Corporal for less than 3 months. Now you can be Mrs. Corporal Charles Weeks...ain't that just grand?

In about two more months I'll be eligible for R&R. Where do you think I should go? Hong Kong, Bangkok, Australia, or Oki? I think that if I do go on R&R, I'll just lie in a hot bath for a couple of days. Smitty got back from Bangkok and he had the clap. They pumped him full of penicillin and then he discovered he was allergic to penicillin, so he got pretty sick. But he said it was all worth it and is ready for R&R again. Don't worry. I promise I won't get the clap- I hear the women are ugly. Ha Ha.

Can you believe it—by the time I go on R&R I'll be 20—not a teenager anymore.

I love you,
Charlie aka Johnny

Fri. Oct 21, 1966

Today is the worst day of my entire, short life. Once again we were in contact with Charlie, and once again we suffered losses. This time it was Trigger, my best friend in this shithole. I'm having trouble keeping my face on straight. You know, I can still feel his presence as I write this letter and hope that I am able to survive and leave this far behind me.

This morning, we were talking about how we were only two years different in age and how we both got married just before coming to this place. He was excited about going on R&R in 3 weeks to meet his wife in Hawaii.

We moved out and surrounded a village that had been taken out by the Cong. We went in on a search and destroy. We were satisfied all was clear when Trig thought he heard a sound in a bunker. We see a mother who died with her baby in her arms. The baby was trying to nurse on his dead mother. Trig started toward the baby and a couple of the guys told him to watch out- the dead body might be booby-trapped. He said "What the hell, we can't leave that baby here," and he picks it up. Then we see a little girl, maybe 5 or 6 hiding behind the dead woman. Her legs had both been shattered and were crawling with maggots, but it looked like someone had been feeding her, trying to keep her alive-maybe the mother before she died. When we got her back to camp the Doc said the maggots were keeping her legs "clean" and keeping her alive by eating the rotting skin and helping slow down the infection. Our interpreter tried to talk to her, but she was terrified. He said her name was "Tune," at least that's what it sounded like.

Anyway, Trig, he hands the baby to me and picks up the little girl and gives her to Candyman. We start back toward camp to get some medical help and get a chopper to take the kids to the Catholic mission.

As soon as Trig takes a step forward to check a compass bearing we hear a click. He turned around and looked me in the eye with a strange smile like the fear of dying suddenly left him. I started toward him and he yelled, "No! Get the kids back," and then he steps off the mine...and his body goes flying into the air. Strange how short a time a half of a second is--the difference between life and death. We carried him back...all of us pretending he was gonna make it...but we knew better. This is an awful place to die - halfway around the world from home.... If there is a place called Hell this surely must be it. How come young men with so much to live for have to die? I hope I can find peace in my daily Bible reading. I hope you can do the same. And I hope those kids survive...what if that was Keni?

I probably should tear this up instead of sending it to you....

C.W.

THIRTY-NINE

1 Corinthians 15:55
[55]O death, where is thy sting? O grave, where is thy victory?

Sarah didn't respond to Rachel. She fixed her attention on the government car approaching the house.

Clouds covered the sun, casting shadows on freshly sprouted seedlings in the flower bed. Rachel stopped pulling weeds. She shaded her brow with her hand and squinted at the darkening sky. She repeated, "Looks like some angry clouds gathering over yonder. Maybe we should get Keni inside."

The car stopped. Two uniformed men climbed out.

Sarah stared into the expressionless faces as the men stepped towards her. The sky pressed down. In an effort to suffocate her, the air refused to pass through her lungs. Her hand grabbed at her throat

Lips moved, words crashed against her eardrums, but she heard only the sound of air rushing past.

Landmine...return body...personal effects...counselor.

She had no concept of how much time passed before the two soldiers returned to the car and drove away. She had no recollection of moving to the living room, nor of Rusty joining her and Rachael there. Unreal. None of it real.

Rachel hovered nearby, tears staining her cheeks.

Rusty leaned against her.

Sarah saw, clutched in her own hand, a government document—crumpled. Someone, she didn't remember who, had pressed it into her hand and closed her fingers around the paper.

From beyond the screen door, a bird sang three notes in monotonous repetition; a meaningless song. Silence followed, and a moment later came the sound of a car passing along the road and moving away. Twice more invisible cars passed and died away.

&

Black dress--Government-issued-folded-triangle flag--everything a widow needs.

"She's resting, poor child." Dee's voice, soft and muffled seeped from the next room. Sarah glanced at her sleeping baby. Dee had adopted the role of gatekeeper, to ward off well-intentioned, but unwanted visitors and the condolences they carried with them.

It was EmmaLee's voice Sarah heard in quite reply.

She momentarily interrupted her search for Charlie's high school ring. EmmaLee, she wanted to see EmmaLee, but not now. She was not yet ready to deal with the flood of sympathy sure to spill over her. She shrugged. Later. She'd see EmmaLee later.

In the bedroom—now hers alone, Sarah returned to rummaging through her jewelry box. Her hand paused on a discolored white box. She removed the lid, fingered the delicate cross inside and taking it out, fastened the chain around her neck. A faint smile briefly touched her lips and vanished.

The window shade allowed the late afternoon sun to lay a ribbon of fading light onto the floor. The peaceful breathing of her sleeping baby harmonized with a mockingbird outside the open window tuning up for his evening song. Sarah put a Beatles album on the turntable and turned the volume down very low. "Good Day Sunshine."

The melancholy reminder of Charlie and their lost future made her grieve more strongly. She reached for a small box on the table next to her. The box of personal effects the Marine Corps had returned to her contained only Charlie's lighter, his wedding ring and his Bible with a photo of Sarah and Keni tucked inside. She ran her thumb across the letters C.T.W. cut into the Zippo lighter.

Memories of that loathsome graduation night swirled through her head. The night when joy and anticipation so quickly turned to revulsion. She watched Keni sleep and wondered if she alone questioned the baby's brown eyes. She was sure Charlie had made a connection before leaving for Vietnam. But she also knew Charlie loved her and the baby, and if he had suspicions, he never mentioned them.

The music mixed with the sound of her baby's breath. Everything ethereal; detached— the Beatles, the sleeping baby, the bird, the sound of hushed voices, and the smell of frying bacon coming from the kitchen, the feel of the

218

lighter in her hand, and the way the light fell on the floor. All surrounding her without any link to how she felt.

Wiping tears from the chrome lighter, she placed it back into the box. She paused, took Charlie's Bible from the box, ran her fingers across the leather cover and turned to the page marked by Keni's photograph. *John 8:3-11*. She wondered if this was just a random placement, or if it marked a significant passage, perhaps the last Charlie read.

> *3 And the scribes and Pharisees brought unto him a woman taken in adultery; and when they had set her in the midst,4 They say unto him, Master, this woman was taken in adultery, in the very act.*
>
> *5 Now Moses in the law commanded us, that such should be stoned: but what sayest thou? 6 This they said, tempting him, that they might have cause to accuse him. But Jesus stooped down, and with his finger wrote on the ground, as though he heard them not.*
>
> *7 So when they continued asking him, he lifted up himself, and said unto them, He that is without sin among you, let him first cast a stone at her.8 And again he stooped down, and wrote on the ground.*
>
> *9 And they which heard it, being convicted by their own conscience, went out one by one, beginning at the eldest, even unto the last: and Jesus was left alone, and the woman standing in the midst.*
>
> *10 When Jesus had lifted up himself, and saw none but the woman, he said unto her, Woman, where are those thine accusers? hath no man condemned thee?*
>
> *11 She said, No man, Lord. And Jesus said unto her, Neither do I condemn thee: go, and sin no more.*

Now and then the mockingbird sang, and then stopped as though it waited for a reply.

The ribbon of sunlight had disappeared from the floor.

Closing the Bible, she hugged it to her chest as if to let the words bathe her body like salve on a wound. She sat silently with her eyes closed for a full minute, clinging to the comfort of the scripture.

Again, the bird sang.

She rose, feeling the need to escape the confines of the room.

Neither Dee nor EmmaLee said a word or tried to stop her as she walked barefoot from the house, across the smooth pebbles, into the corral where Belle waited to be bedded down.

Vicki Olsen

Sunset had given way to twilight and a small cloud formed over the house. Sarah's eyes rolled skyward, she turned her face up to catch the raindrops that had begun to fall. She threw the blanket and saddle across Belles back, inserted her bare toes in the stirrup and swung into the saddle. She dug her heels into Belle's ribs. The mare bolted through the yard with Sarah ducking under branches, she thundered across the pasture, Sarah's loose hair flying in the wind; drops of rain beating against her face, the words echoing in her ears, "Go and sin no more."

FORTY

Matthew 6:14-15
¹⁴ For if you will forgive men their offences, your heavenly Father will also forgive you. ¹⁵ But if you will not forgive men, neither will your Father forgive you your offences.

Rachel handed the phone to Sarah. The tired voice on the other end of the line sounded weak and troubled. She barely recognized Momma.

"It's about your daddy, honey. I come in--I'd done a little work out in the garden--and there he was all sprawled out on the kitchen floor." Dee paused. Sarah braced herself for the inevitable. "It took all their might for Jim Ed and Junior to get him onto the bed. The doctor come out, said there weren't nothing to be done for him. Said we should just keep him comfortable." The words trailed off and then Sarah heard Jim Ed on the line.

"Sarah Jane, I hate to ask."

The muscles in Sarah's face tightened.

"Momma needs you here…to help with Daddy. The way she's going…you know how demanding he is—he hasn't changed. She's gonna be sick too if she doesn't get some rest. Me and Junior, we're no use in a sick-room, and she won't leave Daddy's side for fear he might need something."

Sarah said very little when agreeing to Jim Ed's request. Her daddy's long relationship with alcohol and cigarettes had finally taken its toll, and she would return to her parent's home to become their daughter once again.

Early the next morning Jim Ed parked his pickup next to Rachel's sweet peas and put Sarah's suitcase in the bed of the truck. Holding Keni on her lap, Sarah turned to take another look at the little trailer where she had been Charlie's wife…and then his widow.

Pulling out of the driveway, the two cruised south along the state highway to the junction with the county road. The approach had changed as prosperity had come to the outskirts of the small town, but the disparity in the surface became pronounced as they turned off the highway. The road narrowed as they bumped along the two-lane pot-holed asphalt. The landscape transformed as they passed farm after farm with row after neat, little row of white-topped structures of asbestos-roofed chicken coops popping up from the ground.

A knot formed in the pit of Sarah's stomach as they drove past the metal sign hanging from the fence enclosing Jones Farm. The white chicken encircled by stenciled letters announced her return to a life she thought she left behind the day she married Charlie, three years earlier.

She climbed out of the truck and was greeted by a gangly spotted dog with hound-like flapping ears and the long snout of a hunting dog. Junior followed close behind. The dog circled around her, sniffing at her legs and hands. Deciding that he liked what he smelled, he padded back to join a long-haired bird dog dozing under a tree. The bird dog unenthusiastically lifted his head, sniffed at the air disdainfully and continued his nap.

As Junior started to unload Sarah's things, she wondered how long it would be before she would be able to load them back up again.

At the familiar creak of the spring on the screen door, the doubt and dismay felt only moments earlier were replaced by reassurance at the sight of Cotton coming onto the porch. "Mighty good to have you back home, Miss Sarah Jane," he said and held the door open for her.

Dee pushed herself up from the kitchen table with a sigh and greeted her daughter with tired eyes and an anxious smile. Taking the baby in one arm, she wearily hugged Sarah with the other. Kissing Keni's cheek, she drawled, "Gimme some sugar, baby." The toddler giggled as Dee nuzzled her neck. "I sure am proud to have you home, Sarah Jane. I've missed seeing you and the baby. She's growing too fast I would hardly recognize her if she wasn't the spitting image of you when you was her age except for them big brown eyes."

Sarah squeezed her mother's hand. "I know, Momma, I'm sorry we didn't come around to visit."

Inside the house little had changed. Sarah's head filled with bittersweet memories. The windows clumsily propped open with sticks of wood let in a breeze, warm and heavy with the pong of the chicken yard. She had almost forgotten that unmistakable "smell of money."

Jim Ed had taken her old room but had done nothing to make it his own—it was still her room as she left it. Now, he moved his things back to his old room--the one he had shared with Junior, giving Sarah her room again.

Sarah put Keni down for a nap on the bed covered with a pink spread—the smell of mothballs still clinging to it. How like Momma to have saved it all these years, pulling it out of the cedar chest for her return home. Strange how the familiar smells made her feel at home. She smiled to herself—*mothballs and chicken shit. Add collard greens and I'll know I'm home.*

Turning the knob on the box fan in the window to let the warm breeze blow across Keni's unmanageable red curls, she remembered how she had once suggested they buy a window air conditioner. Jim Ed said something about the wiring in the old house and the subject had been dropped.

Sarah sat on the bed, shuffling through a stack of Little Golden Books Dee had placed on the table. She brushed a wayward tendril from the baby's forehead and began to read *The Little Red Hen*. Before the cat refused to take the wheat to the mill, Keni's eyes had drifted shut, her breathing slowed, and her thumb crept slowly into her mouth.

Sarah left the sleeping child and joined Dee who'd retreated to the relative cool of the porch to escape the unyielding heat of the kitchen. Junior and Jim Ed had returned to the field, but Cotton had stayed to help Dee move some heavy boxes from the barn.

Sarah slid onto the porch swing beside her momma. The rusty chain squeaked as they rocked back and forth; the paint on the floor beneath the swing worn away by the many feet that had rested there. Dee squeezed a lemon wedge over her iced tea, dropped it into her glass and poked at it with her finger.

The rattle of the ice cubes in Dee's glass as she sipped her tea was the only sound in the long awkward silence as both women avoided the subject of impending death

Cotton broke the silence by coming around the side of the barn with two boxes of canning jars stacked on top of one another. Resting his foot on the lower step, he balanced the boxes on his knee. "Where do you want these, Miss Dee?"

Before she could answer, a weak voice from inside the house called, "Dee. Dee where you at?" and broke into a deep fluid filled, wheezing cough.

"Guess I'd better go check on yore daddy," Dee said, looking sadly at Sarah.

Cotton followed her into the house and returned without the boxes.

"Can you sit and talk a minute?" Sarah asked.

He nodded. "I reckon I can sit a spell." Roosting on the porch rail, he waited for Sarah to speak. Pulling a match from a box, he flicked the head with his thumbnail, lit a cigarette and flipped the match into the yard. He sucked the smoke into his lungs and choked it out in a puff of white vapor wafting from his mouth and spiraling upward into the air. His hack drowned out the sound of the muffled tight bark from inside the house.

"I know it ain't easy on you being here, but your momma sure is grateful for your help."

"I haven't been to see Daddy yet. I don't know what to say. I was never too close with him...he never had much use for girls.... He did a lot of hurtful things to me when I was growing up." Sarah's throat burned as she tried to hold back the welling tears. "I blame him for a lot of my troubles, but I want to forgive him." She twisted the wedding ring on her right hand. "Charlie tried to help me find comfort in the Bible, but I'm still too angry." Sarah gathered her thick hair and twisted it off her neck, into a rubber band. "I'm only here because Momma needs me...not for him."

Cotton pulled up the rocking chair opposite her and glided into an easy rhythm. "Every now and then things you don't want just might be the things you need most." He looked straight into her eyes. "Sometimes forgiving folks ain't about them deserving forgiveness...it's about them needing it, and even more because *you* need it. Might be hard to do, but it's powerful hard to move on if you don't."

Sarah rubbed at an invisible spot on her cheek. "You're right, it's something I should do; need to do...want to do. But he won't even allow he's done anything wrong."

"Yep, that's your daddy; he could make a preacher cuss! But forgiving don't mean forgetting... just means you chose happiness over hurt. Truth told, happiness don't mean you ain't got troubles...just means being able to smile, even if you don't feel like it. Smiling don't always mean you're happy neither; it can just mean you're strong."

"But it's hard to be strong; death seems to hang around me; Kenny, Charlie, and now Daddy."

Pulling off his hat and scrubbing one hand through his hair, Cotton stared a few minutes at the short shadows on the ground. "Truth is, death ain't nothing more than change and change's just a fact of life." He wiped the sweat from his brow with a red handkerchief, ran his hand through his hair again and put his hat back on. "Let's see if we can figure this one out...judging from them shadows on the ground there, it's nigh on to noon.

This morning at sunrise our shadows was long. Them shadows change all day from sun-up to sundown; moving directions and growing shorter. Then they start to grow long again, and it starts all over again tomorrow. Sure enough, things is always changing, nothing stays what it is. It's the Lord's will. You can't run from it no matter how hard you might try."

Sarah nodded but wasn't sure she understood.

"Kenny was my best friend…his dying changed me something fierce." Her voice quavered. "I was just a little girl. I'd never known life without him. I felt so alone and scared. I think I'm just now starting to understand that I'll never see him again."

Cotton lit another cigarette, inclining his head to bring the tip into the flame. "Don't be too hard on yourself. When someone you love dies, especially a young'n, so sudden-like, you can't let go of 'em all at onest… you lose 'em bit by bit…in your own good time. That way, it kindly helps in our sorrow."

It occurred to her that Cotton was very likely the smartest person she had ever met. "I'm not the little girl I used to be. I've done things I'm not proud of, but deep inside I'm still that unhappy little girl who believed in Cinderella. There was no one in my life to comfort me and help me understand. Momma had her own pain, and no one else seemed to notice me. It was easier not to think about me, lost in my own little girl version of grief. I was too innocent to understand it…children die, and death is forever." She shrugged. "It's funny, even though only one person is missing--the whole world can seem empty."

"If there's ere a thing to remember…you can think of all the misery what's tearing you apart or you can hold to what was good. Whichever you hold deep, it'll catch up with you…become a part of you. In the end, you don't never get over it no ways."

Sarah sat back and drew a long breath. "I have wonderful memories of Kenny, and I still miss him very much." She hesitated for a moment, and then added, "I wonder who will miss me when I die."

"It's a crying shame, Miss Sarah Jane, you barely 18 years old, and already a widow thinking about your own passing. It don't seem right you having to deal with that much dying.

"I was pretty much prepared for Charlie's death. I knew he was in a dangerous place. I knew what could happen, actually expected it to happen, I just didn't know when…and now with Daddy…. nothing can hurt me anymore." Feeling emotionally exhausted from revisiting her grief, she wanted to change the subject. "Momma seems so fragile...not the rock she's always been. I want to take care of her, she needs me. She won't let anyone else help her; always afraid she might bother someone."

Cotton stretched out his legs and nodded. "Yep, all your aunties took a turn at helping their sister as best they could, but I reckon your momma never learnt how to take help. She's used to being the one doing the taking care. Your Aunt Myra, she offered to come stay for a while, but Miss Dee, she weren't having none of that- said her sister makes her nervous. Your Aunt Willie Mae stopped by a time or two and made Dee eat some soup and drink a little tea."

Sarah sat for some minutes in deep thought, and then with a wistful smile, she rose. "You understand the world and its ways. I always feel better after talking with you." She took hold of Cotton's hand. "I'd better go see Daddy now."

Cotton squeezed her hand and walked off toward the barn.

Sarah continued to sit for another moment, then went into the house.

She cracked opened the door to the bedroom Dee and Otis had shared for over thirty years and peeked inside. The old man was stretched out on his bed, gaunt and wasted. The air coming through the open window circled around her carrying with it the rank staleness of nicotine absorbed into curtains, blankets, and rugs. The smells of the house mixed with a new odor, the stink of dying circled her. Through the dim light of the sick room, frantic yellow eyes peered at her from a skeletal face which hadn't been shaved for weeks.

Gasping for breath Otis tried to rise, pushing back against the headboard, clutching a fistful of sweat-soaked bed sheets. The sight of his face convulsed with pain sent a jolt through her stomach. One thing was clear.

I was called here to see him die. I'll see him die.

The next cough he made produced a splatter of blood that dribbled off his parched lips and caught in the scabby white beard covering his face.

Dee, sitting quietly by his side, stopped reading the newspaper to him and dabbed at the stubble on his chin. She stood and laid a gentle hand on Sarah's shoulder, turned and left the small room.

Sarah apprehensively took the seat left empty by Dee's departure. Feeling alone in the hush that surrounded her, she gazed at the patches of flaking discolored skin on her daddy's cheeks. His eyes fluttered open and in a thin strained voice, he forced out the single word, "water" from his crusted lips.

She filled a glass from the pitcher on his bedside table cluttered with bottles of drugstore cough syrup and made herself look into his eyes. Braced to accept whatever she saw there, she helped him sip from the glass. What she saw…was nothing. No love, no guilt, no regret. How could nothing hurt so bitterly?

His lips moved, and his boney reddened hand twitched on the thin faded quilt. For a brief second, he seemed to want to speak. Maybe he was suffering from pangs of remorse after all, but then his head sank back on the pillow and he sighed deeply, shuddered and gave a weak, dry cough. It was pitiful to see his exhaustion. After a long while the rasping labored breathing took on the uneven shallow rhythm of sleep.

How odd it seemed, to sit at his bedside and watch her father die while the rest of the world simply went about its business.

FORTY-ONE

Matthew 18:21-22

²¹ Then Peter came to him and said, Lord, how often shall my brother sin against me and I forgive him? until seven times? ²² Jesus says to him, I say not to thee until seven times, but until seventy times seven.

1968

Sarah pulled the pins from the tightly braided roll at the nape of Dee's neck. Freeing the hair from the thick braid she let it fall almost to Dee's waist in crinkly waves and studied her mother's reflection in the mirror. The once red hair had faded to a commonplace brown, streaked with yellowed white fingers. Wearing a washed-out cotton robe, Momma looked thin and tired; her once creamy ivory skin, sallow and lined. It had taken some doing, but Sarah managed to convince Dee to sleep undisturbed in Sarah's room for just one night.

Sarah brushed her momma's hair in slow strokes and continued to brush long after it was necessary. She then gently re-braided the dull hair into a single thick braid and secured the end with a rubber band.

"Momma, Cotton told me you wouldn't let Aunt Myra help you...."

"You know how she is. It always seems like she's turning her nose up as if it warn't right the way I done things...turns me into a nervous wreck." Her voice became small and wavering. "Myra and Ella and Willie Mae been taking turns bringing dinner for the boys, but nary a one of your daddy's people has come around to check on him and none of 'em has offered no help neither. We ain't seen 'er one in a coon's age."

Dee's gaze dipped to a framed photo on the dressing table. Her troubled look gave way to a half-smile.

When she was only a girl, Sarah had found the snapshot tucked inside Dee's Bible. Sarah recalled her amazement when she realized the pretty

228

young woman in the photo was her mother. She had found a discarded frame in a drawer and placed the photo on her dresser.

Dee's bony finger brushed across the black and white image of a smiling teenager holding a white cat. Her eyes glistened as she touched the picture. "That's the front of my Momma's house…just before I married your Daddy." Her voice was vinegary with disappointment. "I was just about your age."

She kissed her fingertips and laid them against Sarah's cheek. "Sarah, what's to become of you if you stay in this town?"

Sarah took the photo from Momma's hand, looking at it long and carefully. The teenager stared at her from the photo. She raised her eyes and looked into her mother's face again.

"Sarah Jane, no matter what you do, you'll never be nothing but white trash to these folks. Leave this place. Leave as quick as you can and don't never look back." Dee firmly took hold of her daughter's hand. "Don't let life cheat you like it did me."

Sarah remembered reading it in one of her books…*small towns have narrow minds and long memories*. She could no longer deny that truth. She did not want to repeat her mother's struggles; her greatest fear was falling to the same fate. If she wanted a better life, one that avoided the pitfalls of her mother's choices, she needed to create her own path…and that path led out of Tolerance.

As if she could read her daughter's thoughts, Dee put her arms around Sarah. "I know you got the dirty end of the bargain in life." She whispered, "I ain't been the best momma." She kissed Sarah's hair. "But I done the best I knowed how."

Sarah wanted desperately to say something to comfort her mother, but instead held her tight and said nothing.

Sarah looked from her mother to her daughter. Keni slept at her feet on a pallet Momma had made of a stack of neatly folded quilts.

Dee bent down to pull the sheet over her shoulders and caressed the fringe of wet red curls plastered against the toddler's cheek. "Give this baby a better life than what I gave you."

Sarah realized that she, alone, was the to link between the past, and all the generations of the future.

"Momma, you're tired. You need to get to bed." Sarah helped her mother pull a cotton gown over her head and then with a weary sigh, Dee slipped beneath the covers.

Sarah pulled the chain dangling from the bare bulb hanging in the middle of the room. She eased the door shut and made her way to the bedroom, turned sick room, where she would assume the caretaker role while her momma rested.

❧

The agonized coughing that went on all day and all night had temporarily grown silent. A deep stillness crept through the house as the room sank into blue shadows. Isolated from the routine of the outside world within the four walls Sarah heard no sound but the irregular labored breathing that raised and lowered her father's chest and the ticking of the clock on the bedside table.

Lying motionless, his pale face fading into the whiteness of the pillow, her father looked as if he were already dead; his mouth hanging agape revealing the few brown stained teeth he still had. He stirred, and a breath moaned in his throat.

Sarah studied the rasping figure. How many times had she wished he would die? She lost count years ago.

In the dusky darkness, she recalled the terrible things he'd done to her in this room and grieved for the innocence stolen from her. But that did not cover all the subtleties that complicated this situation. She silently mourned for the father's love she'd never known.

What you did to me is part of what made me who I am.

As the light in the room faded she clicked on the small reading light and settled in with a book, turning her eyes toward her daddy from time to time.

He made strangled sounds deep down in his throat; wasted hands clutched at his sunken belly. An unpleasant feeling swept over Sarah; being alone with him felt vile; unsettling. Her mind a tangle of battling thoughts, she wondered what excuse, what reason could she give for his insensitive words, wounding accusations--his hurtful actions? She became more and more conscious that half her bitterness was not about the callous indifference that bombarded her memories, but instead that he seemed to take such great pleasure in hurting her. No child should have to fear their own father. No child should have to feel shame they don't understand or guilt for something they have no control over.

You tore big pieces out of me and threw them away.

She passed each hour in dread of his waking and being alone with him in this room filled with so many damaging memories. He stirred and began to cough weakly. She wrapped her arms around herself and sat watching him, listening as each short, quick inhalation whined from his throat, knowing each breath could be his last.

It was a soul-sickening moment when she began to be aware she did not feel as a daughter should at the time of her father's death. As she hovered about his bed, she understood his death might be a blessing for her...could mean a new beginning; freedom to build a better life for herself and her daughter. It was because of him she had not brought the baby around to visit Dee, depriving both grandmother and granddaughter of the special bond they should share.

He'd always been unremorseful and belligerent, yet she no longer hated him. She'd hated him for so long she wasn't prepared for any other emotion. Nor had she imagined she could feel sympathy or understanding for the man in the bed. What was she feeling? Anger—guilt—sadness—compassion? She welcomed his death, and that appalled her.

Then, hit with the realization that he was just a human being lying powerless; dying in front of her, needing help and not caring who gave it to him, she felt only pity for him. He was simply a farmer, not a very good one, and that was all he knew. He had found little happiness in life, yet he had never complained or cursed his fate.

With this newfound insight, Cotton's words resonated through her and peacefulness took root deep inside. *Sometimes forgiveness isn't about them deserving it, it's because you need to forgive.* It seemed so clear now, forgiveness is not excusing...it's freedom from anger. It all began to make sense. She remembered what Cotton once said about the meaning of mercy...

It's about not giving someone the punishment they deserve.

She looked at the old man on his deathbed. This was not the man who stole the innocence of her childhood and replaced it with something ugly and perverted, but simply a dying human being who needed her mercy.

Sarah now found it possible to perform the common act of kindness, easing his pain with no bitterness to complicate the deed.

A light warm breeze pushed at the curtains through the open window. The moon shone brightly, and the stars slowly moved on their course eastward as hour after hour passed with torturous slowness. She began to lose a sense of time passing.

Beads of perspiration formed on Otis' forehead. As she bent over the sick-bed wiping the perspiration from his brow and cheeks, his features became tense with pain and he droned into a rambling chant. His eyes blinked open and he looked at her as if he wanted to speak. He raised his head and looked at her with dull, half-closed eyes, then dropped back onto the pillow.

Sarah poured some whiskey into a teaspoon as she had seen her mother do. She lifted the spoon to his lips. "Here Daddy, just a sip." The whiskey went down, and his breathing became freer, his hands stopped frantically picking the air. Those long bitter years of numbing his pain and worry with rivers of liquor had come to this.

"Daddy, do you know me?"

He stared in the direction of her voice. Confused pale gray eyes blinked slowly; his lips moving—talking soundlessly. He continued staring at her blankly for a few moments longer, then turned his gaze to the ceiling.

She gave a bitter laugh. "If you could talk, I don't know what you'd say to me. I don't know you." She bit her lip and glanced away. "I don't know who you are…."

The tip of his tongue flickered between his teeth and his eyes gradually sank shut.

"There's something I need to tell you." She had to release the feelings of the past that she'd locked inside. "I don't know what to say to you. I don't even know if you can hear me or if it really matters…maybe you don't want to hear what I have to say…but I've got to say it now."

The room darkened as the moon drifted behind a cloud and brightened when it emerged.

"What you did to me was wrong, and you knew it was wrong." She shrugged. "Who knows, maybe you don't even remember it—you were always drunk. But I need you to remember what happened…what a miserable life you made for me. Can you understand all I had to endure because of you? I don't know what made you do those things to me. You made me feel dirty deep inside—so deep I couldn't wash it away. I can still feel the dirt you left on me."

A moment passed. He gagged, coughed and gagged again. She wiped a streak of white foam from his chin. His lashes fluttered open and fixed on her. There was a faint, barely perceptible motion of his lips. Did he feel an urge to confess, to ask forgiveness?

She didn't know, but it didn't matter any longer.

"You had complete control over me. If you tell a child to do something, they think they have to do it. I trusted you to take care of me, to do what was right. If you tell a child they are wrong, they believe you. I never said a word about what you did…if I had told someone that would be admitting it happened. I believed I had done something bad to deserve all those things you did to me."

His lips continued to move though he made no discernible sound. She searched his face but saw no remorse in his expression. He pressed himself back into his pillow; the last bit of light died in his eyes and he gazed emptily into space.

Has he forgotten all the things he's done to me? I wish I could forget them too.

"I thought I must not be a good person, that I was unworthy of being loved. First, I hid inside myself, then I spent a lot of time looking for someone to give me the love you couldn't give me. The only way I found my strength was to go outside our family to find the goodness in me. I found Charlie…and now he is gone…but I still feel his love and I still have the strength he helped me find."

She suddenly was unburdened by the blame of the past. The pain was simply gone…taken away. She had given up expecting things from other people; things they chose not to give her.

That emotional prison would never draw her back again.

She spoke softly, wanting to touch her daddy's face but not daring to. She wanted him to know she'd forgiven him. Could he read the forgiveness in her eyes? She wanted to let him die in peace.

Waiting for the faint morning light to signal the end of the long night, she sat for some time.

Just before dawn, Dee came quietly into the room to take her place by the side of his bed. Almost as thin and haggard as her dying husband, her night of rest had not diminished the dark circles underneath her eyes.

Sarah feared her mother was wasting away.

She put her arms around her mother and in an unemotional sickroom whisper said, "I'm afraid he'll not make it through another night."

Dee rested her head against Sarah's shoulder. For a long moment, they stood that way, silent, close to tears. Sarah's grief was for her momma.

FORTY-TWO

Psalm 119:130
¹³⁰ The unfolding of thy words giveth light, giving understanding unto the simple.

He died on a rainy afternoon. The doctor came to the house and pronounced him dead, and the funeral home took the body away.

He'd been quite lucid in the end, but Sarah suspected he died unrepentant. Her father may not have died in peace, but it was a consolation to Sarah that at the moment of his death she was no longer filled with anger and hatred. Though the bad memories were not fully erased, her act of forgiveness freed her.

On the morning of his funeral, the rain ceased, but the humidity left a light misty fog down by the pond. Looking out the bedroom window Sarah saw a mass of pale gray clouds drifting away above the tree-tops. It promised to be a lovely day, the fresh sky left clean and clear after the rain.

The sunlight gleamed off the chrome bumper of Rachel's freshly washed Pontiac. She'd insisted the Jones family use her air-conditioned car to drive to the church. The shiny new vehicle looked unquestionably out of place parked next to Cotton's old blue truck.

Sarah smoothed the skirt of her fitted dress, the same one she wore to Charlie's funeral, checked her hair in the mirror and joined Dee on the porch.

Momma's dark cotton dress hung too loose on her thin shoulders; her collarbone protruding sharply from the baggy neckline. She handed Keni to Sarah and adjusted the surplus of material bunched around her waist, tightly cinched in place with a wide belt.

Junior waited in the car with the engine idling. He pulled at his tie. Cotton and Jim Ed waited near a budding peach tree. A tendril of white smoke rose into the branches. Cotton looked in Sarah's direction, took another puff on his cigarette, threw the butt to the ground and stepped on it.

Jim Ed looked awkward and uncomfortable holding the jacket of the dark suit he'd bought for Charlie's funeral. Sarah realized for the first time that Jim Ed was a handsome man. His blue eyes sparkled against his tanned skin and dark, thick hair. She wondered how he'd avoided marriage this long.

Sarah sucked in the delicate scent of peach blossoms spangling the trees, which momentarily eclipsed the smell of the chicken yard. She closed her eyes, breathed in deeply and followed her family to the car.

Cotton climbed into his old truck and fell in behind the Pontiac as they pulled from the driveway.

Sarah hadn't been inside the tiny church for almost a decade—not since Kenny's funeral. It looked the same.

By Southern tradition, this was a small funeral—nothing like the emotionally packed service that marked Kenny's passing.

Sister Dorothy Jo played some of Dee's favorite hymns as the family passed the open casket and took their places on the front pew. The piano music abruptly stopped after *Amazing Grace,* and Brother Leon stepped to the pulpit. He looked down at the congregation, his hands clutching both sides of the honey-colored wooden podium. The buttons of his powder blue polyester suit pulled a little tighter, straining against his paunchy middle, but his dark hair, freshly barbered, was stiffly sprayed into the same pompadour he had worn when Sarah first laid eyes on him long ago.

He cleared his throat and shuffled the papers laid in front of him. Pulling a neatly folded handkerchief from his breast pocket, he wiped away the beads of sweat glistening on his upper lip and dabbed at the sides of his neck and forehead. He tucked the handkerchief back in his pocket, cleared his throat again and began the eulogy. "I don't pretend to have known Otis Jones well...," and then the minister went on to prove it by extolling Otis' non-existent virtues. Maybe he believed he could fool God and preach Otis into heaven.

Brother Leon's voice stepped up in pitch, and he began to enthusiastically wave his arms in the air. He spoke of sin and damnation, warning the unsaved of their eternal penalty and offering salvation to the repentant. As he droned on, Sarah thought of how Otis always refused to go to funerals. He said a funeral ought to be about the fella who passed away—not about trying to get the rest of the folks into heaven. He would have especially hated this one.

She waited; hoping to hear something to make her feel better. But the generic words left her feeling as if she were at the funeral of a stranger.

When Brother Leon finally brought his tedious sermon to a close, Dorothy Jo began a too loud rendition of *Rock of Ages* that was so high; the buxom soloist was forced to sing the entire rendition off-key.

❦

They buried him in the church cemetery next to Kenny. Sarah stood over the freshly dug grave among rows of leaning stones in the old cemetery. She bent down to remove the tacky stalk of plastic flowers– yellow and pink and red, poked into the ground in front of Kenny's grave. She could not think of a more pathetic sight than weather-worn plastic flowers fading on a grave. With a twinge of guilt, she thought, *someone should have pulled those up before the funeral….*

One of the black-clad mourners standing near her, a woman well into her sixties—she'd been sitting with Daddy's family in the church—turned to her companion and asked in a loud whisper, "Gladys, who's that over there? She ain't from around here."

"Mavis said she's our second cousin…"

"No. I don't think so. Not her. Who's her mamma'n'em'?" The first lady whispered back.

"Mavis didn't say- now hush, Wanda."

"Upon my soul, I do believe your right. She's the baby of the family—Irma Jean--- I haven't seen her in years. How old do you think she is now?"

"'Bout forty-five, I guess," Gladys said.

There was a pause but a few minutes later the whispering started again as Wanda continued her dialogue with Gladys. "Ain't that nice, his final resting place is next to his son. That poor boy got hisself run over by a tractor a few years back. Such a tragedy—I still remember the day….

Sarah tried to block out their voices as she watched her father being lowered into the ground. Tears sprang into her eyes—not for her father, but for the pain she'd felt watching Kenny's coffin disappearing into the grave and how unbearable it had been to see Charlie's casket suspended over a gaping dark hole in the earth. Her whole life had changed with each death. She had struggled, trying first to make her dreams fit God's plan and then trying to make God's plan fit her dreams.

Now she knew her father's passing would mark another change in her path—but this time death brought an unmistakable peace to her heart.

❦

Junior guided the Pontiac past cars and trucks parked along the paved county road that ran in front of the farm and came to a stop beside the barn where he wouldn't block anyone. Cars were still arriving.

The house was flooded with family members in every room and spilled out into the yard, gathering around tables set for the ritual that follows any southern funeral. For southerner's, there's a deep-rooted connection between food and sympathy, and deep pride for having the reputation for making the best potato salad or Karo Nut Pie.

Aunt Willie Mae and Aunt Myra dominated the kitchen, bustling around with Sunday aprons covering their funeral best. A ham was in the oven and two roasted hens resting on a pan full of cornbread dressing were cooling on the counter. The ice box was packed with cole slaw and fruit encased in red or green Jell-O—funeral food.

Dee grabbed an apron and brushed a wayward lock from her forehead. "Lordy mercy, I never expected this many people to come. It's a blessing folks been dropping off food day and night." She went to the stove, took a fork, and turned over a piece or two of the chicken before Myra shooed her away.

"You git—we got it under control--there's plenty of food. Even some of the Methodist from Miz Week's church brought food. Just tell me where you keep Grandma's vegetable dish and go visit with your company."

In the living room, ladies in church hats and funeral dresses flocked around the tables lined with food, piling plates with fried chicken and deviled eggs for their husbands before fixing a plate for themselves. Men lounged outside with ties removed and shirt collars unbuttoned.

Keni was being passed around for all her cousins and aunts to comment on how much she looked like Sarah, intermingled with the chatter of how much she'd grown.

Jim Ed stripped off his jacket and tie, rolled up his sleeves, revealing his sun-browned arms and looked his normal self again. Sarah watched him circle the room, making small talk with each guest and wished she had the poise and confidence to do the same. There was lots of hugging and reminiscing over childhood memories and laughing over old stories. Sarah did little talking herself; mostly she observed.

As she watched two women sitting side by side on the couch balancing their plates very carefully on their laps, it occurred to Sarah that she'd not eaten.

The younger woman was, Sarah thought, Aunt Sylvia and the white-haired woman Sylvia's mother, Florence.

"Why ain't Floyd here?" the older woman asked.

"Sakes alive Momma, eat something. Try some of that green bean casserole." She pointed with her fork at the older woman's plate. "It tastes pretty good even if I did make it."

Uncle Joe returned with a fresh plate of food and sat between the women.

"But why ain't Floyd here?" Florence just held her plate and looked at the food.

"Floyd, he's the oldest one? Adah's boy?" Sylvia asked.

"I think he went to Texas, maybe he don't know his daddy has passed on." Uncle Joe said.

"Oh, nonsense. The obituary was in the papers." The old woman poked at the casserole with her fork.

"Maybe it weren't in the Texas paper," Uncle Joe said. "Or maybe he doesn't like funerals.

"Who don't like funerals?"

"Florence wants to know why Floyd ain't here." Uncle Joe raised his voice. "For Pete's sake, somebody tell Aunt Flo why Floyd ain't here."

She sat silent for a brief moment, then she said, "Just seems to me, a boy would come to his own daddy's funeral. It ain't natural. That's all."

Uncle Joe rolled his eyes and mumbled something under his breath.

As Sarah made her way about the room, overhearing scraps of conversation, she realized how little she knew about her father. There had been another Otis Jones, one she never knew--one who'd disappeared before she was born. There was the teenager who ran away to join the Marines, fought in Hispaniola, caught malaria and came home with a bullet in his hip. Then bought his farm with the money he'd saved. And the heartbroken widower who sat around his house crying, wondering how he could take care of a motherless new-born baby.

"It was so sad when Adah died having that baby. Otis never was the same after that… the whole thing just about kilt him. He talked about her so much that we got embarrassed and nary one of us knowed what to do. We found him a wet-nurse over there west of New Hope. But that was about all the help he'd let us give."

A woman came from the back porch and hugged Sarah. She didn't recognize her at first, but there was something familiar about her eyes. Then she smiled and Sarah recognized her Aunt Ruby, Otis' sister.

"Y'all put him away right nice. What a blessing it quit raining—it's so depressing to have a funeral in the rain. Getting your Sunday shoes all messed up." She squeezed Sarah's hand and scurried toward the couch where she sat next to a motherly old lady fanning herself with a floral print hanky. Otis' Aunt Frances.

"You better come here and hug my neck," the older woman insisted and opened her age-spotted arms to give Ruby a hug. Then pulling away and slowly shaking her head, she said, "He sure didn't look too good, did he? Was a time when he was the best-looking man in the county—so tall and that black hair always just shining so purty." She closed her cataract-clouded eyes. "I sure hope his after-life is better than this one."

Ruby slowly shook her head. "Our pa shore wore mean to him. I don't think a day went by he didn't whup that boy with that big ol' brown belt he kept hanging on the back of the bedroom door. Seemed Otis couldn't do nothin' to suit Papa." She looked down at her hands.

"He was such a sweet, quiet boy...Papa tried to beat it out of him. Weren't nothin' he could do 'cept hurt real bad inside. Ain't nothin' hurts so much as hurtin' inside."

The old woman nodded. "But Otis never laid a hand on nary a one of his own children."

Sarah heard someone call her name and watched as Aunt Pearl pushed through the crowd. "Sarah," she said, "I've been looking everywhere for you." She took hold of Sarah's hand. "Did you get an extra program? I lost mine and I wanted to keep it..." her aunt lowered her voice. "Tell me the truth. Don't you think that preacher dyes his hair? Mary Beth says 'no,' but just look at him...getting a little long in the tooth to not have a lick of gray, don't you think?"

Sarah started to reply but was interrupted as Pearl was momentarily distracted by her sister, Ruby. "What did she give me that look for- did I miss something?"

Pearl joined the two women still deep in conversation. "What have you two been yakking about? You've had your heads together over here for quite a spell."

"Talking about how hard it was for Otis when Papa run off and left Momma with all us kids and Irma-Jean just a baby. Mamma didn't have money enough in the house to buy a sack of flour. Otis weren't but thirteen hisself, but he was the oldest and he had to be the man. He didn't know nothing about farming. He just done the best he could for us."

Pearl shrugged. "It's a good thing Papa left; otherwise he'd of beat Otis 'til Gabriel blew his horn."

"Lord, if that preacher hadn't started coming around to check on Momma, I don't know what we'd a done. He took a fair interest in Otis too… always paid him to come out to his place and lend a hand."

"I thought he was kindly sweet on Momma. But Otis, he had a strong dislike for the man. Never understood why he took such a mighty disliking to him. Funny how he stopped coming around soon as Otis took off for the Marines. Fred-Charles was big enough, that preacher coulda paid him to help out."

Listening to these snippets of conversation Sarah wondered how much more she didn't know about the handsome young man who once had hopes and dreams of his own—that stranger who became her father. The question that bothered her was what caused him to change. What made him give up on his dreams?

࿓

After the guests had gone and the aunts had cleaned the kitchen, washed the dishes and wrapped the leftovers in Saran Wrap, Sarah lay in her bedroom. She stared at the ceiling through the darkness, thinking of all the memories housed in the room. Closing her eyes, she remembered the feel of dirt and grass and mud against her feet--childhood memories, big and small, good and bad; memories of events that defined who she'd become. She did not wipe away the tears trickling down her cheeks leaving a salty taste on her lips.

There was a quiet tap on her door, and Dee entered without waiting for an answer. Standing with the dim light from the kitchen shining behind her was the figure of what had once been a tall, resilient woman— now defeated by life. "I just came to say good-night," she said as Sarah settled back down into the pillows, her cheeks a bit flushed from the tears.

Dee touched her forehead then gently bent to kiss her good night. This was the first time Sarah remembered her mother doing that. She was certain her mother had never kissed her goodnight.

She wondered when one ceased to be one's parents' child and became oneself. One thing she knew for sure, she would never allow herself to become Sarah Jane Jones again. She would be Sarah Weeks—a stronger more confident Sarah Weeks.

But for now, she looked forward to getting back to a sense of routine, to feel the comfort of habit she'd never recovered after Charlie's death.

FORTY-THREE

Isaiah 43:18-19

18 Remember not former things, and look not on things of old.19 Behold I do new things, and now they shall spring forth, truly you shall know them: I will make a path in the wilderness, and rivers in the desert.

Hello, honey." The sound of Rachel's voice on the other end of the telephone brightened Sarah's mood. "Rusty's gone to Texarkana for the day. I'll make a nice lunch and we can spend the rest of the afternoon catching up. I sure do miss seeing you and the baby."

It was a beautiful Friday; no threat of rain and the heat tempered by a cool breeze. Sarah pulled her car into the drive and parked next to Rachel's flower beds. Rays passing through the leafy tree branches covered the ground in dappled shade.

The house looked different in the sunshine—no longer her home. She wondered if it would ever feel like home again, or was it now consigned to her past, never to be a part of her future.

Sarah tapped on the back door and entered without waiting for an invitation. The fresh smell of clean laundry filled the air, and Rachel sat at the kitchen table in front of a cup of coffee, jotting something onto a notepad. Dropping the pen onto the table, she stood and reached for Keni.

"Come over here and give Nana some sugar."

She took the baby in her arms, and amid giggles and chubby legs kicking, kissed both of the child's rosy cheeks and then the top of her head.

Turning to Sarah with concern in her eyes, said, "How's your Momma?"

"As good as can be expected, I suppose," she said, taking a cup from the rack on the counter and filling it with coffee. "She's almost herself again, thank the Lord, and the doctor says she's regaining her weight quickly."

She sat in a chair and sighed. "If he'd waited much longer to die, I'm not sure she'd ever get her strength back."

Sarah's eyes focused on the plump toddler. "Put her down, Miss Rachel, she weighs a ton."

Keni wiggled off her grandmother's lap and waddled toward a basket of toys in the corner of the room.

As she watched her daughter play Sarah wondered, not for the first time, if Keni would have to learn life's lessons the hard way as she did. Was she destined to repeat the pattern, growing up poor, badly educated and without feelings of self-worth?

"I sometimes wonder if I can bring her up by myself," Sarah spoke the words almost to herself.

"You're not alone. Rusty and I are here, so's your momma."

"What's to become of her in this town? At the very best, she'll have a decent life. That's the most I can hope for. I'm afraid I will wake up one morning and realize I'm just wasting my life in this town."

Rachel sat still for a second, looking silently at Keni pulling one toy after another from the basket. Her face tightened as she seemed to labor to come up with a reassuring answer.

"I don't know," she finally said looking away, avoiding eye contact. It was the only honest thing she could say. "But sometimes it's not good to think too much. There's an old Swedish proverb -- *worry can give small things a big shadow.*" She paused before continuing. Then looking directly into Sarah's eyes, she said, "God has a plan for you and you need to let it work."

Sarah wondered if God's plan was to punish her for her past sins, or if He had put her on this difficult path for a reason. "What if Satan also has a plan for me, and it could destroy God's good plan? I haven't always turned to the right people for help."

Rachel sat back and drew a long breath. "Sometimes we do surround ourselves with people and ideas that aren't good for us. But if you want the answers, it's often best to just be still and listen." She got up and, with a plop, dropped her cup into a sink filled with soapy water. Turning towards the icebox, she busied herself taking out the ingredients Sarah recognized would soon be turned into her favorite chicken salad. Then she pulled out a chilled roll of cookie dough wrapped in waxed paper.

Sarah joined Rachel at the counter and started to tear lettuce for a salad. Automatically the two fell into a familiar rhythm working side by side going about the process of fixing a meal. Within minutes, the smell of baked cookies wafted through the air.

It felt good to be in the kitchen with Rachel again slicing tomatoes and thin slivers of cucumber. They talked about Rachel's flowers, the horses, and latest articles in Redbook, but not about Charlie or Otis or Kenny, while they spread freshly made chicken salad between slices of brown and white nut bread. They soon had the meal on the table.

Sarah took the cookie sheet from the oven and looked at Rachel "I've missed this— more than anything I've missed our conversations."

Rachel smiled and nodded. "Me too."

Keni tugged at the hem of Rachel's skirt with her chubby little hands trying to get her attention and chanted "Cookie, cookie, cookie!"

"I think this princess is ready for her lunch," Rachel said, shoving an old wooden high chair out of the corner and setting it by the table. *Charlie's*. She lifted Keni into the chair, put a warm cookie on the tray and poured a small cup of milk.

Sarah shot a feigned disapproving look at Rachel but couldn't hide her smile.

"I know," Rachel answered grinning and placing a small Peter Rabbit plate filled with chicken chunks and apple wedges next to the cookie.

Keni laughed and kicked her feet. "Mmmm," she said mimicking her grandmother.

"Taking care of this little girl seems to be the only thing keeping Momma alive these days." Sarah gently pushed the hair from Keni's forehead.

She took half a sandwich from the plate painted with pink rosebuds. Rachel always called it *Grandmother's Havilland*. Sarah thought it was too nice for everyday, but Rachel insisted it was there to be used.

The dishes came from France many years ago and had been handed down through Rachel's family. Rachel and Rebecca had each inherited half the china as wedding gifts from their mother and Sarah supposed; someday it would belong to MaryAnn and EmmaLee. Suppressing a smile, she pictured Dee's chipped china and mismatched spoons—her inheritance.

Sarah chewed on her sandwich in silent contemplation as if it held the key to some great mystery.

"Miss Rachel, Have you ever tried to put together a giant jigsaw puzzle without having the lid that shows you the whole picture—not knowing what the finished picture is supposed to look like—that's how I feel about my life right now."

Rachel placed her hand over Sarah's. "It's hard to understand why we have to go through the things we do. All the troubles you've had to deal with in your young life have given you wisdom beyond your years, but you have to accept what is and let go of what was—and what could have been."

"I know we all have problems—and we just have to deal with them. Except, suppose I've got it all wrong? I need the box top to look at. It seems like a piece is missing from my life puzzle." Sarah offered a sip of milk to Keni, who rubbed her eyes with goo covered hands.

Rachel slid her chair back, went to the sink and dampened a washcloth with warm water and handed it to Sarah. "Our dreams don't always turn out exactly as we picture them." Her eyes were on Sarah as she wiped clean Keni's mouth and little hands. Looking into the girl's happy sweet face, her eyes went soft with sadness.

Sarah stood, lifted Keni from the high chair and held her against her shoulder as she rocked from side to side. The child raised her head, fretted a bit and rubbed her hand against her nose and eyes.

"Momma thinks I should leave Tolerance and try to make a better life for me and for Keni."

"Maybe you should listen to your momma. Could be that missing piece is not to be found in Tolerance."

Rachel started collecting dishes from the table. "Why don't you put her down for her nap? We can talk some more."

Sarah laid Keni on Mary Ann's bed and returned to the kitchen. She picked up a stack of dry dishes and put them away.

"Your momma is right about leaving here." Rachel dried her hands on a dish towel, filled two glasses with iced tea and put them on the table with a plate of cookies. "This is as good a time as any to talk about this. I want to show you something that might interest you."

She took a small book from a drawer and set it on the table in front of Sarah.

Sarah picked up the *University of Arkansas Undergraduate Catalog*, thumbed through it, and put it down. "Nobody in my family ever went to college. EmmaLee and I used to talk about it, but I never really believed I could go…." Sarah bit her lip. "Especially, you know… after I got pregnant."

"You're a bright young woman, Sarah. There's no reason why being a momma should stop you from getting an education. In fact, Keni's future is a good reason to get one." She placed her hand on Sarah's arm. "It's something Rusty and I have been talking over. You are smarter than most and your vocabulary is extensive thanks to your love of reading." Her forehead puckered. "You even have a kind of sophistication that's out of keeping with your upbringing."

Sarah cut her eyes toward the catalog resting on the table. "I don't know anything about getting into college."

"I do. I can help you. You just have to convince yourself to try. If you're too attached to things you're supposed to let go of, you'll never achieve what you are capable of."

"You know after Charlie..." Rachel held back her tears and didn't finish the sentence. "We put the money we'd set aside for his college in a trust fund for Keni...she's taken care of. But Charlie can still help you. Rusty and I think you should use the government insurance money for your tuition."

Sarah ran her finger across the rim of her tea glass, as questions of the more remote future occurred to her. All her life she'd believed she didn't deserve any better than her abusive upbringing, but she knew her child did not deserve to be raised without affection and opportunity.

It would be difficult, but here was a chance to reclaim her destiny, rather than waiting for her future to come to her. Sure, she couldn't change her past, but she could refuse to be held back by it.

The more she mulled over the matter, the more excited she became thinking about the possibility of a different sort of future. And the more she thought about it, the more complicated and unreasonable it seemed. This would be different from finishing high school when Rachel kept the baby for her and cooked her meals and refused to accept rent.

"What about Keni? I'd have to find a place to live and a job and someone to watch Keni while I'm in class." Looking into Rachel's eyes, the thought was left unfinished... the answer to her question was clear before she asked it.

"How could I leave my baby here; not fold her little clothes, not tuck her in, not brush her curls? It would tear my heart out."

"You can't wait for the perfect moment...it will never come. You leave this town and trust your momma and me to take care of that little girl for you. When you're settled, you come to get her. You will not leave her behind. No matter what happens you will always be her momma.

"Sometimes the hardest part about growing is letting go of what you are used to and moving on to something unfamiliar. You just have to make a decision that you are going to do it and don't worry about how everything is going to turn out." Rachel reflected for a moment and then said, "I think Robert Frost said it best in one of his poems ... *the best way out is always through.*"

Sarah sat for a moment. Gently biting on her lip, she thought about what Rachel said, and yes, it made sense. She nodded, murmuring, "That's right. Sooner or later you'll come out on the other side... just put your head down and keep going and eventually it will be over."

By the time the marble clock on the living room mantel-piece softly chimed four times, Sarah knew what she would do. She would grasp this chance to completely reinvent herself.

It's only a question of how many times I crash before I get it right. She could thank her daddy for one thing. The hard time she had growing up ...that disparagement and disillusionment had made her strong enough to handle any obstacles along her path.

She put the catalog in her diaper bag. Gathering Keni into her arms, she collected the rest of her things, hugged Rachel and made her way out the door.

FORTY-FOUR

Isaiah 54

*⁴Fear not; for thou shalt not be ashamed: neither be thou confounded; for
thou shalt not be put to shame: for thou shalt forget the shame of thy
youth; and the reproach of thy widowhood shalt thou remember no more.*

Ones opportunities in life are often born from the ordinary occurrences
in the lives of others.

Just such an ordinary occurrence created Sarah's opportunity when
Cotton approached Jim Ed, his hat clutched in both hands, his eyes focused
on his boots.

"It's like this…" he said. "I got this here letter from my baby sis, Arnetta,
up in West Fork. My old maid aunt, she was my daddy's sister, she died a
while back and left me and my sister some land— she didn't have no kids of
her own. The land ain't worth nothin' but it's all Arnetta's got, and she can't
tend to it by herself no more. I need to go help her out. You folks have been
mighty good to me, and I hate to leave you high and dry, but family's gotta
come first. I'm mighty proud to have known you and appreciate all you done
for me."

Signs come in many different forms with many different meanings. West
Fork was fifteen miles from Fayetteville, where the University of Arkansas is
located, and Cotton said this was a sign from the good Lord.

For once fate presented Sarah with an opportunity rather than an
obstacle. She could choose to change her direction and her surroundings.

If you want the answers, it's sometimes best to be still and listen to your heart.

At last, she could see the possibility of moving from the shadows of her
past and into the light.

She was leaving everything behind except for a small box packed with some clothes, Charlie's Bible and a few paperbacks she'd rescued from the piles at Hazel's Second Hand Store.

With cautious anticipation, Sarah tossed a shoebox filled with ham sandwiches and two slices of Dee's coconut cake onto the seat of the pickup and climbed in next to Cotton. The sound of gravel under the tires gave way as the truck pulled onto the blacktop road. Sarah raised her hand to give one last farewell wave to her family. Junior, Jim Ed, and Dee, balancing Keni on her hip, returned her wave and watched until the truck was out of sight. She'd come very close to changing her mind, but she knew she had to do this for her own future and the future of her child.

Sarah absorbed the images of poverty and the old ice house as they disappeared in the rearview mirror. The memories of Tolerance made her melancholy, but the moment passed quickly.

The invigorating mountain breezes flushed Sarah's cheeks as the terrain transformed from the flat farmlands of Hallard County to the dense oak forests and inviting valleys of the Ouachita National Forest. The beauty was marred only by the occasional piece of abandoned farm equipment or old pickup truck left to rust in a field.

Cotton motioned toward the dashboard with his head. "Sorry 'bout the radio not working. Never bothered to get it fixed. Back home, 'bout the most important news of the day was the hospital report, telling the names of the folks going in and getting out, and the ones that died. Never got used to listening to nothing else."

Passing through small town after small town, Cotton drove with one hand on the wheel, the other holding his cigarette between his fingers as he changed gears. They drove on winding county roads without names past modest houses without numbers, looking lonely and alienated from their surroundings.

A large shaggy dog bounded past the neatly trimmed boxwoods lining the driveway of one of those houses. The metal screen door was adorned with an ornate letter "S." Sarah wondered who lived there— the Smith family, or did the family living there just not bother to replace the "S" after the Smith's were long gone?

Nipping at the tires, the dog ran along the deep ditches, tangled with honeysuckle that bordered both sides of the road. Cotton tossed the cigarette butt out the window and gently tapped the horn. The dog trotted triumphantly back to his yard, satisfied he'd chased away another intruder.

Sarah threw a crushed square of waxed paper into the shoebox and pulling out another sandwich offered it to Cotton.

"I've had my fill, Miss Sarah, thank you kindly."

As they continued north, the truck gently began to climb into the foothills of the Ozarks. The skinny highway wound through a narrow pass cut into the crest of the hills dotted with tiny towns with names like Acorn and Y-City. Sarah watched the desolate houses shoot past, their mailboxes jutting out on arms reaching for the road.

They drove for a while, neither speaking. Sarah leaned her head back against the seat and shut her eyes. After a moment or two, she said, "I was just thinking. Funny how you're going home and I'm leaving home, but we're both headed for the same place."

He nodded. "I sure have missed that life in the hills. I miss my people too. We was so poor we didn't have two nickels to rub together, but we was happy. I especially miss family music time. Most everyone I knew could play some sort of instrument. We just learned to play by watching. Books and learnin' usually played second fiddle to a lot of other things—including learnin' to play the fiddle." He chuckled at his joke.

Sarah pensively looked out over the mountain peaks in the distant horizon and envisioned this new place where she would start fresh.

As if he'd read her thoughts, he suggested. "The Lord don't care about your past, but a new start is a rare and good thing. When everything is wiped clean, it's life's way of letting you know who you really are and who you can be."

"I'm looking forward to a clean start where nobody knows me. I'm sick of having people look at me like I'm cheap."

"Miss Sarah, if you don't mind me saying so, you need to stop thinking like that...it's a whole lot of nothing. You can't live your life to please people. Please one and the next fellow will fault you for doing the thing that pleased the first 'un. You'll never be happy if you keep on trying to please people. Just live to please yourself and the Good Lord."

"How do you know if what pleases you pleases God?"

"I don't try to figure it out. I ain't never really felt the need for what most folks call salvation. I just try to do what's right."

Cotton pointed out the window toward the west as they passed a sign that read, "West Fork Population 350. My sister's place is down the road a couple of miles. Place called Hogeye, ain't even big enough to be a town. I'll drop you off in Fayetteville."

They drove into town just as lights were being switched on inside the houses they passed. Sarah liked the way the town looked with each illuminated window giving a snapshot of the lives of the people inside. People sitting down to a family dinner, people sitting alone in front of a flickering television, people going about their chores. The images were almost hypnotic as they swiftly flashed past her eyes. It was as if her life just started and all that went before was only a crazy nightmare. She momentarily longed to be back home, to be in her house being the observed, not the observer.

It took her a moment to realize Cotton was speaking. "What do you plan on doing for a job?"

"Oh, I don't know. Like Scarlet O'Hara, I'll think about it tomorrow." She paused for a moment and then continued. "Right now, I just need to find a good cheap room somewhere."

The End

AFTERWORD

According to government research, female victims of child sexual abuse are at two to three times greater risk for subsequent victimization at some point in their lives than women without a history of child sexual abuse. For additional information from the National Institutes of Health go to:

https://www.ncbi.nlm.nih.gov/pmc/articles/PMC2572709/

ABOUT THE AUTHOR

Where are you from? Depending on the day of the week Vicki Olsen might answer Arkansas, Texas, Idaho or I don't know. This is a dilemma familiar to many military brats.

Born in Arkansas, at the age of two she began moving every two or three years with her JAG officer father as he was transferred to air force bases in Louisiana, Texas, Idaho and Illinois as well as Germany.

After graduating from high school in Idaho, she attended the University of Arkansas, earning a BSBA in Marketing. She spent three decades of her adult life in Dallas, Texas where she gave birth to two Texans.

She has held a variety of jobs, including working as an insurance adjuster, a paralegal, and as the owner of a small antiques and gift store.

She currently lives in Arkansas with twelve goldfish and an array of African violets. She is working on her second novel.

https://www.vickiolsen.com/

NOTE FROM Vicki Olsen: Thank you for sharing Sarah's journey. If you enjoyed *A Sparrow Falls*, please consider telling your friends or write a review. It would mean a lot to me.

Amazon: https://amzn.to/39QWtxV

Goodreads:
https://www.goodreads.com/book/show/42408282-a-sparrow-falls

BookBub:
https://www.bookbub.com/profile/vicki-olsen

Vicki Olsen

Next in Series: When Sparrows Gather (Sparrow Series Book 2)

When Sparrows Gather is the continuation of Sarah's story. She leaves Tolerance hoping to put her past behind her and start a new life with Keni. But will she make the same mistakes all over again. But she will soon find that you can't run away from life's problems and there are dangers everywhere. Will she make the same mistakes again, putting her trust in the wrong people and losing her own identity trying to please others?

When Sparrows Gather

"Each has his past shut in him like the leaves of a book known to him by heart and his friends can read only the title.

- Virginia Woolf

ONE

Isaiah 43:18-19
*18 Remember ye not the former
things, neither consider the things of
old.
19 Behold, I will do a new thing; now
it shall spring forth; shall ye not know
it? I will even make a way in the
wilderness, and rivers in the desert.*

"Only those who will risk going too far can possibly find out
how far one can go."
— **T.S. Eliot, Transit of Venus**

1969

The muffled thud of a car door slamming sent her heart soaring into her throat. For the third time in the last half hour, she shifted her eyes to the plate glass window of the Ozark Café. This time the van she'd been watching for was parked at the curb.

Over the weeks Sarah had grown used to seeing that van…everyone in Fayetteville, Arkansas had grown used to seeing it.

Still, it was an odd sight decorated with peace symbols and vibrant designs, large and small, bouncing against one another in every fluorescent color imaginable; *Jesus Loves You* painted in day-glowing orange and magenta on the side. It had become as familiar on campus as the bearded and beaded hippies juxtaposed against the fraternity boys and sorority girls with their pearl and diamond encrusted Greek-lettered pins.

A gust of crisp air swept in as the outer door opened and closed.

He strolled into the restaurant with an aura of confidence coupled with a boyish grin.

Their eyes met. She felt heat rising up her neck into her face as she greeted him.

A strand of untamed black hair had worked its way free from a shaggy ponytail and lay against his cheekbone, threatening to fall into his stunning eyes.

Those blue eyes unsettled her, made her feel exposed as if he could see right through her and knew who she was under the skin.

Sarah took a deep breath. Had those eyes and that smile caused her to be foolish? Or was it her craving for kindness, born of low self-esteem and her painful past that made her want to accept his invitation?

He planted himself in a faded red vinyl booth by the front window. Her table.

She lifted the pot. "Coffee?"

He shook his head. "No, thanks."

This wasn't the first time he'd sat at her table, but this time was different—she'd be leaving in that oddly painted van.

She recalled the day they met. It never occurred to her it would lead to this.

That was eight weeks ago.

Yesterday had changed everything.

With her impetuous decision to accept his offer to stay at the commune, she'd go with this near-stranger to a farm way beyond the boondocks, outside of town where she'd live with a collection of free spirits. Or end up on the evening news...her mangled body found in a tangle of vines between mossy boulders.

But what choice did she have? She'd made a diligent search of the newspaper ads and notices pinned to bulletin boards all over town. There were simply no off-campus rooms available.

Yesterday. Was it only yesterday? Aaron and Caleb settled at her table drinking coffee. They engaged in an enthusiastic exchange, swapping opinions on the real meaning of Christ's teachings,

as they folded piles of mimeographed flyers. The morning light shown through the window, casting rectangles over a stack of underground newspapers bundled beside them. Aaron peered at Caleb through little round wire-rimmed eyeglasses. His sinewy body leaned against the bench; legs stretched out in front of him with the heel of his army boot resting on the ankle of the other. Sarah had always wondered if those boots meant he was a veteran or if they were simply a fashion statement.

When she'd come with the pot to warm up their coffee Caleb had searched her eyes and asked if everything was all right? She thought she'd hidden the tears, but as always, he'd seen what others didn't.

"Nothing's wrong." Her shrugged exposed the lie.

He reached for her hand but hesitated. "Come on Sarah, what gives?" His question reflected nothing but genuine caring.

"Well," she said. "You know...my room in Mrs. Peter's house...the student who has it for the fall semester will be here this week. I'm having a little trouble finding a place to stay...that's all."

She'd quickly walked away before he had time to comment.

As she wandered around the room busing tables the two men drank their coffee and talked quietly, throwing an occasional glance in her direction.

Her interest was piqued. Something about the conversation made her uncomfortable...nervous ...certain they were talking about her.

She made several passes near their table, shamelessly trying to listen to the conversation, but only heard occasional snippets.

"We've done it for others," Caleb clearly said.

"Not a good idea..." Aaron said, lighting a cigarette.

"...a few weeks...Tamar...," Caleb said.

She watched intently. Her curiosity getting the best of her, she wove her way back to the table with a clean ashtray.

Caleb's eyes surveyed the room. "Looks like we're your only customers right now. Can you take a quick break?"

Her gaze darting from them towards the kitchen, she nodded in the affirmative.

"Then," he said, sliding over to make room for her, "sit down. Let me tell you what we have been discussing."

Unsure what was about to happen Sarah shifted in her chair and nervously forked her fingers through her hair.

Aaron made a temple of his fingers and leaned in towards her. He peered at her from behind the thick glasses magnifying his expressive gray eyes.

"There may be something we can do for you. We want to offer you a safe place to live in peace...a place to stay until you can find what you need. You can stay with our family.

She gave Aaron a puzzled look.

He gave a little smile. "We're not related, but we're like a family. We believe we have been chosen by God to do his work and we have all taken a vow to give everything we have to the family. All money and possessions are shared."

"But I have nothing to share," Sarah lied. She thought about her widow's benefit, the money she planned to use for tuition and living expenses, money to support her daughter. Would they expect her to turn that over to them?

Caleb took her hand.

"We're not asking for that. That is only required of members of the family. You're welcome to come stay with us— get to know us and have time to think about it, mull things over. The farm is just a beautiful place where people can live in peace and know God loves them. We welcome people to come and stay for a short time. Some remain, others move on. All we ask is to accept the love of Jesus and share in the chores."

He had a statesmanlike gift of persuasion.

She'd slept little last night as excitement at the prospect of an anticipated new experience gave way to little uncertainties and flashed over into doubts. Misgivings caused her to reflect on her impulsive nature and question the wisdom of her impetuous decision to accept their offer.

Now Caleb was here, the keys to the VW bus dangling from his hand. Surely, he could see her heart pounding through the thin fabric of her uniform.

A quick smile lit up his face. He slung his knapsack over his shoulder, "You ready?" The sleeves of his chambray work shirt were rolled up hiding the fact that they were too short to cover his long arms.

A dry knot of panic rose in Sarah's throat. Forcing herself to breathe she swallowed hard to choke down the lump and called toward the kitchen. "Gus, I'm leaving now."

The balding man behind the order window wiped his big hands on a grease-stained apron and starting to wave a lazy goodbye, stopped mid-gesture and cut his eyes toward Caleb with a bewildered look.

Untying her apron, Sarah hesitantly moved to the time clock and slipped her punch card into the slot.

Caleb caught her by the hand, and she followed him, without saying a word, out to the street where the VW waited at the curb. Placing his hand on the small of

Sarah's back, he helped her into the van, tossed the knapsack in the back and settled into the seat beside her.

Sarah shifted her shoulders in an effort to relieve the tension growing there. This is dumb, she told herself. Caleb turned the key in the ignition. As the van pulled away, she shot a nervous glance in his direction. It was easy to forget she was alone with him for the first time; it felt so natural to be with him.

two

James 3:1
[1] Let not many of you be teachers,
knowing that we who teach will
receive heavier judgment.

"That is just the way with some people. They get down on a thing when they don't know nothing about it."
— **Mark Twain,**
The Adventures of Huckleberry Finn

Sarah had known from the first moment she'd seen him that Caleb was out of the ordinary. She'd realized, even with that brief encounter, that she had a sense of safety with him that she'd seldom felt.

Almost two months ago he'd strolled into the nearly deserted diner. It was shortly after the lunch rush had ended. The only sound had been the occasional clink of dishes being washed in the kitchen and Idabelle behind the counter making a fresh pot of coffee. Every day since Sarah had started working at the cafe the previous

Monday, she'd watched the plump little waitress perform the ritual at precisely 1:30.

Taking long-legged strides Caleb sauntered past the lone customer, a man at the counter reading the newspaper, and planted himself in a faded red vinyl booth by the front window. Her table.

The man looked up from the newspaper to glower at the long-haired hippie and then cut his eyes toward Idabelle. Moving closer to the counter she refilled his coffee cup and lifted a burning cigarette from the ashtray next to his elbow. The two hunched forward as they exchanged small talk and Idabelle rhythmically lifted the glowing cigarette to her pursed red lips. They shared a private joke. The man's quiet chuckle mixing with the waitress' hearty laughter rang out and filled the café.

Sarah had quickly grown used to hearing that sound when one of the regulars would repeat some corny story for likely the hundredth time. Idabelle knew how to make nice with everyone and keep the customers satisfied. Turning her attention to the hippie seated in her booth, Sarah took a deep breath. As she greeted him and placed a glass of water and napkin-wrapped silverware on the table in front of him she hoped her hands weren't shaking visibly and her voice didn't sound as trembling as it felt. She looked away, glancing instead at a couple walking through the door, as she tried to regain control of her breathing and waited for him to make his selection.

Pointing toward the chalkboard on the wall behind the cash register where Gus posted the Daily Special, he said, "I'll have that. Medium."

She scrawled *Cheeseburger Special- Med.* across the order pad and hurried toward the kitchen. Ripping the order from the pad she stuck it on the spindle for the fry cook.

Idabelle caught Sarah's arm and winked. "Someone should tell him it ain't polite to stare." She nodded toward the booth

Sarah grinned. "Do you know who he is?"

"Sure, he's one of them weird Jesus people that hangs out up at the college. They got some sorta church on a farm outside town...come in here all the time with that long hair and blue jeans. You can't tell the boys from the girls."

"Well, there's no doubt in my mind—that one's a guy." Sarah pretended to fan herself with her hand.

"They all smell alike too. Gus says it is something called patchouli oil. Says they wear it so's you cain't smell the marijuana—they all smoke it, you know. I got to tell you, I don't understand how them hippies just showed up out of nowhere one day."

Sarah chanced another look in his direction and found him staring at her. She felt her face flush again, and again looked away.

"Some of these regular old coots around here don't like it so much." Idabelle winked and topped off the coffee drinker's cup. He lifted his cup in salute and returned to thumbing through the paper.

"I told Gus we ought to put up a sign— 'No Hippies Allowed.' He said ifn' they don't cause no trouble and keep spending money, he don't mind them being in here. Said we should just 'go with the flow'...whatever that means. Something he heard one of them hippies say."

Sarah jumped at the 'ting' of the kitchen bell, indicating an order was ready.

Approaching the table with his food, she sensed him gazing at her. Trying to avoid eye contact, she focused on the red plastic carnation in a vase next to the napkin dispenser. His hand brushed hers as he moved his water glass to make room for the plate. Her heart skipped a beat.

Sarah found herself casting more than one glance in his direction as she went about her business.

Sipping a Coke and taking an occasional bite of his hamburger, he'd studied the open Bible resting on the table, sporadically stopping to make notes in the margins.

Taking the last bite, he tossed his crumpled napkin on the plate and motioned for Sarah to come over. She placed his check on the table and he tossed a couple of bills on top of it.

"Keep the change."

Sliding from his seat, he stood, downed the last swallow of Coke and turned to leave, raising a hand in a goodbye gesture as he backed toward the door.

"I'm Caleb, by the way."

"Sarah," she'd said pointing to the name tag pinned to her uniform.

"Well, Sarah, nice to meet you. I'll probably see you around."

She'd struggled for a response, but like an idiot, just stared and said nothing.

The next day, all attempts at concentration on the tasks at hand ended in her mind overflowing with thoughts of Caleb. Her gaze repeatedly darted to the window, searching for a glimpse of the van.

Sarah's eyes brightened when Idabelle pointed a varnished, red fingernail toward the window and facetiously quipped, "You can stop looking—your boyfriend's here."

He came in that day, and every day at the same time, sitting with friends in her booth. Greeting her by name and a friendly smile, his blue eyes penetrated her while he ordered. Beyond that, he'd given her no sign to make her feel there was hope for anything more; never engaged her in conversation. Yet, Sarah found herself thinking about him, her stomach fluttering at the thought of seeing him.

In those first few weeks, Sarah never had a private word with him. But each day, she liked what she saw a little more and each day he seemed to linger a little longer.

He was usually with Aaron. Tall and very blond, with hair curling around his ears, Aaron reminded her of Charlie. She'd noticed the resemblance the first time Aaron came to the café...the rugged features and, sun-streaked hair. His close-cropped beard and the barely visible red wisps above his lip made her remember Charlie's letter. On active duty in Vietnam, he'd written to tell her about the mustache he was growing and how the guys made fun of it. Thinking about it, she smiled before sadness crept in.

She never saw Charlie with the mustache. Only the picture that came in a letter a few days after he'd stepped on a land mine and made her an eighteen-year-old war widow and single mother of a one-year-old. That had been two years ago. The image of the official vehicle pulling up in front of the house carrying two immaculately clad soldiers haunted her still.

She had studied Aaron as he sat across from Caleb. He spoke in a brusque and crisp manner, yet not wholly unpleasant. He was in his mid-twenties, like Caleb, but he had an air of arrogance about him lacking in Caleb. He didn't remove the Greek Fisherman's cap—like the one John Lennon often wore.

While overseeing the activities on the sidewalk, the two would argue about the way modern Christians interpret the message of Jesus.

Sarah had watched through the window, with curiosity, at the scene unfolding outside. A street team comprised of one frizzy-haired boy wearing a tattered green army jacket, and two girls bounced along the pavement, each clutching a wad of handbills and a few newspapers. They hurried towards passers-by, handing out flyers to anybody who'd take one.

From time to time they would find someone, curious about what the group was doing, willing to stop and listen to them advocate their cause. But most accepted a leaflet and kept walking. Usually, it was stuffed into a pocket or glanced at before it was dropped to the pavement or deposited in the trash bin at the end of the block.

When anyone threw a flyer to the ground, one of the girls, her boyish figure hidden beneath a loosely fitting cotton blouse and long skirt would glare or shout, "Littering is against the law. Please don't litter."

The other girl would grab her by the arm and shake her head in disapproval. She'd retrieve the papers from among the gum wrappers and cigarette butts on the sidewalk and add them back to her armload to be redistributed.

As Sarah continued to watch, the timid girl handed her remaining flyers to the boy and came into the café looking flushed and excited. Her large hazel eyes darted around the room. She rubbed her hands on her bell-bottom jeans and smoothed her chestnut hair, plaited into a single braid.

A large middle-aged woman at the rear of the café, well away from the window, had turned toward the girl and gave a long, hard stare as if she'd spotted a fuzzy green worm in her salad.

In the presence of the small crowd, the girl took on the look of stage fright and headed toward the table where Caleb and Aaron sat.

Caleb laughed. "Hannah, are you keeping Abigail out of trouble? Tell her the idea is to engage the folks in conversation, not in battle."

She'd pressed her lips together. "I'm afraid she'll never be able to tame her tongue or keep her mouth shut when she is angry. Even Joshua has no control over her once she starts to boil."

"Remind her to lead with her ears instead of her tongue," Aaron said. "The Bible says *Be quick to hear, but slow to speak, and slow to anger. For the anger of man worketh not*

God's righteousness. Hannah, we're counting on you to maintain some social order out there."

The girl opened a small beaded leather pouch that hung from her waist and deposited a handful of change into a cigar box next to Aaron's elbow. She scooped up more leaflets and a bundle of newspapers and started for the door. Caleb called her back.

"Take your guitar—get Abigail to sing with you. Joshua can sell papers." He reached under the table and pulled out a beat-up guitar case.

Hannah grabbed the guitar and headed out the door. She hefted the papers onto Joshua's arm and sitting cross-legged on the sidewalk in front of the café, opened the guitar case. Resting the guitar in her lap she strummed a cord, twisted a tuning peg and strummed the cord again before lighting into a vigorous rendition of *I'll Fly Away.* Hannah suddenly lost her timidity when she played and sang the praises of Jesus for nickels and dimes tossed into her guitar case. Abigail, her wavy brown hair barely tamed beneath a red bandana, clapping her hands, sat down and joined in. Their voices melded in an appealing tangle.

Joshua, roamed among the cluster attracted by the music, pressing flyers into the hands of passers-by. A single long strand of wooden beads swung from his neck as he threaded his way through the crowd. He ran to a car that idled at the light and tapped on the window, flashing the newspaper. The driver shook his head and drove away as the light changed.

By the time the girls finished their version of *Hallelujah I'm Ready to Go,* they had drawn a small gathering and assembled a smattering of coins.

Sarah cleared dishes into a bus tub and wiped a table with a damp cloth. Her foot tapped in time to the music until an older man in a flannel shirt and John Deere cap came through the door; his eyeglasses filmed with dust.

He clutched one of the flyers in his sweaty fist. His friend Vern followed on his heels.

James Lee. Sarah dreaded what might happen next. He was a nice enough guy most of the time, but often made caustic comments about hippies, when under the influence of alcohol.

Sarah knew about the effects of alcohol. Her father had exerted his impulsive alcoholic behavior on her and her family often enough.

The man's eyes shot about the room before lighting on Caleb and Aaron. Aaron was already on his feet as the man made his way toward them.

He shook his fist at Aaron, still clutching the paper. "Who put you hippies in charge of Jesus? What makes you think you know all about religion?"

"Hey man, we don't pretend to know all about religion. All I know is what a powerful influence Jesus can be." Aaron reached out to touch the man's shoulder.

James Lee pulled back and sneered. "Well, I don't pretend to know all about girls neither, but I know an ugly girl when I see one...and I'm looking at one now. But you sure got some pretty hair."

Vernon snickered his approval.

Gus, behind the counter, newspaper spread before him, grinned and snorted, then went back to his paper.

Aaron walked away, ignoring the cat-calls following him. Caleb gave Gus an apologetic smile.

James Lee and Vern continued to taunt.

Gus stared at them for a bit, took a long drag off his cigarette and exhaled with relish. He coughed and stubbed the smoke out in an ashtray. "I don't want any trouble in here," he said and folded his newspaper.

"Just having a little fun. No harm in a little fun. No need for them hippie kids to get all fired up," James Lee chuckled.

three

Psalms 137:1
[8] By the Rivers of Babylon, there we sat down and wept, when we remembered Zion

"Memory is the diary we all carry about with us."
— Oscar Wilde

B y the time Caleb brought the VW to a stop in front of Mrs. Peters' modest frame house Sarah had pushed aside some of her anxiety. She hurried up the sidewalk, edged with bright yellow mums, and slipped her key into the door lock of the tiny room— a nice room. In the corner, next to a small bed covered with a sunny yellow and white quilt stood her single box of belongings, packed and ready for Caleb to load into the bus.

Last night, while packing, her mind had wandered to a short time ago when she'd enacted a similar scene. Before leaving her childhood home, a small chicken farm in Tolerance, she'd placed a few articles of clothing in a box and lovingly positioned her mementos on top—two wedding bands tied to a pale-yellow ribbon, and a Bible— it had been with Charlie's personal effects shipped back from Vietnam.

Tolerance held a lot of memories; some good—most bad. She ran her fingers across a framed picture of Jesus she'd received the day she and Kenny were baptized. Kenny had been her brother, her protector. Her life had changed forever when she was just eight and he was thirteen. A tractor can slip and take away a life in a split second. She'd been mad at Jesus for a long time after Kenny died.

The only happiness she'd known after that day was the time she spent with Charlie. Smitten from the minute she saw him on her first day of high school, they'd done all the normal things teenagers do in small towns—football games, drive-in movies, and dances at the local hang out. It had been a brief happiness before a grown-up future, doomed by circumstance, intruded. Their shot-gun wedding took place a few months after Charlie graduated and only weeks before he reported for training at the U.S. Marine Corps Recruit Depot in San Diego. Charlie had been 18 and Sarah 16 on their wedding day.

Taping the box shut, she thought about what she'd left behind in Tolerance...the sagging porch with its peeling paint and old swing, her favorite doll, her Nancy Drew books...and three graves. Two, Daddy's and Kenny's, were in the graveyard beside the white clapboard Baptist Church, and Charlie's in the cemetery next to the stately First Methodist Church with its white columns and brick façade.

So far, her short life had been a series of moments of joy followed by sorrow. Was it always to be like this? She wondered if those painful years of grief and loss had, after all, led her through the darkness to this new beginning...or was this just a joyful interlude to be followed by a new sorrow?

Moving the box aside she crawled into this bed for the last time and closed her eyes. She reminded herself why she was here; to forget the sting of memories, starting fresh in a new place, finding a future for herself and her young daughter Keni.

Trying to make sense of what was happening and how she felt about it she pulled the covers tighter over her shoulders wished she could talk to Charlie's mother. Rachel always knew the right things to say. Not the answers, but a way for Sarah to find the answers for herself; some poem or a quote to set Sarah's mind to thinking. Rachel was fond of quoting Robert Frost...*the best way out is through.* Those words haunted Sarah, filling her first with fears, then with encouragement.

She'd woke this morning with a powerful desire for the conviction to stand in the street and distribute leaflets, to pursue a spiritual lifestyle—living off the land, helping others without asking for anything in return. She wanted to understand this dedication.

Now, Caleb stood beside her, ready to take her to a new home...a new life...and somewhere inside, she again began to doubt her choice. Sarah paused, gently biting on her lip. She was divided between gratitude and fear. Were these people who they seemed to be? Had her instincts about him been correct? Her instinct had not always been so good; restraint never her strong point. Should she prepare to be a victim of her own poor decisions again? She looked into Caleb's eyes for confirmation of any delusion she may have.

As she studied his kind face, Sarah realized she didn't even know his real name. Caleb was not the name his parents had put on his birth certificate. All the members of the family had taken symbolic biblical names and referred to themselves by these first names only. She smiled to herself; at least she wouldn't have to choose a new name.

She nodded. *Robert Frost makes sense. Sooner or later you'll come out on the other side... just put your head down and keep going and eventually it will be over.* To change things for the better, she had stop running away. Sarah placed a hand on the doorknob and took a final, slow look around her room in the near darkness. Her face grew hot and her stomach began to feel uneasy. She would accept her life as it is in the moment. She shut the door behind her and followed Caleb to the VW.

Coming 2021
Available In
French and English

Vicki Olsen

Preview

The Duty of Memory

1

The Tailor

Beauvais, France 1994

The white-haired man folds his hands behind his back thoughtfully. He walks across the room toward the window. For a long while he stands there, seemingly transported to another time, another place, his erect figure outlined against the dim light.

He pulls an immaculate white handkerchief from the pocket of his finely tailored black jacket. He cleans his glasses, neatly replaces the handkerchief and positions his

272

glasses on his nose before turning to the nicely dressed young woman seated across the room.

"Are you sure you want to hear the ramblings of an old man?"

The woman nods, removes a tape recorder from her briefcase and places a cassette in the recorder. "I would like to know about your time as a Prisoner of War at Camp Fünfeichen, if you don't mind. I want to understand what motivated someone to risk their lives in the Resistance...hear small stories that defined everyday life within the backdrop of the war; not stories of spies or guerillas hiding in the woods. I want to learn about the unlikely heroes, the butcher, the baker, the candlestick maker, if you will."

The man clears his throat. "I would very much like to tell you the story. I appreciate this opportunity. It's more important to me than you can realize."

The woman moves her eyes slowly over the neat, full waves of perfectly combed hair—as white as his starched and impeccably ironed shirt. Her gaze pauses on his cufflinks—the blue, white and red vertical bands of the French flag.

The appearance of the aging tailor is difficult to equate with a war hero—a cog in the Kummel Network of the French Underground.

"Are you ready?" he asks.

"Yes." Her pen is poised over a legal pad.

"Okay, where should I start?"

"First tell me about yourself—Radziminski—definitely not a French name."

"Let's see...I was born in Germany in 1910. My parents moved there from Poland. We lived a better life in that country than we would have had in Poland."

"Ah, that explains the name. So, Germany was your first home?"

"Yes, my father chose not to change his name—he was very proud of his Polish heritage. I am called *Brünislaüs*. My father, Joseph was a carpenter... yes, yes, I know...." He laughs. "But my mother was not Mary. She was Josepha; she was a seamstress. We were a family of three brothers and a sister. I was the oldest."

The tailor stops talking. The woman sits motionless waiting for him to resume.

"As a child, Mama would hold me on her lap and kiss me on each cheek and then brush the curls from my forehead and kiss me there. When I grew too big to crawl into her lap, she would pull me to her ample bosom and kiss my forehead. My step-father, Michel, would say 'Josepha, you spoil him! He will grow weak.' He was not entirely wrong, but he was wrong about making me weak. The memory of those kisses kept me alive when those evil doers took me prisoner at Dunkerque."

The tailor pauses. "But this is not the story I want to tell; I want to talk of the Resistance—not of myself."

"Yes, we will get to that." The woman nods.

Bruno stares out the window into the distance. Minutes tick away the future before she asks, "Is it painful for you to recall—your time as a POW?"

He looks up briefly yet doesn't meet her eyes. He allows himself a moment of introspection. He'd been a lot of different men after his stepfather found work in the mines of France in 1922 and moved the family from Germany. But at this moment he is a tired old man— A humble tailor, who never wanted to be anything more, yet took pride in what he'd done in a former life. Now, he wants to preserve a legacy.

He glances at a pile of photographs nearby. "You never knew if you were going to die the next day." He picks up one of the faded snapshots. "When you made a friend then, you made a friend for life."

CONTACT ME

I truly appreciate you taking time to read my books and I'd be thrilled to hear from you.

If you'd like to get in touch with me you can do so by email: vicki@vickiolsen.com

Twitter:

https://twitter.com/vickiolsen48

Facebook:

https://www.facebook.com/VickiOlsenAuthor/?modal=admin_todo_tour

Goodreads:

https://www.goodreads.com/book/show/42408282-a-sparrow-falls

BookBub:

https://www.bookbub.com/profile/vicki-olsen

Website:

https://www.vickiolsen.com

Made in the USA
Monee, IL
01 August 2024

63107026R00163